TIMOTHY K. CLARK

The Mice Storm

First published by 4th Story Publishing 2020

First edition

ISBN: 978-1-7362922-0-4

This book was professionally typeset on Reedsy.
Find out more at reedsy.com

For my family...

1

The Ramp

The itching bothered Flynn the most.

He dug his fingernails under the edge of the plaster cast on his leg to scrape at the pale, wrinkled skin underneath.

Once the oppressive heat and humidity of an Ohio summer had finally faded, Flynn had hoped the itching would subside and make the cast slightly more bearable. But *Old Man Winter* hit the city like a ton of bricks. He was always indoors, and people always had the heat cranked up high, so his leg itched even worse – it was driving him bananas.

"Stop scratching, dear. Your leg will get infected," chided Mrs. Easterbrook.

She faced him in his wheelchair, pulling hard on the armrests, trying to drag him across the driveway covered in icy snow. That put her far too close to his face, as far as Flynn was concerned. Mrs. Easterbrook was awfully old to foster a kid, wasn't she? She was battling the onslaught of old age with a rabid determination. The old lady had pancaked her makeup into every crevice and corner of her crinkly face. Her hair was so deeply dyed and heavily hair-sprayed it reminded him of a plastic helmet. She was as round as a balloon, with thick wrists and thick ankles. To Flynn, she smelled like roses mixed with the water that was left over after his mom had boiled him hot dogs for lunch.

Mrs. Easterbrook bared her teeth as she strained to pull the wheelchair, while this ungrateful boy just sat there staring at her. Physical exertion was not part of her plan, but she would overcome this obstacle as… she had no choice.

When they crossed over the driveway onto the small sidewalk, she stood upright and twirled around to face her house.

"It's not much but I'm sure you'll be happy here." Her hand slowly swept along the length of the house like she was a presenter showing off a new-and-improved bar of soap during a TV commercial. The small ranch home was covered by red bricks, with white shutters and empty flowerboxes at each window.

"Although, I must say, when I signed up to be a foster parent, I hadn't counted on hosting a boy… in a wheelchair," said Mrs. Easterbrook.

He kept digging his finger under the leg cast, a plaster disaster that ran from his ankle to halfway up his thigh. His surgically repaired leg was propped up, straight out from the chair, on a metal support. The pesky itch was always just out of reach. At ten years old, Flynn was rail-thin with royal blue eyes, that everyone raved about, and fiery red hair, that everyone teased him about, parted down the middle. His hair had grown out over the last few months and now swooped out over his ears, like wings.

Mrs. Easterbrook turned her attention back to tugging hard on his wheelchair.

"You know… it's easier to push these things than pull," Flynn stated.

She stopped dead in her tracks on the sidewalk, leaned in close to his ear. He winced slightly. That rose bush-hot dog smell again. Roses reminded him of funeral homes.

"And it would be even easier if you would actually help," she fumed. "Dear."

Flynn rolled his eyes, placed his hands on the rubber wheels, and began rolling himself along. They trundled along the walk and stopped at a set of steep concrete stairs.

"Here's where it gets hard," she sighed. Mrs. Easterbrook moved behind the chair, gripped the handles, and leaned him way back. "Now, one… two… three… push!"

2

His hands tight on the narrow rubber wheels, Flynn pushed down with all his might. Up the first concrete step they jumped.

"Again!" She leaned him farther back, put all her weight against the back of his wheelchair. Flynn gripped as far back on the wheels as he could, grunted, and shoved himself upward and onward. The chair hopped onto the small concrete pad. His exposed toes at the end of his cast jammed hard into the front door.

"Ow!"

She ignored his cries of pain, shuffled past him to unlock her front door. Flynn's wheelchair started to move backwards off the small porch, towards the stairs. He frantically caught hold of the rolling rubber wheels. He stopped the chair before the wheel slipped off the edge and sent him tumbling into the snow.

They both struggled to get him over the threshold and through the door. Flynn was relieved. Mrs. Easterbrook was sweating.

She quickly removed her overcoat, adjusted her pink dress, and began to fan herself with her hand. After several deep breaths to recover, she delicately corrected her hair that she had expertly dyed a dark brunette shade. Her nearly perfect work on the perm ensured those curls would remain tight. A little bit of manual labor was *not* going to ruin her day. No siree!

Flynn watched her as he rubbed his sore hands. He thought her hair made her look like a dog.

She noticed him admiring her absolutely gorgeous hairstyle and preened for her audience of one.

"It's called the Poodle Cut. Always a favorite look for ladies with my facial structure," she said.

Poodle sounds about right. He smirked, but let it fade quickly so she would not notice. Flynn looked around his new home.

The year was 1978. But Mrs. Easterbrook's place was mired in the 1950s. He immediately spotted the plastic floor runner old people always had, that ran from the front door to the kitchen, designed to protect the precious carpet underneath from filthy kids like him. He noted the black and white striped mid-century sofa in her living room was also covered in plastic. White knitted doilies covered every surface in the room – the arms of the sofa, the chairs, end tables, and the wooden kidney-shaped coffee table. Old people loved putting crocheted doilies on *everything*.

"Could you take me to my room? I'm kind of tired," he said.

"Oh, well, um, about that," Mrs. Easterbrook's voice became timid and trailed off to a whisper.

Flynn eyed her with suspicion. She searched the room for something, anything, to rescue her from this conversation.

A wave of loneliness flooded over him. He missed his parents, his home. It had been several months since the accident and the boy had endured surgeries and rehab exercises. That this house was to be his new normal scared him. He gripped the canvas backpack resting on his lap tightly to his chest.

"You see, dear, I… well, being a widow – Mister Easterbrook passed a few years ago, may he rest in peace – I wasn't quite sure about our living arrangement, so…" she rambled.

A lump in one of the front pockets of the backpack shifted. Flynn noticed the movement and looked quickly back up to Mrs. Easterbrook. The backpack lump squirmed again, sliding up closer to the zipper. His eyes darted back and forth; he was as uncomfortable as his host.

"We… I-I mean I thought it would be best to set up your bedroom downstairs. In the basement."

The zipper slid to the side, creating an opening of just an a few inches. A whiskered snout pushed out. Flynn's eyes grew wide; he fumbled for the zipper. The head of a small, gray mouse appeared. Flynn shook his head at the small creature.

She leapt behind Flynn's wheelchair, quickly pushed him into the kitchen. Flynn zipped the pocket shut again.

"Wait? What did you say? Basement?" Flynn looked around in a panic. Her kitchen was also lost in the 1950s. There were yellow vinyl chairs surrounding a small green table. Mint green cabinets matched the refrigerator that sat next to an open door to the basement.

She wheeled him to the doorway. Flynn tried to lift himself in the chair to see down into the abyss, but it was too dark to see. He held his backpack tighter.

"Yes, since we're just getting to know each other, I wanted you to have your own private space. My handyman set up a bed for you down there. There's a small bathroom. So, you don't have to come up, and…"

"Don't you have a spare room? On this floor?"

"Oh, dear, you see, I work out of my house. My second bedroom is where I style hair. All the ladies of the neighborhood come to me for their cosmetology needs," she said.

Flynn looked at her in disbelief, then back down the stairs, finally down at his wheelchair.

"But—but how am I going to get down there?!"

"Oh, my handyman made a special ramp for you!"

"A ramp?!" Flynn was incredulous. His face boiled to a dark beet-red color. Anger built up and he began to hyperventilate.

She rolled his chair closer to the edge. Flynn gasped, his hands reaching out to hold onto the sides of the doorway.

"And he installed a pulley and rope on this cupboard behind us," she said, turning to pull the thick twine away from the metal pulley that had been screwed into the side of a mint green cabinet.

"A rope?! You can't use a rope, Missus Easterbrook! Please!"

"You're only ten years old, dear. You can't weigh *that* much." She tied the twine to the front of his chair, knotting it twice. Then a third time. Just to be safe.

She swung the chair around, wanting to get this over with as soon as possible. Flynn frantically searched everywhere for anything to rescue him from the upcoming catastrophe.

"Lady, this is crazy! What if there's a fire?!"

"Oh, relax, dear. You'll be out of that chair in a few weeks or so. This is temporary," she assured. She wrapped the twine around her hands. With her thick feet spread far apart, she pushed him backward down the basement steps, then pulled in the slack on the rope.

Wood panels had been nailed down on the staircase to create a makeshift ramp. Flynn gripped hard on the rubber wheels to stop them from rolling. He looked back but could only see darkness waiting for him below.

"Please! No! Did the foster home people approve this? This can't be legal!"

She put a foot on the seat of the chair and shoved him until he was on the ramp.

"Help! Somebody! Help me!"

"Oh, don't be such a sissy, dear! This. Is. Fun."

Grunting hard, she used her foot to launch him down the ramp. She turned to the pulley, with both hands gripping the twine. The wheelchair lurched, inch by inch, into the dark.

"I'm going to report you, lady!"

"Don't flip your wig, dear! You're lucky… I took… you on." Perspiration poured down her face as she strained to work the rope.

"Pull me back up!"

The small gray mouse popped its head out of the backpack again, nervously looking around to see what the fuss was about. They were halfway down. The wood panel floor creaked as the wheels pressed down.

Mrs. Easterbrook let more and more line through the metal pulley wheel. The twine shook up and down, vibrating from the tension. Flynn had his hands on the wall, trying to keep his broken leg from touching the sides.

"Um…" Mrs. Easterbrook was worried. Her pink high heels weren't helping the situation. She began to slide on the linoleum floor toward the pulley.

Flynn's wheelchair jerked farther down the ramp.

"Oh, dear," she added. She bit her lip hard trying to hold on.

The pulsating twine jumped out of the pulley wheel, caught on the sharp edge of the bracket – slicing the twine into two sections.

Her beady eyes flared to the size of teacup saucers.

The broken twine flew up into the air and the wheelchair was set free.

The gray mouse squeaked and buried himself deep in the backpack.

"Noooo!" bellowed Flynn. The ten-year-old boy instantly saw his short life flash before his eyes. For the second time ever.

His hand could only catch one wheel as he slid backwards. This caused the wheelchair to turn and slam into the wall. But he could not hold on.

He screamed as they picked up speed. Downward. Fast. Faster.

The gray mouse peeked out again, squeaked, and scrambled down into the backpack.

Mrs. Easterbrook gasped; her fingers held on to her bright red cheeks.

"Oh, I've killed him," she whispered.

Flynn cruised off the ramp, onto the gray concrete floor, and into the darkness. His hands covered his eyes. The wheelchair raced the length of the basement.

He left wheel caught on a metal support pole. The chair spun out of control on the slick, bare floor.

Flynn couldn't see much, except for light from upstairs flashing by again and again and again as he spun round and round. His hands grabbed the chair armrests.

The back of the wheelchair finally hit something. Hard. Flynn came to a sudden halt.

A loud crashing sound roared up at Mrs. Easterbrook. She grimaced. Her hand darted out, flipped the light switch to the basement.

More loud sounds emerged as indecipherable objects continued falling to the floor.

"Flynn?! Flynn? Are you okay?"

Flynn sat back in his chair, which was lodged against a long metal shelf. Boxes of all sizes were strewn about. He was covered in artificial Christmas tree branches, a plastic pumpkin from Halloween, and several cardboard boxes. His face was pale. He was breathing quickly from the fear, adrenaline, and anger. Another box, teetering above, finally fell onto his head to complete his humiliation.

"Flynn?!" She leaned forward, struggling to see, or hear, a sign of life.

He tossed aside the decorations and boxes, pulled open the backpack pocket – the mouse was huddled in the bottom, alive but scared.

Mrs. Easterbrook tried to step onto the ramp but knew she would only slip-slide down and injure herself. She felt helpless. She put both hands on the single railing and leaned as far as she could to see down into the room below, but it was no use. Only a small amount of the concrete floor was visible.

"Flynn, dear? I'm so deeply sorry! Please tell me you're all right!" she pleaded.

The first sign of life to roll into view were his blueish-white toes sticking out from the open end of the cast. He wheeled up to the bottom of the ramp. His eyes burned holes into, and then shot daggers at, the old lady at the top of the stairs.

Hand on her chest, she breathed a sigh of relief. "Oh, thank God!"

With raging fire burning inside him, Flynn backed the chair away from her view.

"I'll, um… I'm going to make us some dinner. Let me know if you need… I-I have bandages. I can make you an ice pack! Flynn? I'm so sorry, dear!"

No response. Guilt spread across her face and she closed the door. After a deep exhale, she composed herself with a quick straightening of her pink dress, an adjustment to her Poodle Cut hair, and confidence-boosting march back through her mint green kitchen.

2

The Mouse

Flynn carefully set his backpack on the bed that had been parked in the corner of the musty basement. He struggled to remove his heavy winter coat and threw it hard, from anger and frustration, against the basement wall.

He exhaled once, then again, trying to calm himself down. A social worker at the foster care center told him that breathing would help him control his anger.

He looked around his makeshift bedroom. A twin mattress rested on a rusty metal frame, covered with yellow sheets and a quilted blanket. An old wind-up alarm clock sat on a cardboard box that served as his nightstand. She had provided him a single flat pillow covered with a powder blue pillowcase.

His hands nervously tugged on his favorite shirt – a red, white, and blue Bicentennial long-sleeve shirt that he'd gotten for an elementary school class picture. 1776 to 1976. America's 200th birthday.

He remembered to let go of the shirt and placed his hands on his lap – he did not want the fabric to get stretched out and be ruined. Wait! Something was missing… Where was his suitcase? His whole life was in there! Everything he had left in the world.

At that moment, a worn suitcase slid down the ramp, into the basement, and stopped at the same wooden shelf he had slammed into. He stared at it.

There was a pause when Flynn didn't respond. "You're welcome," Mrs. Easterbrook shouted down at him.

The small gray mouse hopped out of the backpack and scampered across the bed. His nose darted up and down, exploring the new moldy scents lingering in the basement bedroom. His fur was a rather dark gray for a house mouse, with light gray fur covering his belly. He had big eyes, big ears, and a long hairless tail.

"Are you okay, Gray?" Flynn watched the mouse look up at him and nod. "Good."

"I'm hungry," said Gray.

Flynn smiled and pulled out a clear plastic baggie, full of mixed nuts, from the backpack. He tossed them to the mouse.

Flynn shook his head in disbelief. "Only *you* would think of food after *that*. That woman is crazy!"

"I think it's a win, kid! We gotta great little hideout down here!" said Gray.

Flynn smiled when he heard the mouse's New York accent. He had grown accustomed to talking to a mouse, but the accent nearly always took him by surprise.

Gray pulled out a cashew and nibbled on it. "The old lady can't come snoopin' around, ya know? We got it made in the shade!"

Flynn pulled a collection of books from his backpack. He inspected them for damage. Each one was a book about World War II – non-fiction accounts of the battle of Midway, the events of D-Day, as well as guides to military aircraft, ships, and tanks. He put down his books and scooped up the mouse.

"Are you okay?" He looked the mouse, pushed up a paw, poked his ribs. Gray laughed at the tickling.

"Stop! Yer killin' me!"

Flynn smiled at his friend. Gray put his paws on the boy's hand, a serious look on his little face.

He motioned Flynn closer. "Come here, kid."

Flynn held the small mouse up to his ear.

"I bet you can't stand… being in that wheelchair," Gray whispered.

Flynn leaned back in his chair, confused.

Gray laughed hard. "Get it? You can't *stand*? Bein' in a *wheelchair*?!"

The boy finally got the joke, lightly tossed his friend back onto the bed.

"As if talking to a mouse, with a New York accent, isn't weird enough," Flynn said. "I found one who tells jokes."

"Well, like I told you... all mice talk, kid. But none are nearly as smart or articulate as me! You know what I'm sayin'? Heh. Am I right? Of course, I'm right. We don't talk to just anybody, ya know. Only the special ones," Gray said. He took out an almond, chewed on it.

"Why did you choose to talk to me... that day?" Flynn looked closely at Gray.

"You saved my life," said Gray. The almond was good. He nibbled some more.

"Well, yeah. There was that," said Flynn. He decided was a proud of that fact. "So, do you owe me because of that? Is that why you're still hanging around me?"

"Hey, I don't owe you nothin'!" Gray pretended to be mad at Flynn. He shook a paw at the boy. "I think *you* owe *me*! Do you know how lucky you are to be in my glorious presence? New Yorkers would pay top dollar to have a quality mouse like me picking food outta their trash. That city was full of nothin' but rats. Man, I hate rats!"

"But... I did save you."

"That you did, kid. And, for that, I'm grateful. Truly. You're my boy now. We're family," Gray smiled up at the poor, lost, lonely boy with a bum leg, sitting in his wheelchair.

Flynn liked that. He leaned back in his wheelchair. "Good. Although... we don't have a very big family. It's just us."

The mouse dug through the small baggie, looking for a cashew but not finding one.

"Man, what I wouldn't do for a slice of pie right now," Gray said.

"Apple pie?"

"Ha! No, kid. That's what we call pizza in the big city. I love me a good slice," Gray reminisced, went back to his bag of mixed nuts.

11

The boy carefully opened his suitcase, removed all the useless clothes stacked on top, and pulled out his treasures one by one. His Evel Knievel stunt cycle was intact. Both his blue and his yellow Micronaut action figures were safe. He examined his prized Monogram model airplane kits (the Mustang P-51B and the Mitsubishi Zero A6M5) that he never had a chance to assemble, along with some paints and modeling glue. His *Avengers* comic books and *Conan* magazines looked to be in good shape. He wished the social worker who had gathered things while he was in the hospital could have gotten him a few more things but there was only so much room.

"My dad made a good pizza," said Flynn. Memories of his dad flooded back to him, making him break out into a big smile. But reality quickly and effortlessly whisked those happy thoughts away as he caught a whiff of a new scent.

"I think she's making me one of those TV dinners," said Flynn. "I can smell the burnt cranberry dessert."

Gray was preoccupied with a different smell. There was another mouse in the house. Maybe even in this room. His nose worked overtime trying to locate the source, but he was careful not to let his search be obvious. The mouse in question was a female, she was young, and was not related to him or his family back in New York.

"Food is food, kid. Food is food," Gray said.

The ceiling of the basement was the exposed wood joists of the floor above. Hiding at the top of the concrete wall, behind one of the joists, sat a tan mouse with cream-colored fur on her belly. She was called Koko. And she had heard enough.

Like a thief in the night, Koko silently padded along the concrete wall and immersed herself deeper into the darkness.

3

The 1974 Chevrolet Caprice Estate Wagon

Flynn loved the family station wagon. It was big, black, and had the best feature ever on any car he had ever seen – a third row seat that faced out the back window.

Before every journey, he would swing open the back gate and climb into his very own secluded fort where he hid books and pencils and sketch pads. He also stored the windshield ice-scraper back there because it doubled as a machine gun in case enemy ships or planes got too close.

His mom and dad could talk away in the seats up front, while Flynn was isolated enough that he would not be bothered by all their words. They talked a lot.

Summer was the best because the rear window in the back gate could stay open. Wind would whip in as they zoomed down a highway. Just like the cockpit of a Vought F4U Corsair fighter plane. He could set his machine gun on the window edge and fire at the German Messerschmitt 109 war planes that would invariably fly into his sights.

Rat-a-tat-tat-tat! Boom!

Another Nazi fighter plane would bite the dust. After every kill, Flynn attached an imaginary sticker, a silhouette of a plane, to the side panel of his cockpit. He was considered an Ace because he had shot down more than five enemy planes. The number was probably closer to forty, but who was counting? He was a legend!

His last trip in the Caprice wagon was on a warm summer evening. The Myers' family didn't have a lot of money for expensive summer holidays. But they took regular vacations, by car, to nearby states. Even though Flynn hated going by car – it was always about the destination for him, never the journey – the Chevrolet Caprice Estate Wagon made the journeys bearable. Of course, he longed to leave the car behind for a trip to Hawaii so he could visit Pearl Harbor.

Their vacation had started with a trip to New York City to call on some cousins on his dad's side of the family. All those big skyscrapers were pretty cool, but the city smelled. And it was loud. He was happy to be out of there. After they left New York, they drove on to the Great Smoky Mountains of Tennessee. It was a lot like Ohio, except they had those mountains. Ohio barely had hills.

They were headed to Gatlinburg for the week. Their massive wagon floated along on all those curvy, winding roads lined with Frasier fir and red spruce trees.

His parents sang along to a local pop radio station until they drove out of range, then his mom had to spin the dial until she found another one playing songs they liked.

Flynn's back window was down, and he was reading a book propped up between his knees. He was deep into the story of the Battle of the Bulge, one of the last major offensives by the German army near the end of the second World War.

Flynn's head hurt from reading far too much in the car. He felt it was time to take out a few Japanese Zeros. Those enemy planes were never easy to shoot down.

When he lifted the long, wooden ice-scraper out of the side pocket of the wagon, he noticed that a gray mouse hanging from the brush bristles.

The mouse looked terrified.

Flynn was terrified. He screamed.

The mouse squeaked again and again.

"Flynn?" His dad's eyes were wide in the rearview mirror.

"What's wrong, sweetie?" His mom turned toward his backseat fort.

Flynn lowered the scraper, his apprehensive eyes locked on the mouse. The mouse let go of the bristles, landed on his hind legs, and froze solid. They engaged in a staring contest, each waiting for the other to move first. The mouse was a tiny statue.

"Flynn!" said his mom.

Flynn peeked over the edge of his seat to answer his mom. "What, mom? Um, I'm fine. Are we there yet?"

"No, honey! And stop asking!"

Flynn returned to the staring contest. The mouse never blinked. Not even once. But the mouse was scared. For a brief second, he snuck a quick look at the open back window. Flynn followed his gaze. They locked eyes again.

He smiled at the mouse. "You don't want to jump out the window," he whispered. "We're moving pretty fast. That might hurt."

The gray mouse's small nose bobbed up and down.

Flynn grinned.

His parents went back to singing along with one of their goofy disco songs.

The boy slowly, ever so slowly, lowered his open hand down to the carpeted floor. He held it out, hoping the mouse would step onto his palm.

The gray mouse crouched down low, expecting an attack, and sniffed at him. The boy's hand was worrying. He still had a chance to leap up to that open back window and escape the smelly vehicle. Wind whipped the child's red hair.

Something about the boy's goofy smile disarmed the mouse. But he was no fool. The mouse scampered back to the small pocket where he had been hiding. His head popped up and he glowered at the boy, awaiting his imminent demise.

For a brief moment, the mouse closed his eyes and wondered if he had made the biggest mistake of his life. When he opened his eyes, the boy hovered over him with that big grin.

"You're safe down there. Just don't let my mom see you," Flynn assured the mouse. "That would be *real* bad."

The boy opened a Styrofoam cooler hidden behind his leg, pulled out a baggie filled with cheese cubes. He picked out cheddar and held it over the mouse's hiding spot. The mouse sniffed at the cheese cube then ducked back into hiding.

Flynn's brow wrinkled. The mouse must really be scared. He placed the cheese cube at the edge and took his hand away. He was determined not to rush this relationship.

Flynn grabbed his book and pretended to read as his small friend hunkered down in his plastic bunker.

4

The Tribe

The winter sun had set behind the brick ranch house. Light flakes of snow fell, covering the tracks from Flynn's wheelchair journey earlier in the day.

Koko raced along the wood two-by-fours that made up the structural framing behind the walls of the woman's house. She sped through holes that had been chewed open in the wood. She climbed up onto some metal conduit that protected the electrical wiring. Up, up, up she scurried.

She emerged, through a hole in the floor, into the attic. She waited silently, catching her breath. The attic was full of loose insulation, roof rafters, and abandoned storage boxes. It was dark. Quiet.

One by one, over two dozen mice cautiously emerged from hiding. Their pointy noses searched for any new, dangerous scents. Even with poor eyesight, most were able to make out Koko's shape across the attic. These house mice wore coats of dusty tan or light gray fur, with slightly lighter colors covering the fur across their underbellies.

Tate was the first one to come running up to her. He was filled with nervous excitement.

"Koko, what was all that noise?! What is going on? What did you see?! Do they have food?"

She lowered her head, grinned, and waited as Tate peppered her with questions.

Koko winked at Maska as he lumbered up behind Tate. Maska was the largest mouse anyone in the tribe had ever seen. He was tall, with huge muscles rippling just under his light gray fur, and weighed well over three ounces. Maska put his padded paw over Tate's mouth.

"Shh-shh-shh," whispered Maska. Tate rolled his eyes at Koko.

A deep, proud voice echoed across the attic. "What news?!"

Viho stepped from the shadows. Once a fierce warrior, time had caught up with him and he had taken his place as leader of the tribe. His paw held on to the staff used only by a Halona chief. He wore the scarlet and gold leather vest of the leader, as was the custom of the Halona tribe, that barely covered his large belly.

Koko scampered across the joists and nodded to the chief.

"Well? What goes on down there? Should we be worried?" he bellowed.

"There is a new human. A male child," said Koko. The other mice gathered in close.

"And he made all that... commotion?"

"He is in a metal chair, with wheels. He appears lame. The woman of the house tried to lower him down to the floor below ground and... it did not go as planned."

"I see," said Viho.

"She lost control. The boy rolled down a ramp. But he was not injured further."

Viho chuckled to himself, patted his belly. "Ah, humans. They are sometimes dangerous and many times foolish. But then, are we not all?"

His mate, Zaltana, a regal mouse with light reddish fur, moved forward to stand next to her chief. She placed her arm through his. When she stood on her hind legs, she was almost as tall as Viho. Her claws toyed with the ornate necklace, adorned with the teeth of his enemies, around her neck.

"Is there more news, Koko?" asked Zaltana, towering over her mate's little spy.

Before Koko could answer, she noticed the young mouse hiding behind Zaltana. His paws gripping her fur tightly. He timidly peered around her to get a better look at the spy. Koko winked at him, which made him disappear behind Zaltana again.

"Yes, Zaltana. There was a male mouse. With the boy," said Koko.

All the mice gasped. The chief and his mate stood tall, projecting a calm demeanor.

"Was he Matwau?" Viho leaned in, trying to read her reaction.

"He had darkish-gray fur and a light gray belly. But there was no hair on his tail. He is not a field mouse." All the others visibly relaxed. But only slightly.

"And he accompanied the child? The boy knew he was there?"

"Yes. They were… talking to each other," she stated, knowing what would come next.

The crowd of mice were stunned. Paws covered mouths; a few took a step back. Maska pushed Tate behind him for cover. All the mice surged forward, asking a million questions at once.

"He talked to the boy?"

"Are you sure?"

"How could this be?"

Viho put his paw in the air and they were immediately silent. He moved close to her, held onto her shoulders.

"Koko, you are the night. My master thief and the greatest scout that any chief could ask for. I do not doubt you. But I must ask, for my own clarification. The two – the boy and the mouse – they were having a conversation?" He was deadly serious.

"Yes, sir." The tribe stirred again. One mouse ostensibly fainted from shock.

"By Apollo!" Viho spun away, his paw rubbing his fuzzy chin, and paced the attic. "It's been generations since we have spoken to humans."

Koko scampered closer to him. Her voice was a hiss. "They seemed to be… friends."

"This mouse? Did he appear disturbed or manic, in any way? Was he sickly?"

"No. But he did talk… funny."

"'Crazy as old Geronimo' funny? Or laugh-out-loud funny?"

Koko kept her focus. "He had a strange dialect; I could not understand him easily. He is not from around here."

Zaltana stepped in front of the frightened mice, her paws held up and a calming look on her face.

"The sun has set. I am sure you are all hungry. Gather your food now," she soothed. They did not move. "Go on. We have plenty to eat after your courageous raids! Go, my warriors!"

All the mice shuffled off to eat.

Zaltana turned to the young mouse hiding behind her, bent to whisper in his ear. "Yuma. Go with others. Eat something... for me," she soothed, stroking the dark reddish-brown fur on his head.

Reluctantly, the youngster backed away, then scurried off. Zaltana watched him go, a sad look in her eyes.

Tate popped his head around from behind the massive Maska.

"May I go eat, as well?"

Maska grinned and grabbed Tate by the scruff of his neck. "I am surprised you are not already eating!"

Tate resumed chewing the sunflower seeds that were stashed away in his cheeks, "Way ahead of you, big mouse! Way ahead!" He popped another seed in the air, caught it, pranced off toward the others.

Maska watched his chief pace back and forth. With a sigh, he spun around and strode off to a far corner of the attic.

As Maska approached the worktables of Adriel, he noticed everything about this mouse was organized chaos. He wore ugly glasses he had made himself with some wire and pilfered lenses, but Adriel constantly cleaned them and adjusted them to perfection. Even though mice are fastidious groomers, Adriel's tan fur was unkempt and his paws dirty from hard work. But he also had an economy of movement, every step or reach of the arm was calculated and graceful.

"Adriel! How are you, my friend?" Maska bellowed.

Adriel's workbench was full of tools, plans, notes. Maska used one of his claws to spin around one of the drawings but his big paw was slapped away by the engineer.

"Your weapon is not ready yet!"

"What? Can I not simply greet an old friend?"

"You only ever want something from me, Maska. That is without doubt," said Adriel, never looking away from his never-ending work.

The massive mouse leaned down to whisper in Adriel's pointy ear.

"We may be facing a new threat, Adriel. I must be prepared."

"You just want your new toy, Maska."

The big mouse was close to the engineer. Too close. Adriel was nervous. Maska leaned his head back and laughed, full and hearty.

"That is so true, my old friend! So true!" He patted the engineer on the head. "I want my toy… tomorrow." Maska lumbered off.

Adriel adjusted his glasses that were knocked askew from the heavy pats on his head.

In the middle of the attic, Viho finally stopped pacing. He summoned Koko back to his side.

"You are to perform reconnaissance. Search the exterior of the house, but do not go outdoors. Look for signs the Matwau may lurking about."

"At once, sir." Koko disappeared back into the shadows.

Zaltana placed her paw into her mate's and looked deeply into his tired eyes.

"You are hungry, as well. You should eat."

"When the tribe has eaten. We must prepare for battle. We have to be ready. For anything."

"We knew this day might come," she said. "We are ready."

"This is a bad omen for us. I fear the worst," he sighed. "A bad omen, indeed."

5

The Bridge

The Myers' station wagon hummed along the quiet highway through the Smoky Mountains. With the summer sun settling down for the night, bright yellow light shone through the fir trees cast to cast flickering shadows across Flynn's face. His big grin had not faded as he gazed down on the small gray mouse hiding in the corner of his backseat fort.

"What's your name?" He held out the cheese cube, but the trust was not there. The mouse ignored the cheddar as his small, pointed nose worked overtime.

"My name is Flynn," he stated. "That's my mom and dad up there. They're kind of goofy and they can be pretty strict. They never let me stay up late to watch TV. Except on Saturday nights. I like to watch *The Love Boat.*"

The mouse stared at the boy intently. He was worried but realized the boy was not an immediate threat. He hadn't tried to squash him. He also had not alerted the other humans to his presence. He might survive this encounter after all.

"Let's see… what should we call you?" Flynn pondered silently, his thumb and finger propped up his chin.

"What about Jerry? Like the cartoon," he thought out loud. "No. You don't look like a Jerry."

The mouse wondered how he had gotten himself into this mess. This morning, he had begun raiding the dumpster of a Chinese restaurant when he noticed a woman approach and throw away trash from her car. Tired of the Chinese food scraps, he had scampered around to the back of her vehicle while the humans had gone inside the restaurant. He figured he had time to check out the smells coming from the big car and make off with something new for lunch. He was wrong.

"Your gray fur is really cool. Hey! I know! I'll call you Gray!" Flynn tried to whisper but he was too excited.

"What's that, honey?" His mom was annoyed.

"Nothing, mom!" Flynn put his finger to his mouth to shush the mouse, even though he was the one talking loudly. "Yes. It's official. Gray. That's your name now."

Flynn thought he saw the mouse nod – ever so slightly – at his new name.

The truck driver was nearly done with this day. He'd been driving for sixteen straight hours and was ready to park his rig and kick up his boots. His woman had told him, over the CB radio, that she had cooked up a pot roast and had a dozen beers cooling down in the fridge, just waiting for him to get home.

Sure, he was driving a bit fast but… he was an expert. He'd been long-hauling cargo for almost ten years. Almost had his Kenworth paid off.

He came down off a slight grade and drove onto a long, white bridge that spanned one of the many Tennessee gorges along his route. He was getting close enough to home to already taste those beers. Despite his anxiousness, he decided to downshift gears and slow the rig.

The CB radio crackled to life.

"Hey, there, Road Roller, come back at me," said the woman's voice on the radio speaker.

He chuckled to himself, reached for the radio mic. He was tired and his hand hit the mic clip instead, knocking the mic off. It dropped down, dangling back and forth on the extra-long cord.

The trucker reached down, tried to grab it, but his hand only flailed around.

Heading in the opposite direction, the Myers's station wagon rolled along on the freeway toward the long, white bridge.

Road Roller grasped the CB mic cord halfway down but couldn't reach the mic.

"I say, come back at me, Road Roller," she squawked on the speaker. "What's your twenty?"

Frustrated, he took his eyes off the road to get a look at the mic dangling by his cowboy boot. He looked up, adjusted the trajectory of the truck on the bridge, then back down at the mic.

Road Roller could see the headlights of a car ahead as it approached the bridge.

His hand gripped the mic and he sat back in his worn vinyl seat. It was then he realized his Kenworth had veered into the wrong lane. In a panic, he pulled hard on the steering wheel.

The big truck swerved out of the other lane. But the empty trailer slid on gravel that covered the asphalt.

Riding along in his backseat fort, Flynn attempted to gain the trust of his new friend by letting the mouse sniff his fingers. He had seen that work with dogs before.

Brakes squealed. The station wagon dipped forward, as the brakes locked up, and then swerved to the right. Flynn's head banged hard into the side of his backseat fort.

The big rig corrected, and the trailer pulled back into the correct lane – but it was too late for the Caprice Estate wagon.

The car missed hitting the side guard rail of the bridge but shot off the edge of the mountain and into the gorge below.

Road Roller downshifted a half dozen times, hitting the brakes hard as the hydraulics screamed and the tires bit into the tarmac.

The station wagon sailed straight out onto the thin mountain air, arcing through the night sky for a brief moment. The gravity that held the family to their car seats disappeared. Flynn and Gray floated up. Shock and wonder flashed across their faces. The starry night sky was all they could see out the back window.

Flynn grabbed the small gray mouse out of the air, pulled him close to his chest.

When the wagon hit the ground again, both dropped hard down onto the backseat floor.

Then the car started to roll.

6

The Basement

"You've got to be kidding me."

The wheels of Flynn's chair stopped as they bumped into the doorway of the hastily-built basement bathroom once again.

His chin drooped down onto his chest in despair.

Gray looked up from eating a peanut.

"Man, this place is so bogus!" sighed Flynn.

His wheelchair was stuck in the entrance to the small bathroom that the handyman had created for him. The chair was too wide to fit through the door.

"I can't get in the stupid bathroom," he complained. "It's freezing cold and damp down here. There's not even a TV! Is there a phone down here?! I've got to call someone to get me out of here!"

He used his good leg to kick free from the doorway. He searched the room; his eyes were frantic, and the anger was again rapidly building.

Gray noticed that the boy was losing his cool again. Flynn began to hyperventilate, his face turning bright red.

"Hey, kid? Listen up," the small mouse scurried to the edge of the bed to be close. "Take a deep breath there, buddy! Yer gonna blow a gasket, okay? Yo! Look at me!"

His furtive eyes landed on the mouse and he gasped for air. Flynn swallowed hard. Took a long drag of air.

"Breathe."

Flynn let out the air trapped in his lungs, pulled in more. His fists, clenched tight on the armrests, relaxed slightly.

"There ya go. Another breath. We've been through this before, kid. You're gonna okay. Capisce?"

Flynn pushed back in his chair, hard, shaking his head. If he had something to throw, he would have thrown it.

"This is not fair," growled Flynn.

"No. It ain't fair." Gray climbed on the metal frame of the foot of the bed, lithely jumping over to Flynn's good leg. He placed his paws on the boy's shirt.

"But this is where we are, all right? And so… we're going to make the best of it."

"No, we have choices. I think," Flynn stated. He wheeled them closer to the bed. He pulled out a mimeographed sheet of paper from the open suitcase. "They had a list of people willing to take me. Maybe we go to one of these foster homes!"

Gray looked at the piece of paper – two other names and addresses were listed below Mrs. Easterbrook.

Gray's whiskers waggled feverishly. "Where'd you get this?"

"I took it from the clipboard when they made me sign the papers at the home," he admitted.

"I see," murmured Gray. "Well, the problem is that we don't know where these people are, and we got no way to get there. They wouldn't even know we was comin'."

"So… we're stuck here?"

"Afraid so. Besides, we don't even have a way to get you and that hunk of junk outta this basement."

Flynn put both hands on his face, hiding the fresh wave of anger that boiled up within him.

"It's okay, kid. We been through a lot already. Together. This'll get better."

"Before it gets any worse? Or after?"

Gray could see the snow filling up the small egress window at the top of the basement wall.

"I don't know, kid."

7

The Gorge

The sound of cicadas filled the late summer night. A babbling brook cut through a bed of river rock down the middle of the valley nestled between two tall mountains.

The only working car headlight glowed out across the black water. The upside-down station wagon rested on several boulders, with most of the roof crushed in and the mangled back door of the wagon hanging open.

Flynn woke, lying half in the weeds and half on the dry bed of rock. He turned his head toward the wounded car. He could hear distant shouting, from up on the white bridge.

Gray scampered toward him from the wrecked station wagon. Flynn tried to sit up but was racked by pain that crashed over him like a wave. His right leg punished him the most. He tried to reach down to that pain shooting through his leg, to comfort it or try to push it away, but his body would not permit him to sit all the way up.

The small gray mouse stopped seriously close to the boy's face. He held his paws up, almost as a warning.

"Okay, kid," said Gray. "This is probably the wrong time to spring this on you, but—"

Flynn briefly forgot about the pounding pain. He recoiled at the words coming out of the mouse's mouth.

"Yeah. I can talk…"

Flynn's hands went to his head. Was there blood? Had he hit his head? What was going on? He looked at his hands then snapped his fingers, to make sure he was awake.

"Oh, you got problems but... your *head*? Your head ain't one of 'em," he stated plainly.

"But, but... what? I-I..." The fog in his brain prevented him from forming a single, clear thought.

"Your leg, on the other hand? That's pretty bad," Gray said.

Flynn looked down at his jeans. They were muddied, torn in places, and he saw his blood all over the denim and surrounding rocks. It was then that he noticed a bone sticking out, through his jeans, just below his knee.

The boy panicked. His heart raced. He struggled to breathe. His skin turned pale white. He dropped his dizzy head hard to the rocks, closed his eyes. He was going into shock.

"Flynn?! It is Flynn, right?" Gray took a deep breath. "Look, kid, I need you to stay with me. Keep those peepers of yours wide open. Okay, Flynn?!"

Gray stepped closer to the boy. Precariously close, for the mouse. Gray could see the woods just beyond. His survival instincts kicked in, begging him to run. Escape. *Now, you idiot... run!*

"Mom? Dad?" Flynn was groggy. He flailed on the rocks as much as he could. "Mommy!"

"Flynn, please. Just breathe, kid. Help will be here soon. Kid?!"

"Where's my mom? My dad? Where..."

Distant sirens entered the valley, echoing off the mountain. Red and blue flashing lights lit up trees around the gorge.

Gray placed his tiny paw on Flynn's cheek. The boy stopped struggling, looked at the mouse. Tears clouded his vision, but he could still see pain in those small dark eyes.

"I got some bad news, Flynn."

"Where are they? Can't they get out of the car?!" Flynn knew what was coming but didn't want to hear it.

"Terrible news, in fact."

"Help me get over there! I need to help them!" he screamed. His hands reached out for the broken station wagon. "Mom!"

"I am sorry…"

"No! Mommy! Daddy! Please!"

"Very, very sorry," Gray lowered his gaze from the crying boy.

"No," he whispered to himself. "No…"

Bushes rustled, branches cracked, as people worked their way down the side of the hill.

Run, Gray's mind screamed him. *Run!* The mouse shook off the voice in his head.

Humans were arriving to help the boy.

Tears streaked Flynn's face.

He needs me, Gray told that nagging inner voice. *I'm all he has now.*

Gray scrambled across the child and jumped into the front pocket of his torn jeans. There was just enough room to keep him hidden from sight. From the other humans.

He was going to stay with the boy.

8

The Storm on the Horizon

Koko stood on the windowsill, looked out on the crisp snowscape that made up Mrs. Easterbrook's backyard. It was tranquil, quiet. Thick flakes of snow drifted down to add to the heavy amount that had been falling all winter.

She shivered. The house was warm but the thought of being out there chilled her tiny bones.

Koko despised the fact she could not see well. Her vision was better than most mice because her black eyes jutted out farther, allowing her to sense movement more easily. She could detect motion at more than twice the distance of anyone in her tribe.

She aimed her mouth away from the window glass to prevent her breath from fogging up the glass. Koko wanted one last, long look. There was no good moonlight to help her cause. Ready to give up, she backed away from the glass. A gut feeling gave her pause. Koko moved back to the window.

A small whisper fell out of her small mouth, to no one in particular. "Are you there?"

Mice make up for poor eyesight with other senses. Whiskers let them know when they are close to running into something and can help them detect a slight change wind direction or a change in temperature. Their stiff hairs sense slight vibrations. A highly developed sense of smell lets mice differentiate between prey and predator and can help them find food or communicate with their tribe. Large ears give them excellent hearing, and they can detect frequencies most other animals cannot. But Koko put her sense of intuition to use as she hunkered down near the cold glass of the window.

Her hearing was useless because – as she did nearly every night – Mrs. Easterbrook had plopped down in her favorite chair in the living room to watch a box that broadcast an obnoxious light and blaring sound. The whine of electricity, the buzzing of the tubes, dust particles burning off the metal parts inside, and the high pitch of the human voices that came through the metallic speaker were terribly annoying.

But any species that could so efficiently hoard such large amounts of food probably deserved the right to stare at their box of light and sound for hours on end. She chuckled to herself at the thought of not needing to fight for survival every waking moment of life.

How boring.

Mrs. Easterbrook tossed her aching feet up on an ottoman, as she took a long drink from her highball glass. She had lowered down the TV dinner to the boy but had no desire to try to get her tray back. Maybe she would get it tomorrow. For now, the local news was on. More importantly – the weather. And the cute weatherman.

"Winter continues to bear down on the Central Ohio region," announced the weatherman, with his square jaw and flashy, white-toothed smile. "So far, in January, we're experiencing the seventh coldest month on record, with an average temperature of twenty-one degrees."

She poured another shot of warmth down her throat, toasted the handsome man on her television.

"We've already had nineteen inches of snow fall in the new year. And it doesn't show any signs up letting up. The meteorological service is keeping an eye on a new low-pressure system that seems to be building to the northwest, up in Canada. Looks like we're going to continue dealing with a very long, cold, and wet season. Old Man Winter is not through with us yet. Back to you, Larry."

Mrs. Easterbrook shook her head. All that snow, wind, and humidity would be murder on her customers' hairdos. They might stay away from her salon until spring.

Koko had no need for the human on the light box to tell her about the weather. She could sense that the situation was only going to get worse. The tribe might be stuck in this house for a long time. A house with a new and unexpected threat.

"Stay perfectly still, my warriors."

Moki stood motionless on the wood pile. He stared at the house through a broken eyeglasses lens he had found.

"Just a little while longer."

His vision, like most mice, was blurry. But the glasses lens did magnify what he could see. A small dark shape was still huddled on the windowsill, backlit by the artificial light inside.

"One of their scouts may be hunting us still," Moki hissed.

The tribe of field mice waited silently, unmoving, on firewood logs stacked in the back corner of the yard. They had been trained from birth to remain motionless for as long as needed. Each of them had an eye on the house and an eye in the sky, looking for owls and hawks.

Field mice were larger than the typical house mouse. They had dark tan, brown, reddish, and dark gray fur with white underbellies. Their tails had dark hair on the top with lighter hair underneath. These field mouse all wore battle jackets made from scavenged leather, wool, or vinyl. They carried shields, strapped to their backs. Some were armed with bows and a quiver full of arrows or they carried spears. Nearly every warrior had a sword or knife fastened to their belt.

Moki, their leader, was barrel-chested, with powerful front and hind legs and massive shoulders. He was the tallest in the tribe, with more than a few battle scars across his dark red fur. One particular scar ran across his right eye, giving him the menacing look of a hardened warrior that no mouse would want to run across in a dark field.

Dyani stared proudly at her mate as he stood silently atop the wood pile. But impatience quickly overcame her appreciation.

34

"Moki, the weather grows worse. We should attack now," whispered Dyani.

"They are probably in this house, Dyani. All signs have steered us here," he announced. "But we do not know for certain. And our people? They are weary from traveling over this frozen terrain."

She started but held her tongue. There was no point arguing with the stubbornness that is Moki.

"They probably climbed that tree, nearest the house. Jumped over to the roof, set up camp in the attic," he mumbled, mostly to himself. "That is what I would have done."

"This is the worst winter in many seasons," Dyani stated. "We must make our move soon."

Below the wood pile, Chuchip slid closer to Moki. He was First Warrior among the tribe, eager to demonstrate his bravery.

"She is right, Moki. Should we attack at sunrise? Before they wake?!"

"All in good time, Chuchip. Surprise is our friend. They do not yet know we are upon them."

Despite being still as a statue, Moki's cold paw betrayed him. The broken eyeglasses lens slipped a little through his claws. He closed his eyes and lowered his head.

He had made a mistake.

Koko saw a brief flash. A glint. Bluish-green light from a mercury vapor streetlamp had caught something that moved in the back corner of the dark yard. She had spotted Moki's grave error when the lens his slid down in his paw.

"They are here," she whispered to herself.

Koko backed silently from the windowsill, disappearing into a dark corner of the house.

9

The Morning

A small streak of sunlight shone through the lone egress window at the top of the basement wall.

Flynn was sprawled out on the top of the sheets and blanket, still in his clothes from the day before. His cast had forced him to sleep on his back once again, which he hated, for another long night.

Gray was curled up close to Flynn, in a space between the blanket and pillow.

A loud heavy thud from the top of the stairs woke them.

Mrs. Easterbrook's voice drifted down to the boy and mouse. "Oh, dear. That... device is rather large. And... ungainly."

"Lady, you asked for a winch. This is a winch," said a gruff male voice.

Flynn listened without moving. He didn't dare blink. Gray lightly scrambled to the foot of the bed to see if he could tell what was happening upstairs.

They heard the sound of heavy boots trailing off, with the clacking of high heels following close behind. Flynn knew this was his opportunity. He pulled his wheelchair close to the bed, slid into the seat. Gray looked from the stairs to the boy and back again.

Flynn wheeled over toward the bottom of the steps. Gray hopped onto his lap as he rolled by. At the foot of the stairs, they peeked upward, around the corner, but could see nothing.

The heavy stomping sound returned. Flynn backed the chair out of sight. Another heavy thud. A grunt from the man they had heard before. The boy rolled a bit closer.

The handyman had set down a car battery next to the basement door. He took a drill from a toolbox, plugged it into an outlet.

"Oh. Are you sure that's necessary?" Mrs. Easterbrook asked the handyman.

He sighed, heavily, without looking up at her. "If you want to be able to pull him up, the winch has to be locked down."

He proceeded to use the drill to screw something to the wall across from the basement staircase.

Flynn and Gray looked at each other, shrugged, then peeked back upstairs.

"Just know this is temporary. I'll need this gone from my house once the boy can walk again," she stated. A sound outside caught her attention.

"Oh! The mailman!" Her heels clacked away on the kitchen floor linoleum.

The handyman shook his head, went back to work.

Viho, the leader of the house mice, stood in a baseboard hole behind the living room sofa. He held a paw up to keep the others silent and still.

Mrs. Easterbrook tore through the living room, struggling to get her winter coat on, and threw open the front door. She dashed into the cold winter morning.

"We are clear! Quickly, everyone! Quickly" Viho commanded.

The tribe poured from the whole in the wall. The last one through was Sani, the tribe elder. His fur was streaked with white. He was tired and achingly slow.

"If Koko is correct, we have very little time," announced Viho.

A loud thump startled them all – they froze in place.

Viho heard the handyman let out another grunt. "There are even more humans in the house than we expected. Gather supplies as quickly as you can! Go everyone. Go!"

The mice dispersed under the sofa, along the baseboards, and over the back of the sofa. Koko scrambled to the bay window to be lookout.

Sani slowly stumbled along the wall, grumbling to himself about his aches and pains. Viho started to yell at the old one, to hurry him along, but Zaltana put a paw up to his mouth to stifle him. He rolled his eyes at his mate. She smirked at him.

She turned to young Yuma, who nervously chewed on his claws behind her, and dragged him off into the living room.

Outside, Mrs. Easterbrook rushed along the recently shoveled walk toward her driveway, her heels crunching into the fresh snow. Her handyman had cleared snow off the path, but she was running too fast. When she reached the top of the drive, she had no way to stop. She slid on her heels. By flailing her arms, she kept her balance but was stranded in the middle of the icy driveway.

"Oh, dear," she muttered.

Taking baby steps in her high heels, she inched her way to her car. She held on tightly, using the fenders and doors handles to stay upright.

But as she moved downward, she ran out of car.

Mrs. Easterbrook stared down along the rest of her drive to the mailbox. The mailman, in his truck, had buzzed along to the next house down the street and was no help to her.

She let go of the car, took a few small steps. She instantly regretted wearing the high heels onto the ice. The flat part of her shoe lost traction and she slid down the driveway. A high-pitched scream bellowed from deep within.

Down, down, for the last half of the drive, she slid on the slick surface. She was bent forward like an Olympic ski jumper ready to launch off the jump.

When the ground leveled out, she skidded to a stop. Her waving arms had kept her upright. Relieved, she stood up straight and smoothed her dress.

She took a step toward her mailbox but her foot, then nearly her whole leg, sunk deep in the snow. Mrs. Easterbrook pulled her leg to free it from the snow. But her high heel shoe did not come out with her foot. It was buried deep down in there.

"Dagnabbit! Cheese and rice!"

This wasn't going as planned. Breathing hard, she bent over to dig out her lost shoe. Her other heel slid out from under her and Mrs. Easterbrook planted, face-first, down into the cold snow.

From her hiding spot in large bay window, Koko watched the woman try to get back up and fall back down. A puff of snow flew into the air. Koko laughed to herself. Humans. The little round lady crawled to the mailbox on hands and knees. She used the wood pole of the mailbox to drag herself up. She was flushed, gasping for breath.

Mrs. Easterbrook was finally able to grab her mail from the box. Shuffling through the letters, she found what she was looking for – a envelope from county child services.

Mrs. Easterbrook tore it open, found a description of the foster services, and reviewed her expected monthly time and expenses. She held up the check, stared at the amount, and grinned. She was saved!

Her eyes squinted as she scanned her street. Had anyone seen her fall? She had an image to maintain, after all. She adjusted her hair, pulled down on her dress under the coat, and brushed off the wet snow.

Taking her other high heel off, she tip-toed carefully back up the drive to her house.

The handyman lowered a metal rope, with a hook at the end, down the plywood that covered the basement steps.

"Now, take hold of that there," he shouted down to Flynn. Gray was hidden between the boy's back and the vinyl of the wheelchair seat.

"This might be a bad idea," Gray whispered. Flynn nodded his head from side to side, as if say he knew that but there wasn't a whole heckuva lot he could do about it.

"Put the hook on the front of your chair. This thing'll pull ya right up, lickety-split," boasted the handyman.

The boy was able to grab the metal hook. He fixed it to a bar under the seat vinyl, tugged on it to make sure it was on tight, nodded to the handyman.

"Okey-doke. He we go. Hold on!"

The handyman flipped the switch he had rigged up to the car battery. The winch started turning, pulling the metal rope around a cylinder.

Flynn lurched forward when the rope was pulled taut. Worried, he held his hands out to help guide the wheelchair. The wheels turned. The chair tipped backwards, just a little, as it rolled onto the plywood. Flynn swallowed hard.

"There ya go! Lookin' good!"

The old truck winch was noisy. The motor strained as it pulled the boy and his wheelchair up and up from the basement.

"Just a little farther." He coaxed the chair upward with his hands, his fingers summoning the kid upstairs.

Flynn constantly guided the path with his hands.

"Gotcha!"

The handyman pulled Flynn up the rest of the way. He flipped the switch and the winch stopped turning. Gray ducked down farther as the handyman pushed Flynn into the kitchen.

The winter sun, shining off the snow outside, filled the room with light. Almost too bright for Flynn who had been down in the dark pit for some time.

Mrs. Easterbrook burst into the dining room. Her face, hair, and the front of her dress were wet from the melting snow. She grabbed a kitchen towel from the counter to dab herself dry. But it wasn't haven't much effect; she was an awful, soggy mess.

"Here's the boy, lady. Up from his cave," the handyman said.

She stopped primping her hair to give him a dirty look. The handyman chuckled, pushed Flynn toward her, and grabbed his tools.

"Oh, dear! Well, I'm sure I look quite the fright. I mean, I just…" she stammered. With a deep sigh of disgust, she gave up. She stood as tall as she could and put her chin out.

The handyman grabbed his toolbox but noticed something was wrong – it was considerably lighter than when he brought it in. He looked around the floor, down into the basement, up on the counters.

"Here, I made breakfast for you," she said, pushing Flynn's chair up to the dining table. A cold plate of eggs, sausage links, and white toast awaited him.

Flynn watched her as she moved around him, pushed the salt and pepper closer, handed him a napkin, and then suddenly became unsure of what to do with herself. She patted the boy on the back and shuffled into the kitchen.

The handyman was still looking all around. "Have you seen my drill?"

Mrs. Easterbrook pushed the much larger man out of the kitchen. "Thank you very much for your help! Everything looks fine. Works fine. Is fine. Exceptionally fine."

"Um, I'm gonna need that winch back soon," stated her handyman. He was looking over his shoulder for his missing drill.

"You'll get it back! They told me the boy would be walking in a few weeks," she continued pushing on him until they were in the living room. "Then… he'll be able to help around the house."

"Okay, lady. Okay, no worries," he said. "But, uh, there is a matter of the bill."

She managed to shove him through the front door.

"Just send me the invoice! Please, thank you, and goodbye now!"

Out on the snowy street, a shiny new red Oldsmobile Cutlass Supreme docked alongside her curb, close to the mailbox.

"Cheese and rice! Of course, she's early!" She was at a complete loss.

"What?" The handyman looked back at the car, then to Mrs. Easterbrook. She slammed the door in his face.

She spun quickly to face a wall mirror hanging between two faux-metal sconces – wet hair hung down in her face, black mascara ran away from her eyes, lipstick smeared off her lips. With eyes as wide as they would go, she let out a deafening scream.

Back in the dining room, Gray leaned over to get a look into the living room.

The scream startled Flynn, who stopped chewing his food.

"Heh. The old lady just caught her look in the mirror!" Gray whispered loudly. He laughed. Flynn managed to smile.

They heard her run from her living room to her bedroom. She slammed the door hard. Gray laughed harder.

Flynn held up his hand and the small mouse jumped high enough to slap his paw on it. The boy went back to eating the cold breakfast. Gray was glad to see the boy smile. He hadn't seen that since they were riding together in his family's station wagon.

Flynn gave the mouse a piece of the fried egg from his plate, then gave him the crust from the toast.

"Thanks, kid."

Neither one of them saw the electric drill being dragged behind the living room sofa.

10

The Halona

Water drained from the avocado-colored bathtub. Gray stood on the edge of the avocado pedestal sink to watch the vortex of bathwater spin round and round as it drained away.

Gray questioned the entire setup – a giant container to hold hot water, a metal drain to release dirty water, a showerhead above to provide water from a higher vantage point, with a dozen soaps and shampoos lining a small avocado shelf, and a rack of towels for drying off. All *that* was required to get clean? It made no sense to him. He chuckled to himself. Gray sniffed himself and began grooming his fur.

His hair still damp, Flynn dressed in his old clothes. He didn't think to bring anything up with him earlier. But he loved his Bicentennial shirt, so it was cool.

"Now... the hard part." The boy stared at the big plastic bag and duct tape he had wrapped around his cast to keep it dry. Gray winced.

"It's not like you got a bunch of fur to rip off, kid. I ain't exactly sure all the fuss is about."

"Ripping tape off skin isn't exactly fun," said, Flynn. He exhaled, to prepare himself.

He gripped the tape in his fingers, inhaled deeply. Pulling swiftly, he yanked off a long strip stuck to the top of his leg. Then another strip down the side. He switched hands and pulled the last bit from behind his leg. It was red, sore. He rubbed at it but that just made the rest of his leg itchy. He scratched at it.

"You know you shouldn't do that," warned Gray.

Exasperated, Flynn flung himself back in his wheelchair. He threw the tape and plastic away from him. Anger flashed across his young face, his cheeks turning bright red. Gray could see that the boy felt helpless.

No animal wants to be helpless. When mice are born, their eyes are closed. The mothers nurse and care for them for several weeks. During that time, they are defenseless and require care. But after a few weeks, they open their eyes and can see. After another week, they can explore outside of the parents' territory. Unless they become injured, they take care of themselves until old age sets in – if they are lucky enough to make it to old age. *Most do not make it*, Gray mused. Humans were a completely different ballgame. They needed constant care and protection. For many years. They even stayed in their homes long after they could eat, run, and play on their own. But they also lived for a very long time, so there was no real hurry.

Gray turned his attention back to the boy. "You okay?"

"Yeah… This just totally sucks!" Flynn's gaze was aimed at the avocado wall tiles, but he was a thousand miles away. Or several years ago.

"Hey, kid. You know, we all lose people. I've lost a lot of friends and family. It ain't easy. If you want talk about it—"

"I don't want to talk about it. Okay?"

Gray put his head down. From the time the boy woke in his hospital room until now, he had not talked about it. No tears were shed. Just a whole lot of anger.

"It's okay to feel sad. To be sad."

"I'm fine," said Flynn, harshly enough to let Gray know the conversation was over.

Gray ran to the wheelchair and climbed down onto the handle as the boy moved them to the door.

He managed to turn the chair at an angle so he could reach for the door, but the round handle didn't make it easy. His damp fingers kept slipping off. He maneuvered the chair at a better angle and turned the knob. Backing away from the door, Flynn used the toes sticking out of his cast to draw the door open.

Unsure of what to do next, the boy and the mouse rolled into Mrs. Easterbrook's hallway and stopped. They listened. Waited. Voices were coming from one of the bedrooms. Gray and Flynn looked at each other, shrugged, and zoomed down the hall. They stopped before his cast would be visible in the doorway.

Mrs. Easterbrook was talking to someone. "Oh, and you did not hear this from me, but I saw that Daniel Sloane carry in the groceries for Patsy last Saturday morning. I wonder what Kathy Sloane would say if she knew about that!"

Another woman was in the room. "What?! Did they see you?!"

"Of course not! No one is more discrete than I am, Margaret. You know that," said Mrs. Easterbrook.

"I know that," the woman acknowledged.

Flynn rolled his eyes. Gossip. Old folks sure did love to gossip. He rolled the chair, as fast as he could, past the door before they could see him – but he wasn't fast enough.

"Oh, Flynn, dear! There you are! How was your bath? I'd like you to meet Missus Robinson!"

Flynn backed the wheelchair into the doorway, a fake smile plastered on his face. He gave a slight wave.

Mrs. Robinson sat on a black barber's chair with large rollers in her hair. She had a bright-blue mask of goop covering her face while wearing a smock to protect her clothing.

"Oh, he's just adorable! Bless his heart!" She squealed through pursed lips to avoid cracking her facial mask.

Flynn remembered his dad always saying that *Bless his heart* was code that means they think you are either cute or a moron.

He noted the entire bedroom had been converted into a hair salon. Along with the barber chair, there was a black sink against the wall. A free-standing hair dryer, with its big pink dome, stood like a robot behind the chair.

"Oh, Flynn, dear! Someone sent you something. It arrived while you were in the bath. It's in the parlor," Mrs. Easterbrook was done with him, shooing him along with her hand. *There she goes*, Flynn mused. Using fancy terms for stuff. Nobody calls it *parlor* anymore. It's a living room. She probably called her couch a *davenport*. He had heard these old-timey phrases far too often over the course of his many, many years.

As he pushed himself down the hall, voices back in the salon bedroom made him pause.

"So, it must be expensive taking on a foster child," said Mrs. Robinson. Flynn scooted back toward the room, just so he could hear better.

"I'm sure it'll require time and energy," said Mrs. Easterbrook, holding up the check she received from the county in the mail. "But it does have its rewards."

Mrs. Robinson could see the dollar amount on the child services check. She was impressed.

"Goodness. I may have to ask Ed if *we* can take on a foster child," she said. "Momma needs a trip to Florida!"

A bitter looked flashed across Flynn's freshly scrubbed mug. As he hurriedly rolled himself down the hall, he bumped into the living room doorway but didn't care. He pushed his way to the middle of the room, brooding, embarrassed.

Was he just a paycheck to her?

Gray didn't want to interfere. He'd said enough already. He hopped from the handle of the wheelchair over to the coffee table. On it stood an impressive collection of colorful helium balloons, with red ribbons, and a small collection of candies tied down as the base.

"Yo, kid! Someone sent you a gift!"

Flynn repeatedly tapped his good foot on the wheelchair pedal. He stared out the window, eyes full of anger, welling up.

"Flynn? Look," Gray tried to distract him. He pulled the card off the ribbon and held it out for the boy. Flynn turned his head, grabbed the card out of the mouse's paws. He didn't want to read it, but he knew Gray would not stop until he did.

Dear Flynn,

You are brave, you are strong, and you are special! You're also in our thoughts and prayers! Get well soon!
  - The University Hospital team

It was signed by several of the nurses from the hospital – and, maybe, one of the doctors? He couldn't read the signature very well. They must have waited to send the gift until he had a more permanent address than the foster facility.

His anger drained away. Tears welled up. Both happiness and sadness washed over him. He smiled briefly, until a tear finally fell. *No*, he thought, *I'm not a little crybaby*. Flynn quickly pushed away all those emotions. Anger was the only thing he wanted to feel in that moment. He tossed the card away, sat up straight in the chair, stared out the window.

That was the kind of card his mom would have thought to send. He quickly remembered all the *get-well* cards and even a few condolence cards she had forced him to sign over the years. She was always thinking of others. He had no idea how she had the time or energy to always make those small gestures.

Gray studied Flynn carefully. He needed something to snap the boy out of his funk.

"Hey, you got some candy over here, too!" Gray held up the small mesh bag tied to the end of all the balloons.

Flynn gave the candy a small glance. He shook his head. "You can have it."

Gray sighed when the boy turned his gaze back out the front window. "Are you sure? It does look rather tasty."

Worried about Flynn, the mouse made a big show of unwrapping the candy bag. He put his sharp teeth on the mesh, then stepped between all the ribbons holding up the balloons. His paws and teeth pulled open the bag. He picked up a piece of taffy.

"What do we have here?" He tossed the taffy aside. "That don't look good. What else we got?" He inspected a butterscotch, threw it away.

Flynn glanced at the mouse.

"Nothin' is really grabbing my attention here," said Gray. He examined the candy necklace but set it down. The *Tootsie Rolls* were tossed aside. *Jolly Ranchers?* Certainly not.

"Um, Gray…"

As the mouse took out pieces, the mesh bag became lighter and lighter. The balloons lifted off the coffee table.

"Gray!"

The mouse ignored him, continually pulling out candy, as the ribbons lifted his midsection.

With less weight on the base, the balloons floated up toward the ceiling. And Gray was airborne. He pretended to suddenly notice.

"Oh, crap…"

As the bag lifted, the remaining candy fell out. He drifted out into the middle of the living room.

Gray adjusted himself so he could see his friend below. Flynn half-smiled, reached out to grab him but missed. Up and up, Gray spun in the air, holding tightly to the ribbons to keep from falling. The balloons gently tapped the ceiling and bounced downward. A slight breeze, pumping from the heating vents, pushed the balloons toward a far wall.

Flynn wiped at the drying tears on his face.

"Gray, get back down here! What are you doing up there?!" His grin turned to a smile. Then a chuckle as he kept reaching up in the air for his friend.

"*This…* is totally bogus!" Gray shouted.

As the balloons sailed through the room, Gray looked down at the living room. He could see the decorations Mrs. Easterbrook had placed on every flat surface. He was able to see behind the ceramic figurines, the candles, picture frames, small glass globes, and souvenirs from trips long past.

Standing behind every knick-knack, on every flat surface – was a mouse.

Every member of the Halona tribe stood motionless, hiding behind the room decor, until they realized Gray could see them.

Viho sent out the warning signal. Mice communicate in high-pitched squeak that humans cannot hear. And Viho put the tribe on notice with his squeak – it was time to run! Zaltana grabbed young Yuma's fur, hurried him along, as she raced from behind an old photo of Mr. Easterbrook. Tate helped the old-timer Sani away from a thick, round candle. Maska vaulted off an end table, only to hit the floor with a thud. The mice swarmed out of the living room.

"Quick! Come get me!" Gray shouted to Flynn. "I gotta jump! Park yer carcass underneath me!"

Flynn, distracted by all the mice running through the room, turned his attention to Gray and positioned his wheelchair until he was under the floating mouse.

Gray dropped from the sky and fell into Flynn's hands.

"Follow that mouse, kid!" Gray pointed at Viho, who stood in the kitchen doorway guiding his tribe from the room.

Flynn spun the wheels on the chair hard, launching them toward the door. Viho galloped on all four paws into the kitchen. A half dozen mice scrambled to keep up with their chief.

Gray held onto Flynn's jeans with his claws, as the boy heaved the wheelchair around the corner and into the kitchen. Viho and the other mice shoved the basement door open, wide enough for them to squeeze through.

Gray waved the boy on. "Don't let 'em get away!"

Flynn slammed the two brake levers on the wheels and the rubber tires bit into the linoleum floor. The wheelchair screeched to a halt. Gray ran out along the boy's leg, onto the cast, until he reached the toes. He reached, pulled the door wide open.

The mice scrambled down the ramp into the basement.

Flynn handed Gray the metal hook from the winch and flipped on the switch. The mouse attached the hook to the chair, as Flynn spun around and backed them up to the top of the basement stairs. They descended down the ramp.

When they reached the concrete floor, Flynn unhooked the cable and turned the wheelchair to face his basement bedroom. There was no sign of any mice. The only sound was the winch continuing to unspool the metal rope onto the floor. Flynn and Gray both scanned for signs of movement, listening intently for the slightest sound.

Gray sniffed the air.

"You guys can come out. I can smell each and every one of ya," said Gray. He placed his paws on his hips and waited.

Up in the kitchen, on the top of the steps, Koko moved out from the shadows. With no sign of the lady of the house, she switched off the winch motor and pulled the basement door closed behind her. Koko quietly scurried down the ramp.

Flynn saw his blue pillowcase moved slightly. "You! Behind the pillow! I can see you."

Viho proudly marched out from behind the pillow and stood up on his hind legs, whiskers and ears back and his chest out. Several warriors stationed themselves beside their chief, including Maska, who towered over Viho. The big warrior crossed his arms and focused on the boy.

"Aww, they're so cute!" Flynn grinned at the small group.

Over two dozen mice, from every dark hiding hole and crevice in the basement, leapt out with long bows in their paws. Arrows were notched. Bow strings were drawn – ready to fire on the boy and mouse. More mice rushed out with sharpened spears held high, prepared to hurl. The only one without a weapon was Yuma, who hid behind Zaltana.

Both Gray and Flynn gasped. "Whoa," exhaled Gray.

Viho strode forward. "You now have twenty-seven arrows and six spears—!"

Old Sani stood atop the nightstand with a spear held high but his arm quivering from the weight. Then the spear fell out of his paw, clattered down onto the nightstand.

Viho sighed. "Make that... five spears pointed directly at you! And they are waiting for my command to fire. Turn over your weapons now and I may let you live!"

Gray slowly padded out onto Flynn's cast, holding his paws up in the air. Bow strings tightened as the mice warriors aimed at him.

"Hey there, cousins," Gray offered. "We got no weapons, as you can see. We're new around here. We don't know your customs. We're here in peace, ya dig?"

"Why are you here?!" Viho bellowed. "Did the Matwau send you? And why, in Apollo's name, were you speaking the human tongue with this boy?!"

"This guy? This here's Flynn. He's my… brother."

Many of the mice inhaled, their eyes wide. Viho marched to the edge of the bed to get a closer look at Gray.

"Have you… *gone Geronimo?*" Viho sniffed at him.

Gray grinned. "No, I ain't crazy. Ya see, this kid saved my life. I was lookin' for some food and got… caught in his family car. Long-story-short, they took me a long ways away from my city. On the way here, we got in an accident, and when we crashed the kid held onto me. Real tight like. We rolled down a big hill. I escaped with no harm. But the boy was injured tryin' to take care of me. His father and mother, well, they died in the accident. So, he's my family. He's all I got and I'm all he's got. His name is Flynn."

"I see," pondered Viho. "And what is your name… cousin?"

"My name is…" he paused, looked back at Flynn. "I'm called Gray. I'm from New York City, which is pretty far east of here. After the accident, they got the kid healed up and sent him back here. He's from *this* city. But since his parents died, those in charge stuck this kid with the lady who lives here."

"What of your mate? Your children?"

"Well, I was kinda young and a bit of an idiot when I got myself locked in the kid's car. I got no family of my own." Gray decided it was time to stop playing defense. "But, uh, you got me at a loss, bud. I got no idea who you are and why you got all these pointy sticks aimed at us."

"I am Viho and these are my people. We are the Halona."

"Yeah, okay. That doesn't really help me out all that much," Gray chided.

"Well, my young city mouse, we are a tribe. These warriors are *my…* family. Our ancestors were originally from the Middle Place in this land but, over several generations, have moved east to find greater access to food," Viho announced. "We are being hunted by a tribe of Matwau. But you are safe here with us."

"I see," pondered Gray. He stared intently at all the arrows and spears still aimed his way. "Look, I messed up. Okay? I talked to the kid. I know we're not supposed to, but he's the only human I ever talked to. I was afraid he was gonna die on me and I wanted to try to keep him alive. And I—"

"Stop," proclaimed Viho. A look of worry crossed Gray's face. "You do not need to explain. I understand. Just know this… we have no quarrel with you."

Viho held his paw in the air and his warriors instantly lowered their bows and spears.

Gray let out a huge sigh, plastered a fake smile on his furry face, and turned to look at Flynn.

"What's going on?" Flynn asked Gray.

Gray deftly climbed onto Flynn's shoulder, watched the tribe mill about below.

As the warriors put away their weapons, hushed murmurs and quick stares filtered out across the tribe.

"I heard about things like this. A lotta mice across the Midwest and way out West still follow the old ways, the old traditions."

"What old traditions?"

Gray pointed to the boy's Bicentennial shirt, with the 1776 to 1976 dates on it, and looked up at him. "Before your people got here, there were the First Humans. I think you call 'em Indians. They respected mice. All creatures, really. My distant ancestors would work with 'em and they'd help each other out. The First Humans taught us how to talk. We taught them to use screams and shrieks to frighten their enemies and communicate with each other," explained Gray.

"You mean like this?" Flynn put his hand to his mouth, started the ululating war cry he'd seen in the old Western movies they showed on Sunday afternoons. The warriors instantly retrieved their weapons and aimed them at the crazy, screaming boy in the metal chair.

Gray waved his paws in the air. "No, kid! Don't do that!"

Flynn winced and held his hands in the air to show he meant no harm.

Gray got closer to the boy's ear. "You're gonna get us killed, kid."

He sighed and sat down on Flynn's shoulder, leaned against his neck. "Anyway, a lot of mice picked up the Indians' culture and these yahoos apparently got a beef with some other tribe of mice. Problem is, we're caught in the middle of it."

"And that's... bad news?"

"It might be, kid. It might be."

Koko watched from her perch near the top of the steps, her icy gaze fixed on Gray.

She was startled by movement from above – footsteps approached the basement door. She darted into a shadow.

The door flew open, Mrs. Easterbrook peered down the stairs.

"Flynn! Are you down there?" Mrs. Easterbrook had her coat on but was wearing her more sensible winter boots. "Oh, Flynn, dear?!"

"Yes, Missus Easterbrook?!" He shouted up but turned to look at the stunned mice warriors, who had notched their arrows once again.

"I have to run to the bank before they close! I'm sure you'll be fine down there, yes?!"

Flynn motioned with his hands for the tribe to calm down. "Uh, yeah! I'll be fine! Um, thanks!"

Everyone listened, waited, for the woman's footsteps to fade away before they decided to move again.

A small, fiery mouse rushed out past Maska, full of bravado, a spear locked in his paws.

"I will take them all on!"

Maska scooped him up by the scruff of his neck, leaving him dangling and in shock. Maska laughed hard.

"Easy, little Wamblee! The fight will be here... soon enough!" The other laughed along nervously with the big mouse. Wamblee was slightly humiliated but instead tried to laugh along with the others.

11

The Preparation

M oki, the hardened leader of the field mice, observed the house as his tribe slept all around him in their encampment on the firewood. Even the ever-vigilant Chuchip snored peacefully by his side. He beamed at the young warrior.

Without smelling or hearing her, Moki was startled when the stealthy Tala appeared next to him.

"By Apollo, Tala! Do not do that to an elder! My heart practically halted in my chest!"

Tala grinned. She was good at sneaking up on others. Her name meant Stalking Wolf. The moniker fit her well. The stealthy scout even wore a similar coat of gray fur.

"Well, speak child. What have you learned?" Moki enquired.

"The Halona are in the house. But I believe they know we are here. They are preparing," she said.

"We have lost the element of surprise then. Eh, we should have attacked at sunrise," he sighed.

"There were too many humans coming and going. We had no choice."

"We always have a choice, Tala. Always."

"The people are gone now. We should wake the others and strike!"

Moki looked at the long shadows cast by the afternoon sun, shook his head.

"We leave when it is dark. There is still little moonlight at night. We will not give them the advantage." Moki looked at his recon expert. "Get some rest."

She shook her head. "There is work to do," announced Tala. She skulked away.

More pride filled the old warrior's heart as she disappeared behind the firewood. Moki went back to scanning the house for activity.

"What a surprise. Taima is fast asleep," said Tarsha.

Taima dozed on Flynn's bed, up against a pillow. Her paws held behind her head, with her bow and quiver of arrows across her lap.

"Are we being attacked?" asked Taima, her eyes still closed.

Tarsha struggled to contain the collection of spears resting on her shoulder. She turned to look at Bodaway, their fire maker, who carried an armload of fire arrows.

"No," said Tarsha. "We are not being attacked."

"Then it is time for sleep," said Taima. She rearranged herself against the comfy pillow.

Tarsha shook her head at Bodaway, slapped his arm, and they resumed hauling the weapons of war across the bed.

In the opposite corner of the basement stood a workbench, long abandoned with the passing of Mr. Easterbrook. Adriel nodded to his helper, Fala, to plug the cord for the electric drill into a nearby outlet. She struggled at first but eventually managed to wiggle it into the socket. Adriel turned the chuck key on the drill, to tighten down the sanding wheel he had attached. He motioned for Fala to lean her weight against the drill trigger.

She shoved her back against the big orange button on the drill handle and pushed with her lower legs until they shook. Instead of turning on the sanding disc, the drill itself began to spin in a circle on the workbench. Adriel ducked down as the drill passed overhead.

"Fala, stop! Fala!"

Adriel tried to get her attention, but the young mouse kept pushing the drill around in circles. Maska placed his big paws on the handle, stopping

Fala and the drill from spinning round and round. The drill motor spun to life, startling most in the basement, and the sanding wheel whirred into motion.

Adriel rubbed his paws together, grabbed from a stack of wooden sticks, and held a single spear up to the wheel. The sanding disc quickly sanded away on the wood to reveal a deadly sharp point in mere seconds.

Maska let out a hearty laugh at Adriel's ingenuity, until their engineer handed the next blank stick to the big mouse.

"Now... *you* know how to do it. There are two hundred and forty more to go." Adriel pointed to the stack of sticks. Maska grumbled, accepted the stick. Adriel patted him and moved on to his next project.

"What about my toy?" Maska shouted, but the engineer simply waved a paw to dismiss him.

Fala shoved in the drill button again. Maska held the noisy spinning machine motionless, sanded away at the next stick, and sang an ancient song about warriors going off on a hunt.

Flynn had parked his wheelchair in front of a stack of cardboard boxes. Seated in a circle on top was Viho and his mate Zaltana. Sani, the elder, sat next to them puffing on a paw-made pipe and blowing smoke rings into the air. Koko was huddled on all fours next to Sani.

Gray walked around the circle. He looked for an opening, for a place to sit among the group, but they offered none. He backed away, his dark eyes observing each of the tribal leaders closely.

Viho used a piece of pencil lead to draw on the cardboard between them. "I believe they will come into the house the same way we did – up the tree, at the rear of the house, and in through the attic," said Viho, pointing to his crude pencil drawing of the house.

"What is your plan?" asked Zaltana as she held onto his paw. Her eyes darted to the strange mouse standing near them.

Gray noticed the young mouse that Zaltana had called Yuma. He waited as close to the circle as he could get. Gray noted that the mouse was young but rather large for a house mouse. His dark reddish-brown fur set him apart, as well.

"We know this house better than the Matwau," Viho announced. "We will have the advantage if there is a fight. However, we will be on the main floor so that we have means to escape if we fare poorly in battle. We will have an escape route ready here and here." He pointed to the front and back doors. Viho had drawn them slightly ajar.

Flynn sniggered, loudly enough for the mice to hear him.

Viho marched close to the edge of the box, pointed his pencil lead at the boy. "You have something to add, young one?"

Flynn sat up straight in his chair, cleared his throat. His face burned bright red. He felt like a teacher had caught him whispering to a friend instead of paying attention to the lesson. Gray grinned at his friend.

"Um, no, sir. I'm sorry," Flynn gulped. "It's just that you guys, you know, umm—'

"Yes?"

"Well, you talk funny. You're all so stiff and formal. 'We must have a means to escape if we fare poorly in battle!' You, like, don't ever use contradictions and stuff," he said.

Viho looked at Gray, confused.

"The kid's talkin' about *contractions*, cousin," Gray explained. Viho was still not sure what the boy was talking about. "I think…"

Viho cocked his head to the side, as if the child were speaking a different language. Gray sighed.

"You guys say things like 'cannot' or 'will not' while most say 'can't' or 'won't', ya dig?" Gray added.

Viho tried to unravel the puzzle that was Gray. He turned to Zaltana. "He thinks *we* speak funny?"

Zaltana shrugged.

Sani, the elder, groaned as he stood. With a paw on his aching back, he limped forward, pointing his pipe at the boy.

Viho sighed, rolled his eyes at Zaltana. She gave her mate a disapproving look.

"We do not talk often," said the white-haired old mouse. "We can communicate just as easily with smell and sound as we do with words.

However, the gift of the First Humans was speech, and we respect their teachings. Language has beauty but also has great power. Those who could communicate had an advantage and so... most mice refused to be left behind. We are much smarter than your people know. Many can read, most can speak, and all can think. So, in short, we respect the human language."

"You were smart not to let humans know it," said Flynn, mostly to himself.

"That is why were shocked to discover Gray's... *transgression* with you," added Viho, inserting himself back into the conversation.

"Transgression? That's bad, right? Look, it wasn't his fault, I swear!" Flynn feared a reprisal against Gray.

"Do not worry yourself, Flynn," Viho smiled. "We are saddened at the loss of your parents but rejoice that you found a brother in Gray."

Gray bowed his head, glad for the acknowledgement. He hopped onto Flynn's cast and scampered up the boy's shirt and sat on all fours on his shoulder.

"The Halona tribe welcome you. All of us shall, from this day forward, refer to you as... Dakota," announced Sani the elder, making it so.

Gray leaned over to Flynn, motioning him closer. The boy put his ear close.

"I bet the old geezer called you that because he doesn't remember your name," whispered Gray.

Flynn smiled but turned his attention back to Sani. "Dakota? Isn't that an Indian tribe?"

"Yes. I believe there is a human tribe with that name, from the Middle Place. But it is also a word we use that means friend. You are now our ally. Our Dakota." Sani gave a quick nod to make it official. He slowly squatted back down in his spot in planning circle.

"He definitely doesn't remember your name," said Gray.

They both settled in to watch the tribal leaders resume plotting their escape.

12

The Battle

Tala waited at the barren, gray tree towering over Mrs. Easterbrook's brick home. She listened. Her nose sniffed the cold winter air. No signs of any enemy activity. She motioned for the tribe to advance and then scurried up the bark of the tree to gain a better vantage point.

Ahiga, with his coat of tan fur, was the first one to arrive. He was eager, ready for action, with eyes shifting back and forth for anything sign of an approaching mouse. Ahiga wore his red battle jacket made from a scrap of vinyl. On his back, he had strapped his bow and quiver of arrows. Stuffed into a stretched-out leather belt was a small ax, another knife, and a sword – he was prepared for battle.

"I can smell their fear from here!"

Ahiga dug his claws into the bark, preparing to climb up the tree, his tongue hanging out in anticipation, when a paw grabbed his shoulder and yanked him back. A tall albino mouse spun him around and pointed a sharp claw at his face. She was called Enola. Her white fur made her almost invisible in all the snow, but Ahiga could easily see those light pink eyes staring him down.

"Calm yourself, Ahiga." She adjusted her bow and quiver, looked back at the approaching mice. "Your time will come."

He shoved her paw away from his shoulder, stepped in close to her. Enola rose up higher on her hind legs, her stare instantly more menacing. Ahiga would fight just about anyone, at any time, but he had to admit – Enola scared him. Just a little bit. He groused to himself, backed away from her, and paced back and forth, waiting for the others to arrive.

Chuchip, the chief's righthand mouse, and Moki were the next to arrive safely at the tree. Their deep exhalations sent white clouds of steam into the night air. Chuchip knocked snow off the chief and then away from his own fur and weapons.

"This snow is treacherous! We will be in fine favor with Apollo if we all make it inside the house alive," complained Moki.

Kiona and her mate, Elsu, were next to travel through the long trench of snow that had been trampled by the others. They held paws, Moki noted. Ah, young love. It made him smile for a brief moment.

His fire expert, Hakan, led Chayton to the barren backyard tree. Hakan removed his quiver full of flame arrows, inspected each one to ensure they were dry. While Chayton stared up at the tall tree, he accidentally bumped into Ahiga.

"Get off me, you fool!" Ahiga pushed Chayton down in the snow, ready to pounce on him. Chuchip yanked the angry Ahiga away, got up close, nose to nose.

Chuchip pointed to the house, then pushed Ahiga back a step. "Save all that fire in your belly for them!"

Chayton spat out a huge mouthful of snow, pushed himself off the ground. "You are not very nice."

This made the angry mouse even angrier. Ahiga leapt at Chayton once again but Chuchip managed to hold him back.

"And *you* are not very smart!" Ahiga snarled at him. Chayton jumped behind Chuchip for protection.

Another two dozen mice completed the trek, flooding the area at the base of the tree. Hinto, the clever engineer, arrived with his tools in tow. Sakari followed behind him and dropped two more of Hinto's sacks into the snow, collapsing into a snowbank to catch her breath. Dyani, the chief's mate, brought up the rear as she had to escort old Nodin, shaman of the tribe.

He pushed her away and leaned on his trusty walking stick, hacking and coughing with every exhalation.

Moki counted his troops, surveyed the area, and climbed onto the bare roots of the tree to be seen by all.

"We are not safe in the open like this! Remember the plan – up this tree and into the house. They are expecting us," he barked. "Use caution, my warriors!"

In single file, his tribe of field mice dashed straight up the tree with their sharp claws digging hard into the bark.

Mrs. Easterbrook pushed her heeled foot down on the brakes of her Mist Blue Plymouth Valiant when the traffic light changed to red. She placed her hand on the bank book and envelope of cash to keep them from sliding off the passenger seat.

Flakes fell on her windshield and her old wipers pushed melted snow off the glass. On the other side of the intersection, through each cycle of the wipers, she could see the VFW hall. A sign hanging over the front of the hall was surrounded with light bulbs, announcing the evenings main event.

It was *Bingo Nite.*

Mrs. Easterbrook bit her lip. She cast a quick look down at the envelope of money she had withdrawn from the bank.

The sign was calling to her. Bingo. Tonight only. 7 p.m. to 9 p.m.

The traffic light turned from red to green. Mrs. Easterbrook's heel does not leave the brake pedal. A car horn, from behind, startled her. She slowly eased forward, staring at the VFW hall sign.

"Oh, I'll just play one game," she announced the justification to herself.

Mrs. Easterbrook pulled the steering wheel hard left, guiding the car into the VFW hall parking lot.

She adjusted the rearview mirror to check her hair and makeup more easily. She was on a mission – she had money to win.

Fresh, thick snowflakes fell in the darkness that enveloped Mrs. Easterbrook's brick ranch house. The lamp post at the bottom of the drive was off. No adult was home to turn on the porch light.

A lone lightbulb over the kitchen stove was the only illumination in the house. Flynn pushed his wheelchair into the living room as Gray stood out on the end of the cast on the boy's leg.

"I can't see a thing," Flynn whispered.

"We can, kid." The mouse carefully watched all the other mice scurry about.

"What are they doing?"

"I got no idea," said Gray, distracted. "I thought their plan was to bug outta here... but it looks like they're preppin' for war."

Gray scratched at the fur on top of his head. Two or three mice hid behind every picture frame, candle, fake plant, and tchotchke in the room. They held tight to bows and spears and had neatly stacked quivers of arrows, knives, and swords within reach.

Bodaway rushed past him, sprinting along the coffee table, headed for the brick fireplace. He had two quivers full of arrows with oily cloth wrapped around the points.

"Hey, son!" shouted Gray. Bodaway slid to a halt. "Where's the fire?!"

The wiry mouse, with dark brow fur, straightened his blue sleeveless leather battle jacket and smiled.

"Right here!" said Bodaway. He patted his quiver full of arrows.

"What are those?" Flynn asked, genuinely curious.

"Flame arrows," whispered the mouse. He made swift, furtive glances to either side to make sure no one had eavesdropped on his secret.

"What do ya mean *flame arrows*, son?" asked a stunned Gray.

Koko raced onto the coffee table and rushed Bodaway along. "Get into position." Koko threw a vile look at Gray.

Gray leaned out over the kid's cast to get closer to her. "Can you tell us what is goin' on around here?"

"The battle is upon us," Koko glared at Gray.

"Battle? I thought you guys were gonna pack up and hightail it outta here. You're stickin' around to face your enemy?!"

"Yes. We are mice. We do not run from a fight," Koko sneered at him.

Gray knew it was meant as an insult but let it slide.

"So, you're just going to burn down the kid's home?" asked Gray.

"We have the right to defend ourselves."

"Why are you fighting here?" Gray placed his paws on his hips, stood as tall as he could.

"I apologize that our survival is an inconvenience to you," Koko hissed.

"Then maybe you should survive *out there*," said Gray, pointing out the bay window. "Instead of *in here!*"

"We are in the middle of winter, city mouse. We would be pursued, hunted down, and killed with an enemy at our backs in this snow. We fight, here and now." She threw her head back, bared her teeth, and ran off into the darkness.

"What the heck are we supposed to do?" Flynn asked his friend.

Gray watched the boy's fist clench up tight and his other hand scratch digging into the skin under his cast.

"We gotta boogie, kid. Get outta the line of fire," said Gray. He scampered down Flynn's cast to take his seat on the armrest of the wheelchair.

Viho had monitored the entire conversation from an end table next to the couch. He glowered as Flynn backed his wheelchair out of the living room. He had hoped the boy and the strange mouse might help defend them. He was wrong.

Moki and Dyani stood in the middle of the dark attic, surveying the room. Their warriors were fanned out, bows taut and arrows notched, with noses and ears searching for the enemy.

Tala rushed in to face the chief from a shadowy corner. "This floor is clear. But there is activity below. That is where they wait."

"Then let us join them… shall we?!" bellowed Moki.

His tribe grunted in agreement and they pumped their paws in the air. They streamed across the attic and disappeared through holes in the floor.

"Did I ever tell you the one about this mouse I was fightin' with? He was wearing camouflage and sitting' in his wheelchair?"

Flynn had parked his wheelchair in the spare hair salon bedroom and was staring down the hallway through the slightly open door. The room was as dark as the rest of the house. Gray stood on the arm of the chair, right below the boy, staring into the black hall with him.

"I said to him, 'You can hide, but you can't run!'"

All was eerily silent.

"Do you think the battle has started yet?" whispered Flynn.

"Naw, it's too quiet out there."

They waited. Watched. The air felt electric to Flynn. The red hairs on his arm stood straight up. Was it static? There was tension… maybe some fear? He could not put a finger on the emotions coursing through him. Maybe it was excitement? Was he excited about the looming battle?

The furnace downstairs kicked on, causing both of them to nearly jump out of their skins.

"Holy smoke, kid!" whispered Gray.

"Yeah. I know," Flynn gulped.

In the living room, the Halona tribe tightened grips on their weapons. Watchful eyes searched the pitch-black room for even the slightest movement.

Tarsha turned to the sleeping Taima, who was curled up in a bowl of peppermint candies on an end table. Tarsha rolled her eyes and then kicked the bowl with her hind leg. "Wake up, Taima!"

Taima opened an eye, halfway. "Are they here?"

"They are on their way!"

"Wake me then." She closed her eye.

Tarsha marched off, muttering to herself.

All around them, a piercing high-pitched scream echoed off the walls. Another scream joined in. The Halona pulled their ears back. Some shielded them from the pain. A third squeal came, then a fourth, and finally… dozens of screams pervaded the dark house.

The mice searched everywhere for the source of the battle cries. The screeching came from everywhere and nowhere at once.

"They are here…" Taima sat up, rearranged her quiver, and hopped out of the candy bowl.

"Quite the brilliant one, you are," Tarsha stated sarcastically from across the end table.

Back in the bedroom, the war screams caused Gray to double over, hold his paws over his ears.

"Aww, geez! That is *not* cool!"

"What is it? What's wrong?" Flynn asked.

"Screams! Loud ones. From the bad guys," cried Gray. "Aw, man that hurts…"

"I don't hear anything!"

"You can't. It's too high-pitched for you. Only mice," he stammered. "They're tryin' to scare everyone out there."

The loud squeals stopped. Gray stood back up on his hind legs.

"Well… it's about to hit the fan."

They peered down the long hallway.

Through holes that had been chewed into the walls, the field mice rushed into the dining room. Teams took up positions on the dining table and on both sides of the open doorway to the living room.

Viho could make out their movements; he stood on his hind legs and held his spear high.

"There! The dining room!" bellowed the chief. "Attack!"

His archers unleashed a volley of arrows into the dark room. The small, feathered fletching on the back of each arrow caused them to spin. The spinning created a screeching whine as they zipped through the air.

Dozens of arrows sank into the carpet, the walls, and the side of the dining table.

The field mice ducked out of the way. Arrows whooshed overhead, searching for a target.

Moki yanked Dyani out of the way as two arrows dug into the wood on the table where she had stood.

He leapt forward, paws held beside his bared teeth, and raged at his tribe. "Return fire!"

The house mice leapt out of the way as arrows and spears from the field mice landed all around them.

From the doorway, Tala saw movement on the top of the couch. She launched her spear.

Maska ducked down low as the spear tip sunk deep into the wall plaster above his massive head.

"Was that your best?!" Maska screamed down and fired his spear back at Tala.

She slipped behind the wall, but the spear went through the plaster and exited above her ears. She gasped at the power behind that throw. Maska pulled Tala's spear from the wall, his big eyes searching for a new target.

The young mouse, Wamblee, scurried from his hiding place behind Maska and threw his spear. His little spear went just far enough to pierce the pillow at the end of the sofa.

Maska laughed, patted him on the head. "Nice try, little one. Get your hips and back behind your throw!"

Maska hoisted his spear and heaved it into the dining room. It shattered a coffee creamer shaped like a cow, that was sitting on the buffet behind the dining table.

From the salon bedroom, Gray and Flynn heard the loud crash. Then another volley of arrows whistled through the air. They could hear picture frame glass being shattered, dull *thunks* as spears impacted with walls and furniture, and screams and shouts from both tribes.

"Dude, it's a total war zone out there!"

"Sounds like it," said Gray, shaking his head.

More blustering and shouts reverberated down the hallway. Arrows could be heard whistling back and forth

Gray watched Flynn, who was glued to the opening in the bedroom door, on the edge of his wheelchair seat, moving his arms and hands, as if the boy were fighting alongside the mice.

"Hey, kid. Maybe we should, ya know, shut the door, and lock it? Wait for this to... blow over?"

Flynn ignored him. This was kind of exciting. He'd only ever read about war in his books or watched an old war movie on TV. There was an actual battle going on ten feet away!

On the end table, Viho turned to his mate and grabbed her by the shoulders. "Take warriors, go around through the kitchen, and attack them from their flank!"

Zaltana nodded and rushed off, motioning to Koko and several other house mice to follow her. They hopped off the end table and disappeared into the kitchen. Yuma, unsure of what to do, paced back and forth. As arrows whistled past over his head, he quietly slipped behind a lamp teetering on the edge of the end table.

Viho shouted to archers along the couch and on top of Mrs. Easterbrook's favorite chair. "Fire!"

The Halona drew their bows and launched arrows, pushing back an advance by Chuchip's team at the living room doorway.

In a fit of rage, Ahiga threw himself from the top of a dining room chair onto an armchair in the living room. Hearing sounds over his shoulder from the bookcase behind him, the little warrior backflipped over to land on a dark shelf with his sword in hand.

Ahiga rushed forward, slashed his sword down hard. "Prepare to meet Apollo, scum!"

He was met with stiff armor but was undeterred. He pulled out his blade and swung hard again. In a flurry, he cut at his opponent a half dozen times. Breathing hard, he pulled back. Even though it was dark, we wanted to review the damage inflicted.

A car passed the house and light from the headlights flew across the bookshelf.

Ahiga looked closely at his opponent. He had thoroughly sliced up a picture frame containing a black and white photo of Mrs. Easterbrook from back in the *good old days*.

Chayton, lying on the shelf above, stared down at the infuriated Ahiga.

"Wow. Nice, Ahiga!" Chayton giggled. "You really showed him who is in charge."

Ahiga glared up at the oaf, a fury quickly engulfing him. He pulled his sword back to throw it at Chayton, but his hind paw slipped off the edge of the shelf. The angry mouse dropped down into a wicker waste basket, beside the armchair, with a thump. He let out a scream so loud that everyone involved in the battle pauses. For a brief second.

Then, the arrows and spears resumed their flights.

A large stereo console stood against the wall, farthest from the dining room entrance. The top panel had been slid to the side, revealing the stereo turntable. Fala, the young Halona mouse, stood on top of a small 45 RPM record on the turntable. In her paws, she gripped two nylon cords with a leather pouch in the center. Fala placed a pearl in the pouch. A broken string of Mrs. Easterbrook's pearl necklace laid to the side of the turntable. She reached out her hind leg to flip on the record player. The record began to spin fast, faster. Around and around she spun. Fala then swung her paw-made sling around over her head. At the right moment, she released the sling cord. The shiny pearl zipped out of the pouch and fired across the living room. It shot through the doorway, like a bullet, and over the dining room table.

Moki stooped as the pearl missed his head. The ball shot into a curio cabinet, shattering a decorative plate. The pearl ricocheted through the cabinet, exploding every cup and saucer and plate it encountered. Shards of ceramics and glass showered down on Moki's head.

Angered, Moki signaled for Hakan to fire his arrows. Hakan grinned at his leader, nodded approval.

"Light them up," Moki snarled.

Hakan lined up a half dozen fire arrows on the table. He pulled a single match from his quiver, kicked the head of the match with his paw against the dining table. He set the lit match in the gap between the table leaves. He held his first arrow to the fire – the small piece of cloth, dipped in accelerant, burst into flames.

Over in the living room, Viho spotted the fire burning in the dining room. He spun around to face his archers. "Concentrate your arrows on that flame!"

The Halona warriors drew their bows back, aiming for the dining table, and launched.

Arrows rained down around Hakan, sinking into the tabletop, but he ignored the peril. He notched the first flaming arrow into his bow and fired into the living room. After seeing where the first landed, he shot the remaining five burning arrows at his enemies.

Flynn had opened the bedroom door wider to get a better look. "Um, I think I see fire..."

"Oh, boy," stated Gray. "That is not good."

Flynn backed up his wheelchair. Using his cast, he threw the bedroom door and rolled himself down the hall. Gray held on tight as Flynn pushed his wheelchair at warp speed.

In the dining room doorway, Chuchip and his team launched a round of arrows. He motioned to his team and they scampered into the living room.

Several flames burned at the tips of the arrows scattered across the room, shining light on the Halona mice.

Moki dug his claws deep into the dining table wood, pushing apart the table where Mr. Easterbrook used to add an extra leaf during holiday parties. Tala, Hinto, and Sakari shoved a heavy metal candelabra into the gap where it dropped down in the middle of the table. Candles had been removed and a rubber glove had been tied to the candle holders. The engineer pulled back on the glove, stretching it as far as he could. Tala joined him, yanking hard on rubber.

"Sakari! Quick!" Tala squealed through gritted teeth. "The ring!"

Sakari nodded and rolled in a metal napkin ring to Tala and Hinto, as they strained to keep the rubber glove taught. She placed the metal ring onto the glove.

"Aim to the right. A little more! There!" grunted Hinto. "Release!"

They let go of the glove simultaneously, firing the metal ring missile into the living room.

Standing on the far end of the coffee table, Tarsha turned to the mice around her. "Take cover!"

At the end of her coffee table, Tarsha saw Tate fumbling with an arrow he was trying to notch. She tackled him out of the way as the giant napkin ring bounded across the coffee table. The metal ring clipped her hind leg, sending her spinning off the table.

The napkin ring flew up to strike through the lampshade on an end table, knocking the lamp to the floor, before burying deep in the plaster next to a wall mirror. A frightened Yuma stood trembling where his lamp had used to be. He hurriedly looked around for Viho and ran straight for him.

Tate was gasping for breath as he looked all around for Tarsha. He sat up on the carpet, dazed and shaken.

"Tarsha? Tarsha!" He peered into the darkness. He spotted her, limping under the couch, as she waved to him. He sighed in relief and picked up a spear lying on the floor, rushing back into the fray.

Chuchip and his team scrambled deep into Halona territory, stopping only to unleash a volley of arrows at the mice they could spot in the flickering fire-arrow light.

Big Maska jumped down to a couch cushion and flung his spear hard at Chuchip's marauders. His spear missed its mark, piercing a throw pillow that had fallen to the floor. His strong throw sent feathers from the pillow billowing up into the living room.

After banging into the hallway walls and the entrance to the living room, Flynn skidded around the corner in his wheelchair. Gray held onto the leg of his jeans for dear life.

Every mouse in the battle turned toward Flynn, frozen.

The boy quickly surveyed the scene – small flames burned around the living room, smoke and feathers filled the air, mice were scattered on nearly every surface, and arrows and spears were stuck in everything.

From the dining table, Moki ignored the boy and swung his arm toward the enemy in the living room. "Fire!"

A dozen arrows flew at the Halona and some toward Flynn. Gray jumped behind the boy's cast for cover. Flynn shielded himself as arrows hit his shoulder, his cast, his hand, and bounced off his wheelchair.

"Ow!"

Viho jumped out onto the boy's cast, waving his arm toward the Matwau. "Return fire! Protect the child!"

The Halona notched and fired arrows back at their enemy. Spears sailed through the air.

Flynn reversed his wheelchair out of the room, into the hallway. He pulled out the tiny arrow from his shoulder, removed the one stuck in the palm of his hand. The boy's eyes turned to the salon-bedroom – immediately seeing what he needed.

"Kid, you okay?" Gray inspected the arrow damage. "Wait! What are you doing?"

Flynn rolled into the salon, grabbed a cup full of rubber bands, and a jar full of bobby pins. He hurriedly backed out of the room and into the hall.

"Let's talk about this," pleaded Gray. "Come on, kid! You're gonna get hurt out there!"

From the top of Mrs. Easterbrook's TV chair, Bodaway lit several flame arrows. One by one, he fired them toward the dining room. The flames illuminated the table, the smashed curio cabinet, the bookshelf, and the floor – the Matwau were exposed.

Fala spun herself on the record player again. This time, she had three pearls resting in her sling. She launched them all at once. They sprayed out with one striking the bookshelf and the other firing through the television screen. The TV sparked and crackled, with smoke pouring out from the broken screen. This made Koko grin as she stopped fighting to watch Mrs. Easterbrook's beloved light box die a quick death.

The last pearl soared into the dining room. Moki was hammered by the round rocket as it struck him in the ribs, bowling him over and knocking out his wind.

The spinning record player threw Fala off. Dizzy and stumbling, she bumped into the turntable arm. It lifted automatically, rested on the spinning 45 RPM record. After a few seconds of crackling, the song *Mi Casa, Su Casa* began blasting across the house.

Maska hopped off the coffee table, landed before Chuchip and his warriors, and swung his big spear in an arc. He knocked some of them on their backs. Maska swung back around again and knocked over the rest of them. He howled into the air as the Matwau scurried away from the giant mouse.

Flynn rolled up to the doorway with a rubber band between his thumb and forefinger. He loaded one of the bobby pins into the rubber band and took aim. He saw Ahiga struggling at the lip of the waste basket, trying to climb out, and he released the rubber band.

Ahiga heard the approaching metal bobby pin before he saw it. His angry, beady eyes were wide as he let himself drop back into the trash can. The pin shot through the wicker basket and out the other, right where Ahiga had been trying to climb out. The basket flipped on its side and he was rolled out onto the carpet.

On the end table, Adriel and Taima pushed a wooden knife block into position. In preparation for the battle, Adriel used the knife block to create a catapult. He had added wheels and used a black plastic spoon for the launch arm. Thick rubber bands were stretched back and ready to launch their missile.

"Load the weapon!" shouted Adriel, as he aimed the block.

Taima lifted a red pin cushion onto the spoon. The pins had been pushed through the small stuffed cushion and forced all the way out. The pointy section of the pins now stuck out, like a medieval mace without a handle. When Taima was clear, Adriel shoved away the clip holding the spoon back. The rubber band released all its stored energy, launching the pin cushion high and far into the air.

"By Apollo," muttered Moki. "Run!"

The warriors on the table scattered as the big pin cushion hurtled toward them. They leapt from the table as the pin cushion smashed down on the wood table and followed them off the edge.

Moki covered Dyani as the red pin cushion sank into the dining room carpet, just a mouse whisker away from spearing them.

Flynn fired another bobby pin off his rudimentary slingshot. The pin bounced off the shelf wall of the bookcase, struck Chayton, and knocked him off the shelf. He dropped straight down, toward Ahiga.

"Mother..." whispered Ahiga, as the oafish Chayton fell directly on him.

Zaltana, Koko and a few of her warriors had circled around the kitchen to come up on the Matwau from the side, through the second dining room entrance. With the chaos caused by Viho's troops in the living room, they had surprise on their side. Koko and Zaltana notched arrows. Several more squatted next to them with bows drawn. Zaltana gave a slight nod and they released arrows at the backs of Matwau, startling them.

Moki had seen enough. He pulled Dyani close. "Fetch Chuchip! We must retreat."

"No, we must fight!" Dyani protested, her eyes looking off to the living room.

"This is not our day, my love. Not our victory," stated Moki. "Everyone! Retreat!"

Moki grabbed several of his warriors by the fur, pushed them toward the living room doorway. Dyani scrambled off, shouting for Chuchip and the others to withdraw.

Flynn loaded another bobby pin when Gray stayed his arm, pointed.

"I think it's over, kid. They stopped firing," he said.

In a single file line, the Matwau ran behind the couch. Every few steps, Ahiga would kick Chayton in the tail, still furious at the fool.

Maska, standing on the top of the couch, looked down at the warriors scurrying away. He held up his spear for another throw.

Viho rushed to the side of his massive soldier. "Make the throw, Maska!"

Maska lowered his spear. "It is over."

"For now," ruminated Viho. "But one of those warriors you just saved may be the one to take your life in the next battle."

"Perhaps."

Within seconds, the field mice had disappeared into the hole in the wall, and the fight was done.

13

The Aftermath

Flynn reached his hand up the wall, searching up and down and side to side, for a light switch. After a few seconds of fumbling, light from the only unbroken lamp flickered on and flooded the room. The house mice stopped collecting their spears and arrows from the battlefield to briefly look at the boy, then they returned to their work.

Gray stood on Flynn's shoulder as they surveyed the damage. It was extensive. Feathers from the shredded pillow still floated down, kicked up by the hasty exit of the Matwau. A few small fires burned from the flame arrows. Mice attempted to stomp them out with their shields and paws. Blackened marks from fires were on the carpet, the couch, the coffee table, even the walls. The stench of burnt plastic, polyester, and nylon filled the air. Black smoke had settled in a thin layer across the living room. Spears and arrows were embedded in the walls, furniture, photos, and candles. Plaster chunks had fallen away from the walls, exposing the wood lath strips behind. A light bulb blinked on and off in a lamp laying nearly sideways, held up by the stretched out electric cord.

Shards of glass and ceramic from picture frames, plates, and shelf doors covered every surface in the dining room. Mrs. Easterbrook's tchotchkes and mementos were knocked over, shattered; most of her collection gone forever. Glass from the broken television screen had glittered the carpet around Flynn's wheelchair. The needle on record, that continued to spin on the smoldering turntable, played final notes of the song over and over.

Flynn rubbed at his shoulder where the dried blood had made it itch. He looked down at the small arrows lodged in his cast. As he stared around the room, he noted several of his bobby pin missiles stuck in walls. The excitement of the battle had worn off and the real damage to his new home hit him like a ton of bricks.

"We might be in big trouble, kid."

"Well, you're not," said Flynn. "But I am."

Gray watched as headlights flashed across the walls and a car pulled in the driveway. "Umm, she's back…"

Unsure of what to do next, Flynn's heart sank. He reached to turn off the light switch but stopped halfway. With a final look around the room, he knew nothing could be done to make any of this mess even slightly better. The mice scattered, leaving no weapons or any sign that had been there.

"I got a feeling that *this*… will go down on my permanent record," whispered Flynn.

Sitting in the driver's seat of her Valiant, with her engine still running, Mrs. Easterbrook stared down at her envelope. What had once contained several hundred dollars… now held twelve measly bucks.

It had been a rough *Bingo Nite*.

Mrs. Easterbrook let out a deep sigh, shut off her car, and clambered out. Light flakes of snow fell, landing on her hair, eyebrows, and eyelashes. This winter had taken its toll on her. She was over it. It was too cold and so much snow had fallen. She looked forward to spring and warm weather and a new hairdo. Her boots crunched on the snowy sidewalk as she approached her front door. Thankfully, some light coming from the living room guided her path; she had forgotten to turn on her porch light.

She unlocked the front door and crossed the same threshold that Mr. Easterbrook had carried her over twenty-seven years earlier. After she stomped her boots on the rug, to rid them of the melting snow, she surveyed her living room. What caught her eye first was Flynn, sitting in his wheelchair, with his head down and hand covering his eyes.

What she couldn't see was Gray, who had hidden behind the boy with his back to Flynn's back. The mouse stared at the ceiling, waiting for the cries of anguish and despair that were sure to follow.

And follow they did. But not at first. Air had quickly gushed from Mrs. Easterbrook's lungs as she took in her living room... no, her sanctuary! She inhaled slightly at each broken picture frame and each carpet burn and each hole in the wall. She gasped at her decimated television where she watched Cronkite every night on the evening news. She had eventually gasped in enough oxygen to let out a bloodcurdling scream.

Flynn knew it was coming but winced anyway. Gray merely closed his eyes, covered his ears. The scream echoed out the open door, bouncing off the expanse of snow covering every lawn in the neighborhood.

14

The Escape

Amy Regula drove her ten-year-old rusty green Pontiac slowly over the icy roads, taking turns looking up at the houses and down to the address written on a note in the case file. When she saw the police car parked in front, she knew the brick ranch house was her destination.

She was in her late twenties, but her exacting job had taken its toll. The long hours, low pay, and depressing cases showed Amy, in her rearview mirror, a person who had given up years ago. Makeup had become a waste of time and cost her money she seldom had. In that moment, she realized that having her hair tied back in a ponytail made her head look small – she pushed the mirror aside rather than make a change or look away.

A long, deep groan helped her gather herself. *Here goes another soul-crushing exercise in futility*, she thought. She scooped up the manila file folder and her heavy purse.

Her long, brown boots and tan overcoat protected her from the cold wind and blowing snow as she marched up to the house. Amy's hand went to knock but the door pulled open first. The police officer was looking back at an older lady, who looked like she had been crying all night and had fought hard to cover it up. If what had been described to Amy over the phone had been true, the lady probably had cried all night.

"I'm sorry, ma'am," said the officer to the lady. "Unless you want to press charges against a minor, there's nothing much we can do here."

Mrs. Easterbrook was bewildered, apoplectic. "But what about… all this?!"

"Contact your insurance, ma'am," he stated. "They'll be able to help assess the damage. Good day to you."

The officer turned, noticed Amy standing before the door with her hand still raised to knock. He looked at her hand, then gave her his best fake smile. "Ma'am."

He tipped his cap to Amy, walked off toward his patrol car. She said nothing but wanted to scream she was not old enough to be called *ma'am*.

Amy did not wait to be invited in. She knew she had to project authority, or the foster parents would try to walk all over her. She pushed past the lady, as she stared at the case file to re-confirm names she already knew. With a quick glance, she could see Flynn waiting at the kitchen table in his chair, his head down.

"Missus Lily Easterbrook? I'm Amy Regula, with Franklin County Child Services. You have an incident to report involving the ward," she said, scanning the file. "Flynn Myers?"

What Amy could not see, from her vantage point, was a small gray mouse standing on the boy's shoulder. But Gray got a good look at Amy as she talked with Mrs. Easterbrook. He leaned close to Flynn's ear. "I ever tell you the one about my ex-girlfriend. She dumped me… so, I stole her wheelchair. And guess who came crawling back?"

Gray watched him for a reaction.

Flynn sat in silence. He was humiliated. He couldn't remember a time he had ever been in this much trouble. Even that time he got caught copying a friend's homework because he forgot to do it. Mom and dad were super-mad about that, he remembered.

Mrs. Easterbrook stood flabbergasted in front of the young woman, clutching at pearls that were not there – because the broken necklace was still scattered on the record player.

"Incident? Incident?!" She gestured around the living room. "Does this… look like an incident? This is a disaster!"

Amy scanned the room. She was shocked at the condition of the room but knew she could not show it. She had to remain neutral. Objective.

"Was the child injured in any way?"

"The-the child? Why… I… I don't think he's human! He's a monster! Look at what he did!" She gave another grand gesture at the battlefield damage.

"Children who have been through a traumatic experience have been known to act out by—"

"Act out?! This isn't 'acting out', dear. This is flat-out vandalism!"

"I understand you're upset, Missus Easterbrook. If we could just sit down and talk—"

"No. There will be no *talking*. I want that b-beast removed from here! At once!" She began to hyperventilate and was forced to fan herself as she tried to catch her breath.

"I'm going to talk to the child now," announced Amy. Emotions were running too high. She had seen the boy sitting at the table and strode past the agitated woman, who immediately sat on the arm of her chair.

Gray slid down behind Flynn's back. He put his back up against Flynn's back and pushed, as if to support him.

"Hello, Flynn." She sat on a chair closest to him, placing the file on the table. "I'm not sure if you remember me but we talked a few times. At the group home? Before we placed you here? My name is Amy."

Flynn didn't answer or even look up. "I remember."

She noticed small smears of blood on his arm and hand. "Good. First, I must ask… are you injured?"

"I'm okay."

"Are you sure?"

He nodded his head. Amy noted that the boy would not look at her.

"That's good," she said. "Flynn? Can you look at me?"

Flynn looked up but did not make eye contact for more than a brief moment.

"Umm, can you tell me what happened here last night? Please?"

The boy finally looked at her and his mouth opened, as if he had a thousand things to say. He kept forming words, but nothing came out. She could almost see how fast his mind was racing. Finally, she watched him give up, without saying a word.

"Yes?"

"Nothing," sighed Flynn.

"Nothing happened? Clearly something *did* happen."

"No, I… I mean… I meant that I didn't have nothing to say," stammered Flynn, at a loss. He could feel Gray push a little harder against his back, letting him know the little mouse was there for him. "It was all my fault. I'm sorry. I'm so, so sorry."

"Were you angry at Missus Easterbrook? Did she do anything wrong?"

"No. No! This wasn't because of her. I… I was just playing and… things got out of hand."

"Playing, Flynn?"

He held up his blue and yellow Micronaut action figures. Gray had dragged them up from the basement for the boy after they had concocted their excuse.

"They were having a battle. And there was lots of explosions and stuff. And, well, like I said, things got outta hand."

"But walls and furniture were burned. There are gaping holes in the wall, Flynn. Help me understand that," she pleaded.

"I was playing and shooting at them with rubber bands. And then I was throwing things. But I just kept getting more out of control, I guess. I'm sorry. Tell her I'm real sorry, would you? I won't do it again, I promise."

"So, you got angry… would you say?" He paused but then nodded to her. "You let your emotions get the best of you?"

The boy had picked a point on the wall and could only stare straight at that spot. "Why?"

"Excuse me? What was that?" She could hear him but needed to bring more out. "What did you say, honey?"

She could tell that he wanted to let loose, share his side of the story. But… did he have a *side* to tell or was the boy just acting out?

"You can talk to me, Flynn."

"Why? W-why is this happening to me? It's not fair! I didn't ask for this!"

Amy closed her eyes for a second, then focused on the details in his file that showed how much this kid had gone through in the past few months.

"I know you didn't ask for this, Flynn," she said. "And life isn't always fair. I'd love to be able to snap my fingers and make it all better for you. But it doesn't work like that. You and I both wish that it did, but we don't have a say in the matter."

She closed her eyes, instantly regretted trying to say anything. She knew she was not making sense but had burning need to say something, anything.

"Look, let's gather your things and get you back to the group home. We'll—"

"What?! Why can't I stay here? I don't wanna leave... go back there. I don't want to go anywhere! Please?!"

"I'm sorry, Flynn. But we need to find you a new foster home. Can you collect your belongings while I talk to Missus Easterbrook and have her sign some forms?"

Flynn could only stare down at the kitchen table. "Okay."

"Good. Let's get started then," she said, standing up from the kitchen chair.

A new wave of anger flooded the boy, but he could only push it back down again. "You're gonna have to help me get downstairs though."

"Excuse me?"

"My stuff. It's in the basement."

"The basement?" She looked from his wheelchair over to the basement door. She spotted the winch, the battery, and then the metal cable and hook lying on the floor. She walked to the door, flipped on the light. She was speechless when she saw the wooden ramp leading down into the basement.

"You... were down *there*?"

Flynn nodded.

"Are you *kidding* me?!" she shouted to herself but also as a forewarning to Mrs. Easterbrook. Amy stormed through the kitchen, into the living room.

Gray hopped back up onto Flynn's shoulder. He wanted to watch this.

"Missus Easterbrook, am I to understand that you put this child – a child in a wheelchair – in the basement?!"

Mrs. Easterbrook hopped away from the arm of the chair, positioned herself behind her favorite chair, and covered her chest with her hands. She was on the defensive.

"Well, I—"

"I need to know now, ma'am. Was he housed in the basement?"

"You see, I... well, w-we didn't feel that it was appropriate to have a male in close approximation to—"

"He's ten years old, lady! What is wrong with you?! What if there was a fire?!"

"I-I'll remind you that he was the one playing with fire! I am not the bad guy here. He's the little pyromaniac," she stammered. "I'm the victim!"

Mrs. Easterbrook looked away from Amy in shame. That was when she noticed one of her napkin rings lodged deep into the wall next to her mirror.

Waiting at the top of the basement steps, Koko listened carefully to everything being said. She scurried down the ramp into the basement. The tribe was scattered about the room, resting and recovering from the battle.

Viho stood on his hind legs, awaiting Koko's arrival. "What news?"

Koko stopped before her leader, lowered her head out of respect, and then stood on her hind legs to talk closely with him.

"The boy has accepted the blame for the confrontation," she whispered. "Surprisingly, he did not mention us at all."

"It is no surprise. They would not have believed him. He is wise beyond his years."

"The lady of the house, however, no longer wants the boy here. A different female is here to take him away."

Viho eyes shifted over to the boy's bed. He noticed his backpack and suitcase.

"This is an opportunity for us," said Viho.

Zaltana approached, her paw holding Yuma's as he trailed her behind her. "How so?"

Viho turned to his mate and smiled, his paw reaching out to itch behind Yuma's ears. Yuma loved that and closed to eyes to focus on the scratches for as long as they lasted.

"Have the tribe gather only their weapons, some food and their posses-sions now. We will be leaving very soon... in that," said Viho.

The chief's paw pointed a single claw at Flynn's suitcase.

"Are you sure that is wise, Viho?" stated Zaltana, drawing Yuma close and hugging him tight. "All of us trapped in that box? With no escape route... and very little air."

"If we stay here, the Matwau will return. There is no doubt about that. If we travel with the child away from here in the human's vehicle—"

"The Matwau will not be able to track our scent! We could end up many days journey away in just a short amount of time!" She grew more excited the more she thought about the prospect. She hurried away, with the youngster in tow.

His gaze returned to Koko. "You are going to be our ears and nose out there. Return to the case as soon as you believe the female is ready to take Dakota on his journey to his next home."

Koko nodded and scampered off toward the basement steps. Viho was unsure of his decision. The woman may forget to make the boy take his case. She may inspect its contents before leaving. Any number of scenarios could go badly for them. But he had little choice. He turned back to his people.

"Gather everything at once, my warriors!"

Moki laid on his belly on the snow-covered wood pile in the backyard, letting the sun warm his dark red fur. He held the broken eyeglass lens to his eye, watching for any sign of activity.

Tala appeared next to him from out of nowhere, startling the old warrior.

"By Apollo's bones, I wish you would not do that, child!"

Tala smirked briefly and slid onto the wood pile, next to Moki.

Dyani noticed her return and closed the gap to better hear.

"What have you learned?" asked Moki, without taking his eye off the house.

"It would seem the boy in the metal chair is being punished by the parent for our battle. She summoned several people of authority to her home. There were many arguments. If I had to guess, I would say the boy is being banished," said Tala.

"Banishment? Of a child? For some minor damage? Especially a lame child? Heh. I will never understand humans."

Dyani scurried up onto the wood log next to them, no longer able to contain herself.

"This is good news for us, Moki," asserted Dyani. "He aided them during the attack! With the boy out of the way, we will have no problem overtaking them during our next campaign."

Moki stare at his beautiful mate for a second. He could see the heartache in her eyes.

"Yes. We know the terrain better now. We will return with a better plan of attack and..." Moki paused. "Does Viho know the boy is to be banished?"

Tala nodded. "I believe so."

"Then... that is a problem." Moki turned his eye and broken lens back to the house. "You are certain the boy is to be forced away from this house?"

"Yes," said Tala.

"I am willing to bet that the Halona will be going with him."

"What?!" bellowed Dyani. "Why would they leave with the child?"

"Think it through. The house is no longer safe. We are here and know they are, as well. The boy was an ally. But if he is gone, he can no longer help. Why not go with him in one of those... metal machines? We would hardly be able to track them."

"That would be a huge risk on their part," said Tala.

"Yes, but a risk I am convinced they will take. I would, if the situations were reversed..."

"Well, you can be an old fool sometimes," stated Dyani.

"And a wise leader at other times, my love."

Moki shifted his attention to Tala, resting his big paw on her shoulder. "I have a mission for you," he said.

She nodded, knowing she couldn't say no, to him, no matter the request. "It will be dangerous, and you may never get back to us. Are you sure?"

"Yes, I am sure. Whatever is needed."

"If, and only if, they take the boy away – you need to be in that vehicle. Stay with them until they reach their final destination. Then, if you can... return to the tribe."

Tala nodded again before she had a chance to absorb what he was saying. Thoughts swirled around her mind of what all she would have to do to succeed, and what could go wrong, as she bounded off the wood pile and sprinted toward the house.

Moki watched her go, wondering if he would ever see her again.

He heard Chayton snore loudly, behind him. He turned to watch the sleeping fool roll over on the woodpile... and fall right off. He woke for a second, pulled a piece of bark over himself, and went back to snoring.

He might not mind if he never saw that one again. Moki granted himself one last smile.

15

The Journey

Viho peeked out from inside the suitcase as he lowered the top down over his head. The zipper was drawn across, but a two-inch gap remained so he would still be able to see the basement.

Koko ran down the plywood ramp and leapt onto the bed. She jumped up as Viho used his head to push open the gap and she wiggled her way into the suitcase. The zipper moved across the close it up.

The Halona tribe settled themselves under Flynn's clothes and books to prevent discovery. Each used their extraordinary hearing ability to listen for signs of danger. They tensed their hind legs, ready to dive from the suitcase and away from danger.

Amy Regula held on tight to the handrail leading down the steps. Her boots found enough traction to keep her from sliding the rest of the way down.

"This is absolutely ridiculous," she confirmed.

When Amy finally reached concrete, she let go of the railing and surveyed the room. Her eyes fell on the door to the bathroom – she could only shake her head, making a mental note to add to the file that the doorway was too small to accommodate a wheelchair.

She saw Flynn's backpack and suitcase resting on the bed. The realization that the woman had given the kid a bed almost caused her to laugh out loud. Almost. Her eyes scanned the room for other possessions that might belong to Flynn, but everything was, surprisingly, neatly packed up. What little boy packs stuff up?

She heaved the suitcase up, shocked at how heavy it was. "What's he got in here?!"

The mice near the top of the case tumbled to the bottom, landing on others and bouncing off the books and model airplane boxes Flynn kept in there.

In her living room, Mrs. Easterbrook stopped pacing. She realized now that it was a mistake to call Children Services. But what was done, was done.

She plopped in her favorite chair and instantly regretted sitting down. "Cheese and rice!"

Lily Easterbrook dragged herself off the seat cushion, removing the sharp wooden stick she had sat on. She examined it – a pointed end with small feathers that had been attached to the other end, like some tiny, fancy cocktail stir stick. Her eyes rolled as she tossed it aside.

Mrs. Easterbrook threw herself back into her chair causing a puff of smoke, ash, and burning-orange embers to enveloped her. In utter frustration, she waved at the remnants of the small fire.

At the foot of the basement stairs, Amy stared up the dangerous ramp facing her. She put the backpack over her shoulder, grabbed the handle of the suitcase, and pulled on the handrail. She looked up, one final time, at how far she would need to climb.

"I am not getting paid enough for this."

Her boots slipped on the first two steps she took. But she managed to catch the head of a nail, partially sunk into the plywood, to gain a foothold. She made it halfway went her foot slipped. Despite her weight and that of the bags she carried, she held onto the railing. She pulled the dangling leg under her and carefully inched her way up the ramp.

Flynn watched from the kitchen table as his suitcase slid through the doorway and into the kitchen. One boot appeared as the social worker threw herself the rest of the way up from the basement. She was breathing hard and rubbed her aching hand, once she was able to stand up straight.

"I believe I have everything, Flynn. You ready to go?"

The boy lowered his head, the fear and disenchantment in his eyes visible to her across the room.

She set the heavy suitcase on the floor, handed him his bag. When Flynn saw her look away, he slid open the backpack zipper, pulled his elbow from his side, and let Gray dive inside.

"I'm ready," he said. "I guess."

Tala waited patiently underneath the green car, letting one of the rear tires shield her from the harsh wind. She could see where rust had begun eating away at the metal vehicle. That would be her entry point into the trunk.

She watched the younger woman lower the boy in his rolling chair down, step-by-step, and away from the house. The older, round lady watched at the door, not saying or doing anything to stop the child from leaving. Tala noted that the older woman looked somewhat distraught, at least, which meant she had some emotional reaction to her child being taken away.

Snow fell from the sky. Thick, gray clouds slid in front of the winter sun and Tala could sense in her whiskers that it was going to be another cold night. She paused to sniff the air, the neighborhood, trying hard to memorize everything so she could find her tribe once again. Smoke from a nearby chimney, as well as the awful fumes from the car, did nothing to aid her sense of smell.

The younger woman slowly wheeled the child down the driveway.

Tala aimed her nose at a few nearby evergreen trees, searching for unique scents. She memorized the smell of a few bushes, plants, and the pine needles surrounding the house. Cold, crisp air was all around her. Fewer smells than during a hot summer day. This was not going to be easy. Her olfactory receptors worked overtime but there was little there for the mouse to home in on.

The thought of never seeing her tribe again sped through her mind. Instinctively, she shook her head to clear away the fear. After sniffing the air, Tala finally caught the scent of her camp hiding out in the backyard of the house. The pheromones of each and every member of the tribe drifted into her nose. She smiled to herself – she was going to find her way home.

She hunkered down below the tire when the woman approached.

Tala watched as the woman wheeled the boy to the side of the car. She helped him move the hefty suitcase from his lap and to the snow. The woman lifted the boy to get him into the seat. Once his cast was secure, she closed the creaky metal door. Next, she dragged his wheelchair to back, managed to fold it up, and hoisted it into the trunk. Finally, she hauled the heavy suitcase to the trunk, slamming it down hard. The woman took a few moments to catch her breath, leaning against her car.

The light gray mouse, known to her tribe as Stalking Wolf, slipped silently up through the rusted hole in the trunk. She sat quietly on all fours, using her whiskers to map out the nearly pitch-black area around her. Tala used her sensitive sense of smell to make sure she could detect the boy was in the car. But then she identified other mice. Nearby.

She panicked. The other tribe was here. In the trunk with her. Probably in that big case beside her. Moki had guessed correctly – they were using the woman's vehicle to escape.

The realization dawned on her that if she could sense them, they would be able to recognize her scent. Tala darted through the rusty hole in the car, hopped onto the axle of the car, and huddled close to the smelly gasoline tank. That might help keep her from being detected. Hopefully.

The car started. Her heart pounded almost out of her chest. She heard a clunking sound as the big metal vehicle shifted and began rolling along the slushy ground. Using every claw, she held on to the axle as chunks of ice and snow pelted her from the spinning tires. Cold wind cut through her damp fur.

A few seconds into her journey, she was miserable. But her tribe was counting on her. She would survive this.

Amy Regula stood inside the phone booth, balancing Flynn's file on the small steel shelf under the phone. She tried to keep the sticky phone far enough from her ear that it wouldn't touch her skin and still hear the person on the other end. Her boots stuck to the floor as she shifted her weight back and forth, trying to keep warm.

The cold breeze blew the falling snow against the dirty glass of the phone booth and drifted up against the side.

Flynn saw her end the phone call and hang up. She picked up the receiver with only two fingers again, inserted another coin, and dialed another number.

Gray watched Amy from the dashboard. "That phone booth's seen better days. Looks like pretty much all of 'em back in New York. You had to be seriously down on yer luck to go into one of those boxes."

Gray wiped his paw across the windshield to clear the fogged glass. He kept his eyes on the young woman so he would have time to hop into his hiding place.

"I wonder if she's calling *this* family?" Flynn held up the mimeographed sheet of paper with the list of foster families. Gray did not look over, so the boy inspected the names and addresses again.

"No idea, kid. But she probably doesn't wanna take you back to that group home and then uproot you again when she finds you new digs."

"I hope they're nice," said Flynn, his fingers lightly touching the names on the paper.

Gray finally turned to look at his friend. "Well, I'm glad we got away from those whack-job mice back there."

"The Halona weren't so bad."

"Kid, they almost burned that old lady's house down! You got shot!"

"By a toothpick," said Flynn, cocking his head to the side and giving the mouse a questioning stare. "But seriously, though. They got attacked. All I did was help."

"I get it. Look, we just gotta mind our Ps and Qs. If we get kicked out again, nobody's gonna want us, capisce? We need to keep our noses clean."

"By we, you mean *me*… right?"

"I'm just sayin' that you only get so many shots. They stop tryin' to put you in a foster home and they'll leave you at the orphanage. That place was depressing. Those cold concrete walls. The thin metal cot you had to sleep on. It was like prison. And I oughta know – I visited a friend's uncle who lived over in the trash bins on Rikers Island when I was a youngster. Scary place. Terrible food. Too many rats..."

The driver's side door opened. Gray pushed the panic button – he hopped off the dash and landed beside the boy's good leg.

Amy was too preoccupied with her purse and Flynn's file to notice a gray mouse disappear into the backpack.

"Good news, Flynn. We've got a family willing to take you on short notice," she announced. "But don't worry. They've already gone through the pre-placement training and...they have already fostered other kids. There were no issues reported."

Flynn could only stare at her with a look of worry plastered on his face. Once more into the unknown.

Under the car, Tala heard the clunk of the transmission as it shifted into gear. She shook all the dirty melting snow from her fur, closed her eyes, and steeled herself for another grueling leg of the insidious journey.

Amy drove so slowly, so carefully through the driving snow. She hated snow. The rear-wheel drive car was constantly sliding around turns, slipping as she braked on the icy roads. What compounded the problem was that this was the worst winter ever, in her memory. Two feet of snow covered the ground, accompanied by bone-chilling temperatures, with more falling every day. It was still only January; she had two more months of this crap.

She held on to her silly high school dream of moving to California. Sunshine, palm trees, the sandy beaches, all of it called to her. Maybe it was one of the movies she'd seen or something on the TV shows she watched... something had sparked the dream, or maybe that song that talked about how it never rains in Southern California. She didn't care. She just wanted to get away from... winter.

As more wet flakes pelted her windshield, she cranked up the wiper speed. She stole a look at the boy next to her. His hands were balled fists, knuckles white, holding tight to his backpack.

"Flynn? You're going to be okay."

She saw him give a short nod from the corner of her eye.

"I was saving this for a surprise, but I guess I can go ahead and tell you now. The house we're going to is handicap-accessible," said Amy. She gave him a look to gauge his reaction. He looked puzzled. "The Ciminellos are a couple. Arthur was injured in the war and uses a wheelchair. The house has a ramp and even has an elevator."

"An elevator?"

"Well, it's probably not a fancy one that you'd see in a big building. But it would still allow you to get up and down easily."

"He was in World War Two?" Excitement flashed across his face.

"No. Vietnam. They're a fairly young couple. Closer to your age, I guess, than Missus Easterbrook." She noted that the enthusiasm faded from that young, fresh face. "This could be a really good opportunity, Flynn. It could be long term. And that's what you want, right?"

"I don't know," he said. Tomorrow seemed too far away.

"I can't imagine what you're going through. But I know you're—"

"You're right... you can't imagine," he whispered, out loud. He didn't mean to do that.

Amy grimaced. She had tried to fill the silence and had failed. Again. She felt a burning need to talk to him, reassure him, but she had no words. Nothing original. Just the same stuff that people say to each other over and over. *I'm sorry for your loss. Things are going to be okay. Life doesn't give you things you can't handle.* Stupid platitudes that had long sense lost their meaning.

"I'm sorry," said Amy. It was the only thing to say that made sense.

Despite her best judgement, she reached her hand over and held his. Flynn stared straight ahead, his face bright pink from anger, embarrassment. To her surprise, he didn't pull away. He did not squeeze back but, for the first time in a long time, she felt like she had done the right thing.

16

The New Family

Flynn let Amy pull him from the car and plant him into his wheelchair seat. He felt helpless, useless, like a toy being passed around. The skin just under his cast started to itch like crazy. Without concern for causing damage, he scratched the itch.

Snow fell harder as she dragged his heavy chair onto the sidewalk and retrieved his suitcase.

Flynn took the moment to get a better look at the house. It was one of the older homes in town, built in the 1920s. There were two floors, and the outside was covered in cream-colored stucco. He studied the steep pitched roof, brown wood accents, and diamond-paned windows. A long wooden ramp ran from the driveway to a large porch.

Amy placed the suitcase in Flynn's lap as he pulled the backpack over his shoulder. She turned him, ice crunching beneath the wheels, and pushed his chair up the drive. Gray stuck his nose out from the front pocket of the backpack. He grinned and winked at Flynn, who gave him a weak smile in return.

Elaine Ciminello burst from the front door, in her bell-bottom jeans and orange floral blouse and bare feet. As soon as her feet touched the freezing cold ice, she whirled around and dashed back through the front door. In a whirlwind, she managed to hop back onto the porch as she slid on a pair of suede ankle boots. Her long curly blonde hair swirled and bounced around her long nose and even longer face.

"Oh, hello there! Let's get you inside! It's so cold out. You gotta be freezing," she said, talking very fast. She grabbed hold of his cast to pull him up the ramp but immediately realized that was a bad idea. "Oh, your toes! They're blue!"

She turned around and ran back into the house. Amy rolled her eyes, blew fallen hair away from her face, and pushed hard on the wheelchair handles. Elaine returned with a red knit cap in hand. Flynn recognized that kind of hat. His mom called them toboggans, but a friend told him that was what Canadians called a sled. Words were always so confusing to Flynn. *Everything had to have fourteen different names*, he thought.

The woman stuck the cap onto the end of his cast, covering his cold toes. She jumped in next to Amy, grabbed one of the wheelchair handles, and helped get him the rest of the way into the house.

"We got you. We got you," she assured as they rolled Flynn to a stop in the foyer of the house. "Now, let's get a look at you." Elaine stood back, hands on her hips, and smiled at him.

"Hi, Missus Ciminello. I'm Amy—"

"Isn't he the sweetest thing! Just adorable!"

"—Regula. From Child Services."

"Oh, where are my manners?! I'm so sorry. We talked on the phone," she said as she shook Amy's hand hard, throwing her arm up and down. "I'm Elaine!"

Artie Ciminello burst into the foyer through French doors that led to the great hall. "Whoa, whoa, whoa... what do we have here?!"

His hands, covered with fingerless gloves, grabbed the wheels on his wheelchair and he slid to a stop next to Flynn. The boy recoiled slightly, unsure of what to do next. The grinning man reached out his hand and Flynn returned the handshake. The man's powerful grip hurt, so he tried to squeeze back just as hard... like dad had taught him.

Artie was thirty years old with a round head covered in thinning light brown hair. His scruffy beard already had hints of gray. His arms were covered in cheap bluish tattoos, from his adventures overseas. He sported the typical black concert t-shirt every guy wore these days, Flynn noted.

His eyes were immediately drawn to Artie's faded jeans – they were loose-fitting, he quickly realized, because the man's muscles had atrophied from lack of use. Flynn's own legs had already started to get smaller, thinner. The fear of not being able to walk or run well again quickly overwhelmed him.

"All right, man! Strong grip! Far out!" Arthur Ciminello beamed proudly at Flynn. "Welcome to our humble abode, muchacho!"

Flynn glanced around the large house. Brown paneled wood enveloped every wall. A dark, heavy wooden staircase ran upstairs. A Persian rug had been laid over the slate tile in the foyer, but wide oak boards covered the floor throughout the rest of the first floor. That would make it easy to roll his chair over.

"Artie Ciminello. This here's my old lady, Elaine," he said. "And you're Finn, right?"

"Flynn," said both Amy and Flynn.

"Flynn! Oh, man, sorry about that. Flynn, Flynn, Flynn… Got it. Flynn," he stammered. "Elaine, why don't you take his bags? Here, man, hand me your coat!"

Elaine lowered the boy's heavy suitcase to the floor. She reached for his backpack, but he pulled it close to his body. She let go and smiled as an apology. Flynn removed his coat and Artie snatched it from him. He watched as the man rolled backwards with ease and tossed Flynn's coat up on the newel post on the staircase.

"Nailed it! First try!" Artie fist-pumped the air, drove up next to Flynn's chair, and grinned at him. "Come on, man. I'll show you around. You ladies probably have some papers to sign or something?"

Amy hesitated. The couple seemed nice. But it was all moving so fast. Too fast? She didn't know. Couldn't tell. Wasn't sure.

"Um, yes, I—"

"Good! We'll leave you to it. Let's roll, man," said Artie.

She wanted to object but had nothing to object to, so she turned to the smiling Elaine. "Would the kitchen be a good place?"

Tala clung to the car axle for a few moments longer, soaking in the last of the heat from the tailpipe, with her eyes closed. As the heat dissipated, ice quickly formed on her fur. She pulled her claws away from the axle, dropped to the cold snow below.

Night was coming. The woman and the boy were still in the house, which meant this was likely his final destination. She also knew the night was going to get even colder once the winter sun fell below the horizon. She needed to find shelter or get indoors.

Tala peaked out from underneath the car. The big house was surrounded by old, tall trees. Trees were the bane of existence for mice. Predators waited there to strike unsuspecting prey. The house was far back on the lot and up on a small hill. This was going to be a dangerous run. But Tala had no choice.

She rubbed her paws together for warmth, took two deep breaths, and scrambled on all fours for the house.

Tala stopped at a large rock with a house number painted on it, listened for flapping wings or feet crunching on the snow. She could smell no predators in the vicinity, but her nose and whiskers never stopped searching.

Sprinting as fast as she could, she scurried toward to the nearest tree.

She smelled the hawk first, then heard the wings. It was a light, smooth ruffle of air. Nothing loud, but enough to scream out danger.

Closer and closer, the sound of the wings descended upon her. She was exhausted but knew her life depended on summoning her last reserve of energy. Tala's paws dug hard in the snow, launching her forward with each leap.

The wings were almost on top of her, but she ran in a straight line. Just a few seconds more. A shadow fell across her. One more second, and... now – Tala dived hard to the right, then bounded off the icy snow to her left. Sharp talons from the hawk bit into the snow next to her, barely missing her. Ice sprayed over her fur. The red-tailed hawk flapped its wings hard to launch back into the sky.

She never stopped running until she stood next to the tree, panting hard to catch her breath. She sniffed the cool air, trying hard to reacquire the hawk's scent. Tala only had seconds before the hawk could climb to the optimal altitude to make another run at her.

Tala raced into the open yard. The hawk had circled around and was diving from the opposite direction. She couldn't see a shadow, but the smell wafted across her nose and the slight, muffled sound of those wings.

Go, Tala, go, she whispered to herself. Closing her eyes, she dug deep to find the very last ounce of strength that would carry her to safety.

As she ran, she lurched from side to side, scurrying as fast as her little legs would carry her. She bounded over a small mound of snow and felt the flapping wings push air down hard on her fur and whiskers.

Tala neared the wheelchair ramp in front of the house. She was close. So close.

But this time – the hawk caught her. A set of talons gripped her lower back. The other squeezed around her tail. She lost contact with the ground.

"No!" she screamed. Tala struggled within the grasp of the massive bird.

As she was lifted to her impending doom, the bird's wing hit the railing of the wooden ramp. The hawk made a terrifying screech, frightening her. The talons dug in deep, trying to crush the life from her.

The bird's wing hit the ramp railing again, throwing it out of balance. As hawks tend to scoop prey up and then fly off, this one could not do both at the same time. Tala shifted her weight back and forth, heaving against the hawk's grasp. The predator let her go, shifted away from the structure, flapped hard enough to lift off, and flew off into the cold night. Tala dropped a few feet into a mound of snow. She scrambled to her paws, dashed under the ramp.

Laying on her back, breathing hard, she stared up at the wood planks. The ramp had saved her. Every part of her body hurt. She rolled over to survey her surroundings, noticed blood on the ground. She closed her eyes, trying to sense if she was mortally wounded or not. After a long sigh, she relaxed. She would live.

Tala slowly, tenderly crawled along under the ramp to the house.

The suitcase stood upright in the middle of the foyer.

Flynn and Artie were rolling through the house as Amy reviewed paperwork with Elaine in the kitchen.

The zipper on the case unzipped from the inside. Koko popped her head out and waited, listened. She could sense no humans close by. She jumped off the suitcase, paws landing silently on the Persian rug. After a pause, she dashed around the case for a better look – the coast was clear. She gave off a high-pitched signal that only her tribe could hear.

Viho opened the zipper all the way down and was the next mouse on the rug. He ran to the closest baseboard, his whiskers feeling out his surroundings. He looked for an opening, a weakness in the structure. When he found a gap, Viho put his teeth to work. The mouse quickly chewed at the wood until there was an opening large enough for Maska to fit through. He chirped out a message to the others. The Halona poured from the suitcase. In single file, they dashed across the oak floor and through the hole Viho had created. In mere seconds, they were gone.

From outside one the diamond-paned glass windows in dining room, Tala watched the enemy tribe disappear into the baseboard – giving her the proof she needed that they had occupied the house. She limped away from the window to find shelter and warmth.

Hopping off the porch, Tala carefully hugged the foundation of the house until she turned the corner. She quickly found a safe spot under the siding and just above the dryer vent from the basement. She pulled out loose insulation from the siding, gathered dried leaves, and fashioned a tiny nest for herself. Tala curled in a ball and fell fast asleep.

Inside the house, Artie and Flynn wheeled their chairs from the dining room and into the kitchen. They sailed past the kitchen table where the women were talking.

"And this is the kitchen. You've seen a kitchen before," Artie said. He looked back over his shoulder as Flynn slowed down. "Come on, man! You got to keep up!"

Flynn struggled to get back up to speed. Amy grinned at him as they sped by.

On they rolled, past French doors that looked out on the backyard, through the pantry, mudroom, laundry room, and then into the great hall. Flynn had never seen so many rooms on the first floor of a house. He looked up in wonder as he rolled into the hall. The room was two stories high, with wood beams running across the coved ceiling. Several dusty chandeliers bathed the room in a golden light. The walls were covered with old tapestries, along with several pairs of antlers and several deer heads. A large Tudor-arched fireplace was the centerpiece of the room, surrounded by several seating areas filled with older sofas, chairs, and ornate tables.

Flynn stared up at the Great Hall ceiling. As he reached the center of the room, he turned his wheelchair around to see a hallway protected by a dark wooden bannister, up on the second floor, that looked down on the room.

"Wow. Are you rich?"

"Ha! No way, man. This pad has been in my family forever, which means… it's all been paid for," said Artie. "My mom kicked the bucket when I was a kid and my dad's in an old folks' home because of his memory. Or lack thereof. He doesn't remember who I am anymore."

"I'm sorry," he said.

"No, it's cool, man. I get disability comp from the VA and my old lady waits tables down at the Steak and Ale. So, no… we're not rich."

"Oh, okay." Worry crept into Flynn's head again. Was he just another paycheck to these people, too? Artie rolled up next to his chair, facing the opposite direction.

"Hey, man," he whispered, looking back toward the kitchen. "It's totally cool. That woman, from Child Services? She dropped the dime on the other lady you were staying with. No way we're doing this for the cash, man. Elaine really wants kids, but… I'm injured. We were thinking about adopting, you know? But that takes years and years, they told us. So, we're going the foster kid route, you dig?"

Flynn wanted to breathe a sigh of relief. But showing any emotions, this early, seemed a risky prospect. He gave the man his best fake smile and nodded.

"That's my boy!" Artie playfully punched Flynn's shoulder, which kind of hurt. He kept up his fake smile as Artie spun his wheelchair away, and then rubbed his sore arm.

17

The New and Improved Basement

Flynn turned from Amy, who was saying her goodbyes, to his backpack pocket. Gray's snout popped out and the mouse took as many fresh breaths of air as he could.

"Yer killin' me, kid," whispered Gray. Flynn shushed him, tried to gingerly stuff the mouse back into hiding spot.

Amy startled him when she leaned down to say goodbye. "You're going to be okay here, Flynn."

He nodded. She pinched his cheek and gave him one last reassuring smile. Adults always go for the cheeks. If he ever became president, he would outlaw the pinching of all kids' cheeks by any grownup.

"Thanks again for all your help. And for this opportunity," said Elaine.

Amy gave the couple a final visual inspection.

Artie pushed himself up, sitting a little straighter in his wheelchair, and gave her a half-wave. "Little man's gonna be fine."

Amy smiled at Flynn and opened one of the double front doors. "He is."

"Be careful out there. The snow just never stops coming down," said Elaine, stating the obvious.

"Yeah," Amy replied. California dreaming, she told herself, as she closed the door.

"Well, let's get you situated," Elaine said as she picked up his large suitcase. With the zipper still open, most of the contents from the case spilled out onto the floor.

"Oh, no." She quickly chucked his clothes and toys back in but not before Artie scooped up one of Flynn's model plane kits. He inspected the Monogram Mustang model.

"What do we have here?" Artie flipped the box over and over, peeked inside to see the boy had not started the model yet. "Nice, nice. P-51 Mustang. The most aerodynamic pursuit plane in existence, back in the day."

Flynn was stunned. "You like airplanes?"

"Do I like airplanes?" Artie smiled at Elaine, who playfully rolled her eyes at him. "Follow me, man!"

Artie stopped in front of a small closet door. He pulled the door open as Flynn rolled up.

"Back yourself in there," Artie gestured inside the dark closet. A light finally flickered on. He could see the same brown paneling found throughout the rest of the house. Flynn turned to look at Artie, who just grinned at him. "Go on. It's cool."

Taking a chance, the boy spun his wheelchair around and backed slowly into the tiny room. He could not take his eyes off Artie.

"All right, here we go," he said. Artie adjusted his chair so he could reach into the closet. His fingers found a button with an arrow pointing down. "See you later, alligator!"

"Wait!"

Two metal doors folded in to enclose the closet. Flynn could hear a motor hum to life above his head. The closet was an elevator. He held tight to his wheelchair armrests as he lowered slowly to the basement.

When he hit bottom, the motor stopped the steady hum. The metal doors automatically unfolded. As quick as he could, Flynn pushed his wheelchair away from the box as Gray popped out of the backpack. The humming cranked back up as the elevator returned to the first floor.

Flynn and Gray rolled into the room. It was the typical finished basement that Flynn had been in dozens of times in his young life. Fluorescent lights encased in a suspended ceiling. Dark paneling on the walls. A turntable and equalizer were set up, with tall speakers on both sides. He saw vinyl albums stacked in old milk crates. The room had all the basement man cave trappings – lava lamps, a tattered couch, orange shag carpet, a bean bag chair, blacklight posters of Hendrix and smiley faces and peace signs, some candles, and beads hanging down in every doorway.

The elevator brought Artie down into the basement. He rolled past Flynn as Gray burrowed back into the backpack.

"You're gonna like this," declared Artie.

He cruised through the beads into another section of the basement. He flipped on the lights, spun in a circle, and waited for Flynn to fight his way through the beaded curtain.

This side of the basement had not been finished. Flynn noted the concrete block walls and gray floor. His eyes were instantly drawn to several model planes hanging from the ceiling and resting on surfaces all over the room. There was a workbench holding a few projects already in progress, as well as a variety of tools and spare parts.

Flynn's mouth fell wide open. "Whoa… sweet."

He wheeled up close to get a better look. Many of the planes were remote-controlled – they could actually fly. He saw biplanes and the triplane masterpiece that the Red Baron had flown in, the red Fokker Dr.1. He recognized the WWII classic Mustang P-51. There were quite a few from the Vietnam war: a B-52 bomber, a Douglas F-4 Phantom fighter, and a few helicopters… the Sikorsky S-61R and the Bell UH-1 Iroquois. It was, Flynn had to admit, quite an impressive collection.

"Very cool, Mister Ciminello," Flynn said.

"Hey, man! You can call me Artie, cool?"

Flynn nodded. He was worried the man was going to ask him to call him dad. That was something he had not considered yet. What if someone, someday, asked him to do that? He didn't think he would ever be able to call someone else… dad. Not in a million years.

Flynn's worried look caused Artie to fret about his planes.

"Hey, I know you're probably more into World War Two planes. Am I right?! Well, we can get some more of those, man. Build 'em together, you know?"

Artie grabbed one of the biplanes off the workbench and examined it. He held it up to boy to hold. Flynn grabbed it – it was lighter than he was expecting.

"But these are really fun to fly. We can take them out back this Spring. There's plenty of room to take off and land and to do stunts. I like the biplanes better because they're slower, heavier, easier to control. I'll turn you into an ace in no time, man!"

Flynn gave a weak smile. Artie had no idea that he was already an ace and had shot down more than forty planes from his cockpit in the Caprice station wagon. That was now down at the bottom of a gorge in Tennessee.

A funk quickly descended on the boy. Artie noticed.

"Hey, mi casa su casa, compadre. You dig? What's mine is yours. I won't get mad if you want to come down and work on your stuff. Use my tools, man. That's what they're here for. Whatever you need. Comprende?"

Flynn comprende'd.

"Remote-control planes are my release," said Artie. Flynn handed the biplane back to Artie, who examined it once again. "My freedom. I'm stuck in this stupid chair for the rest of my days, man. But you? You're lucky. You'll be walking again real soon, right?"

"Yeah. In a couple of weeks or so."

"I envy you," Artie said, falling into a funk of his own. "I was a star on my high school football team. Running back. Man, I was *fast*. But I could not outrun shrapnel. Grenade went off behind me, shot up my back. Woke up in a hospital in Da Nang and that was the end of my military career. Army didn't want me no more. People back home didn't want me. The government just said, 'Thanks for your service', wrote out a check, and that was it."

The room was filled with an uncomfortable silence that Flynn always hated. When he was younger, or not stuck in a wheelchair, he could easily slip away without anyone noticing. But he could not think of anything to say. And he could not leave the room.

Artie slammed the plane down onto the workbench, enough to startle

Flynn and cause him to jump up in his seat. Artie slid his wheelchair next to his, leaned in close, as his furtive eyes darted around the room.

"Never trust the government, man. Never." Artie sat back, inspected the boy's reaction. Satisfied, he held onto Flynn's arm and leaned back in. "This is just between you and me, but they're trying to control our minds, man! They tested all kinds of drugs on us over in 'Nam and now they are running their experiments on the rest of the country. They put chemicals in the water, in our food, to keep us happy and dumb us down so they can manage us. You know how I know?"

Flynn did not know how he knew.

"Disco, man. Disco. Have you heard that crap? People are out there dancing to that garbage and it's terrible! *Get Up and Boogie, Play That Funky Music, Stayin' Alive…* You'd have to be on mind control drugs to dig those tunes!"

Flynn was torn. Some of those songs were ones his parents played on their stereo and they would dance to them. *They didn't seem like their minds were being controlled*, he thought.

"But they know I'm on to 'em. The government's been watching me. I haven't seen them, but I've heard their unmarked black helicopters hovering around the house at night. I know they're there!"

Now Flynn was really confused. If Artie had not seen these helicopters, how did he know they were unmarked and black?

Artie stared at the ceiling of basement, listened hard, with his mouth hanging open. "Do you hear that, man?! I bet they're up there right now!" Artie let go of Flynn's arm, patted him hard, pushed his wheelchair out of the workroom.

Gray waited until he heard the wheelchair roll onto the elevator to pop out of his hiding place. Flynn examined one of the remote-control planes.

"Wow! That guy's a few sandwiches short of a picnic, kid," stated Gray.

"Maybe. But he's got some pretty cool stuff. Check it out," said Flynn. He held the airplane out to the mouse.

"What is that?"

"It's a World War One biplane," said Flynn.

"Kinda small, ain't it?"

"Well, it's just a model. The real one is big enough to hold a man and fly him through the skies. He could sit right in there." Flynn pointed to the cockpit.

"All the planes I seen flying over the big city only had one wing. This one's got two," observed Gray. He pulled out his bag of mixed nuts, opened it, and started chewing on a walnut.

"Back then most of the planes needed both wings because they didn't know how to make them strong enough to fly," said Flynn. "By World War Two, they were building Spitfires and Corsairs that would fly circles around the biplanes. They were stronger, faster, and more maneuverable."

"It doesn't make that much sense to me. Everyone buildin' bigger and better weapons just to kill each other. Live and let live, I say," said Gray. He took another bite of the walnut. "Why not spend all that time and money makin' more nuts like these."

"So, that is a weapon?" said Viho.

Both Gray and Flynn jumped when they heard the voice of Viho. He was standing on the end of the workbench, his nose and whiskers working furiously. Maska stood silently behind Viho. He was a daunting figure, looming over his chief.

"Holy smokes!" exclaimed the mouse. He dropped the walnut and clutched at his heart. "Dude! What are you doing here?!"

Gray scanned the room for the rest of the tribe. "This is not cool!"

"How does it work?" Viho ignored Gray's hysterical reaction. "Show me."

Gray was irate. "Show you what?!? You can't be here. You guys practically burned down the old lady's house and got the kid thrown out!" Gray pointed a paw at the chief.

Maska stepped between Gray and Viho.

"Back off, Enormouse!" seethed Gray.

"Calm yourself, cousin," soothed Viho. He strode past Gray to the boy, his paws in the air to show he had no weapons and meant no harm. "We traveled this great distance with you. The Matwau will probably never find us here."

"Probably?!" Gray paced back and forth on Flynn's backpack. "You okay with this, kid?"

Flynn looked down and away, his fingers played with the backpack zipper. He shrugged.

"You *are* okay with it! What's wrong with you, kid?"

"What? It's like he said. Those other mice are miles away. They can't find us now," said Flynn.

Gray stared at the boy.

"Show me what this is," asked Viho. Flynn set the biplane on the workbench. He went to pick up the mouse leader but paused.

"Can I?"

Viho was unsure of what the boy wanted to do but nodded his consent. Flynn scooped up Viho and set him down in the cockpit of the biplane. He fit perfectly.

"This is an airplane. A model of an airplane, actually. The propeller, here, spins around fast enough that the plane can fly through the air."

"I have seen the false birds in the sky," acknowledged Viho.

"Good. Okay, planes like these were used during battles. They were first deployed during World War One, about sixty years ago."

"Why?" asked Viho. Flynn explained air-to-air combat to him.

Gray exhaled. Viho was a smart cookie. He was showing interest in things the boy liked. Gray used to watch an old man, back in the city, that would fish off the pier in the waters of the Hudson River. He would put a worm on a metal hook and dangle it in the water to lure in fish. Every once in a while, he would catch one and reel it in. Sometimes he threw fish that were too small over to Gray. Viho was dangling a hook in front of Flynn's face right now.

"If you control the air in a battle, you have superiority. If you knock out the other side's fighter planes, you can protect your bombers and move troops and supplies to where you need them. If you own the skies, you can bomb their cities and strafe their troops on the ground. You can even cut off their supply lines."

"Very interesting. You are smart indeed, Dakota," said Viho.

Flynn smiled. Pride swelled in him. He remembered how he would show his books or a new model to his dad, who always took an interest in all Flynn's hobbies. He knew his dad wasn't as passionate as he was, but he loved that his dad cared enough to listen.

Gray slapped his own face with his paw. Hook, line, and sinker.

18

The Lull

Tala woke from her restless sleep. She was sore all over and parts of her fur were stiff where the blood had dried. It was dark out but that was always the way in Winter. She sniffed the cold air for signs of an imminent threat, though no creature loomed nearby.

She needed food soon but knew she needed to start her journey. Tala focused hard, cleared the hunger from her mind. She let her sense of smell soar through the night.

With her eyes closed, she took in the assorted food smells, exhaust from their wretched cars, smoke from chimneys as the humans settled in for the evening. Scents from a few predators caught her attention but she sailed past them. Her mind searched desperately, sifting away any smell that did not matter to her quest. She managed to concentrate to a higher degree and caught a whiff of Hinto, their expert builder. His grooming was not nearly as perfunctory as the others as he was always caught up in his projects. The odor from the entire tribe eventually washed over her and she knew where they were located.

Her eyes opened; she grinned to herself. Tala pointed her entire body in the direction she was going to have to travel to find the tribe again.

Food was next. A birdfeeder, over a nearby wooden fence and across a street, that was along her path, still had a few seeds that would tide her over.

She hated the thought of leaving her makeshift nest next to the dryer vent, but her mission was critical. Staying close to the house foundation, she ran along concrete blocks for protection. When she reached the end of the massive house, she stared out into the black of the expansive backyard.

A familiar scent drifted across her tiny nostrils. She stole a quick glance at a snow-covered, dirty egress window that looked in the basement. She shook off the smell and returned her attention to the yard.

It was time. She took several deep breaths and told herself it was now or never. As fast as her four legs would carry her, she sprinted into the night.

And her long journey began.

Gray stood at the cold egress window that was just above ground level. A strong scent crossed by his nose causing his whiskers to flitter about. Another mouse must have passed by outside. He stared hard at the glass for long minute but could see no movement.

It dawned on Gray that he really needed to improve his ability to smell. These house mice were finely attuned with the sense, but he was not. A lifetime spent in the city – surrounded by tall buildings, hordes of people, unique foods, garbage, animal and human waste, smog from the cars, all of it, had dulled his olfactory ability. But he knew he was learning. Gray had recognized the scent that had just passed by outside. The smell was certainly a field mouse and most likely one of the Matwau, he was sure of it.

"Noticed her scent, did you?" asked Koko.

Gray nearly leapt out of his skin. She was standing right behind him on the window ledge.

"Oh, for cryin' out loud!" He clutched his chest as he tried to regain his breath.

Koko laughed at him. Silly city mouse. She knew Gray was not cut out for this. She surmised that the city mouse probably grew up lying around in a trash can, eating perfectly good food that had been tossed out by overfed humans, without so much as an owl stalking him day and night.

"But, yeah, I smelled something out there," he admitted.

"Good. We'll make a real mouse out of you yet," said Koko.

"So… those field mice are here? Already?"

She laughed at him. "No, city mouse. No. Even though the human drove slowly, there was no way they could have kept up with the car for that long. But I do believe a Matwau scout stowed away in the car, along with us. I did not catch her scent, but I was trapped in the suitcase and could detect nothing but his foul-smelling socks."

"Yeah, his feet can get pretty ripe," conceded Gray.

"The scout is more than likely headed back to her tribe. If she survives the trip, she will reveal our location, and they will come looking for us."

That was the last thing he wanted to hear.

"Hey, I gotta ask? What did you guys to do to make this other tribe so mad?"

Koko thought about her response and then looked him in the eye. "We have been fighting each other for a while now. It is just the way it is."

"Naw, that don't make a whole lotta sense. I can see if you guys moved into their turf, they'd fight back. But this is starting to look more like an obsession."

Koko shrugged, silently scurried along the sill, and disappeared.

Gray shifted his attention down to the basement workroom. The entire tribe was hustling and bustling around the room. Some mice returned with food found upstairs. Others were fashioning new weapons to protect their new home. Viho barked orders and answered questions.

Flynn was meticulously describing the model airplane to Adriel and his assistant Fala. She was writing notes for Adriel on a small pad of paper with lead that had been removed from a pencil.

Zaltana watched over Yuma as he and Wamblee threw a small, red plastic ball back and forth with Sani, the elder. Gray jumped down to the top shelf of the workbench, then to the work surface, and approached the young ones. He noticed the protective Zaltana take a step closer, but stop, when he got close to Yuma.

"What's shakin', youngbloods?"

Both the mice looked at him, then each other.

"What did you say?" asked Wamblee, grinning slightly.

"I asked how you kids are doin'. Slip me some skin," said Gray. He held out his paw, but the young mouse just stared at the padding on his palm.

"Here. Like this." He slapped the palms of his paws together, then held out his paw again. Wamblee was unsure what to do next. He tentatively held out his own paw. Gray slapped down on it. "That's slippin' me some skin. It's a way of saying hello."

"Sure," said Wamblee, but he wasn't sure. "You say funny things."

"That is no lie, little man. What's going on?"

"Oh, we are playing with Sani," said Wamblee. He turned to point to the mouse. Sani had his paws up, waiting to catch the ball.

"Ah, a little pitch and catch! Nice."

"Yes, but…" Wamblee leaned in to whisper to Gray. "He is not very good. He is really, really old. Watch!"

Wamblee tossed the small ball at the old mouse – it sailed right past him. A second later, Sani finally moved his paws over to try to catch the toss.

"See?" said Wamblee. Sani slowly spun around, nearly toppling over, and shuffled off to collect the ball.

Gray smirked at the kid, winked. "He is almost four Springs old!"

That declaration caught Flynn's attention. The boy turned his wheelchair to get closer to Wamblee.

"What was that?" asked Flynn.

Wamblee had no fear. He hopped closer to the boy to loudly whisper to him. "I said that Sani is really, really old."

"Yeah, I heard that. How old is he?"

Gray looked down, dreading what was coming next.

"I said 'He is almost four Springs old'. Can you believe it? He is ancient!"

Flynn looked directly at his friend. Gray looked everywhere but at Flynn.

"How long… do mice usually live?" Flynn asked the young Wamblee.

"Typically, about eight seasons."

"Eight seasons? That's only two years," said Flynn, his mind swirling. Anger built up quickly. The mice sensed his rage, stopped what they were doing to watch. He pushed his wheelchair away from the bench, his face bright red, his knuckles white on the chair armrests.

"Hey, kid," said Gray. He scurried quickly to the edge of the bench, stood on his hind legs. "Are you okay?"

Flynn felt the need to get up and run away, as fast as he could, but knew he was stuck in his chair. His hands were balled into fists. He wanted to throw something, punch the wall. But he had nothing to throw, no wall nearby. Flynn did the only thing he could – he spun his wheelchair around and rolled out of the room.

"Did I say the wrong thing?" asked Wamblee.

"No, kid. No. He's human – they live a lot longer than we do."

"Is that not good?"

"Well, he lost his parents a while ago. And now he's worried he's going to lose me next." Gray could only watch the empty doorway, hoping the boy would come back.

Flynn parked his chair at the far end of the finished basement, staring up at the fingernail-shaped moon outside the egress window. A slight amount of blue light lit up his face. His lips were pursed, his jaw clenched and unclenched, his fingers sore from balling into fists.

Flynn believed in God. His parents had taken him to Sunday School every week and he used to say his prayers, with his mom, before bed every night. While he stared out the window, it dawned on him that he hadn't said his prayers since his parents were killed. *Was that the reason everything kept going from bad to worse*, he wondered. He wondered if this was a test. After the accident, when Flynn woke in the hospital, a nurse waited at his bedside. She confirmed that his parents were gone, and he remembered feeling shocked, scared, confused. But he could not recall being sad.

Now, he had just learned that his only friend, a mouse he had named Gray, would probably not be at his side as he grew up. The anger seeped back in. He directed his anger at God.

"Why is this happening to me? What did I do to deserve this? Am I being punished?"

He waited, listened. There was no response. The moon was quiet, too.

Back in his hospital bed, he had asked the nurse just one thing, "Why?"

She gave him a sad smile – the one that adults always gave when they felt sorry for you – and stroked his hair behind his ear. "You've been through a lot. But you're going to be okay. It's just going to take time. God will never give you more than you can handle, Flynn."

As the moon moved ever so slowly across the window, he could feel it mocking him. The moon just sailed through the night sky. The world would keep spinning whether he was there or not. Flynn had never felt so small, so insignificant. Useless. What he wanted did not matter. He was no different than the snowflake he watched falling to the ground outside.

That was more than he could handle. "Please. Please? Give my parents back to me…. please?" he said to no one. Not even the moon. He wanted to cry, wanted to be sad, but no tears would come. He was empty.

Artie tried to tuck Flynn into bed but only managed to move the blankets back and forth. The boy stared at the ceiling.

"I ain't gonna sing you a lullaby or anything, amigo," laughed Artie. "Nobody wants to hear me sing! Heh."

"Where's… um," stumbled Flynn.

"Elaine? She had to go to work. But she said to say goodnight. If you need anything, we're down the hall. Just shout."

Flynn returned his gaze to the ceiling. Artie gave him a half-smile and turned off his light.

"Night, Flynn. Sleep tight, man" he said. He wheeled his chair out of the room, pulling the door closed as he rolled out.

Normally, Flynn would be a bit scared – a new room, in the dark, with moonlight casting shadows through the tree branches on the walls, and wind howling against the windows. On this night, nothing frightened him. He put his hands behind his head on the pillow and counted the ceiling tiles.

"Did I ever tell you the one about a guy in a wheelchair who went for a job interview?" said Gray, from behind the lamp on the nightstand. "The manager asks, 'What's your biggest weakness?' and the guy points to his wheelchair and says, 'Um, that I'm handicapped?'"

"I'm not in the mood, Gray."

"And so, the manager then asks, "Where do you see yourself in five years?' and the guy says, 'Here, in the wheelchair.'"

"Gray…"

"Finally, the manager asks, 'Okay, what's your dream job?' and the guy sighs and says, 'Ya know, I always wanted to be a stand-up comedian.'"

Gray waited for the boy to laugh at his jokes. "Ha-ha! Okay, that was *hilarious*, kid! I got a million of these!"

Gray hopped over to the bed, crawled along Flynn's blanket, and stood on his chest.

"You okay?"

"Yeah," said Flynn.

Gray tilted his head to the side, gave the boy a skeptical look. Flynn grabbed Gray in his hand, sat upright, and held the mouse close to his neck for a long hug.

"I can't lose you, too!"

"Aww, kid. It's cool. I ain't goin' anywhere any time soon."

"But Wamblee said mice usually live two years! Only two!" Flynn held Gray out in front of his nose. Gray put his paws over the boy's thumb. "I don't know how old you were when we met, but we've already been together four months – and that's like half your life!"

"I'm guessin' math ain't your strong suit," smiled Gray.

"You know what I mean!"

"Who knows how much time we got together? Whaddaya say we make the most of it?"

"But you should be out there, living your life… maybe find a girlfriend, or something. Start a family. Not wasting it with some dumb orphan kid stuck in a wheelchair," pleaded Flynn.

"Can I tell you something without you getting' all weepy and emotional on me?"

Flynn nodded his head. Gray rested his chin in the palm of his paw. "I did start a family. With you."

The boy gave his friend another big hug. Too big.

"Ouch! Careful, kid! Or I won't make it to my first birthday!"

Flynn relaxed. But just a little. He didn't want to put Gray down again. Ever. Gray closed his eyes, hugged the boy's neck as hard as he could.

19

The Big City

The broom came down hard.

The old lady cursed in Italian. She pulled the broom up and slapped the straw head again at young Gray and his mother, scattering them in two different directions. Gray ran toward their opening in the baseboard. His mother was trapped in the corner.

Gray was small, just a few weeks old, but was growing bigger by the day. He had only been running around and playing with his mother in this dusty apartment for a few days. They took a break from learning how to talk, when the old lady went shopping, to practice climbing and jumping. But the woman returned early, having forgotten her purse, and caught them on the counter. She had grabbed her broom and chased them around her Brooklyn apartment.

At the baseboard, Gray turned back to find his mother. The old woman turned her broom around, pointed the handle at the mouse stuck in the corner.

"Die, rodent! Die!" screamed the old lady.

Gray watched as his mother stood on her hind legs, ready to fight, when the broom handle struck her hard. She crumpled into the corner. Her body motionless.

Despite his age, young Gray knew what had happened. His mother was gone. He screamed so loud, in such a high frequency, that every mouse on the block was able to hear his anguish.

Gray ran toward his mother, but the old woman turned the broom on him. She whacked the floor a half a dozen times, trying to strike him down. He gave up trying to get to his mother, returned to the hole in the wall.

"Parassiti!" exclaimed the old lady in Italian.

He hid just inside the wall, trying hard to catch his breath, as the tears fell.

The broom handle shoved through the hole as the old woman attempted to crush him. Gray scrambled away on all fours as far as he could.

When he stopped running, he was in an alley between apartment buildings. Rain was falling and distant lightning lit up the late afternoon sky. Gray raced behind a dumpster to find several mice splitting up the remains of a Coney dog that someone had thrown in the trash.

"Guys! Help! My mom! She's been... I think she's—"

A large mouse turned away from his tasty hot dog to look the youngster up and down.

"Whaddaya want, kid?!"

"My mom! I... she's been hurt real bad! She might be dead!"

The big mouse leaned in close enough that Gray could smell the onions and chili sauce on his breath.

"Them's the breaks, kid. Beat it!" The mouse kicked Gray in the stomach, sending him rolling away from the dumpster and out into the rain.

He was hurt, wet, scared. He stumbled away, eyes searching for anyone who would help him. Gray backed his way to the other side of the alleyway. When his wet fur hit the brick wall, he huddled down under a milk crate. Rain pelted him as he shivered in the cold Spring air.

"Mom?" he whispered. "I need you..."

Gray woke with a start. He was panting hard, unsure of where he was. He sat up on the top of the pillow next to Flynn's head. The boy was fast asleep, breathing slow and steady. Gray clutched at his own chest.

"It was just a dream," he said out loud. But he knew it was not a dream. He was reliving what had happened to him, to him mother, all those many months ago.

Waves of memories washed over him. He was taken back to his days living on his own in the big city. The sounds, the smells filled his brain. He laid back on the pillow, stared at the same ceiling tiles that had consumed the boy.

He had been on his own for a long time. His dad had been caught in a mousetrap back when his eyes were still closed so he didn't even remember what he smelled like. After he lost his mom, Gray fended for himself. He had tried hard to break into a few of the families in the neighborhood, but no one wanted anything to do with him.

He knew he had to stay away from the sewers and the subway tunnels. His mom had ingrained that into him while he was young-blind – the rats down there were dangerous.

Gray managed to hang around with groups of stray mice living in alleys, empty lots, or under bridges but that was short-lived. They were only out for themselves and had no intention of forming a family with him. He had traveled over to an island, a human prison out by the airport, to find a distant cousin. That mice crew was barely a step above living with rats, so he forced himself to move on.

The mouse rolled over on the pillow, as a grin fell across his face. He was forced to grow up fast, but it had baked him into a pretty tough cookie. What a crazy journey he'd been on.

He took a few moments to watch the kid sleep, then decided to close his eyes – maybe he, too, could get some much-needed rest.

20

The Plan

Tala threw her back against the wall of the dry cleaner's building. Her breath was ragged, fur matted down, and legs like rubber. Tala heard the cat howl as he raced around a snow-covered parked car towards her.

She pushed off the wall, leapt out onto the snow, and raced away. She was light enough to stay on top of the frozen surface of the fallen snow, her tiny claws leaving slight impressions. The cat howled again as he closed in on her. But the striped tabby weighed considerably more. When he hit the same snow drift, his paws sank deep and slowed him.

Tala was exhausted and knew she could not hold out much longer, even with the advantage of the deep snow. She raced off the snow and doubled back to the building. Big paws were directly behind her, crunching through the ice as the cat galloped closer and closer.

Near the rear entrance to the dry cleaner, Tala spotted a drain in the ground, covered in white plastic. Tala bet her life that the drain cover was loose. She launched off the snowpack, landing on the white plastic grate. The tabby cat growled as he covered the distance between them.

Tala dug her claws into the plastic cover. She leaned backwards, taking the grate with her. The cat jumped through the air, claws extended. The white plastic cover fell on top of her but her hind legs fired like pistons. She threw the grate away as she backflipped through the air.

The small grate hit the cat in the nose.

Tala's flip landed her a few inches above the drain opening. She rolled forward, diving straight down into the drain. She hit the bottom of the pipe on frozen ice. The tabby dug his paw down into the drain, claws extended, trying to capture her. At first Tala slipped on the ice, then managed to scramble out of his reach. She crawled along the drain and away from the cat's long arm.

Her heart pounded in her chest as she paused to look back. The cat growled and meowed at her.

After a deep breath, Tala sprinted along the rigid plastic drainpipe. Tala had no idea where this would take her, but she had no choice. She simply ran, knowing that she was at least headed in the right direction.

Chuchip raced up to his leader, who stood atop the wood pile watching the house, with a look of excitement splashed across his face – he could finally act instead of waiting around. He hated waiting.

"Moki! Tala is—"

"On the move. Yes, thank you," said Moki. "Stalking Wolf's scent is once again in the wind, which means she is returning to us."

Chuchip looked down in disappointment. Moki gripped his shoulders. "You did good. But I have been at this a long time. However, I am old and needed you to confirm my conclusion." He ruffled the fur on top of Chuchip's head and got a grin in return.

"Gather the others. We will not wait for her return," said Moki.

His announcement caused Dyani concern.

"We will meet her midway in her journey."

"Is that wise?" asked Dyani. "What if she is unable to track us because we are on the move?"

"We have no choice. It would take her days to get back to us here. But we cut that time in half if we leave now. We do not know if this new parent will reject the boy or if Viho will even stay at that location for long."

"Then we must gather our things and leave at once!" announced Dyani to Moki and for the others to hear.

"A wise decision," said Moki sarcastically to Dyani, then flashed a grin at Chuchip.

Flynn heard the noisy elevator doors close behind him as he rolled his way into the kitchen.

Artie pushed away from the table to reach back for a box of cereal sitting on the counter. "Morning, muchacho! You sleep okay?"

"Yeah," answered Flynn. "Thanks."

"Cereal all right for breakfast?" Artie shook the cereal box.

Flynn grinned. He really liked cereal. "Sure."

"Cool, man. Cool." Artie did a quick spin with his wheelchair, grabbed another cereal box. "I had Elaine pick up a couple at the store that I thought you'd like. Did I do okay?

Flynn saw a box of *Count Chocula* and a box of *Boo Berry*. He smiled at Artie, nodded.

As he poured out the *Count Chocula*, Gray hopped onto Flynn's leg. "No, kid! Get the *Boo Berry*!"

Flynn waved his hand at the mouse, trying to keep him quiet but also letting him know that he liked *Count Chocula* better.

"Personally, I like *Franken Berry*," said Artie as he poured out cereal in his own bowl.

Flynn took a piece of the brown cereal, held it under the tabletop for Gray.

The mouse took the piece, looked at it, and tossed it on the floor. "No, kid! Don't give me that crap! Give me the marshmallow!"

"*Franken Berry* is the best. You want to know why?"

Gray looked in the direction of Artie, confused. "Who does this guy think he is? *Franken Berry* ain't the best!"

Flynn tried to pay attention to Artie, but Gray was very distracting.

"It's because the *Franken Berry* makes the milk strawberry-flavored," said Artie.

"Strawberry milk is disgusting. This guy must've been dropped on his head as a kid," whispered Gray.

Flynn giggled, tried to disguise it.

"Oh, that's funny, huh?" said Artie.

"No, no. Not funny at all," said Flynn. He handed a few marshmallows down to Gray to shut him up.

"Everyone knows there is nothing better than chocolate milk!" muttered Gray.

To cover for the noise Gray was making, Flynn took a few noisy bites with his spoon clanking on the ceramic bowl.

"You're darn right. Nothing funny about strawberry milk," said Artie. Flynn could tell Artie was enjoying the conversation, even though he was pretending to be mad.

"Well, it's kinda funny... strawberry milk looks like Clifford the Big Red Dog peed in a bowl," murmured Gray.

Flynn laughed out loud. Artie was surprised. Gray fell backwards, laughing so hard at his own joke. Artie tried laughed along with Flynn, but he was a bit taken aback by this kid.

"Okay, well, maybe it is a little funny. Right?" said Artie, confused. "Anyway, listen... I don't want you to think that I'm leaving you or... abandoning you, or anything.

Flynn's smile faded away.

"But I've got to go to physical therapy at the VA on Tuesdays. They come by and pick me up in a van. So, I'll be gone for a few hours today. Is that cool, man?"

"Oh, yeah, no problem."

"Okay, as long as you're sure?"

"I'm fine here. I'll ... read my books," said Flynn.

"Righteous! Okay. Elaine is upstairs sleeping if you need anything. I gotta get ready, man." Artie gave the boy his best smile, took a last big bite of his cereal, and rolled his wheelchair out of the kitchen.

Artie rolled back in through the kitchen doorway. "Oh, and if you hear the black helicopters outside, stay away from the windows. Otherwise, you'll need to put tinfoil on your head to block their electromagnetic mind-control radio signals."

"But what if the aluminum amplifies certain frequencies and actually makes it easier for them to read your mind or control it easier?" queried Flynn. Gray covered his mouth so his laugh wouldn't be heard.

Artie was stumped, a quizzical look crossed his face. "You may be on to something, man. They may have been the ones who put that story out there. Oh, man, this is *not* good!"

Flynn tapped his finger on his head.

Artie was in full-on paranoid mode. "Not good at all." His eyes darted around, his ear titled up to scan for sounds, and then he raced away from the kitchen.

Flynn and Gray bumped their chocolate marshmallows together and then popped them in their mouths.

The elevator slowly eased Flynn and Gray down to the basement.

"Just so you know, kid. That other tribe of mice the Halona fought with? They're on their way here," said Gray.

"What?! How?"

"I think one of the bad guys hitched a ride on the car we came here in. She's probably on her way back to spill her guts on our location," said Gray.

"Well, that's good. We'll have more time to prepare," said Flynn.

"So, you're not worried about getting' thrown outta here?"

Flynn's jaw clenched as his gaze focused on the opening elevator doors. "I've got to protect my friends. Besides… I think Artie is nuts."

Gray lowered his head in disappointment. "Out of the frying pan, into the fire," he muttered to no one in particular.

Flynn wheeled them into the workroom, flipped on the lights. There was no movement, no sound.

Viho popped his head around from behind an old oil can. He made a high-pitched squeak, alerting the others that the coast was clear to resume work. The tribe flooded back into the room, returning to their tasks to prepare for the arrival of the Matwau.

When Flynn was close enough, Gray hopped onto the workbench. Wamblee was the first to greet him. He held out the palm of his paw.

"Slip me some skin!"

Gray grinned at the young mouse. He ran his paw across Wamblee's paw. "Get down with your bad self!"

Wamblee looked confused but lowered himself down to the surface of the workbench.

"Ha! That's just a saying, kid! You don't have to literally 'get down'. It just means keep doin' what you're doin' because you're too cool for school!"

All the mice nearby hooted with laughter and Wamblee self-consciously chuckled along.

Zaltana stepped close to her mate, whispered in his ear, "That rebellious mouse could be a bad influence on the young ones."

"It is all harmless fun, my dear." soothed Viho. "Let them be."

Zaltana scowled at Viho but eventually broke into a grin.

Adriel inspected the remote-control biplane model on the side of the workbench. He used the large tape measure to gauge the interior of the cockpit. He quoted numbers to Fala, who furiously wrote everything with the pencil lead on a small bit of paper.

The massive Maska nonchalantly strolled up to Adriel and leaned against the side of the model plane.

"So, Adriel…"

"Yes, yes, yes! I know! You want your weapon!" bellowed the frustrated engineer.

Adriel pushed the tape measure over, stormed off underneath the model plane. When he returned, he held the surprise behind his back. Maska could barely contain his excitement. He rubbed his massive paws together.

Adriel revealed a makeshift aluminum gun to the warrior. Maska reached for it, but the gun was withdrawn.

"Patience, Maska. Patience," said Adriel. He held it up to show how it worked. "This gun is powerful. You pull back on this lever to lock the spring in place. Load a metal ball bearing in here. And the trigger is, here, underneath."

Adriel held out the long tube of hollow metal. The trigger was a piece of metal that rotated back and forth to release the spring and fire the metal

124

ball bearing.

Fala handed Maska a bag full of shiny metal balls, which Maska accepted with a nod.

"I cannot thank you enough, Adriel! You have done me a great service," said Maska.

Adriel waved him away so he could get back to work.

Viho beckoned for Flynn to approach. The boy shifted his wheelchair to get closer to the other side of the worktable.

"Hold out your hand, Dakota," commanded Viho.

"Yes... sir," said Flynn. That caused Gray to raise an eyebrow. Flynn put his hand down on the table and Viho stepped up onto his palm. He motioned for the boy to lift him up so they would be at eye level.

"I want to apologize to you," said Viho.

"How come?" said Flynn. Viho had never heard that expression before – he cocked his head to the side. Flynn smirked. "I'm sorry. Why did you want to apologize?"

"Our skirmish endangered your relationship with your new parent and forced you to pick up and move here."

Gray slowly made his way closer to Flynn so he could hear their conversation.

"Oh, that... yeah. It's okay, I guess."

"No, it was not fair to you. I deeply regret all you have been through and offer my sincerest apology. We would have understood if you had let your people know we were to blame for the damage inflicted," said Viho.

"You know what's funny? A lot of people believe in the Loch Ness monster, and Bigfoot, but I doubt they would believe two tribes of mice had a major battle in some lady's house," said Flynn.

Viho nodded in serious agreement, his paws clasped together like a teacher gathering his thoughts before sharing a new theory with his students.

"I fear we may be faced with a similar situation yet again. Koko has warned me that the Matwau have discovered our new camp and will soon be upon us," said Viho, his eyes locked on Flynn's face as he waited for an angry reaction. Flynn, instead, nodded his head.

"I know," said Flynn. "And I want to… help you guys."

Viho glowed with a sense of pride at this young human. Whenever he thought they could no longer surprise him, they always managed to do just that.

"You truly are Dakota," acknowledged Viho. "May Apollo always be at your side."

"Apollo? Like the Greek god Apollo?" asked Flynn.

Flynn's question piqued Gray's interest. He kept hearing these mice swearing to Apollo but had no idea why.

"The very same. The stories that have been passed down to us from our ancestor have always included Apollo. The Greek humans respected the mouse. They knew us to be fierce creatures because we were a hearty species. Apollo was the Greek god of light and truth and was known as a healer. The Greeks felt that mice were capable of healing, as well, so Apollo was often called the Lord of the Mice. Our people have always prayed to him," said Viho.

"Nice," said Flynn. "Then hopefully Apollo will be with us all. Can I ask something?"

"Certainly."

"Did you lose anyone in the last battle?"

"Apollo was smiling upon us, Dakota. We did not lose a single warrior," assured Viho. "We suffered various injuries but have all lived to fight another day."

Gray interjected. "Probably because you guys have seriously bad aim! You're terrible shots."

Viho turned to look down on the mouse leaning up against Flynn's arm.

"You guys couldn't hit the broad side of a barn if you were standing two feet in front of it."

"Well, we mice do not exactly have the best eyesight, do we?" said Viho. "Do you have a suggestion on how we could do better?"

Viho signaled to Flynn that we wanted to be lowered back down. He set the leader down on the table.

"Sure, cousin! You nutjobs could just boogie on down the highway to some other house! Leave this kid alone!"

"As you have taken the boy in, we have as well. He is family. But if he wishes us to leave, to go out into this Winter storm, we will. What do you say, Dakota?" said Viho. He turned to look up at Flynn. Gray could only roll his eyes.

"No, I don't want you guys to go," said Flynn.

"Well, of course he's gonna say that! You can't put him on the spot like that!" barked Gray.

"Gray, it's fine. I already told you this. They are… family and they need us," stated Flynn, his determination and confidence rising.

"Thank you again, Dakota," said Viho.

Gray threw his paws in the air, walking away from the situation. He was worried about the kid. But he also knew it was going to take the loss of another foster home and the return to that horrid group home for him to realize his mistake.

It hurt Flynn to have to fight with his friend. He watched Gray march off and wanted to stop him, but he didn't know what to do, what to say.

"Do you have a plan, Dakota?" asked Viho, pulling him back into the conversation.

"What?" said Flynn, returning his attention to the chief.

"I sensed that you might have a plan in mind. A way for us to defeat our sworn enemy," said Viho.

"As a matter of fact, I do…" stated Flynn. He gave one last look toward the departing Gray, who gave him a look back over his shoulder. "I think we can scare the crap out of the Matwau."

With a few hops and a quick climb onto a metal book shelf, Gray separated himself from the mice going about their busywork in the basement. He plopped down, dangled his hind paws off the edge of a shelf.

Had he made a mistake hitching his wagon to this kid? Nope. Not going to go there. He shook off the negative thoughts racing through his mind. Not everything was going their way, but he had to chalk it up to bad luck. Gray looked back on his time in the big city and remembered the overwhelming feeling of loneliness. Back then, he was restless. He had no purpose. But now, somehow, this injured child, who had saved his life, gave him something to focus on.

He watched the kid talk to the chief. Flynn's arms gesticulated wildly as he got more and more excited. Gray shook his head as he watched Viho acting all wise, pacing back and forth while his claws scratched his chin.

Things were going to be all right, Gray mused. The kid had a purpose now, too. It was a misguided purpose but... that was all part growing up, wasn't it? You have to figure out how to make your own decisions, even if they were the wrong decisions. And learn from that.

Watching Viho made Gray have to scratch his own chin. As he checked his surroundings on the shelf, he noticed Artie also had quite a collection of military books. One that caught his eye was a translation of The Art of War. He padded over, pulled out the paperback, and started reading to kill some time.

Flynn turned his wheelchair around and pushed himself to the center of the workroom. Unsure of himself, he sat a little taller in the seat, cleared his throat.

"Can I, uh, have your attention? Everyone. I just wanna... say something," said Flynn.

The mice stopped what they were doing. They looked from the red-faced child to Viho, who gave them all a slight nod.

"Okay, first I've got to ask – do you want the Matwau to go away?"

Flynn received murmurs and nods from the tribe.

"Sounds like all of you. All right then. I'm going to help you," said Flynn. The mice let out a cheer. Zaltana smiled, hugged the young Yuma to her side.

"But... I'm not going to help you kill them, or anything. Okay? I think we can scare them so bad they'll leave you guys alone, like, forever. *Without* burning the house down..."

Another cheer and paws went up from the warriors. Viho beamed at Flynn.

"Let's get started," said Flynn.

Gray smiled at the boy, flipped a page on his book, and went back to reading.

Adriel, Koko, and Viho gathered around as Flynn drew up close to the workbench.

"I need your help. And this will probably sound strange but I'm looking for some fireworks." The mice were indeed puzzled. "Once a year, every summer, humans are always blowing stuff up. Loud bangs, lights in the sky – sound familiar?"

"Yes," acknowledged Adriel. "We thought they were battling each other!"

"And have terrible aim, like we do," added Viho.

"This dude is a veteran so I'm betting he always goes crazy on the Fourth of July. We need to search for some leftover fireworks. They're made of gunpowder, so they smell like… sulfur, but you don't know what that is… so… eggs! Rotten eggs! Look for small paper packs that smell like rotten eggs! And bring them to me," said Flynn.

"I will handle it," stated Koko.

"Good. Probably in the garage or maybe down here in the basement somewhere," said Flynn.

Koko slipped off the table and was gone.

"Now, I need to find someone willing to fly in one these model planes," said Flynn. Viho and Adriel exchanged a concerned look.

He reached over for the remote-control biplane and set it in front of Adriel. "Well, not actually fly it. I'll probably be able to do that part. But I need a volunteer to ride in here." He showed them the cockpit.

"Probably?" Adriel was worried.

"Yeah, how hard can it be?" Flynn scooped up a controller for the remote plane, examined it.

Adriel shook his head, shuffled away. "Then I will *probably* be able to find your volunteer."

"And Viho… we need to talk about your fighting style," Flynn looked directly at Viho. "I've got a strategy that might help. It's what helped the Nazis take over most of Europe in World War Two."

"Go on, Dakota," said Viho.

"It's called the Blitzkrieg. It's a German word that means Lightning War.

They used it when they invaded other countries. In the first world war, both sides stayed kinda far from each other and moved slowly when they did. But in the next war, the Germans shocked the enemy with surprise by moving fast. *And* with air superiority."

"Ahh, I am beginning to see where this is going," admitted Viho. "Continue."

"You guys were smart when you surprised the Matwau at Missus Easterbrook's house," said Flynn. "When you attacked them from the other side of the dining room, you gained the advantage. Remember?"

"I do indeed," said Viho.

"Well, we need more of that. Surprise. Speed. With a higher concentration of your warriors in a single movement, a single action, that overwhelms the enemy. It works better than sitting back and just firing arrows at each other."

"Blitzkrieg..."

"We're going to need to train your people," said Flynn. "Get them ready to stop this war for good."

21

The Test Flight

The sunlight found an opening through the drawn curtains in the Ciminello master bedroom. Elaine was fast asleep when the harsh light fell across her face, causing her to stir.

She padded her way to the master bathroom. With her eyes barely open, she grabbed a bottle of sleeping pills and let a single one drop into her hand. She popped the pill, drank water to chase it down. Her shift at the restaurant ended well after midnight so it was too early to be awake. She had to work again that night.

Elaine fell back into bed, pulling a sleeping mask over her eyes. In a few short minutes, Elaine was snoring once again.

Bodaway watched all of this from the hallway, through a small opening in the bedroom door. He reached under the door, pulled it closed, and scampered down the hallway.

He raced down the massive staircase, two steps at a time, and into the foyer. His tiny claws scraped and slipped on the oak floor as he zipped off into the kitchen.

Gray and a team of mice waited at the kitchen table with Flynn, who sat in his wheelchair with a remote-control plane resting on his lap. It was a yellow Sopwith Camel biplane.

Bodaway slid to a halt on the wood floor.

"Is she still asleep?" asked Flynn.

"She did wake and went to her bathroom to swallow something that was stored in a cabinet," said Bodaway. "She is now fast asleep."

"Really? Sounds like she took a sleeping pill. Those used to knock my mom out for hours. That's cool!"

Flynn gave a nod to Tarsha, who waited up on the kitchen counter, and set the plane on the wood flooring.

Tarsha hopped onto a flour canister, stood on her hind legs to give her enough height to reach the radio underneath the upper cupboards. She flipped the switch – music poured out from the speaker.

With the biplane on the floor, Adriel used a paw to block the carburetor and then flipped the propeller around six times to prime the tiny engine. Flynn turned on the remote and signaled Adriel to turn on the power switch on the plane.

Gray stood on Flynn's shoulder, closely watching everything the boy was doing.

Adriel pushed down hard on the propeller and leapt back. It didn't start. He pushed the prop blades again. The engine *almost* caught on. The engineer sighed. He gripped the propeller, pushed with all his might, and jumped back. The engine sputtered, started up, whirred to life.

The spinning propeller created a loud buzz. Flynn listened as the sound resonated through the house – it was loud, but... not *too* loud. Music from the kitchen radio helped dim the buzzing. He grinned, examined his remote-control transmitter.

"Let's see. This is the throttle. Rudder. Ailerons. Elevators... we're good!"

He increased the throttle speed and the engine hummed louder. The plane rolled forward. He adjusted the rudder and the plane turned to the left. He pushed it again, the biplane shifted right. Another smile.

After a quick look at the clock – time was running out – Flynn jammed the throttle hard and the plane zipped away. The mice, with mouths wide open, all leaned in to watch as it zoomed across the kitchen floor.

Down the hallway, the plane picked up speed and jumped slightly, side to side, as Flynn found his bearings. Faster and faster.

The small model biplane lifted off the oak floor. The buzzing increased.

A puff of smoke came from the engine as it took off. Flynn steered the plane hard to the right, over the big staircase, and into the great hall.

Then he lost control. The biplane stopped turning and veered straight ahead.

"Oh, crap! I've lost the signal!" shouted Flynn. He looked at the walls between him and the biplane. "The wall! There's metal in the wall – it's blocking the radio waves!"

Flynn tried pushing his wheelchair with only one hand, but this caused him to spin in a circle. Adriel watched how the wheels worked, motioned to the team of mice to push both wheels at once. They scurried around Flynn's chair and, as a team, helped spin the wheels forward.

The biplane flew directly at the far wall. Flynn pulled back on the throttle to slow it down. With the slower engine speed, the plane lost altitude.

The mice rolled him to the kitchen doorway where he regained the radio signal. Flynn worked the transmitter controls, throttled back up, banked the plane hard to the right.

"Whoa! Too close, too close!"

The biplane landing gear lightly tapped the wall as it made its turn. He adjusted the controls, leveled off the plane.

"Oh, wow… we made it!" Flynn sighed.

The engine buzzed along as the plane sailed through the great hall. He chewed on his lip as he tested his piloting skills. Ailerons down and the biplane flew up. Rudder to the right or left and the plane turned.

The biplane flew too high, close to a dusty chandelier. Flynn panicked, pushed the aileron up and the plane dived down and to the left. The wall got closer and closer. Flynn adjusted the controls again, the plane banked left… toward the fireplace.

"No, no, no…"

He flicked the controllers hard and the plane corkscrewed through the air, barely missing the hearth. He circled it back into the wide-open great hall. Flynn sat back in his chair, breathed a sigh.

The mice watched in awe.

"Okay, let's bring it down…"

He flew the plane over his wheelchair, causing everyone to instinctively duck down. It soared through the kitchen. The throttle was cut, ailerons and elevator slid down to grab at the air. The biplane lost altitude. Flynn shifted the rudder to force it down the hallway. The plane roughly bounced and then touched down on the floor. The wing was too close to the wall as the plane landed, causing it to veer to the right. The balsawood tip of the wing touched the wall and spun the plane in circles. It finally slid to a halt in the foyer. Flynn and the mice leaned backward to see down the hallway, holding their collective breath. The motionless plane was still in one piece. No damage. Sighs of relief all around.

A song on a radio ended and the voice of a newscaster came on.

"Success, Dakota!" Viho shouted.

"Thanks," said Flynn, surprised at his own ability.

The local news anchor on the radio shared several headline stories.

Flynn shut down the transmitter, pushed down the antenna, and rolled out of the kitchen. Gray stood on the boy's shoulder, patted his neck.

"You did good, kid. That was some fancy flyin' right there."

"Too many close calls. And I need to figure out what to do when I lose control because of these walls. But... it was a good test run."

The news anchor introduced the weatherman for his report. "Good morning, Columbus! It doesn't look like winter is showing any signs up letting up. Temperatures will remain *below normal* for this time of year. In fact, we're now on record as being the second coldest month in the Ohio Valley region, with a chilly nineteen-degree average. Our high today will only be *eight* degrees. For the month, we've had twenty-two inches of snow fall and one to two more could fall this evening..."

Flynn tuned out the talk of an impending low-pressure system and stared at the clock. They were running out of time. "We gotta get out of here. Mister Ciminello will be back from therapy any minute now."

The mice darted down the hallway. Each grabbed a section of the delicate wooden plane and guided it toward the elevator.

Flynn wheeled his way into the elevator when the doors slid open. He picked up the plane from the mice, put it on his lap.

"We have air superiority," said Flynn to a proud Viho, as the elevator doors closed.

22

The Weary Traveler

The half-moon cast a blue veil on the tiny mice paw prints that had been trampled into the snow.

In a single file, Moki's tribe scrambled along the front of a yellow split-level house as fast as they could. Their wide eyes scanned in every direction in search of the predator.

Moki was sure he had heard a barn owl fly overhead, somewhere up there – an owl that was waiting for the right opportunity to swoop down and scoop up a tasty morsel. It was so difficult to hear an owl fly. When most birds fly, air swirls over their wings and makes a distinct noise. The wings of an owl are larger, so they flap less, and their feathers are serrated, like a comb, to break down the turbulence caused when they move through the air. They are silent, deadly hunters of mice.

"Quickly! This way!" bellowed Moki.

He dashed under a parked car in the driveway of the faded yellow house. One by one, the mice sprinted under the cover of the snow-covered car. Both Kiona and Elsu were on either side of the shaman Nodin, supporting him, as they ran for safety. Chuchip brought up the rear, protecting their flank. He slid on his backside, under the car fender, as the screeching barn owl dived down and just missed his tail.

"That was too close!" shouted Chuchip. He grinned, as he hopped up his hind legs, and wiped snow and ice off his back.

"Tala is near. But we cannot cover much ground with that owl in pursuit," protested Moki.

"I could run out there and draw it away. Everyone could make a run for those trees behind the house," said Chayton.

Ahiga rolled his dark, beady eyes. "No, you fool! You are about as fast as a rock! That owl would feast on you in no time! Wait a minute... what am I saying? Never mind. Sure, start running, idiot!"

"Stop, Ahiga," warned Moki. "We do, however, need a distraction."

Without a word, the albino mouse, Enola, sprinted from under the car, toward the street, and away from the house.

"Enola! No!" shouted Moki. But it was too late. He knew her intentions, so he gathered the tribe up near the front of the car. "Be ready to run for those trees!"

She bolted across the snow in a straight line, presenting herself as bait to the circling owl. Enola was nimble, quick on her paws. She knew the attack was coming but kept running directly for the mailbox, believing the tall post might deflect the owl. When she felt the wings flap within inches of her whiskers, Enola darted away from the mailbox. Her new target was a young, thin tree about ten feet away.

The barn owl made a turn in the air, aimed down at the white mouse dashing across the snowy strip between sidewalk and street. Enola took in huge gulps of air, filling her lungs, as she felt her leg muscles burn from fatigue. She had been running, jumping, and climbing all day and exhaustion had caught up with her.

Moki saw their chance. "Go now! Run like the wind!"

With the preoccupied owl bearing down on Enola, he pushed his tribe out from under the car, one after another.

Enola sensed the wind change around her and drove herself down into the deep snow. Her claws furiously dug through ice and she burrowed farther down. The owl grabbed at Enola but missed and landed on the snow.

An enraged Ahiga drew his sword from his homemade scabbard. He stepped out of the line of escaping mice, ran toward Enola and the owl in the yard, screaming as loud as he could. The barn owl spun around, threw out his wings, and screeched back at Ahiga. The angry mouse stopped in his tracks, eyes wide, mouth wide open.

"Oh, no, no, no!" stammered Ahiga.

Ahiga spun around, raced back under the car. As the owl staggered toward Ahiga in the thick snow, Enola saw her chance. She hopped out of her hole in the snow and ran up the thin tree, claws digging into the bark. This drew the attention of the hungry owl. Enola ran up the trunk, sliding around to the opposite side so the owl would have to follow her.

"Come with me, bird brain!" shouted Enola.

The owl ran along the snow, flapped his wings, and squawked loudly in an attempt to scare her.

Enola ran out along the first strong branch that would hold her weight. It was covered with snowy ice. The owl paused, watched her path, and took flight. Enola had started slowly on purpose, then took off running as the bird landed on the weighted branch.

"Don't stop now!" teased Enola.

The barn owl inched along the branch as the albino mouse raced out toward the tip of the branch. The weight of both creatures caused the branch to bend down. When the owl saw a clear path to her, he took flight. Enola reached the end of the tree branch and paused. As the owl got closer, Enola jumped off.

The snow-covered branch flew back up – smacking the flying owl in the face. Shrieks of surprise and pain filled the night air.

Enola landed, rolled away on the snow, laughing. "Let that be a lesson to you!" .

She bounded along on the snow, on all fours, to catch up with the tribe, as the owl struggled to take flight behind her. She grinned as the barn owl continued to squawk out his embarrassment.

When she sprinted past Ahiga, he recoiled in fear as if she were another attacking predator.

"Relax, Ahiga! I took care of that big, bad beast for you!" said Enola.

He gave her his most angry glare, but she never looked back at him. "Oh, I really hate that white witch." When he heard another screech from the barn owl, he hurried to catch up with the tribe.

When everyone in the tribe arrived next to Moki, he was sniffing at the wind under a group of pine trees. Despite the smell of pine needles, he eventually picked up the right scent. Moki gestured for the others to follow. In their single file line, they dashed past a chicken-wire fence, surrounding a snowy garden, and around a small wooden backyard shed.

The determined Moki led the charge, moving fast while still watching the sky for danger. He surged over rocks, bolted around snow drifts, and ducked under fallen tree branches coated with ice.

He pointed his paw at a small dark spot in the distant snow. "There!"

The tribe raced over to find Tala lying on her side. Her chest barely moved up and down as she struggled for breath. Her wet fur had iced over, and she was covered in mud and debris. Her eyes were closed.

"Tala! Can you hear me?" implored Moki. He sat next to her, pulled her onto his lap, and wrapped his paws around her. "We have you now, little one. Your difficult journey is over."

Other members of the tribe pulled off their cloaks and covered Tala up. Dyani used her cap to dry off the exhausted mouse.

"Gather what is needed to make her a travois," commanded Dyani as she took Tala from her mate. Dyani held the young mouse in her arms.

Chayton and Hakan rushed off to find twigs. Sakari pulled netting from her pack. Chuchip grabbed his knife to cut up strips of fabric from the buckskin war shirt he wore. Dyani cupped snow in her paws, fed melting water to poor Tala.

Moki stood up and marched forward, away from the triage work being performed by the tribe. He was able to track the direction she had taken through the neighborhood and beyond – he knew the path they would have to take.

The mice began piecing together the travois for Tala. The First Humans had used them to carry weapons, food, and injured warriors. This knowledge had been passed down from their ancestors. The pull-sled consisted of two long poles with smaller poles attached across to form a triangle. Chayton and Hakan laid down several thick branches to form the travois base. Chuchip tied the wood together and added the cross members, and Sakari attached her net in the center.

Ahiga and Chayton carefully placed the frail Tala on the paw-made sled. She stirred slightly after they had set her down. Moki ran to her side, held her paw, as she looked up at him with tired eyes.

"You did it, Stalking Wolf. You did it," whispered Moki. "Rest now. You have shown us the way." She smiled slightly, closed her eyes.

Chayton grabbed the two sticks at the front of the sled and waited for the chief.

"No time to waste, people. The journey continues," said Moki.

Everyone gathered their belongings and followed Moki as he strode northward through the blowing snow. The sticks of the travois lightly dragged two lines on either side of the line of paw prints in the snow.

23

The Fireworks

"Did I tell you I heard the helicopters yesterday morning?"

"You did?!"

"I was trying to sleep. You were probably still at therapy. I could hear one buzzing around outside the house, but I was way too out of it try to take photos," said Elaine.

"We need that proof, baby." Artie slammed his fist on the table in frustration. "The Man is tryin' to bring us down and we can't let 'em get away with it, you dig!"

Elaine sipped her coffee and nodded her agreement. They were sitting around the kitchen table, eating cereal.

"Did you hear the helicopters, Flynn?" asked Elaine. She poured out more cereal since she still had extra milk in her bowl.

"Um, helicopters? Uh, no, I don't think so," stammered Flynn. "I was building one of my models in the basement, so…" He pictured the remote-control biplane zooming past her bedroom door.

"You like my workroom, don't you? That's awesome, man. So what model were you building?"

Flynn panicked. He wasn't really building a model, but he couldn't bring himself to admit he was working on an airplane because that might give away what he was really doing. "Uh, I was building the lunar lander from the Apollo Eleven mission."

"Ha!" squawked Elaine.

"Oh, no," said Artie. He leaned in closer to the boy. "Don't get her started, man!"

"You know that whole thing was faked, right?" Elaine put both palms on the table, her chin jutted out in defiance. "There's no way we put a man on the moon! We don't have that kinda technology. It was all just government propaganda to scare the Russkies and calm down the Americans. Win the space race to the moon because they were flyin' Sputnik satellites over our heads. What a bunch of bunk!"

Wow. She's crazy too, thought Flynn. "Interesting. May I be excused?"

Artie winked at the kid. "Of course, man. Go build your lunar lander."

Elaine hopped up from her chair, rummaged through a stack of old mail on the kitchen counter. She didn't even realize Flynn had wheeled his chair out of the room. "I've got a pamphlet around here somewhere. 'We Never Went to the Moon' or something like that. Where did you put that, Artie? It said we had the technology to put those astronauts on the moon but not enough to get 'em back. He was a rocket scientist, too! You really should read it, Flynn. Flynn?"

"He's gone," said Artie. "You and your crazy conspiracy theories."

She smiled down at her man and gave him a big kiss to say thanks for putting up with her.

Flynn fed a few *Count Chocula* marshmallows to Gray as they rolled out of the elevator. He pushed the wheelchair into the workroom and coasted up to the bench. The Halona mice emerged from their hiding spots.

"Good morning, Dakota," announced Viho. "We have a surprise for you."

Flynn rubbed his hands together, smiled – he had a good idea what they had found.

Koko was first out, dragging a bag made from torn fabric. She dumped it on the wooden table. Dozens of firecrackers rolled out. Tarsha and Tate were next, pushing another bag from behind. They had found a variety of round and cylindrical fireworks – smoke bombs, cherry bombs, some mortars and a few M-80s. Big Maska managed to drag in several Roman candles, each about a foot long. Young Wamblee struggled to carry in his collection of tiny Lady Fingers. It was a great assortment of fireworks.

"Nice job, guys!" yelled Flynn. He began inspecting the fireworks, explaining what each one would do when lit with a flame.

Gray shuffled off to his shelf. He cracked his Art of War book open to where he had left off. When he heard a rustling sound coming from the floor, Gray peered around the side of his book. He watched as Adriel and Fala walked around Flynn's wheelchair. They whispered to each other, pointed to sections of the chair, and she would write down notes. Adriel made wide gestures with his paws and rolling motions and indications of size. She would nod and ask questions. They made a great team. It reminded Gray of how his mom would explain things to him. She was like the old Italian women in the apartment where they lived. They always talked with their hands. He suddenly felt alone again. Before he let any emotions overwhelm, the mouse held his book back up and focused on reading.

Flynn took a pen knife off a shelf and cut down the length of one of the firecrackers.

"Okay, watch this. All of these fireworks are filled with gunpowder," said Flynn. "See?"

He poured out black powder into the metal jar lid. Looking around, he found a book of matches and took out a match.

"By itself, gunpowder isn't really dangerous," explained Flynn. "But... when you add a flame to it..."

This caught Bodaway's attention. He shuffled close as Flynn lit the match.

"It burns hot." Flynn dropped the burning match into the jar lid. The flame lit the gunpowder – which burned in a bright flash, crackled, and flamed out.

All the mice backed up or turned their heads in fear. Except Bodaway, who moved even closer with his eyes wide and a big smile plastered on his whiskered face. Smoke billowed across the table.

"But when you pack it tightly – like this firecracker – and light it, well... then it explodes!" All the mice gasped in awe.

He showed them an unburned firework, with the wick sticking out of the top. "This wick gives you time to light it and move away before it blows up.

Pretty cool, huh?"

"Cool," said a spellbound Bodaway.

He stared at the black burn mark on the metal lid. The sulfur smell from the burnt powder was like the overwhelming scent of wildflowers in the field to him in that moment. "Explode one!

Even Gray was amazed at the pyrotechnical display. He set his book down and hopped over to the workbench.

Trying his best to be nonchalant, Gray leaned against Flynn's forearm that was resting on the tabletop. "Pretty impressive, kid. So, we're throwin' these bombs at the other mice now?"

"No, that's not the plan at all," protested Flynn, keeping his voice low enough that the others could not hear. "I'm trying to help my friends."

"You know, I've been reading this really smart Chinese guy and he's got a lot of thoughts on—"

"Sun Tzu. Yeah, I noticed your book. It used to be required reading for the Japanese generals and admirals in school. I read somewhere that the book was assigned to the library of every Japanese ship bigger than a destroyer. But they thought it was out of date by the time World War Two came along," said Flynn.

"Yeah, and how'd that work out for them?" laughed Gray.

"Well, they lost but they had the right strategy. The Japanese didn't have enough fuel supplies, so they took over islands and countries that had fuel. Then, they used surprise to attack the American fleet. One section of that book talks about mystifying, misleading, and surprising your enemy."

"True, true. But if they didn't eventually win the war, even though they had surprise on their side, what did they do wrong?" asked Gray.

"Well, the Japanese saw the Germans doing really well over in Europe, so they were pretty confident. They attacked Pearl Harbor, but the American aircraft carriers weren't there. And when they attacked the island of Midway, they didn't expect their carriers to be there... but they *were*. Most of their own carriers got destroyed by our Navy planes. Then we took back all the islands they had won and cut off their fuel supplies," explained Flynn.

"I'm seeing the picture now, kid. Sun Tzu said something about how, with many calculations, one can win... but with few, you can't. It seems like they hoped things would go very well but... they didn't do their homework," said Gray.

"Yes, the Japanese should've conducted more intelligence. They depended on their weapons and strategy but didn't know what we were up to," admitted Flynn.

"Do we know what the Matwau are up to? Where they are? What their plan is? This Sun Tzu cat also said if you know the enemy and yourself, you shouldn't be afraid of a hundred battles. These Japanese folks didn't know their enemy and lost. If we don't know what's goin' on or what the Matwau even want, maybe we shouldn't be fightin' them?"

Anger quickly took over Flynn. His jaws tightened and his fists clenched. "Look, all I know is that this other tribe knows we're here and they're coming to hurt us. I'm just trying to defend these guys."

"Well, maybe another battle with them ain't the answer. This Sun Tzu guy said that the art of war is to beat your enemy without fighting, you dig?"

"That's what I'm trying to do here, Gray!"

"By building bombs?"

"No! Yes. I don't know. I just want to scare the daylights outta these mice! If this works, they won't bother us anymore! Sun Tzu also said that when you surround an enemy, leave them a way out. Don't push too hard against a desperate opponent because they'll fight even harder to survive. If we intimidate them hard enough with the remote-control plane and the fireworks, then they'll run for their lives and not come back. You see?"

Gray hadn't read far enough into the book to come up with any more useful quotes to win his argument. But he couldn't shake the feeling that he was missing something.

"We can do this. I don't want to hurt them, just scare them off," said Flynn.

"I gotta wonder if their backs aren't already up against a wall. We mice are territorial, but these yahoos are travelin' miles in the worst winter storm ever... for what?" asked Gray.

Frustration set in with Flynn. He couldn't understand why Gray was defending mice who were attacking their friends. He was done arguing about it. The boy tried to roll his wheelchair away but hit something hard. Flynn tried to look behind him, tried to push back again. He was stuck.

"What's going on back there?" said Flynn.

"Stop moving!" demanded Adriel, from below the wheelchair.

Gray peeked over the edge of the table to spot the engineer and Fala working on the frame of Flynn's wheelchair.

"Adriel's doin' something to your chair down there," said Gray.

"What's he doing?"

"What are you doing?!" shouted Gray.

"Working!" Adriel climbed up onto the axle of the wheelchair. Maska staggered into view, loaded down with tools he'd found around the workroom.

Gray nodded, looked up at Flynn, and shrugged. "He's working..."

Flynn rolled his eyes. "Yeah, thanks. I heard that part."

Bodaway approached Flynn with several firecrackers in his paws. He laid them down and tugged on Flynn's sleeve to get his attention.

"Can you show me more, Dakota?" said Bodaway.

Happy for the distraction from whatever was happening below his wheelchair, Flynn picked up a firecracker and his knife. "Sure, I'll light up another one. But then we've got to get to work, okay?"

Bodaway nodded excitably, holding up the pack of matches, and gave the boy a big grin. Flynn smiled back at him, cut into the paper holding the precious black powder.

Gray was hungry. He needed more than the cereal the boy had provided. He scurried away from the workbench. The tribe was smart to gather food and stockpile it in several locations throughout the basement, in case one storage spot was compromised. As he bounded along on all fours, Gray let his nose do the guiding. He could detect sunflower seeds over in the corner of the room. He found the stash underneath the metal base of a standing drill press.

As he squatted on his hind legs, chewing on the seeds, it dawned on him that Flynn was craving a fight the way he had craved food. After all that the boy had been through, anger had replaced love. The happiness, contentment, and security he had known was gone. Fear, guilt, and resentment had filled that hole. Gray had been in the same spot as the kid. He understood the anger, but he had no idea how to turns things around for the boy.

As he finished his snack, Gray noticed young Yuma huddled in a nearby corner of the basement. The youngster's back was wedged against the concrete block walls, with his tail was curled around his hind legs, and his eyes darted nervously around him.

Gray set down his seed and approached Yuma slowly with small steps and his paws out wide.

"Hey, there," soothed Gray.

The young mouse pushed himself farther back into the corner; his dark eyes growing wide.

"It's okay. It's all good, my man. I'm not going to hurt you," said Gray. Yuma grew even more frightened. "In fact, I'm just going to stop right here. Cool?"

Surprising Gray, the youngster scurried directly at him, his paws grabbing Gray's fur.

"Whoa, whoa! Relax, kid!" said a stunned Gray. "Take it easy…"

"You are the new one here! The outsider?" asked Yuma, in a panic. Even though the reddish-brown mouse was a youngling, he was as tall as Gray. "Right?"

"Uh, yeah, guilty as charged, kid."

"What?"

"Nothing. It's something they say in the big city. Me and the human are … outsiders," said Gray.

"I think I am an outsider, too. Can you help me?!" begged Yuma.

Zaltana's voice rang out from behind the drill press, around the corner. "Yuma?! Yuma!"

Yuma released Gray, ran back to his concrete corner to cower in fear.

"Help you? Help you do what?" questioned Gray.

Zaltana marched from around the metal base of the drill. First, she spotted Gray and then saw Yuma trembling nearby. She glared at Gray and ran to the side of the young mouse.

She picked him up from all fours, inspected him, and soothed his fur. "Yuma, are you okay? What happened? I could not find you?"

Yuma nodded his head quickly. She gave another look at Gray. "Did he hurt you?"

Yuma shook his head, but she was not convinced. Zaltana raced over to confront Gray.

"What is going on here?" she demanded.

Gray turned to pick up another sunflower seed. He held it up to her face, then took a bite and chewed. "Lady, I'm just here for a snack."

"Did you bring him here?" Zaltana pointed at the youngster.

"No way, no day! I was looking for seeds. I saw him cringing over in the corner there. That's a fact, Jack," stated Gray.

She didn't want to believe him but had no proof of anything. She gave him another stern glance for several seconds and turned away.

"Although, I gotta say…"

She shot back at him with another dirty look.

"You're holding those reigns pretty tight. He's a big kid. You might wanna let him off the leash every now and then. Just my two cents," said Gray.

"He is my responsibility. So, kindly keep your whiskers out of my nest," commanded Zaltana.

Gray started to speak but stopped. Her response set off an alarm and he knew better than to ignore it.

"You are an outsider and, as far as I am concerned, no longer welcome in our tribe. Dakota has chosen us so you might consider… moving along." Her imperious stance and the condescension in her voice sent a clear message – she wanted him gone.

He held his paws up, giving in.

She marched off, grabbing Yuma by the paw. The young mouse gave a quick, anxious look at Gray and then they were gone.

Gray took another bite off a sunflower seed as his mind raced. Why did Yuma think he was an outsider? What help did he need? Why did Zaltana say the youngster was her "responsibility"? That was weird one for a mom to say about her kid.

Tate zipped around the corner, interrupting Gray's train of thought. "There they are! Sweet nectar of the gods!"

Gray backed up as Tate dove into the sunflower seed storage, shoving a handful into his mouth.

"Take it easy there, bud," said Gray.

"Oh, you do not understand! They hide these from me!"

Gray laughed as Tate spit out half of what he was chewing by trying to talk. "I can see why."

"These seeds are so good! Mmm-mmm." Tate ate another handful as a thought popped into his head. "You ever noticed that when you eat healthy, like fruit and vegetables, that you actually get hungrier while you are eating them? No? My stomach actually growls when I eat anything green. Just me?"

"Hey, bud. I got a question," said Gray. Tate raised his eyebrows to let him know he was ready to answer, as he took another bite of sunflower seeds. "What's the deal with Zaltana and her kid, Yuma? Does that whole situation seem strange to you?"

Tate stood up straight, stopped chewing, and his eyes opened wide. "Oh, sorry. I just remembered. I-I have a… thing I need to do."

Gray watched as Tate scrambled away as fast as his paws would carry him, leaving Gray even more confused.

"No? Just me?" Gray said.

24

The Night Moves

Small, wet flakes of snow pelted the deluged city. Moonlight struggled to shine through thick winter clouds.

The mammoth plow, on the front of the city truck, rammed its way through the new fallen snow. The weary driver and passenger had stopped for some fast food, hopped back in their truck, and went right back to the grind. The had plowed this same road yesterday but all the new snow and the drifts that had been blown onto the streets forced them to plow again. Neither of the city workers had noticed their new passengers, hiding under the truck.

Moki and over two dozen mice were huddled on every flat surface around the frame of the truck. They held on tight to the gas tanks, the chassis, and even the bouncing rear axles. Snow and ice kicked up at the small mice, but they were determined to catch a ride.

"Stand strong, my warriors! This beast will carry us to our destination with great speed!" bellowed Moki, over the roar of the diesel engine. "If it does not kill us first," he muttered to Dyani. She held on to his paw for a few seconds before gripping the gas cap to keep from falling off the tank.

Moki turned to Tala. She was lying on tank, bundled up but still shivering, and holding on to a welded seam on the gas tank. Wet snowflakes bombarded Moki as he laid a paw on her back.

"Are you sure about this, little one?" asked Moki.

"I am. The job of this vehicle is to remove snow along their streets. It is not going to any particular destination," said Tala. "This one is headed toward the Halona camp."

"Let us hope you are right," sighed Moki.

The mice heard the elevator doors open upstairs, on the main floor. Every one of the Halona tribe froze in place, their ears turning toward the sound.

Flynn looked up from wrapping several firecracker wicks together. "Guys? What's up?"

He got his answer when he heard the elevator motor start up. "Ah, crud…"

He watched the mice flee in every possible direction. From under his wheelchair, he saw Adriel and Fala jump off the base of his chair and scurry away.

The mice were smart to take all the tools and supplies they had in hand, so that everything in the room appeared as normal.

When the elevator opened up to the basement, Flynn hid the firecrackers and spun his wheelchair away from the workbench. A quick look at the egress window let him know it was dark outside. They had been working all day long.

Flynn glanced up at the shelf where Gray was usually camped out. His book was there but his friend was absent.

Artie zoomed into the basement workroom, a big grin on his face.

"What's happenin', man?" probed Artie. He looked around the room as rolled up next to Flynn. "Hey, not tryin' to cramp your style or nothin'. Wanted to give you your space and all that. Hope I'm not interrupting?"

"No, it's… it's cool," said Flynn.

"Righteous, man," said Artie. "What have you been up to down here?"

"Nothing. Just working on… my models," said Flynn as he looked at the workbench and there were no models in sight.

"Really?"

"Um. Yeah."

"Well, I think you've been up to more than that…"

Flynn's face burned bright red and his mouth dropped open. He had no idea what to say or do next.

"A lot more than just models, man."

"You see… I, uh, well, um," mumbled Flynn.

"You're totally busted, dude." Artie smirked at him, backed up his wheelchair, pointed down.

Flynn tried to look down around his chair, at what Adriel had been working away down there for hours, but he could not see a thing.

"Is that what I think it is?" asked Artie.

"What? What is it?" Flynn was confused. He tried to back up his own wheelchair to get a better look. The wheelchair was heavier than normal.

"You've been holding out on me," said Artie. "You've made your own electric wheelchair, man!"

"I did? I mean, I did. Yes, I-I did," said a very confused Flynn.

"Let's take a look," said Artie. He rolled around Flynn's chair, inspecting everything. "What do we have here? That's the two-hundred-and-twenty-volt motor from my old washing machine!"

A large cylindrical metal motor had been placed in a wire cage and suspended under the seat. Gears from the motor had been mated with a thick, metal tube that traveled to both wheels.

"There's my transaxle from that old go-cart I had as a kid. Do you have it plugged into the battery charger?"

Flynn noticed wires from a battery charger, that was resting under the work bench, ran to a spot underneath his chair. And he noted that the charger was plugged into a long extension cord, which was plugged into an outlet in the wall.

"Uh, yeah…"

"Dude, that charger has a lot of power – it runs sixty volts. How are you controlling it?"

Flynn looked lost. He searched the basement in vain for something, anything, to help. He noticed Adriel hidden under a nearby desk. The little engineer pointed to the side of the chair, Flynn reached his hand back, just behind the wheel, felt a plastic box. He pulled up the box and noticed that it was a remote control, just like the ones used for the model planes. Adriel gave a smile and salute to the boy. Flynn set the controller on the armrest of his wheelchair.

"Nice! Remote control!" said Artie. "Let me see it in action, man!"

"Well, it's not really ready yet. I've still got to test it and—"

"Perfect! This'll be your maiden voyage! Give it some gas," said Artie, rubbing his hands together.

Adriel waved wildly, trying to get Flynn's attention. He mouthed out the word "No!" over and over.

"Okay," said Flynn. He used his hands to roll backward a few feet. Adriel covered his eyes; he couldn't watch what was about to happen.

Artie grinned ear-to-ear like he was about to bite into a thick, juicy steak dinner. "Come on! Fire it up!"

Flynn took a deep breath. "Okay. Here goes nothing…"

He timidly placed his hand on the remote controller. He placed his finger on the joystick, gave a little push, and the motor roared to life.

The wheels rotated so fast they spun on the concrete floor. When the rubber wheels gained traction – Flynn and his wheelchair flipped backwards.

The boy screamed as he was slammed down on his back. The shout stopped as soon as the wind was knocked out of him. The motor was so powerful that the wheels could not spin fast enough, which turned the entire chair over onto the concrete.

Adriel looked out from behind his paws, after hearing the loud thud on the concrete.

"Whoa!" screamed Artie. "You okay, man?!"

Flynn was still in his chair, with his broken leg sticking straight up in the air. His hands gripped tight to the wheelchair armrests. He gasped until his lungs expanded and was finally able to breathe again.

Now down at Adriel's level, Flynn turned his head to the side to look over at the engineer. The mouse awkwardly shrugged and put his paws up in the air.

"That was awesome!" shouted Artie.

Flynn did not think it was awesome. Artie rolled his chair close to Flynn, positioned himself behind chair, and lifted up on the handles. The weight of Flynn's cast helps pull the boy upward and forward – until his chair slammed down hard on all four wheels.

"There ya go, man. Right as rain!" said Artie. "I think you might want to use one of my twelve-volt batteries. You'll have a little less pep in your step."

"For sure," agreed Flynn. He rubbed at the back of his head with one hand and his sore shoulder with the other.

"But that's still pretty amazing. You did all that yourself?" asked Artie.

"Um, yep. All by myself," said Flynn. Without thinking about it, he scratched at the skin right where the cast on his broken leg started.

Artie looked the boy up and down, from his young face to the cast on his broken leg. "How?"

Flynn could see the skepticism crawl across Artie's weathered features.

"Well..." started Flynn. He looked around the room to see what Adriel and Fala could have used to do all that work to his wheelchair. He saw small parts and wires on the floor, a folding metal chair nearby, and tools on resting on the workbench.

"Well, it's obvious I did this all myself. It's not like there's anyone down here with me. Right?" said Flynn. He feared to even take a breath as he watched for a reaction from Artie.

Artie stared at the boy sitting in the wheelchair. He looked around the room and noticed the folding chair, tools, and wires on the floor. He finally smiled at Flynn. "Wow.... you're all right, man! If I can get my hands on another washing machine motor, you gotta hook *me* up with an electric chair!"

Artie patted Flynn hard on the shoulder he had fallen on, causing him to wince and force a fake smile.

"Elaine's not working the steakhouse tonight. She's got dinner ready upstairs. Clean up down here and join us when you're ready, man."

Artie rolled out of the workroom toward the elevator. Flynn heard a click from below and looked back to see Adriel unplug the extension cord from the battery charger.

154

"What the heck was that, Adriel?" asked Flynn. "You could've told me what you were doing!"

"I apologize, Dakota," Adriel stated, his head bowed. "When I am caught up in my work, it is all I think about. I hope you are not injured."

Flynn rubbed the back of his head instinctively. "Yeah. No, I'm fine."

"That is good," said Adriel. They both turned to watch as all the mice returned to their tasks. "You are vital to defending us when the Matwau attack again."

"Vital?"

"Your use of the radio-controlled device was hampered by the walls of the house. If you cannot control the plane, your plan may fail. Since we are too small to effectively move your chair during battle..."

"You made my chair electric so I could move myself," said Flynn. "Nice. But... you still could've warned me."

"This is true," admitted Adriel.

Flynn looked around the room at the other mice diligently working. "Hey, have you seen Gray?"

Adriel put his paws together, thought for a moment, and shook his head. "I have seen not much more than the bottom of your seat for most of my day."

"Got it," said Flynn. He took one last look at Gray's book resting on the shelf. "I sure hope he's okay."

The city truck plowed through the fresh powder on the nearly empty Columbus streets.

When the truck stopped for a red light, Tala signaled to Moki – it was time to jump off.

"Warriors! Dismount!" shouted Moki.

Dozens of mice jumped from their positions across the big truck and onto the snow-covered street. Moki waited until everyone was off, then helped Tala stand up so she could jump with him. After the two launched off the top of the gas tank, Moki landed in the snowdrift. But Tala did not fall next to him. He looked back up at the truck. Tala's war coat had caught on a rivet sticking out from the gas tank. She dangled there, struggling to remove her jacket so she could fall to the earth.

The light turned green and the big snowplow pulled away.

Moki sprinted after the truck as it picked up speed.

"No, leave me! I will catch up with you!" shouted Tala.

"Never!" screamed Moki, over the rumble of the truck engine and wheels crunching on the icy slush covering the street.

Moki caught up to the mud flap that waved back and forth in his face. He leapt forward, dug his claws into the rubber, and pulled himself off the snowy road.

The truck accelerated. As he reached the top of the mud flap, he swung around to the side facing the rolling tires. Snow and ice sprayed him as he worked his way, paw over paw, to the truck chassis. Moki gripped the edges of the frame as he crawled past the rear axle. He ducked under the rear axle support beam and reached up to grab hold of the frame again. More water and ice chunks pelted his fur as the next set of tires rolled underneath him.

"What have I done to deserve your wrath, Apollo?!" he screamed out in anger.

Still trapped by her coat, Tala broke a claw trying to tear the thick fabric designed to protect her during battle. Her weight pulled on the hooks on the front of the jacket, keeping her stuck in the coat. She reached back to try to pull herself back onto the top of the gas tank, but she was facing away from it and had no leverage. When she tried to use her hind legs to kick off and away from the side of the tank, she flopped around in vain. Her energy was waning fast.

As Moki crawled along the chassis, the truck hit a bump in the road. He flew up in the air, lost his grip, and shot straight down. His tail reached out, caught a brake line, and held him hanging in mid-air.

Using the momentum of the truck rocking back and forth, he swung himself toward the gas tank. When he got close enough, Moki let his tail go. He landed on the top of the slippery tank, slid all the way to the other side, and dug in his sharp claws to keep from falling off the other side.

Moki scrambled to the edge, reached down, and pulled Tala up by her coat.

Without wasting a moment, he stood Tala up, threw her over his shoulder, and jumped off the side of the truck. They landed in a small pile of snow that had drifted onto the street.

"Are you well?!" he shouted as the loud snowplow drove off into the night.

"I am. Barely," she smirked at the chief.

He wiped snow and dirty water from her fur, inspected her for injuries. "You will live. For a little while longer."

"Why did you come after me?" asked Tala. "You jeopardized the mission. You should have let me go and gone on with the others. I am just one."

"Where there is one of us, there we all are. And where we all are, there is but one. We could never leave you behind. That is the point of the mission," stated Moki, his paws on her arms.

She smiled at him, nodded.

"We must hurry," said Moki. The two climbed out of the drift and ran back down the street.

25

The Enemy

In his bedroom, Flynn fidgeted back and forth, desperate to find sleep or at least lie in a somewhat comfortable position. When he shivered from cold, he pulled up his bed covers but then pushed them back as soon as he was too hot. The moonlight outside, shining through bare tree limbs and casting scary shadows on his walls, pushed the hope for sleep farther away. Even worse was the wind whistling through every crack and crevice in the siding that surrounded the old house.

Where was Gray? Flynn glanced at the nightstand and back over to the other pillow next to his head. *He should be here by now*, he thought. Flynn closed his eyes hard to force sleep to come to him.

Within the walls of Artie and Elaine's Tudor house, Gray hurried along the old wood framing. He climbed up a stud and out through an opening some mouse had chewed open many years ago. He paused for a moment to look back along his path. The house was quiet with the humans settled down in their bedrooms. He heard soft muttering from the foster parents. He could tell Flynn was still awake by the sound of his breathing and rustling around in bed. The mouse could make out the high-pitched squeaks from the Halona mice working away down in the basement.

Gray sighed, turned away slowly, and darted back into the hole in the wall to continue his journey. Eventually, he emerged into Flynn's bedroom through a hole in the back panel of the built-in bookcase. He was extremely quiet this time – he did not want to let Flynn know he was there.

His first mission was to find a small pencil or piece of lead that he could carry. He searched the top of an old wooden desk in the corner of the bedroom. Gray found one that had been sharpened down to a nub. He pulled the lead out of the tiny pencil with his claws, placed it in his mouth, hopped to the floor, and clambered into Flynn's suitcase.

Inside the case, Gray found the mimeographed piece of paper. It was the list of names of foster parents willing to take on Flynn. The mouse used his pencil lead to write an address down on the corner of the mimeograph paper. He slowly, quietly tore off the corner of the paper. Gray popped his head out of the suitcase and listened. Flynn was still awake but had his eyes closed and did not detect Gray's presence. He scrambled out of the case, up the bookshelf, and out of the room.

In the master bedroom, Artie was seated in his wheelchair beside the bedroom window that looked onto the backyard. He held up the AN/PVS-2 Starlight scope to his eye. The night vision rifle scope was one of the toys he brought home from Vietnam. It was terrible for targeting the enemy but pretty useful in watching for the government black-ops agents who were trying to spy on him.

"Have you spotted them?" asked Elaine. She was standing in their bathroom, brushing her teeth.

"Shh!" warned Artie. "They might be listening!"

Elaine rinsed the toothpaste from her mouth, marched over to a dresser, and picked up his tinfoil hat.

"Then you should be wearing this." She placed it on his head. Artie smiled up at her, patted her hand.

"You're always thinking of me," said Artie.

"Speaking of which, you should get some sleep," said Elaine.

He shrugged, returned to scanning the backyard for secret agents. "I need you to go to the hardware store for me tomorrow."

"Have you seen how bad the roads are out there? I am so sick of this snow," said Elaine.

"I found some mice poop today. We need some traps," said Artie. "Maybe get some poison."

"Mice? Oh, no..."

"What?"

"Don't you get it? Mice! The government has been training animals for covert operations! They could've attached little helmets to the mice to infiltrate the house, listen in our conversations, take photos, you name it!"

Artie processed this information. "You're right! Man, those jive turkeys will stop at nothing..."

Elaine put on her tinfoil hat, sat on the bed next to his wheelchair, and patted his arm. "We have the advantage, honey. They don't know that we know."

"Roger Wilco, foxy mama." Artie resumed his night-vision surveillance of yard. "Roger Wilco."

The kitchen was dark except for the bluish moonlight shining in through the windows. Koko sat at one of the windowsills, eating a stale crouton she had found under one of the counters. Her big eyes searched in vain for any movement out on the lawn. Koko's strong sense of smell was hampered by the woman's excessive use of garlic and onion in her cooking. She needed to move to a better vantage point.

She hopped off the windowsill, ran toward the back stairs that lead up to the second floor.

Gray watched her bound up the stairs from his hiding spot in the pantry room. He set down the clove of garlic he held in his paws and waited for enough time to pass that she would be well out of range to sense his movement.

He darted quickly across the kitchen floor and under the table. He listened, let his whiskers sense his surroundings. The coast was clear. He hopped on a kitchen chair and then onto the table. He waited for another few seconds, listening and sniffing the air again.

Gray jumped from the table to land on the same windowsill Koko had occupied. He had been hungry, but the pangs vanished quickly because her lingering scent – there was something about her he did not like. He didn't know what it was about Koko that bothered him but knew he should not trust her.

"Nobody 'nose' how bad you smell," Gray sang to himself. He smirked briefly, but it was time to get to work.

Gray cleared the condensation from the window glass, stared out at the vast, white backyard behind the house. Even though his eyes were useless, he could make out shapes. The heavy snowfall throughout the month had made the nights so much brighter now that the moon was out. He could see the shape of a small shed out there – exactly what he was hoping to find. But there was a lot of open ground between this house and the shed. Open ground sent a shiver down the spine of every mouse. He knew if he was to save Flynn, he had to make the trek out to that shed.

First, Gray needed a way to get out of the house. He tried to lift the window directly in front him. His paws pulled up hard on the brown wooden frame, but it was either locked or frozen shut – probably both.

He scanned the kitchen. There were several other windows that would also present the same problem as this one. He saw a door past the pantry, but the gap was too small at the bottom to squeeze under and there was no pet door. Gray loved pet doors. They were a mouse's best friend.

The range hood over the stove caught his attention. Those hoods had a fan that vented smoke out of the house. There weren't many escape routes from apartments in the big city, so his mom had pointed out the range hood over the old Italian lady's stove in Brooklyn.

He leapt back to the kitchen table. Another jump put him on the top of the chair. A final jump put him on the countertop. He rolled, slid, and almost fell off the other side of the slick counter.

"Whoa!" exclaimed Gray. Using his arms, he maintained his balance and stayed upright.

He sprinted to the stove, a wide eight-burner model with a large metal hood hanging above. Gray looked straight up at the vent. Too high. His eyes landed on a plastic flour cannister. With all his weight behind it, the mouse shoved the cannister over to the stove. Instead of sliding onto a burner, the cannister tipped over. Gray sighed, rolled it under the vent opening, and used another burner to brace the base so he could tip it upright again. He leapt up to the top of the lid and looked up – the vent was still too far. He looked around for other options.

Hopping off the cannister, he began shuffling around items onto the stove and all around it. When he had everything where he wanted it, he was ready. He had knocked over the thin roll of paper towels and placed a serving tray over it, to act as a seesaw. Gray had slid two cans of soup onto the serving tray, farthest from the cannister. Next, had had tied a piece of string around another can of soup, rolled it up the tray, and placed it on the lid of the flour container. He took the string back to the other side of the serving tray, removed each of the soup cans, and then stood on the edge of the serving tray. He took a deep breath and pulled on the string. The can of soup dropped onto the opposite side of the tray and the falling weight launched Gray into the air. His claws barely caught on the wire vent cover of the fan. Swinging back and forth, he exhaled. He made it.

Getting through the exhaust fan cover was his next challenge. Gray hated the taste of metal but had no choice – he began chewing at the wire. Hanging by his paws, his sharp teeth ground down the metal until he had a large enough opening. As he pulled himself through a piece of wire caught cut his skin, just under the fur.

Breathing hard, sitting in the vent, Gray surveyed the damage. The cut was superficial but still hurt. He hopped up, grabbed a vent fan blade, and pulled himself through the fan. After that, he only had to run the length of the duct pipe that went to the side of the house.

Gray kicked out the lower section of the metal cover that was designed to keep animals and birds out of the duct. Looking down the side of the house, he realized it was quite a drop.

"Here goes nothing..."

Gay plunged down into two feet of snow and disappeared. The scrappy mouse dug his way out of the perfectly smooth hole he had created in the snow and plopped down on a patch of ice, gasping for breath.

Out in the surrounding woods, a bird screeched. Gray sat straight up; his eyes were wide with terror.

"Oh, crap!"

He scrambled onto all four paws and bolted for the shed. Gray galloped along, on the surface of the deep snow, with his claws sending up sprays of ice as he ran.

The same red-tailed hawk that had harassed Tala easily spotted the dark shadow moving across the white snow. The hawk silently dropped off his perch in the oak tree.

Gray raced along, breathing hard, toward the shed. His nose detected a new scent… something was approaching. Maybe it was a bird? Pigeons flourished in New York, but they were just flying rats competing for food scraps and not real predators. Whatever was coming could scoop him up and have him for dinner.

The muscles in his legs were burning, he could feel himself slowing down. He was only halfway to his goal. Gray knew he wasn't going to make it.

The whooshing of the wings startled him as he ran across the snow. He turned his head to see the hawk swoop in close, sharp claws extended, to grab hold of him.

Gray closed his eyes but kept running. He waited for the sharp piercing pain from those claws to stick into his sides.

Unexpectedly for a swift and silent predator, the red-tailed hawk shrieked loudly.

Gray dared to turn his head to look back at the hawk – he noticed a small arrow stuck in the side of the bird's leg. Wings flapped hard to keep the bird in the air, but his claws had retracted.

Another arrow zipped directly in front of the beak of the hawk. The bird realized quickly it was too dangerous to snatch this small mouse. A strong wind blasted Gray as the bird took flight and disappeared up into the dark trees surrounding the backyard.

With his legs about to give out, Gray ran straight into the door of the shed, thumping hard against the wood. He threw his back against the door, fighting hard to steal as much air as he could away from the cold night.

Gray spun, frantically searching the shed for any hole or crack he could use to get inside. He had no plans to give that hawk another shot at him. He found a section of wood at the base of the shed that had rotted away, easily chewed out a wood fragment, and squirmed inside.

The shed was dark and quiet. He pushed aside a dusty oil can and scurried into the room. Moonlight shone down across an old workbench and across the cracked concrete floor. Gray's nose was assaulted by fumes from a red gas can, burnt oil caked onto a grass-stained lawn mower, and turpentine from a dented can on a nearby shelf. Then a familiar scent filled his nostrils.

His whiskers twitched. She was here. The same mouse he detected outside the basement window several nights ago.

"Tell me why I should not put an arrow through your head right now?" she said.

"Because you'd probably miss. And that would be embarrassing," mused Gray. "You guys are crappy shots."

Tala walked out from the shadows and into the blue moonlight, a bow with a notched arrow in her paws. "I took out the bird that was about to have you for a night time snack. So, I think I am a decent... shot."

"So that was you I gotta thank for that?" asked Gray.

"Yes," said Tala.

"Much appreciated. Any reason why you decided to help me?"

She began to circle him. He stood still as she passed behind him.

"Let us just say that I owed that hawk some... retribution," said Tala. "It was a fool's errand for your leader to send you out here looking for supplies."

"Looking for you actually, gorgeous," said Gray. He worked up his most charming smile.

Tala tried to keep a stern face but could only laugh at him. "A fool's errand, indeed."

She pointed her arrow at Gray and pulled back her bow string.

"Wait! Wait! I really am here to talk to you," Gray said, his paws in the air. "I'm assumin' the rest of your gang is around somewhere?"

"We have no time for your words, Matwau."

"Matwau? No, me and the kid were just hangin' with the *Halona*. They're the tribe back inside the house," said Gray. "I thought you guys were the Matwau?"

Moki strode from the darkness behind her. He was an impressive warrior

– tall, strong, battle-scarred. He had his fur puffed, making an already imposing figure even scarier. Gray took a step back.

"Let me clear this nonsense up for you, fool." Moki crossed his arms. "We are the Shoshone tribe. They are Matwau. They are the enemy. That is the meaning of the word."

"Ah, I gotcha, big guy. Matwau means enemy. So, Halona means, what, friend?"

"No. Halona means fortunate in our tongue. I grow weary of this," said Moki. He turned to Tala. "Kill this fool."

Tala aimed her sharp arrow at Gray's head once again.

"Whoa! Whoa! Hang on a second! I… can help you beat them!"

Moki froze, raised his head, but did not turn to look at Gray.

"Go on," commanded Moki.

"I know what they're plannin' to do if you folks go rushin' into that house. I know what you're up against," said Gray.

Moki turned, rushed right up to Gray, and poked a claw into his chest. "Why should I believe a cowardly traitor who turns on his own tribe?!"

"My tribe? Cousin, I ain't with them. I'm with the kid!"

"You mean the boy who was banished by his own mother?" queried Moki.

"That wasn't his real parent. It was a foster parent," said Gray. He noticed Moki's paw reach for his knife and quickly realized that explaining the human foster parent program would probably get him killed. "His real parents were killed a while back. That other woman was just watchin' out for him. Anyway, yes… me and the kid, we're our own tribe now."

"I see," said Moki even though he didn't really see. "Speak quickly then. My patience lessens with every beat of your heart."

Gray chuckled to himself. "I love the way you cats talk. Okay. Hear me out. You got a bunch of well-rested, well-fed warriors in that house and they got a ton of new toys – stuff you ain't never seen before – to throw at you. The kid is showing them how to build bombs and they even got an airplane to use against you."

Tala lowered her bow. "Airplane?"

A frustrated Moki pushed her back. "Not now, Tala. I will handle this."

He turned back to Gray. "Airplane?" Tala rolled her eyes.

Gray put his arms out, made an airplane noise, and flew around in a circle. "Airplane. You know. The noisy metal birds in the sky?"

Moki looked up, at shed ceiling. "They are going to use this... airplane against us? Where would they hide such a massive machine?"

Moki laughed, faced Tala, and pointed at Gray. "This one has gone full *Geronimo.*"

"No, it's not *full-size* airplane. It's smaller. A toy. They control it remotely," exclaimed Gray. He looked around the shed.

Hanging from the ceiling on fishing line, covered in dust, was another remote-control single wing plane. Gray smiled, pointed up.

"Just like that one..."

Moki and Tala both looked up to see the model airplane. The formidable leader placed his paws on his sides, giving Gray a menacing look.

"You said this child was helping them now. Helping them fly this airplane. Building bombs for them. Does that not make you Matwau—?"

"I know how it looks. But he's a youngster, very impressionable. They've got him wrapped around their little claw. He's lost his mom and dad, his first foster home, and these mice are treatin' him like royalty. But I've got to get him away from them. He don't know what I know."

"Which is?"

"That the Halona kidnapped one of yours, didn't they?" asked Gray. "And you want him back."

Moki turned his head to exchange a glance with Tala. His demeanor changed instantly. His shoulders relaxed; his fur was no longer puffed out. Moki held out his paw, signaled to Gray to follow them.

"Come with us, brother. We have much to discuss," announced Moki.

Gray followed Tala into the shadows with Moki marching behind.

"So, uh, what's your name?" asked Gray.

Tala hopped along on four paws ahead of him. "Does it really matter?"

"Yo, I'm not tryin' to yank your chain here. Just makin' conversation," said Gray.

She stood on her hind legs, buried a claw in his chest, and stared him down. "What language is this that falls from your tongue? What rathole did you crawl out from?"

"Rathole?! Listen, toots, I'll have you know—"

"Toots?!" seethed Tala.

"Stop this now. We have no time for a lovers' quarrel…" announced Moki. He pushed past them both and continued the journey.

Tala followed Moki, pulling on his fur. "Lovers' quarrel? What are you talking about? Why would you say that?"

Her voice trailed off as Gray watched Tala scurry after Moki, objecting to his choice of words.

He smiled. "That one's got a lotta moxie."

Gray followed the two behind an old dry sink cabinet. They hopped up onto the first shelf. Gray took a quick look before jumping up to their level. Dozens of Moki's tribe were laying all about the cabinet. They were cold, wet, and tired. Some sought sleep where they had collapsed, others bandaged their paws, a few ate what scraps of food they had left.

Over in the corner, Chayton gently removed Ahiga's quiver and bow. Ahiga sniffed the air. When Gray came into view, Ahiga pushed Chayton back and drew his sword. He let out a wild scream that startled the entire tribe.

"Die, Matwau scum!" screamed Ahiga.

Moki gave a slight shake of his head to Chayton.

As Ahiga rushed toward Gray, sword raised high, Chayton grabbed him by the scruff the neck. Ahiga ran in place, his hind legs pumping uselessly in mid-air.

"Put me down, you dolt!" demanded Ahiga.

Moki surged forward, his paws out, to calm the weary troops. "We are safe! He is an ally. Get your rest, my warriors."

Wary but exhausted, the tribe settled back down. Moki motioned to Dyani and Hinto, his engineer. Chuchip and Nodin, the shaman, also closed ranks around Gray.

"Gather food and drink for our guest. We must meet now," commanded Moki.

"No, you guys ain't gotta feed me. I'm fine," pleaded Gray. "I could probably stand to miss a few meals, to be honest."

"Nonsense, brother. You are our guest," said Moki. "Come, let us gather by the fire."

A bottlecap had been placed upside down on the floor of the cabinet. Small pieces of wood and as sliver of coal had been gathered and lit on fire. Moki added more wood chips to stir up heat. Dyani laid a wool blanket around Gray's wet shoulders and sat beside him. Chuchip handed Gray a cup of melted-snow water. Hinto handed Gray the last of his acorn nuts, tossed the empty bag to the side. Nodin waved a few owl feathers at Gray, granting his blessing on their guest. Moki and Tala were the last to sit in the circle.

They exchanged names and backgrounds. Gray was shocked out how welcoming they were to a complete stranger. They listened eagerly to his stories about the big city and making his way to this house with the boy. He knew they wanted nothing more than to find out about the defenses of their enemy inside that house but remained patient with him.

"Thank you for sharing your journey, Gray," said Moki.

Gray tossed a few pieces of wood into the bottlecap fire. "Not a lot has gone our way. I wanted you guys to know that – even though he's *working* with them – he's a good kid. I want to help you get what you want… but I also need to make sure he's not harmed."

"That is now our need, as well," said Dyani. She tried to smile at him, but Gray could easily see the tension burning a hole in her heart behind those eyes.

"So, I gotta ask – who is Yuma?" asked Gray.

Moki put a paw on Dyani's shoulder. The others put their heads down, unable to look at their chief.

"He is our son," said Moki. "My only son."

"I see. Now it all makes sense," said Gray. "I knew this wasn't about territory. You guys are way too determined."

"We need to get him back safely," stated Moki. "You can help?"

"I think I can."

"Do you have a plan?" asked Dyani.

"Yep. And we're gonna kill two birds with one stone."

"I am happy to kill birds," said Tala matter-of-factly.

Gray grinned at her. Moxie. "I bet you are. But first, you all need to get you some rest."

"No! We must start preparations now, brother!" decreed Moki.

"Not a chance, chief. That bunch ain't gonna come out here to attack you. They're waiting for us. So, we got time on our side. You need to be ready for what's to come," said Gray.

26

The Prerequisites for Combat

T he next morning, Tala woke with a start. She was lying on the hard-bottom shelf of the dry sink cabinet, with her quiver under her head and a small piece of cloth for a blanket. She shivered from the cold as the fire in the bottlecap had gone out. She sniffed around the room. Gray wasn't close so she hopped onto four paws and stretched. Tala raced out of the cabinet.

She looked around the interior of the shed. The sun shone bright light down through the lone window. Her breath steamed around her mouth, nostrils. She saw slight movement from above. As she stared upward, a grin slid across her face.

With ragged claws, worn from her journey across town, Tala scaled the wooden leg of the workbench. She stood on hind legs on the plywood surface, crossed her arms, and stared at Gray.

The remote-control single wing plane was no longer hanging easily on three strings of the fishing line. Instead, the small plane was hanging by one long line, on its side, and dangled above the workbench surface.

Gray had been caught in the line and was swinging back and forth against the plane fuselage. He had been trying to get the plane down, it had fallen, and trapped him in the fishing line.

"What are you doing?" asked Tala.

"Oh, just hangin' out…" said Gray.

Tala began to laugh.

"Ha-ha. Very funny," said Gray.

She laughed harder still, until tears came to her eyes.

"A little help would be nice."

She laughed so hard, it hurt her sore ribs.

"Can you please get me down from here?"

She laughed until she fell onto her back, holding her sides.

"Okay, now you're just being ridiculous," said Gray. He finally cracked a smile.

"All right. Enough fun," said Tala. She sat upright. He gently kicked away from the side of the plane to swing back and forth easily. Tala shook her head at Gray.

She put her small knife in her teeth and jumped onto the tail section of the remote-control plane. Careful not to scratch the exterior of the airplane, she crawled out to where his fishing line had gotten stuck. Using her knife, she sawed at the string.

"No! Wait!"

Too late. She cut the fishing line and Gray dropped hard on the plywood bench, on his back, knocking the wind from his lungs.

"Thanks. For. The. Warning," stammered Gray, once the air returned to him. She smiled down at him. "But stay up there... where you are, okay?"

Gray stood on his hind legs and grabbed the wing that was hanging closest to him. Once he had both paws on it, he gave her the thumbs-up sign – which confused Tala.

Gray pointed to the fishing line that was still holding the plane in the air. "Cut the line, please."

She nodded but then gave him the same thumbs-up sign, wondering if she was doing it correctly. Tala scooted along the fuselage, knife in her teeth. When she reached the string, she used the sharp blade to saw it in half.

He smiled as the line snapped. His paws lifted the wing as the plane dropped onto the landing gear wheels. Tala was thrown across the workbench and into a pile of shop rags – oomph.

She popped out and glared at Gray, her eyes burning holes into his head.

He smirked at her.

"Payback," he stated.

"How can I help?" asked Hinto. Gray leapt straight up in the air. Hinto was standing directly behind him, close to the wing of the model plane.

"You people are gonna give me a heart condition!" panted Gray. "Who are you again?"

"I am called Hinto. It means blue. The kind of blue that is the color of the sky and—"

"I got it! We're good. You're the, uh, builder around here, right?" asked Gray.

Hinto nodded.

"You the man! Cool. Okay. I'm lookin' for a black box, with a metal antenna on it and a bunch of nobs and sticks on it. Could you find something like that for me?" said Gray. Hinto nodded again, dashed off across the workbench.

Tala dusted herself off as she approached Gray. "What do you need from me?"

"I need fuel. It's probably in a metal container about twice as tall as us. It stinks to high heaven," said Gray. She cocked her head to the side, not understanding. "It smells really, really bad."

"Everything in here smells really bad," stated Tala. "Present company excepted of course."

"Of course," smiled Gray.

"What is the purpose of this machine?" asked Tala.

"Well, since they got one... we need one. We can't let 'em have somethin' the kid calls 'air superiority'. It messes with his plan," he said.

"By Apollo's beard, you might just be useful yet," said Tala. She winked, hustled off to find the fuel that Gray needed.

For the first time, Gray noticed a large map that had been pinned to the wall behind the workbench. It was a map of Columbus, Ohio. A detailed street map.

Gray took off his cloth backpack, removed the torn piece of mimeograph paper, and unfolded it. He looked at the street name, then climbed to the top of the shelf on the workbench. He searched and searched until he found the street he needed. Then he began to memorize how to get there.

Flynn watched a hawk fly past his bedroom window. The sun was shining and, for the first time in a while, no new snow was falling. Wind had whipped around all the dry snow and deposited it against the houses, trees, and partially buried cars parked in the driveways on the street.

He was dressed for the day, sitting in his wheelchair, but had no desire to head downstairs and deal with the Ciminellos. Or the Halona. All he could think about was Gray. Where had he gone? Had he left the house for good? Why didn't he say goodbye?

The feeling of abandonment swept over Flynn. He should be getting used to it by now, but it still hurt so much. Couldn't Gray see what he was trying to do for his friends? They just wanted to live in peace and not be constantly attacked. Was that too much to ask?

"Are you okay?"

Flynn's head snapped in the direction of the voice. He saw Viho, standing on the same pillow that Gray usually slept on.

"Oh, hey, Viho."

"You look angry," said Viho. The chief pointed to the boy's hands. Flynn tightly clenched the armrests of the wheelchair.

Flynn relaxed his grip, shook away the pain in his hands. His jaw relaxed and he gave Viho his best phony smile.

"Yeah… I mean, no. I'm not… I'm fine."

"You worry about your friend. I know it can be difficult when friends forsake you. Just know that the Halona tribe are here for you."

"Forsake?" said Flynn. "No, he hasn't left or anything. He's around here somewhere. I think he's just mad at me."

"In that case, I wanted to thank you again for your help. We must be vigilant. My scouts tell me the Matwau are here."

"What?! They're here? *Already*?!" said Flynn. "I thought had days before they made it all the way here in this weather."

"The Matwau are very resourceful," said Viho. "And determined."

Flynn's mind raced. Everything needed to be in place. The Halona needed to be protected and ready for the Blitzkrieg tactics.

"We've got some work to do. I'll meet you in the basement," said Flynn.

He tentatively touched the joystick remote control for his wheelchair. He pulled back slightly on the stick and the chair rolled back against the wall. Flynn moved it forward and to the left and the wheelchair spun around and zoomed him out of the room.

"We await your expertise," said Viho. As the boy disappeared around the corner, Viho smiled to himself.

The last rays of sunlight pushed through the dirty window of the shed. All of Moki's tribe were filling their bellies with the remains of their food and water supplies, prepping for the big battle to come.

Gray and Moki huddled over the small fire burning in the bottlecap. Tala watched Gray as he talked but also gestured with his paws, pointing back and forth, and motioning over his head. She grinned as she loaded arrows into her quiver. Their new guest had an odd way of talking, but he smelled nice.

As Gray explained the last details of his plan to the chief, Moki slapped him on the shoulders and nearly dropped poor Gray to his knees. Moki threw his head back and laughed heartily, dragged Gray over to the rest of the tribe.

"Gather around, warriors!" shouted Moki.

Dyani assembled everyone as the two approached.

"Are we ready to face our enemy?!" barked the chief.

The tribe screamed back they were ready and eager. "Yes, we are!"

Moki turned to Gray, pushed him forward to present him to the warriors.

"You will listen to our brother here – he is going to ensure our victory!"

The crowd of mice cheered for Gray. He grimaced at the leader. "Geez, chief. You got these guys worked up like a bunch of Jesus freaks expectin' the second coming or something."

Moki and the entire tribe tilted their heads to the side; they were perplexed.

"Okay, here's the skinny. We're not just gonna go rushing in there, guns a-blazin'," stated Gray.

At this point, Tala could see that Gray was losing the crowd.

She stepped up next to him. "What he means is this – we would not be smart to charge into the fight just firing off our arrows with no plan," said Tala. She looked to Gray, who nodded his agreement.

"No, we gotta play it smart. We're gonna pull their wool over those cats eyes before we take 'em down a notch," said Gray. He looked Tala to translate.

"We are going to be wise. Our plan is to… deceive?" she said, getting approval from Gray. "To deceive the enemy in order to win the fight."

"First things first, we can't let them lay their peeps on our secret weapon – that fancy schmancy airplane we got," said Gray. He threw a thumb in the general direction of the plane.

"Prior to the attack, we cannot let the enemy discover our secret weapon in advance," translated Tala. She pointed to the remote-control plane. "The flying toy that our brother knows how to operate."

Gray nodded to her, grinning wide. "Yeah, so, what we gotta do is make a big show of moving all your battle gizmos and pointy things from here to the crib across the way."

"So, we'll make a show of force by moving our weapons from this shed to the house," said Tala.

"Yep, and that'll make the morons inside think everything's kosher and this is just gonna be a straight-up throwdown," said Gray.

"So, this will lead the enemy to believe we are to use conventional ordnance in one of our typical battles," said Tala.

"Totally! And then, when it gets dark, they'll stop watching us and go do their own preparations. That's when we'll sneak that plane over," said Gray.

He turned to Tala, who smiled at him and then the tribe. "Ain't you gonna translate that?"

"I think you managed to actually say something they could understand," said Tala.

"Oh, okay. Cool," said Gray. He turned to the tribe. "So… let's light this candle!"

No one responded. Gray nodded to Tala.

"Let us begin!"

The warriors cheered, raised their paws high, and raced away to grab their weapons.

"Nice job, Tala," said Gray. He held up the palm of his paw to high-five her.

She stared at it for a few seconds, then walked away.

"Tough crowd..."

27

The Line of Attack

In one of the spare bedrooms of the house, Koko wiped away the condensation fogging up the pane of glass. She stared out the window, searching for movement, looking for dark objects running over the contrasting white snow.

She waited and watched until she spotted three shapes dart away from the shed and race directly toward the house.

Elsu and his mate, Kiona, followed Gray through the snow. Their claws threw ice shards in the air as they scrambled across the flat expanse of the Ciminello backyard. Bows, quivers, and swords were strapped to their backs, weighing them down. They had made it halfway when they heard the wings of the hawk.

Chuchip and Tala stood on the roof of the shed, watching them run toward the house.

The red-tail hawk made his dive toward the three mice on the open plain of snow.

From the window, Koko smirked when she saw the shadow of the hawk on the ground closing in on the shapes.

Chuchip turned to Tala. "Now?"

"Not yet," said Tala, who looked from the blurry hawk to the mice sprinting across the snow.

The hawk flapped his wings once more to give that final push. His claws reached down to lift up a mouse.

Moki, Dyani, and Hakan waited at the door to the shed. They had bows, swords, and packs strapped across their backs.

"Go!" Moki shout-whispered to the other two. They took off running on top of the deep, white snow.

Gray braved a quick look up at the hawk – it was only a few feet from landing on top of him.

"Come on, Tala! Take this sucker out!" he wheezed as his paws drove him across the icy surface.

"Now?" asked Chuchip.

"Yes," said Tala. They raised their bows, lining their eyes up their target along the shafts of the arrows. She had waited until the shadowy shape of the bird moved even slower.

"Now." Release. The arrows whistled away from their bows.

The hawk lowered his claws onto Gray's back. Gray could feel the talons grip his fur as the arrows struck the hawk in the wing. Both he and the bird tumbled forward. The hawk freed Gray as he skidded across the snow, squawking in anger.

Tala and Chuchip notched a new set of arrows and launched at the hawk. One missed, sailing in front of the bird's beak, but the other drove into his neck. The hawk flinched and let out a wail that echoed across the backyard. Moki and Hakan stopped to fire arrows at the retreating hawk and took off sprinting toward the Ciminello home.

Gray jumped back onto all fours and sprinted across the snow, catching up with Elsu and Kiona. They skidded to a halt at the foundation of the house. Moki and his two companions arrived a few seconds later. Dyani watched the hawk limp off toward the sanctuary of the trees.

"Good riddance," Dyani announced, smiling at the others.

Moki waved to Chuchip and Tala that the passage was clear.

"Everyone! Go now!" screamed Tala down to the rest of the tribe from the shed roof.

In a single line, the field mice scrambled out into the yard with their packs and weapons on their backs.

Gray watched as the tribe made their crossing. He looked up the windows of the Ciminello house. He knew Koko, the ever-watchful eye, was up there in one of those windows. His eyes met Moki's and they nodded to each other – they made it across. Now all they could do was wait for darkness to fall.

Flynn was a field general, overseeing his troops from his wheelchair. The living area in the basement was his battlefield. Fierce drawings of field mice on paper cut-outs were his enemy.

Viho was perched on Flynn's knee, anticipating the false battle to come.

"Charge!" shouted Flynn.

House mice poured out of hiding in a five-wide line of attack. They raced out from everywhere over the battered couch, across the orange shag carpet, around the lava lamps, and from behind the massive brown stereo speakers. As a group, they notched arrows and fired volleys – all missing their paper targets. Flynn breathed a sigh of relief that they couldn't hit anything.

"Okay, freeze!" said Flynn. He turned to Viho, pointed to the troops. "You see, normally, you guys all stop there and just fire back and forth at each other."

"True, true," said Viho.

"And... unfreeze!" bellowed Flynn. "Second wave!"

Another line of mice rushed out from the same hiding places as the front line. They hustled passed the first group to create a new front, notched their arrows, and fired their rounds.

Flynn crossed his fingers as the new volley of arrows flew past or short of the paper cut-outs. Whew! They were closer but still missed.

"Third wave!" screamed Flynn and threw his arm out toward the enemy paper figures.

Maska led a final wave of warriors, swords held high, from their hiding spots. He let out a roar that scared Flynn and shocked Viho. Wamblee ran beside him, his tiny blade in his paw, and let out his own subdued war cry. Maska grinned down at the wee one running at his side.

Tate brought up the rear of the wave, chewing on a cracker. He tried to let out his war cry but spewed crumbs across the shag carpeting.

The third surge of troops rushed past the new front line to confront the paper enemy up close. The original wave fired arrows farther into the basement toward enemy cut-outs. The second wave also launched their arrows even further than the first. The first two lines of warriors chased after the new group to create a wall of oncoming troops.

In a short amount of time, they had overwhelmed and sliced up the pretend enemies.

Wamblee stood over one particular cut-out and slashed his blade down again and again until small pieces of white paper fluttered around him. Maska grabbed him by the fur on his neck and lifted him in the air so they could stare face-to-face.

"I think you got him, wee one," smirked Maska.

"Yes, I did!" bellowed Wamblee. "Slip me some skin!" He held out his paw and Maska put his on the youngster's paw, enveloping it completely.

Flynn leaned back in his wheelchair, grinning at Viho. "That's how it's done, Viho!"

"And this… this is the Blitzkrieg?"

"It sure is! You overpower the enemy with speed and fierceness. They'll turn tail and run off, scared half to death, after that!" stated Flynn.

"What if they do not run?" queried Viho, holding his paws together with his claws lightly touching.

Flynn gulped. He hadn't thought of that. "Well, then they'd be in big trouble, I guess. But they'll run. I know they will." They *have* to run, he thought to himself. Or else they are toast.

"Let us hope you are right," said Viho.

Koko silently hopped from an end table onto the arm of Flynn's wheelchair. She stopped behind Viho, leaned in to whisper in his ear.

"You are safe to speak in front of Dakota," Viho told her. "He is our ally."

"The enemy is upon us, Viho," she said to her chief but stared at Flynn. "They are gathering outside the house."

"We must prepare for the fight to come," stated Viho.

28

The Second Battle

As night fell, the winter clouds had blown off to the East, allowing the half-moon to bounce its bright bluish light off the white snow. If one were to look closely, one would see a trampled path, made by dozens of mice paw prints, leading out from the shed. One would see that the path wound around the side of the house and up to the front, then along the wooden wheelchair ramp where path halted at the double doors.

Breathing hard, Moki's tribe of mice leaned against the siding or were slumped on the cold concrete porch. Sitting near them was a scaled-down version of a P-47 Thunderbird airplane. It was covered with olive green paint on top, gray paint on the bottom, and U.S. Army decals. The remote-control plane was ready for the mission; the weary mice were not.

Down in the basement, Flynn worked on a Monogram model kit of the Mitsubishi Zero A6M5 alongside Artie. Both had pulled their wheelchairs up to the work bench. Artie held one of the wings together with his fingers, waiting for the modeling glue to set.

"There! That ought to hold it," said Artie.

Flynn kept looking at the clock. "Cool. Thanks again for helping me put this together."

Artie noticed the boy peeking at the clock. grinned. "You got somewhere you got to be, man?"

"Uh, no. I was just... hungry. Almost time for dinner, right?"

"Almost. Elaine went off to work but she left us a lasagna in the oven."

"Cool, cool," said Flynn. He snuck another look at the clock. "Hey, I need to head upstairs to go to the bathroom. I'll be right back."

Artie shrugged. He checked the model wing pieces to make sure they were sticking together. He grabbed the tube of modeling glue.

"Man, we probably shouldn't be down here without the windows open. These fumes could have us trippin' real hard."

Flynn pulled on his joystick and the wheelchair backed away from the workbench. "Good thing we're almost done. All right, I'll be back."

Artie nodded to the boy. *I'm making progress,* he thought. *The kid's really taking a shine to me.*

He added a touch more glue to a gap between the wing pieces and pressed hard. When Flynn was out of the room, Artie waited to hear the elevator doors open upstairs and then tentatively inhaled from the modeling glue tube. It was so strong it made him cough and blink hard as his eyes began to water. Bad idea...

When Flynn reached the main floor, he drove his wheelchair onto the hardwood floor. The rubber wheels squeaked loudly when he turned toward the kitchen. He nodded his head to Bodaway, who was standing on the kitchen table. Bodaway shifted his position, just enough to nod to Tarsha, who stood on a shelf in the mudroom. In turn, she whistled to Taima, who was fast asleep on top of the electrical panel box. Taima remained asleep so Tarsha whistled louder.

Taima opened an eye and the let out a big sigh. Using her tail, she lowered herself to the main circuit switch, within the electric panel that supplied power to the whole house. She hopped onto the power switch, with all her weight, but it wouldn't budge. Taima jumped on it but it stayed in the upright position. Finally, she hopped up and down on it until it finally tripped – the switch dropped down and she slipped off the plastic surface and fell behind the bench.

"Ow," Tarsha could hear Taima exclaim.

Tarsha grinned ear-to-ear from her perch on the shelf. *Serves her right for always sleeping on the job.*

All the lights in the house went out. Flynn turned his back to see that the elevator doors had stayed open. He grinned – Artie was trapped in the basement.

Out on the porch, Gray and Moki observed the lights shutting off inside the house – they exchanged a look, nodded to each other.

Flynn spun his chair to face the double front doors. He drove up close enough to reach the handles, quietly opened one of the doors a few inches. Flynn knew the field mice would use this as an entrance… and hopefully an exit.

Down in the basement, when the lights went out on Artie, he heard scraping and banging and the sounds of little feet on the floor overhead. "What is going on?"

He set down the modeling glue and wheeled his way to the elevator in the pitch black. He pushed the button, but nothing happened – power was out in the whole house.

Moki stared at the front door that had just opened slightly. He signaled the others to be ready. Every part of him screamed that all of this was an obvious trap. He turned his attention to Gray, who was busy preparing the remote-control plane. A calm fell over the old warrior. He instinctively trusted his new comrade. If he were to die today, then today was a good day for it.

Flynn raced his wheelchair into the kitchen. Adriel pushed the remote-control transmitter across the table to Flynn and dashed back across to where Yuma was cowering, behind the salt and pepper shakers, and huddled with him to keep him calm.

Fala waited on the floor next to Flynn's model biplane, the yellow Sopwith Camel, adorned with British Royal Air Force insignias, with her paws on the propeller.

Flynn positioned his chair in the entrance to the great hall, gave a quick thumbs-up signal to Viho, who nodded back and gave a silent signal to his troops to be ready.

The lone light in the house came from the roaring fire in the large fireplace, adorned with a Tudor-arch mantel that held several lit white candles. The bright orange light from the fire reflected in the eyes of Viho's warriors, with the exception of Taima who was fast asleep on an end table.

Flynn looked around the kitchen for any sign of Gray. "Where are you, Gray? You should be here for this," he whispered to his absent friend.

The field mice, led by Moki and Chuchip, cautiously moved into the foyer and spread out to provide cover, their swords and bows drawn. Chayton, Ahiga, and Hinto helped Gray drag the World War II fighter plane inside the house. They left the door open to prepare for their escape. Wind blew a spray of snow and cold air into the home. The breeze fanned the flames of the fire in the great hall.

Moki stood behind Gray as he guided the plane to a halt on the Persian rug. "It is time."

"Stick with the plan and this will work. Go!"

Moki grinned, rushed off toward the great hall, with more than half of the warriors falling in behind him. They let out their high-pitched war cry as they advanced.

A handful of mice stayed in the foyer with Gray. They were based in front of the dark, massive staircase, keeping them hidden from anyone in the kitchen.

Moki slowed his team down in front of a pair of antique Queen Anne reading chairs as they notched their arrows. They silently advanced to the second seating area, careful not to expose themselves. They stopped at a large round coffee table, surrounded by two sofas. Moki knew the smart play would be to split into two teams and hop onto each sofa. But he stayed on the hardwood floor, to move between the sofas. This opened them up to an ambush from those on higher ground.

"Should we not climb up there?" whispered Chuchip to Moki, pointing to the sofas.

"No," responded his chief. "Follow the plan."

"This is dangerous, Moki."

"I am aware..."

They scurried forward, along the floor, between the sofas.

Over in the third seating area of the great hall, Viho leapt up onto the back of a semicircle couch. Moki noticed him because his silhouette was framed by the giant diamond-paned window with the moon shining through.

With his sword raised, Viho screamed as loud as he could. "First wave! Attack!"

A group of house mice jumped into the open, bow strings pulled taught and arrows drawn.

Moki leaned close to Chuchip. "It begins," he whispered. "Spread out, warriors!"

The mice on the floor fanned out wide, taking cover behind the sofas and under the massive oak coffee table.

Arrows sailed through the air, landing all around Moki's group.

In the basement, Artie was panicking as he uselessly spun his wheelchair in circles, bumping into every piece of furniture in his way. "Hello?! Flynn?! Can you hear me?! Flynn!"

Zaltana lead the second wave of troops past the first group of archers, launching a volley of arrows at the field mice. A broad smile washed across her face as she ordered her warriors to launch a second round of arrows – the boy's plan would work.

Flynn gave a quick nod to Fala. She had already primed the motor and knew it was ready to kick on. With all her strength, she yanked down hard on the propeller. Nothing. She grabbed it again, pulled hard, and the engine started up. Fala fell backwards, scared by the rotating blades and noise of the propeller.

Gray heard the noise of a motor starting up. He motioned to Hinto to start their single-wing plane. The field mouse heaved with all his might on the propeller, but it did not turn over. Hinto pulled again. Then again. Still no start. Gray motioned for Hinto to keep trying.

Flynn switched on his remote transmitter. Fala sighed, climbed into the cockpit of the biplane, and strapped on her tiny homemade goggles. She nodded to Flynn. He pushed the remote control stick forward. The biplane rolled down the kitchen hallway, toward Flynn sitting in the kitchen doorway. Adriel and Yuma covered their ears as the remote-control plane approached.

Gray gave an exasperated look at Hinto, who had worn himself out spinning the propeller.

"Oh, crap! We didn't prime it!" shouted Gray. He counted how many times Hinto had had tried. It had been about seven, maybe eight turns. "It should work now! Try one more time!"

Hinto gave Gray a stern look, took a deep breath, and pulled hard – the airplane motor roared to life. Stunned, Hinto backed away at the ferocious sound.

"That's my girl!" Gray smiled at the remote-control plane.

"Oh, really?" said Tala, as she marched passed Gray and hopped into the cockpit of the airplane.

"No! You can't get in there!" screamed Gray. "I've never flown this dang thing!"

She shrugged, slammed the plastic canopy closed.

"Tala, no!" bellowed Gray. "Agh! Yer killin' me!"

Tala slid the canopy open. "Oh no. Yer killin' *me*… if you don't get this right!"

Gray planted the palm of his paw on his face. The sound of Flynn's biplane taking off gave him no choice – he pushed the joystick forward and the plane rolled along the foyer floor.

Tala waved as the plane rolled by. He half-waved and gave her a smile, then turned his attention to the remote-control transmitter.

Out in the great hall, Maska rushed forward with the third group of warriors. Moki and his tribe fired off a round of arrows, trying to slow down the attack.

Bodaway stood on the mantel, near the lit candles. With the flame from a candle, he lit the wick on his homemade bomb. He swung himself in circles, released, and the bomb flew between the two sofas in the middle of the hall. The bomb bounced off a couch cushion and rolled off – the explosion shook the room. The shockwave knocked Moki, Chuchip and others to the floor. The sound was deafening to their sensitive ears. An orange bloom of fire and heat flashed over their heads.

Downstairs, Artie was overwhelmed. Alone, in the dark, he heard the model plane motors and then the explosion of the small bomb. He hyperventilated as sweat beaded on his temples and the back of his neck. A white-hot rage enveloped him.

"The black helicopters! They're comin' for me!" he erupted. "You won't take me alive, man!"

Panting hard and grumbling loudly to himself, Artie aggressively pushed his wheelchair into the work room.

On the floor of the hall, Chuchip shook his head at the ringing in of his ears. Moki pulled him onto his hind legs.

"We must get out of here!" cried Chuchip.

Moki shook his head. "We must stay! For a while longer!"

Chuchip grunted but pulled out his bow, grinned at Moki, and launched arrows at the oncoming wave of warriors. Moki laughed heartily, fired his own arrow.

Driving his wheelchair under the doorway for better access, Flynn used his transmitter to bank the Sopwith Camel biplane into the great hall. With another hard-right turn, the plane was on a path toward the middle seating area.

Inside the cockpit, Fala pulled out a metal safety pin that Adriel had heated up and stored inside a metal sheath. She used the red-hot tip of the pin to light the wick of firecracker. She dropped it over the side of the cockpit, grabbed another firecracker and lit the next one.

Below, Ahiga and Chayton fired their arrows and ducked as incoming arrows zipped by their ears. When the first firecracker landed, Chayton obliviously picked it up and watched the wick sparkling as it burned.

"What are you doing, ignoramus?!" shouted Ahiga as he slapped it out of his paw. Chayton was confused until the firecracker blew up a few inches away.

"Aww, you like me!" said Chayton, trying to give Ahiga a hug. Ahiga struggled to free himself from the big oaf.

The next firecracker fell right behind Chayton and the blast knocked him forward. He landed hard on top of Ahiga.

"Get off me! Get off me!" bellowed Ahiga. The big mouse rolled off as

Ahiga pounded his paws against the big mouse.

As the biplane soared on toward the big window, Fala lit another firecracker. It dropped to the floor, exploding in front of Maska and his group. They cowered from the bright flash and loud bang, slowing down the forward progress of their wave.

Maska cupped his paws over his mouth. "Be careful, Fala!"

"Oh, that was not good..." Fala leaned out of the biplane cockpit. "Sorry!"

Flynn banked the model plane again and it flew over his head, through the arched-doorway, and into the kitchen. He adjusted the aileron to roll the plane, then the rudder causing it to turn down the narrow kitchen hallway.

In the foyer, Gray taxied his plane to the kitchen hallway. As Fala's biplane zoomed past him, he shoved the throttle forward on his transmitter and Tala's P-47 Thunderbird model plane rushed down the hall. Remembering how Flynn flew his plane in the test run, Gray pulled back on the controls and the little plane lifted off the oak floor.

Flynn ducked as the Thunderbird flew by. "They've got a plane?!"

He was stunned. He looked all around and then down the hall. He saw Gray controlling the plane with a plastic transmitter. The mouse banked Tala's plane and dragged the transmitter to the entrance to the great hall.

"Gray?"

Gray stopped in the doorway. He knew he had lost control of the plane because of the walls. Tala's plane was flying right toward the far wall. Working the transmitter, he gained control of the plane again. He turned it hard to the left and up at the same time.

The Thunderbird soared up toward the two-story high ceiling, then veered toward the fireplace. Tala's claws dug deep into the interior of the balsawood cockpit. The plastic canopy rattled. Landing gear narrowly missed the dusty window curtains.

Anger overcame Flynn. Gritting his teeth, he turned his biplane around to head directly toward Gray's remote single-wing plane.

Bodaway threw another homemade bomb from the mantel, creating a huge fireball in air between the sofas. The field mice covered their ears before the shockwave hit.

"Fall back and spread out!" shouted Moki. They fired off their arrows, scrambled backwards, and launched another round. Moki's group took cover back near the first seating area as Maska's warriors took over the central area with the twin sofas, near the fireplace.

Gray paused for a brief second from his remote-control transmitter to nod to Dyani. She grabbed Enola and took off running. Elsu and Kiona followed her into the dining room.

Down in the basement, Artie wheeled over to a tall metal cabinet, fumbled for the keys in his jeans, and quickly opened both doors. This was Artie's survival cabinet. He grabbed a flashlight and shone it on the contents of the cabinet – it held everything he needed in case the aliens or the government invaded: an inflatable lifeboat, food rations, ammo, pistols, clothing, passports, disguises, cash, maps, you name it… it was there.

"Not gonna take me alive, man! No way!" Artie shouted to the listening devices he was sure were planted throughout the house.

Artie grabbed everything he could. He filled a backpack with cash, guns, ammo and food. He ripped off the self-adhesive backing on a fake mustache and slapped it on his face.

As all three of the battle waves of Viho's tribe pressed forward, they fired their arrows and reloaded from their quivers.

Maska dropped his bow and removed the special metal gun from the leather strap on his back. He pulled the lever on top of the metal barrel all the way back to load the spring, locking it in place. From the cloth bag tied to his waist, he pulled out a small ball bearing and loaded it in the gun barrel. With a huge grin on his face, Maska aimed his gun and fired. The gleaming metal ball whistled through the great hall.

Chayton fired an arrow just as the ball bearing struck his shoulder, glanced off to the side and buried into the wood leg of one of the Queen Anne reading chairs. Chayton flew back off his hind legs – the sound of a few bones breaking in his shoulder echoed out – and onto his side. Writhing in pain, Chayton gripped his injured arm as tightly as he could.

Moki signaled for several warriors to carry the injured mouse to the foyer. He notched an arrow, pulled back the bow string. He couldn't see where the ball bearing came from in that darkness, with his poor eyesight, but he aimed the arrow in that general direction. Moki released the string and arrow zipped off across the room.

As Maska pulled back his string to load another metal ball, Moki's arrow struck him in the hind leg. Maska screamed in pain, pulled the arrow from his leg, and snapped it in half in anger. Holding the wound, he limped toward the back of the great hall. Zaltana rushed to Maska to help him. She put his arm around her shoulder, but he was so large he pushed her nearly to the floor. He rested his paw on her for what little support she could give.

As Gray was quickly learning on-the-fly to control his plane, Flynn turned his biplane directly at the Thunderbird. Both planes were on a collision course. Tala saw the biplane headed for her and loudly shouted and pounded on the plastic cockpit dome. Gray looked up from his controller to monoplane.

"Oh, no! No, no, no, no!" mumbled Gray. He turned the ailerons and the Thunderbird rolled to the side.

Flynn's biplane flew by with the lower wing grazing the left wing on Gray's monoplane. Flynn smirked as he worked the remote control to turn the plane around for another run – he knew he could beat his friend.

Gray put the flaps up on his plane, pushed the throttle forward. As Tala dove down, she let out another yelp. Gray gave the plane more speed as he then adjusted the flaps back to level and then pushed the flaps further down. The Thunderbird swung back up and up and up... until it flipped over, nearly touching the high ceiling. Tala panicked as the plane turned upside down. Gravity let her go and she floated up toward the canopy. As the plane looped over, Gray rolled it back over and eased off the flaps. Tala's monoplane was suddenly behind Flynn's slower biplane.

"Now the mouse is chasing the cat, kid!" said Gray.

Both planes veered into a turn, zooming through the kitchen. Flynn ducked as both planes flew over his wheelchair. Adriel and Yuma ducked behind the salt and pepper shakers.

Gray kept his Thunderbird on the tail of the Sopwith Camel as they flew through the kitchen hallway and into the foyer. Flynn pulled back on the throttle, allowing monoplane catch up and pass by, and the tilted the biplane wings quickly – his wing caught the wing of the Thunderbird. That little push sent the monoplane careening off to the left, out the open front door, and into the cold night air.

"Uh-oh," said Gray.

Gray dragged the transmitter to the front door. He held the black box and its long antenna up in the air, re-acquired the signal, and worked against the winter wind to bring the plane back toward the house.

Dyani and Enola scaled the cabinets next to the stove and waited to be attacked. No one was there.

Flynn drove his wheelchair back to the doorway, picked up Fala's biplane signal, and steered her back to the battle.

Dyani spotted Adriel and Yuma, with their backs to her, over on the kitchen table, watching the battle. Dyani ran toward Yuma, with Enola right behind. They scurried on all fours as quietly as they could. Every so often, they would stop to wait and listen, but there was too much chaos in the next room. When they reached the end of the counter, Enola jumped over to the kitchen table first, followed by Dyani. Adriel clutched Yuma's arm as he watched the attack raging below him. Enola tapped Adriel on the shoulder. When he turned, she threw her arms in the air and screamed at him. The sight of an albino mouse to the anxious engineer scared Adriel stiff. His eyes went wide, mouth fell open, and he backed off the edge of the table in fear. Yuma turned and looked as Dyani ran up to him, threw her arms around him, and hugged him tight. The youngster cried out in relief but Dyani cautioned him to be quiet by holding up one claw to her mouth. Yuma nodded and all three looked around to see if they had been spotted.

On the kitchen floor, Elsu and Kiona ran beneath Flynn's wheelchair. Kiona chewed rapidly on the straps that held down Flynn's joystick controller, pulled hard on the cord. The controller whipped off Flynn's armrest and Elsu reeled it in, setting the remote control on the wheelchair battery below. Kiona swung down off the rubber wheel and joined Elsu on top of the battery – they had control of the wheelchair.

In the basement workroom, Artie was ready for action. He wore an overstuffed backpack on his chest, a fake mustache, a baseball cap over a blond wig, and dark sunglasses. He checked his shotgun to make sure a round was loaded.

"Come get me," whispered Artie.

He spun his wheelchair to face the workroom doorway, but the footrest hit the self-inflatable raft that had been stuffed into the bottom rack of the cabinet. The metal footrest dragged on the auto-inflation pull-cord – instantly inflating the boat. The raft inflated, fired out of the cabinet, and into Artie's wheelchair. The releasing pressure from the raft shoved him all the way across the workroom. His head struck the far concrete wall, knocking him off the wheelchair and onto the floor. Artie was out cold.

Flynn flew the biplane back into the great hall and dove it toward the fleeing mice of Moki's tribe for another bombing run. His hand reached up to move his wheelchair farther through the doorway, but he could not feel the joystick. Flynn looked down – the controller was gone. He peered over the side to try to locate it. He looked all around.

"Flynn!" screamed Fala from the cockpit of the biplane.

Flynn looked back into the great hall. The Sopwith Camel biplane was headed straight for the floor. "No! No!" he shouted. He pulled back all the way on the flaps and ailerons.

The biplane flew down, down, racing to the oak floor. Fala screamed again, gripping the sides of the cockpit. The plane dipped down between the two sofas and the coffee table. From the momentum of the dive, the wheels on the landing gear tapped down on the wood surface. The flaps finally grabbed air and sent the plane soaring back up.

Flynn added more throttle to keep the plane from falling with the drag of the flaps. The little engine whined as the biplane climbed up and up.

"Get me out of here!" shouted Fala as the plane flew past Flynn.

"Sorry," winced Flynn when she sailed by. He banked the biplane again to turn it back around in the great hall to meet with the enemy once more.

Arrows fell all around Moki and his warriors. He could see the biplane approaching from across the hall. He pulled Chuchip close. "It is time! Get everyone out of here! Now!"

Chuchip scrambled away, shouting for everyone to retreat. Moki helped Ahiga carry the wounded Chayton from the great hall. His troops fired their arrows before bolting from the big room. Another bomb went off near the reading chairs, knocking down several mice as they sprinted from the room.

Under the wheelchair, Kiona pulled backward and slightly left on the joystick. Flynn's wheelchair spun backwards and turned to the side. The chair hit the doorway and Flynn's cast banged against the wall. Dust fell onto Flynn from the plaster above. Kiona overcorrected and the wheelchair spun back to the right as it rolled back and hit the kitchen table.

Enola, Dyani and Yuma fell as the table slid from under them. They recovered and ran toward Flynn, climbing up the chair and hiding out behind his shoulder.

Kiona worked the joystick until the chair rolled forward, this time toward a row of cabinets. Flynn screamed, holding his arms out to protect himself. The field mice slid down to his lap, joining in on the screaming. Kiona managed to veer the chair to the right and they zipped down the hallway to the foyer.

It suddenly dawned on Flynn that, despite their wheelchair run down the hall, Fala was still stuck in the biplane flying in the great hall. He couldn't see her plane – the wall was between them – so he lightly pushed the flaps down to make sure she was traveling upwards. He pulled back on the throttle, slowing her down.

Gray stood in the front doorway, remote control transmitter in his paws, as he guided Tala's plane down to land on the wheelchair ramp. This was his third attempt to try to land the plane. The wind, and his lack of experience, made the situation seem hopeless. He had gotten a little better after each try and she was coming in slow enough that it didn't look like she would hit the house. He hoped. Gray gulped hard as he pulled back on the throttle, lowered the ailerons and flaps all the way. The plane touched down the wheelchair ramp, bounced, and then bounded in through the open front door. Gray dove out of the way as the Thunderbird skidded into a slide, bumping against the foot of the stairs. He rushed to the cockpit of the plane.

"Tala! Are you okay?" he yelled, climbing onto the wing.

She pushed the plastic canopy up, rubbing at the new knot forming under the fur on her forehead. "I have endured far worse," she said. Gray helped her out of the cockpit.

At the top of the massive stairs, Sakari pushed hard against a suitcase. Pulling hard on the handle, was the shaman Nodin. They managed to get Flynn's case to the very edge of the top step.

Flynn's wheelchair skidded to a halt in the foyer. In view of the great hall again, Flynn was able to gain control of the biplane. He aimed the plane toward the foyer doorway. As it got close enough, he dropped the remote transmitter into his lap, reached both hands in the air, and caught the biplane. He shifted the plane around, shutting off the motor.

He carefully pulled Fala out of the biplane cockpit and set her on the floor. In a sheer terror, she darted off into the great hall. Fala flew past Moki and the rest of his tribe as they emerged into the foyer.

"Do you have him?!" bellowed Moki, as he slid to a stop next to Flynn's wheelchair.

Dyani popped her head over the handle of the chair, a grin plastered under her whiskers. She pulled Yuma up close so that Moki was able to see his face.

"Yes!" said Moki. "Everyone, we must leave at once!"

Flynn spotted Tala and Gray running from the staircase toward him. "Gray?! What's going on?!"

"I can't explain it now, kid!" shouted Gray, as he helped Tala climb up the wheel of the chair.

"You're working with them?! They're the enemy!" said Flynn. "Dude, how could you?!"

From the top stair of the staircase, Sakari and Nodin shouted a war cry. Flynn watched as both mice rode on the top of his suitcase down the stairs. The case slid smoothly down each wooden stair tread, then hopped as it glided onto the foyer floor, and shot straight out the front door.

Flynn and Gray watched the suitcase go out the door and then stared at each other.

194

"Do you trust me, Flynn?" asked Gray.

"Y-yes. Yes, of course," admitted Flynn.

"Then please, just do what I ask. I promise I can justify all this whacko craziness! I swear to ya, kid."

"But—"

A dozen arrows flew through the foyer. Viho and his tribe were racing toward the foyer.

"We don't have time!" cried Gray.

Moki and the rest of the tribe swarmed the wheelchair, climbing onto the motor and battery below, the armrests, and Flynn's lap.

Kiona pulled the joystick backward. The wheelchair lurched to the staircase, stopped instantly.

"Grab that plane!" yelled Gray.

"What?!"

Arrows rained down on them from the doorway of the great hall.

"The plane! The plane!" screamed Gray. "We might need it!"

Flynn scooped up the P-47 Thunderbird remote control plane and held it in one hand, with the Sopwith Camel biplane in the other.

Spears and arrows hit the floor around them, stuck into the vinyl back of the chair, a few struck Flynn in the arm. A few arrows bounced off the hard cast on his leg.

"Go, Kiona! Go!" Gray shouted, as he slapped the side of the wheelchair with his paw.

Kiona rammed the joystick and the wheelchair hopped forward, front wheels popping up as the back wheels spun on the hardwood floors. They surged out the front door, the side of wheelchair striking the door jamb, and onto the porch.

Sakari and Nodin stood on top of Flynn's suitcase, down along the ramp, and Sakari waved her arms in the air.

Gray put his paws over his mouth, shouted up to Flynn. "Pick up the case!"

Flynn looked down at the two planes in his arms. "With what?!"

Gray turned to Moki. "Get your strongest warriors out onto his cast!

195

Now!"

The chief grabbed Chuchip and several other field mice and they followed Gray onto Flynn's broken leg.

Kiona could see the suitcase lying in their way, as well as the mice assembling out on Flynn's cast. She turned to Elsu. "Slow down... now!"

He pulled back on the wheelchair remote and they slowed to a crawl on the ramp.

Gray grabbed Moki's arm, just above his paw, and formed a tight grip. "Everyone, lock arms! Form a chain!"

The mice formed a line, arm-in-arm, along the length of Flynn's cast with about ten warriors. Gray pointed to Ahiga at the other end, motioned for him to jump off to the right side of the cast. Then Gray jumped off his side. Ahiga launched himself over his side. The entire chain of mice dangled across Flynn's leg and down both sides.

"Grab the handle of the case after they get on!" Gray barked to Ahiga, pointed at the suitcase.

Sakari helped Nodin climb up onto the chain of mice, then followed him up the line. Once they were safe, the wheelchair rolled forward letting both Gray and Ahiga dig their claws into the leather handle of the case. With everyone holding tight, they pulled the suitcase. It dragged on the wooden ramp until it flipped up, then rolled forward, and was pulled along behind them.

The suitcase was too heavy. The handle slipped out of Gray's grasp, then Ahiga could no longer hold on. The wheelchair slammed into the case as it spun on the icy ramp.

"Come with me!" shouted Gray. He let go of Moki's paw and dropped to the ramp. One by one, the other mice fell to the wood deck. Gray ran to the back of the wheelchair and the others followed him.

Viho and several of his warriors arrived at the front door. They fired arrows and heaved spears.

Miko ducked as a spear flew past his head. "Do we need this case?!"

"Yeah, we do! I want to make a clean break from here," said Gray. "Help me stand it upright!"

Moki motioned for his team to push on the suitcase. Arrows stuck in the side of the case as it slowly stood up behind the wheelchair.

"Flynn! Pull it up!" screamed Gray. Flynn turned his head back and looked down at Gray. The boy nodded his head.

Flynn rested the two model planes in his lap and reached an arm behind his wheelchair. His fingers waggled just above the handle, unable to touch it.

"I can't reach it!"

"Crap," said Gray.

Several arrows struck Flynn's hand, making him recoil in pain. He plucked the tiny arrows from his hand and dropped his arm over the back of the wheelchair again.

Gray scrambled up the side of the case, dodging a spear as it sailed past his shoulder. He moved to the middle, pushed the handle straight up into the air. Flynn's fingers were finally able to touch it. He adjusted in the chair, grabbed the handle, and lifted Gray up with it.

"Put it on the chair handle!" bellowed Gray. Flynn plopped the suitcase handle over the plastic handgrip on the back of the wheelchair. Flynn picked up the model airplanes. The case swung back and forth on the hand grip. Gray was satisfied.

"Let her rip, Kiona!"

Kiona pushed the joystick ahead with both paws. The wheelchair motor whirred to life again. The wheels churned on the ice, caught the wood, and drove the chair down the ramp.

Flynn and the mice ducked as arrows poured down on them. They chugged down off the wooden ramp and onto the empty driveway. Kiona veered the steering stick to the left and the chair followed by locking the left wheel and spinning the right. The rubber wheels whipped through the shoveled drive and into the street. A final round of arrows fell harmlessly in their wake.

Gray stood on Flynn's shoulder as a wheelchair, holding a boy, dozens of mice, two remote-control planes, and a suitcase, zoomed down a snowy street late at night.

Viho and Zaltana stood in the doorway of the Ciminello house, watching them fade off into the darkness.

"We have lost," sighed Viho.

Zaltana put a paw on his shoulder. "Let us follow them. They cannot get far."

"We fueled Dakota's device up before the battle. He will be able to escape our grasp."

Koko, listening in on the conversation, quietly slipped out the door and onto the porch. She could see the trail in the snow where Miko's tribe had walked the toy plane around from the shed. The guilt hit her hard. She had stopped spying on the enemy, allowing them to bring their airplane to the battle. Koko hopped down into their worn path and followed it through the snow.

The powerful washing machine motor easily pushed the wheelchair through the worn ruts in the snow.

"I'd like my controls back, Gray," said Flynn.

Gray sighed, leaned close to Flynn's ear. "Can I trust you?"

"Well, I can't go back there now, dude! They think I turned on them. They shot me!" He held up his hand, pulling out the tiny bloodied arrows that were stuck in his skin.

Gray cupped his paws around his mouth. "Elsu, give the kid back his joystick!"

Elsu gave a look to Kiona; she was clearly worried. But Miko had said they could trust their new friend and he had not let them down yet. She nodded to Elsu, who pushed the wheelchair remote control across the battery to put it within the boy's reach.

Flynn felt around from the side of the chair until he touched the box. He quickly set the controller on the arm of the wheelchair.

"Okay, Gray... where are we going?" asked Flynn.

Gray scanned the name on the upcoming street sign. "Turn right here."

Flynn pushed the joystick right. The chair bounced through the ruts until it landed in fresh tire tracks in the snow.

"Now where?!"

"Just keep going straight. For three more streets," said Gray.

"But where are we going?!" said Flynn.

"Um… you'll see," replied Gray.

"I'll see? Gray, come on," said Flynn. "What's going on, dude?"

"I got these directions memorized, kid. Don't mess with me right now," said Gray. "Turn left… here!"

Flynn reluctantly steered the wheelchair to the left, down another snow-covered suburban street.

In the backyard of the Ciminello house, Koko slipped through the front door of the shed. Even though she doubted any Matwau remained, she stood still for several moments and listened for signs of danger. When no enemy mice revealed themselves, Koko moved around the shed in search of clues.

She climbed up the leg of the dusty workbench and sniffed around. She recognized the scent of fuel, for the model plane. There were old batteries and a few rusted tools scattered about on the bench. The smell of field mice overwhelmed her.

Koko saw a large sheet of paper pinned to the wall, just above the workbench, that was covered in squiggly lines and human writing. She recognized Gray's scent coming from the top shelf, so she climbed up for a closer look. There was a torn piece of paper with writing on it. Two push pins in the sheet of paper held it to the wall. She moved closer to the pins. She glanced at the address on the torn piece of paper. The name on the paper matched a name that was pinned on the wall. The piece of paper on the wall was a map. She realized the address was most likely their destination. Koko put the torn mimeographed paper in her mouth, dashed off the workbench, and sprinted out of the shed.

Taima climbed up to the electrical box in the mudroom. She reached down and pulled up the main power switch, lighting up the house once again.

Viho and Zaltana watched as the tribe retrieved arrows and spears littered about the great hall. Maska limped to his chief, a fresh bandage covering his hind leg.

"What can we do, Viho?" asked Maska.

"There is nothing we can do. They have taken Yuma away and turned the boy's allegiance against us. All is lost," stated Viho.

"There is hope yet, Viho!" shouted Koko, as she ran up to them with the piece of paper in her claws. Breathing hard, she showed the address to Viho. Confused, he gave the paper back to her.

"Speak, child," said Zaltana.

"I know where they are headed," announced Koko, between gulps of air.

"What does it matter?" asked Maska, perplexed.

Zaltana turned on him, poking a single claw in his chest. "It matters a great deal. I, for one, am not giving up. And if I cannot have the child back then… I will have my revenge."

Viho grabbed her by the shoulders, away from Maska, and stared into her eyes. "You are so very right, my beloved. Apologies to you that my faith wavered."

"We all can have a moment of weakness, my dear," said Zaltana.

Without looking away from his mate, Viho addressed Maska. "Prepare the tribe to leave before the sun rises."

The big mouse stared at Viho for a moment too long. "Yes… sir." He bowed his head and limped off into the great hall.

"Do you have a plan?" asked Viho, spinning to face Koko.

Koko looked around the house, then back at her chief. "If the humans follow their same pattern, I believe I do."

"Good. We must be ready," said Viho.

29

The Long Way Home

Mother Nature showed no sign of releasing her cold, icy grip on the city that night. A harsh wind and enormous snowflakes blew hard across the quiet streets. The moon was a soft golden haze, interrupted constantly by rolling storm clouds.

Flynn's wheelchair was running low on battery as they slowly cruised through deep channels of gray slush covering the road. The boy used the model plane wings to shield himself, and the mice he carried on his lap, from the sharp winds. They had traveled out of the suburbs and into the outskirts of the city where the temperature dropped noticeably lower.

"Are we almost there? Please say we're almost there," pleaded Flynn.

Gray carefully inspected the house numbers on each mailbox they passed. "Almost."

Flynn sighed and then shivered uncontrollably, as pangs of hunger and waves of exhaustion took turns jabbing the boy. He looked down at Dyani as she hugged the Yuma tightly to her chest, a permanent smile fixed on her face.

"This might be it," announced Gray.

Excited, Flynn shifted his gaze to the farmhouse at the end of a long driveway. He saw a two-story white home with black shutters, a large front porch, and a matching white barn on the other side of the drive. A two-tone copper and white Chevy pickup truck was parked between the house and the barn. Snow-covered corn fields enveloped the farmhouse on both sides, with a row of tall trees framing the back of the property. Smoke poured from the chimney and yellow light spilled from the windows.

"Whose house is this?"

Gray marched down the boy's cast to get as close as he could. "Remember that list of potential foster parents you took from child services?"

"Yeah," said Flynn, as his mind quickly pieced the puzzle together.

"This is the third – and *final* – foster home that was able to take you in," said Gray.

"How did you find it?"

"Does it matter? We're here now. We got to get inside or we're gonna freeze to death, kid."

"Okay... Let's go, I guess," stammered Flynn. Another shiver spread through him, from the cold and the nagging fear of the unknown constantly whispering in his ear.

Flynn turned the wheelchair off the street and onto the driveway. The motor whined as it struggled to push them through the heavy snow.

"Everyone is going to need to hide," said Flynn.

Gray looked at all the mice covering the boy. "You're right. Can you hand me the case?"

Halfway across the drive, Flynn stopped the wheelchair. He set the remote-control airplanes on the ground and pulled the suitcase off the chair handle.

"Let's all get inside, folks!" said Gray.

Moki and Gray helped the tribe climb into the suitcase. Tala started to pull herself in and paused, looked carefully into Gray's eyes.

"It's okay. You can trust me," said Gray.

Tala held his gaze for a moment and then nodded. Moki guided her up and over the wall of the suitcase and followed her in.

"What am I supposed to say to these people, Gray?" asked Flynn. "How do I explain this?"

"Tell them that Child Services just dropped you off. That they couldn't stick around, or somethin' like that. By the time they talk to each other and get it all figured out... they'll just go with it. It'll be fine, kid."

"Okay," murmured Flynn.

"You can do this, my man! I got faith in you!"

Gray patted the boy's forearm and hopped into the case. He gave a quick nod to Flynn, who zipped the lid closed. He set the case upright, causing the mice and all the contents to slam hard on the bottom.

"Sorry!" he whispered loudly to his suitcase.

Flynn placed the case on his wheelchair handle and grabbed the airplanes. With a deep sigh, he plunged the joystick forward and sped on to the house.

In the farmhouse kitchen, Mark Dobson listened for the popcorn on the stovetop to stop popping. When there were several seconds between pops, he removed the foil-covered container from the heat.

Mark tried to carefully tear open the top but his thick hands, strong from many seasons working the farm, split the thin foil and popcorn scattered across the counter. He was thirty years old, but the sun and wind and dirt had distressed his skin, making him look older. His high-and-tight cut blond hair was more of a fit for a military uniform than the farmer's flannel shirt and worn jeans he wore. He scooped up the stray popcorn pieces and placed them in a yellow ceramic bowl.

Out in the living room, six-year-old Laura used her screwdriver to remove the speaker from the transistor radio. Her thick red curls, a gift from her mother, glowed from the roaring fire in the fireplace.

Mark brought the popcorn in and saw the mess of electronic parts on the coffee table. "Oh, no, honey. Not my radio, too."

"Sorry, daddy," said Laura, with her best super-sad face. "I just wanted—"

"To see how it works. Yeah, I know, kiddo," said Mark. He set the yellow bowl down and scooped up the remains of his radio.

Laura's pouty face broke his heart. It always did. It was his wife's face. His daughter had him wrapped around her tiny finger.

"It's okay. I don't like music all that much anyway," fibbed her father.

Laura crawled up into Mark's lap with the speaker in her hand. "What does this do?"

"Well, that's the speaker. It's where the sound comes from."

"How does it work?"

"Um, well… vibrations from the music—"

They heard something strike their front door. They looked at each other. Then another thump hit a window beside the door. It was a dull smash that sounded like… a snowball.

"I better see what that is," said Mark.

"You better," said Laura, giving her permission.

Mark opened the door and a blast of cold wind followed. He could not see anyone standing outside his screen door, so he flipped on the porch light.

What he saw caught him off guard. He stood there, frozen, unable to speak. There was a boy sitting in the falling snow, at the bottom of his steps, in a wheelchair, with a cast on his left leg.

After a few seconds, Mark opened the screen door for a better look. "Uh… Can I help you?"

"I hope so. Are you Mister…" Flynn looked down at his mimeographed sheet of pink paper with one corner torn away. "Mister Mark Dobson?"

"Y-yes?" said Mark, completely unsure of anything in life at that very moment.

"Hi, um, my name is Flynn Myers. And, well, you were on the list… I mean, you wanted to be a foster parent and… What I mean is that you were approved to be my foster parent but there was a mistake—"

"Wait. Whatever it is, we need to get you in the house right now," said Mark.

Mark rushed down the stairs, in his wool socks, and grabbed both handles on Flynn's wheelchair.

"You hang on, okay?" said Mark.

Flynn nodded as Mark spun him around and pulled him up the first step. Flynn bounced in his chair but grabbed his case and the planes tighter. Mark pulled him up all three stairs and wheeled him backwards through the open front door.

Laura came running as her dad pulled the boy into their living room. "Daddy, who's that?" she asked.

"Laura, honey, I need you to grab those blankets on the couch for me, please," said Mark.

He pushed Flynn's wheelchair up close to the fireplace. Laura retrieved two blankets and handed them to her father. Mark set down Flynn's suitcase and remote-control planes on the floor. He placed a blanket around Flynn's shivering shoulders and another across his legs.

"There, that should help," said Mark. He pulled his reluctant daughter next to his side. "Hi, I'm Mark and this is my daughter, Laura."

Laura approached his wheelchair, looked him up and down, and held out her hand for Flynn to shake it. "I'm six."

"Hi, Six. It's nice to meet you. I'm Flynn."

Laura giggled, ran back to hide behind her dad's leg.

"Can I get you some hot soup? Or hot chocolate?" asked Mark.

Flynn could only nod. Mark disappeared into the kitchen. Laura approached him, a sly grin had crawled across her face like she knew a special secret and was willing to share. She held up the speaker from the transistor radio.

"Do you know what this is?" asked Laura, with no intention of letting Flynn answer. "It's a speaker. It's from a radio. Sound comes out of it – from vibrations – like music and stuff. Do you want it?"

"Um, no thanks," answered Flynn.

Little Laura set the speaker in his lap. "Okay, here ya go!" She floated away to finally enjoy that buttery popcorn that patiently waited for her.

Mark turned on the stove burner to warm up milk in a small pot. He pulled a stack of papers out of a drawer – notes, coupons, business cards, receipts – until he found the card he needed. Using the phone on the wall in the kitchen, Mark dialed a number. He stared at the business card with Amy Regula's name and the Child Services logo.

The phone rang in his ear as he watched the heating pot of milk out of the corner of his eye. He looked at the clock on the wall – the lateness of the hour suddenly dawned on him. He placed the receiver back in its cradle and attended to the milk. He tried to pour it out into a mug but spilled half of it on counter. He smiled, then laughed at himself, for a brief moment. He was, at least, predictable. That's what Candace had always called him when she wanted to tease him.

He searched the cupboards for the can of chocolate powder, then a grabbed a spoon from another drawer. He really missed her. It had been three years since cancer had taken Candace from him, from their young daughter. He knew Laura barely remembered her mom. But he made sure to pull out their family album to show her the old black and white photos, tell her stories about Candace. Mark shook his head, to try to physically wipe away memories in his mind that would have kept him standing in that kitchen for an hour. He scooped up the mug and carried it into to living room.

"Here, this will help. Drink up," said Mark, handing the mug to Flynn. He cleared a space on the coffee table and sat down to be on the boy's level.

"Thanks," said Flynn. He took a sip while staring at the large man sitting next to him. Fear and cold melted away as gulped the hot chocolate.

"So, I met with a woman from Child Services a while back. We did the whole interview routine, but she called and said they were going with someone else. And—"

"That was probably Amy. Um, Miss Regula. Was that her?" said Flynn.

"Yes. That's her. So, you're saying that—"

"She just... dropped me off. But she couldn't stay. Said she had some kind of emergency. She was real sorry she couldn't be here in person. Because... she had an emergency."

Mark looked at the thawing snow dripping off Flynn's wheelchair. The boy's clothes were damp but mostly on the front. His hair was wet, his cheeks and nose bright red from exposure.

"So, you were living with another foster family up until now?" asked Mark.

Flynn took a long sip from the hot chocolate mug, afraid to say anything more. "Uh, Amy said it was just a paperwork mix-up or something like that. I was supposed to come here to live but somehow... well, anyway... I'm here now," stammered Flynn.

"Yeah, you are."

"Oh, and Amy said she's going on vacation. Starting tomorrow. So, she won't be back in town for quite a while," said Flynn, regretting it as soon as the words came pouring out.

"I see," said Mark. "You know what? We'll get it all straightened out later. As long as you're here and you're... safe, I'm happy. You happy?"

Flynn gave a decent fake smile. "I am."

"Good. Okay, you should probably get changed into dry clothes. I haven't really had a chance to get it ready, but we do have a spare bedroom for you."

"On this floor?" asked Flynn.

He smiled quizzically. "Yeah, on this floor."

"Far out," said Flynn.

Mark grabbed hold of the handles on Flynn's wheelchair. "Take as long as you want to get settled in. If you're up for it, since it's Friday night, we were planning on watching *Double Chiller Theater*. It's a—"

"Oh, I know it! Back-to-back horror movies! With Fritz the Night Owl!" exclaimed Flynn. "I was never allowed to watch it... before."

"Well, I won't tell anyone if you don't," Mark smiled.

"Deal!"

Flynn scooped up his suitcase, placed it on his lap, and watched Laura remove the power supply from the transistor radio as Mark wheeled him down the hall.

"I'll make you up a sandwich if you're hungry," said Mark.

"Oh, I'm hungry," said Flynn. The hunger grumblings in his stomach had replaced the fear butterflies.

"Good. Ham okay?"

"Uh-huh," agreed Flynn.

He stopped the wheelchair in the doorway to dark bedroom, flipped on the ceiling light, then slipped past him to put away the many boxes that had found a long-term resting place on top of the bed.

"Sorry. I would've had this all set up for you if I knew you were coming."

"It's cool. I... we did sort of spring this on you," said Flynn.

Mark reached for the suitcase but paused. "May I?" he asked, pointing to the case. Flynn pushed it off his lap, nodding his head.

With the suitcase on the bed, it dawned on Flynn that the tribe of field mice were in there. Mark placed the luggage on the top of the blanket and started to unzip it.

"No!" shouted Flynn, his hand reaching out to grasp at the air.

Mark grinned, held his hand up in the air as if the police had drawn their guns on the thief caught red-handed stealing the jewels.

"I'm sorry. It's just that I got all my things in there. You know, like, underwear and stuff," stumbled Flynn.

"Hey, I get it, Flynn. That's your whole life in that case. I know what that's like," said Mark. "I was always on the move as a kid, too. Broken home and all that."

"Is that why—?"

"Why I wanted to be a foster parent? Yes, but mostly because – and you have to keep this between you and me – I don't think I'm the best father in the world."

Mark sat on the bed, his hands together, and looked down at the floor. "It's just Laura and me now. Her mom, my wife, passed away a few years ago. She was an amazing woman. She knew how to do *everything*. And she was a great mom. But I had no experience at being a parent since I didn't have one growing up. So, I'm sort of learning on the job. And I thought I could use a little help. That's where you come in..."

"You want me? To be a parent?"

Mark laughed out loud. "Ha! No, sorry. See? I'm not even good at explaining things. I'm just looking for a little guidance, another voice, someone who needed a family and who could help complete our family. When Miss Regula told me about you, I thought 'Now there's a kid who grew up with a mom and dad and he could help make sure I was doing the whole parenting thing right.' You know what I mean?"

"You mean like not letting your six-year-old stay up late to watch horror movies?" said Flynn. He had a huge grin on his face.

Mark blushed. "Yes! You see? You've helped me already." He slapped his jeans with both hands and stood up. "Okay, you get settled. I'll make some food. Come out whenever you want or just crash for the night. Either way... welcome to our home."

He walked out of the room, closing the door behind him. Flynn wheeled up next to the bed as soon as he heard Mark lumber down the hallway. He unzipped the suitcase, threw open the lid.

All of Moki's mice had their spears held high and their arrows aimed, ready for battle.

"It's okay, guys," said Flynn. "You can come out now."

The warriors lowered their weapons. They flooded into the room with all their gear in tow.

Gray threw his arms over the edge of the luggage and exhaled a huge sigh of relief. "It worked, kid! You did great."

Flynn peered over at the bedroom door, then back at Gray. "I like them. They're *really* nice."

"I'm glad for ya, kid. I really am. This might be the one. Now, we just got to hope that the Halona don't find us."

Everything came rushing back into Flynn's mind all at once. "Wait! What happened? You promised you'd tell me what's going on!"

Gray threw himself over the side of the case, strolled to the edge of the bed and sat down. He rubbed his whiskers. "I did, didn't I?"

After another long sigh, Gray explained to the boy how the house mice had kidnapped the son of the tribal leader of the field mice. When he found all this out, he told Flynn that he was determined to help this Shoshone tribe and that is why he had basically abandoned the boy.

Flynn took in Gray's explanation and sat in silence; a stony look etched into his face.

Gray could see the anger once again building up in Flynn's eyes. He noticed the clenched jaw and the hands that were balled into fists.

Gray walked carefully over to the side of the wheelchair and placed his paw on the Flynn's hand. "I know none of this is easy to hear, kid."

"They used me, Gray. The Halona took advantage of me, of what I know. Just like Missus Easterbrook only wanted me for a check. Like Artie probably just wanted me there to make his wife happy," said Flynn. "Is Mark using me to? Does he really just want me here so I can be a parent to Laura?"

"From what I heard from him so far, I think you were a pretty good judge of character. He seems like a real straight shooter, kid."

"Why can't people just want you... for being you?" asked Flynn.

Gray exhaled, pulled himself up onto the armrest of the chair, and leaned on Flynn's forearm.

"We all want somethin', kid. Each of us. We want a mate, we want kids, friends, and we want family. But it doesn't always work out the way we want. That's just a fact of life. So, desperate times call for desperate measures – I think that's the saying – and it leads folks to do not-so-good things to get what they want. They make a bad decision to get what they want, and they usually end up regretting it. Or they keep making bad decisions until things get out of control."

"A lot of people around me are making bad decisions. Am I making bad ones, too?" said Flynn.

"The way I see it, you don't get to choose what family you're from, right? No. Ya don't. But we had our families taken away from us. Now we get to choose our own family this time around. *We* get to choose. And that's—"

"That's never a bad decision," finished Flynn.

"You got that right, kid," said Gray, patting the boy's forearm. "You got that right."

30

The Pursuit

In the morning, Viho's troops hauled out a huge number of supplies from of the Ciminello's house. Like a line of ants carrying food from the picnic, they conveyed their bows, arrows and spears, as well as an assortment of Artie's fireworks, batteries, motors, fuel cans, and remote controls.

"Move with haste, my warriors!" commanded Viho

He watched several mice slide down the small hill in the front yard on one of the model airplanes. Adriel had strapped tongue depressors to the landing gear wheels of the radio-controlled airplanes, allowing the mice to skate them easily over the deep snow. They had stolen the Fokker triplane and the Mustang P-51 fighter.

They had waited, along the side of the house, for the sun to come up with all their gear ready to move. Koko was convinced that the same woman would return once the boy was reported missing – and she did finally arrive. When the female from Child Services went into the Ciminello home, Koko signaled the others to begin their organized supply chain operation. They dragged the planes and weapons to Amy's green Pontiac GTO parked on the street.

"I almost have it open!" shouted Maska. The large mouse was hanging from a metal file that he had stuck through the keyhole on the trunk of Amy's car. He used his weight to turn the file hard to the right and was rewarded with a metallic click as the lock released. The trunk springs lifted the lid high into the air and Maska's smile disappeared as he was jerked up with the lid. He bellowed loudly as he rolled down the trunk and into the back window of the car.

A dozen mice scrambled up to the trunk and lowered strings down to the first model plane in the queue. Mice on the ground attached the strings and helped lift the airplane as it was pulled up. The next plane was rolled into position, below the first.

Koko climbed up on a windowsill to spy on the humans. She could see them sitting around a table, talking, so she nodded to Viho that there was plenty of time to load supplies.

Agitated, Artie rocked his wheelchair back and forth. He was still wearing the baseball hat, blonde wig, and fake mustache. Elaine kept clacking her fingernails over and over on the wood tabletop. Amy wrote notes in her folder to avoid eye contact.

"And, I'm tellin' you, man. That was the last time I saw him," said Artie.

Amy read back through her notes. "So, he went upstairs… and then the power went out?"

"That's what I said. It wasn't long after." At this point, the fake mustache adhesive was giving out on one side and it was starting to fall off Artie's upper lip.

"What time did you get home again?" asked Amy, turning her attention to Elaine to prevent staring at Artie's dangling fake mustache.

"It was after midnight. I don't know exactly," sighed Elaine. Exhaustion, from lack of sleep that night, had consumed her. "I came home, and the front door was wide open. The lights were on. I went downstairs and Artie was knocked unconscious and laying on the floor."

Amy turned back to Artie but could only stare at the fake mustache flapping around above his lip. "Wait, you got knocked out? Did someone attack you?"

"Um, well, no… not really," mumbled Artie.

'What happened?" asked Amy. His mustache waved at her.

"The, uh, you see, it was… an inflatable raft. It accidentally opened and, um, knocked me back into the wall," said Artie, followed by another mustache flap.

Amy tried hard not to smile. "I see. Well, no, I don't. Why did you need an inflatable raft?"

"Is this really important, man? What about the kid?! They've got him! Don't you see—"

"Artie... don't!" warned Elaine.

"Don't what? Who's got Flynn, Mister Ciminello?"

Elaine issued another warning. "Artie..."

"She's got to know, Elaine! We have no choice now!"

"What do I need to know?" interrogated Amy, in her most official tone.

Artie leaned forward in his wheelchair. Amy leaned forward, staring into Artie's furtive eyes. Elaine leaned forward and ripped Artie's hanging fake mustache off his lip.

"Ow!" wailed Artie.

"Get on with it," said Amy, still trying not to laugh.

"Okay, we've been under surveillance by a secret society within the government. They have sent their black helicopters to spy on the citizens who aware of their plot to take over this country, man! And they must've heard enough because *they* came last night," whispered Artie.

"The black helicopters?" said Amy.

"Yeah, they were here! I heard them flying around outside when the power went out! They're unmarked, black Hughes helicopters that they used in Vietnam to place phone taps on the enemy. They got these low-noise contraptions on 'em so they're hard to hear. Now, they're using them... on us! There are men in them wearing all black suits and dark sunglasses. Some say they are CIA, but I think they might be aliens. And they were here to kidnap me, man! They knew Elaine was at work, but they didn't know about *Flynn*!"

"Flynn?" asked Amy.

"Yeah, Flynn. He's a male, in a wheelchair, just like me! And it was dark, so they thought they were grabbing me, but—"

"They grabbed Flynn instead?" said Amy.

"Exactly!"

Amy looked at Elaine, believing that she was being pranked, but his wife nodded right along with Artie.

"Okay, well, we... we need to call the police and file a *missing persons* report," stated Amy.

She sat back in her chair, her fingers rubbing at her temples to try to thwart the oncoming headache that was brewing. Amy stared out their frost-covered kitchen window. She did not suspect the Ciminellos of foul play or that they were trying to cover anything up. They seemed to genuinely believe that... aliens had stolen the boy. She worried that Flynn was out there on his own, in the harshest winter she could remember.

Amy's day only got worse. Over the phone, the police argued with her because the boy had only been missing for a short time. She knew it was a myth that people need to wait a day or two before filing a report, but police had to deal with so many cases of runaway children from foster homes they were reluctant to venture out. Amy listened as the Ciminellos told the police what had happened – the cops traded skeptical reactions. She had mentally crossed the family off the list of future foster parenting assignments many hours ago. She watched as they searched Flynn's bedroom, trailed behind as they inspected the basement workshop.

While waiting for the police to finish, Amy plopped down on a sofa in the great hall and began to notice odd things around her – burn marks on the floor, pin holes in furniture and the walls, the lingering scent of fuel and burnt sulfur. Her thoughts started racing – what if this kid was some kind of pyromaniac, hell-bent on burning a house down, and he just wasn't very good at it?

"What are you up to, Flynn Myers?" she pondered.

31

The Barn

Mark spent the morning clearing snow paths to his truck and the barn, as well as working his daily chores around the farm as the kids slept. He gently carried Flynn's model airplanes out to store on the tool bench in the barn.

When he finished, Mark came in to find Flynn and Laura at the dining room table playing a board game. He grinned when he saw the assortment of boxes of cereal, as well as the cartons of orange juice and milk, still sitting out on the kitchen counters. Laura had obviously helped make Flynn feel welcome by providing breakfast for their guest.

Gray gnawed on a peanut as he and Tala watched Mark fish a business card from his jeans and dial the yellow phone hanging on his kitchen wall. The two mice were nestled between the toaster and the bread box on the counter. Gray offered Tala a piece of the peanut, which she took from him and chewed on while never taking her eyes away from Mark.

The man turned the rotary dial on the phone and then waited, with his ear to the receiver.

When no one talked back, he hung up the phone. He shook his head, staring at the card. "Of course, she's not there, stupid. It's Saturday."

He slid the business card between phone and the wall, walked off to join his daughter and Flynn as they played their board game at the dining table.

Tala nodded to Gray, saying nothing, and raced across the counter. She moved as close as she could to the phone for a better look at the business card. She could make out the name Amy on one side and the words Child Services. Tala hopped off the counter and raced off toward the bedrooms.

Gray turned his attention to the kids. They were playing a game called *Life*, which made Gray grin and shake his head. Little Laura was winning, obviously, and let everyone know it.

"I'm gonna send you guys to the Poor Farm!" she declared to Flynn and Mark, as she spun the spinner in the center of the board. She was practically lying on the table in order to reach the board.

Flynn looked at his short money pile. "I don't doubt that for one second."

Gray finished his peanut and sighed. The boy seemed happier here than any place so far. He hopped from his perch on the counter and ran down the hallway to the bedrooms.

In Flynn's room, the morning sun was shining through flowery curtains covering the window. The room seemed empty, but Gray knew better. After uttering a high-pitched squeal, Moki and Tala emerged from behind a picture frame on the nightstand. The photo was of a beautiful woman holding a baby in her arms and smiling at the camera, with sunlight highlighting her red hair from behind.

Gray swiftly climbed on the bed and dashed over to the two waiting on the nightstand, exchanging looks.

"Yo! What's shakin'?" asked Gray.

Tala and Moki looked at other, shrugged. "We are not unwell," announced Moki. "What news do you have for us, brother?"

"Well, the kid seems to really dig the place. The dad and daughter are pretty cool. I think this foster home might actually work out well. Which, um, leads me to the awkward part of the conversation…"

"You would like us to leave," said Moki.

"Um, well, yeah," said Gray, looking away from them. "It's for the best, I guess."

"What about you?" asked Tala.

"What about me? I mean… what do you mean?" Gray stammered, not expecting the conversation to turn back on him.

"Are you going to stay with the boy? Or would you like to... join us?"

Gray stared at her, lost in her eyes. They were amazing eyes. Laughter from the dining room, where the humans were playing the game of *Life*, pulled him back to reality.

"We need time to rest and gather stores for a journey. Will tomorrow be sufficient?" asked Moki. "You are welcome to come with us. We could use a warrior with your wisdom in our tribe."

"No, you don't have to haul outta here by tomorrow. Take some time. I know you guys have been through the wringer. I doubt those losers will ever catch up with you," said Gray.

"It would be best for the child if we set up camp out in the barn for our remaining few days. We thank you, brother," said Moki.

Gray looked from Moki to Tala then back to the chief. "Oh, the barn. Okay. You don't have to go to the barn but—"

Moki bowed his head in respect and backed away. His paw reached out to pull Tala away, as well, as her mouth had opened to add to the conversation. She gave Gray a final look and then disappeared behind the picture frame.

Gray wanted to say more as well, to call Tala back so he could talk to her, but he heard them jump off the nightstand and then pad away through a hole in the wall.

"Smooth, Gray. Real smooth."

Tala raced along between the walls, trying to keep up with Moki's long strides. He was older but still very nimble for such a large field mouse. They emerged from a newly chewed hole in the back of a long bathroom cabinet. The entire tribe of field mice were scattered among the cleaning products and rolls of toilet paper. Some took inventories of their limited supplies, treated wounds from their battle, or tried to sleep.

Dyani laid beside her child, Yuma, against a box of tissues, as Moki and Tala approached.

"I'm sorry I don't remember, momma," said Yuma.

"Shush, my little one. You were incredibly young when they took you. Your eyes had not even opened yet," soothed Dyani.

"But I did recognize your scent and your voices," said Yuma, smiling as

Moki approached. "As well as father's when you both entered the house."

Moki motioned for Kiona to approach the tissue box. "Yuma, my strong warrior. I need you to go with Kiona. She will find you food. We need to talk with your mother."

Yuma was hesitant to leave Dyani, but the young mouse took Kiona's paw and followed her toward their food stash.

"Is there a problem?" asked Dyani.

Moki and Tala huddled down on the warped, water-stained floor of the bathroom cabinet. Dyani crouched down on all fours to join them.

"We must relocate to the adjoining barn and prepare for battle," warned Moki.

"Battle? You believe Viho will find us here?" said Dyani.

"I do. Gray had a great plan to rescue Yuma, but I fear he did not consider the consequences. By removing the boy from his foster parents, those in charge will be forced to come looking for him. Tala saw the man of this house trying to communicate with the woman who drove Viho's tribe to the last house in her vehicle. If he summons that woman to this house..."

"Viho will, naturally, sneak aboard her vehicle and they will come with her," surmised Dyani.

"Yes, and we must be ready," said Tala.

"We have Yuma back! Why can they not accept defeat?!" bellowed Dyani.

"To do so is not in Viho's nature," admitted Moki. "Just like we could not give up."

"What if we simply leave here? Leave Flynn behind?" said Dyani. "They will have no easy way to find us!"

"They will not stop. We must end this, here and now," said Moki.

"Help me prepare the others for our move to the barn?" asked Tala, hoping to distract her from what was to come. Tala held out a paw and waited for Dyani to lead her away. She accepted Tala's paw, and they marched off toward the tribe. Moki beamed with pride as Yuma joined them and showed off the green grape he had been given.

Amy shifted her green Pontiac into *Park*, turned it off, but the old engine continued to cough and backfire for several humiliating seconds. She rolled her eyes and grabbed her manila folder on Flynn Myers, flinging open the squeaky car door. Struggling to stay upright, she marched off through the heavy snow toward her apartment.

Koko stood on the rear tire, under the shelter of the car wheel well, and watched Amy unlock her front door and flip on the porch light. More lights turned on inside the apartment. From the woman's actions, Koko surmised this was not the house of the next foster parent. She jumped to the rear axle and climbed up through the rusty hole in the trunk.

Viho crossed his arms as he waited for his scout to arrive. He could sense from her demeanor there was no good news in his future. "Well? What is the situation?"

"You were right. We will not find the Matwau here. This vehicle is parked outside the woman's home," said Koko.

"She may not know where the boy is located," said Viho. He stroked his whiskers in deep thought and paced back and forth on the floor of the trunk.

"We were wrong to travel with her?" queried Koko.

Without looking to her, he waved away her suggestion. "No, no. She will undoubtedly find the boy. She is, apparently, in charge of Dakota… I mean, Flynn. Since they left the last home without warning, questions will be raised, and this woman will be tasked with tracking him down."

Viho paused to watch Adriel working diligently inside the cockpit of one of the remote-control planes.

"We will wait then?" said Koko.

Viho looked around at his tribe in the trunk. They were all hard at work, preparing for their next battle. "We will wait. We have shelter from the winter storm growing outside. We have supplies. And we now have time to ready ourselves for the Blitzkrieg that we will bring down on the Matwau once and for all."

A mischievous grin fell across Koko's face. Her hunger growled at her from deep down and she responded, bounding off to find a morsel from their food supplies.

The giant barn was in better shape than most of the ones that Moki had set up camp in. The constant heat and cold of the demanding Ohio seasons had not yet taken a toll on the wide siding boards. The roof had no leaks. Floorboards were strong and the windows still held solid glass.

Moki waited patiently while the shaman Nodin, who had fervently insisted, performed his ritual. Nodin used ancient chants, passed down from their ancestors, and a rattle, to incarnate the good spirits living in the barn and warn away the bad spirits.

As Nodin finished his ritual, Moki marched forward and spun around dramatically, drew out his battered sword and waved it in the air – he wanted their full attention.

"Listen to me, my warriors!"

The murmurs and shuffling stopped. Moki's tribe looked up at the mighty warrior.

"I am going to ask those who are willing to make one more sacrifice! Our child has been safely returned to us!" stated Moki. He looked down at a smiling Yuma, as Dyani held him tight to her side.

The entire tribe shouted in triumph, bringing a smile to the old warrior's face.

"I do not know when, but I am sure they will come. Viho will want his revenge. So, if you have grown weary of the cold and the fighting and the running... and wish to part ways, you may do so.... with my respect. I will face them on my own, if I must. But I will run no longer! I will stand my ground, *this* ground, and fight!"

The mice in his tribe looked at each other and all around, then returned their gaze to the chief. Each pulled out a weapon – a sword, a bow, a knife, a spear, or a balled-up paw – and raised it in the air, followed by high-pitched battle cries that would have startled any foe they might have faced. Not one mouse turned to walked away.

"Then we must be ready, my warriors! This barn will be our battleground. This time, we will have the advantage – we will build our defenses, ready our weapons, and lay our traps!"

The tribe shouted out once again, pumped their paws in the air and held their weapons higher.

"Chuchip!" bellowed Moki. The strong, young warrior rushed to his side. "I want you to sharpen the swords and make sure we have more arrows than we could ever need."

Chuchip rushed off, gathering a few mice to help him.

Moki turned to his engineer. "Hinto, prepare those cursed wooden birds for a fight. We will need them both ready to fly," said Moki. Hinto nodded sagely and turned to the remote-control planes up on the tool bench.

"Kiona and Elsu!" He grinned at them as the handsome couple scrambled closer to him. "We should take advantage of the tall beams and ropes in this barn – I want a collection of swinging missiles we can release to combat their remote birds."

Both of the mice grinned at Moki, stared at each other, and dashed off into the barn.

Hakan, his fire expert, shuffled up to him. "My friend, here is where I need your expertise! Our enemy had a powerful advantage in our last encounter. We need to counter their bombs with a few explosives of our own. Can anything be done?"

Hakan flashed a devious smirk, fire blazing in his dark eyes, as he pointed a claw to the corner of the barn. Moki followed his gape. He saw several sealed cans of fertilizer for the farm.

Moki looked back at Hakan. "This is good?"

"This is *very* good," said Hakan, making an explosive sound and his paws mimicking the billowing of fire and smoke.

Moki clasped a big, strong arm around Hakan as they marched off toward the canisters of fertilizer. Yellow and black stickers, emblazoned on the sides of the cans, warned that they contained the highly explosive ammonium nitrate.

32

The Storm is Coming

The moon cast its gaze down on the frozen fields surrounding the Dobson farm.

Gray stood in the dark kitchen, on the skin windowsill, and chewed methodically on a baby carrot. He scanned the white barn across the snow-covered gravel lot, looking for movement. Every few minutes the cold wind blew the powdery snow in gusts, grabbing his attention.

"You guys are workin' pretty hard out there," said Gray to the darkness. He could sense Tala was just out of view.

She scampered up onto the sill to join him. He bit off a piece of carrot and handed it to Tala without looking at her.

"We're getting ready for our journey," said Tala.

"Sounds more like you're getting ready for another battle…"

"We are doing both. In the event they find us," said Tala. Her eyes were locked on his profile, trying to read his reaction.

He finally turned and looked her in the eyes. "Just in case, huh?"

"We could use a clever fighter like you. Join us."

Gray looked away, resumed watching over the driveway. "A city mouse runnin' with a bunch of field mice. My poor dead mother would roll over in her dumpster in shame."

"The boy is very special to you," said Tala. "But humans live for an exceptionally long time. Several generations. He will be without you…

someday."

"I know, I know. But I need to make sure he's settled, safe... and finally happy again. And that ain't gonna happen with your two tribes constantly throwin' down with each other."

"Why does a human matter so much to you?" asked Tala.

"Because he's family, Tala. He's all I got."

Tala sighed, reach out and held his paw. "You are a good mouse, Gray."

"I got good intentions. But that's about all," exhaled Gray.

Still holding onto his paw, she joined Gray in looking out the window.

Down the hall, Mark said goodnight to Flynn and flipped off his light. He strolled away to tuck in Laura.

Flynn tried to roll over in his bed, but the heavy cast on his leg threw him onto his back. He sighed loudly. He was so ready to get rid of that stupid cast. He scratched at the skin just on the edge of the cast.

"Hello, friend," said a voice.

Flynn grinned, looked around the bed to try to locate Gray. He did see a mouse, but it was larger than Gray. Flynn sat up in bed and looked down on Moki.

"Hey," said Flynn. His eyes quickly scanned the room to see if they were alone.

"We have not had the chance to formally meet. I am Moki, leader of the Shoshone tribe."

"I'm Flynn."

"I wanted to thank you for helping me return my son to his mother," said Moki.

"Well, I was kinda fighting for the other side," mumbled Flynn. "But I think I know what you mean."

"The fact is – you trusted your friend, Gray, and had faith in his judgement. That tells me a lot about your character. And, for that, I am thankful," Moki bowed his head in respect.

"Where is Gray?" asked Flynn.

"He is talking with Tala, one of the warriors in my tribe," said Moki. "They have formed a friendship, I believe."

"Isn't Tala a girl?" said Flynn. He wrinkled up his nose. Girls were gross.

"She is female, yes. I also wanted to let you know that we are leaving soon," said Moki. He watched Flynn's face to gauge his response.

Flynn looked away, lost in thought. He had images in his head of Gray and this Tala chick dancing through the corn fields, holding hands, and... kissing. Yuck!

"Is Gray going with you?" he asked, without looking at the chief.

"Gray is a cunning mouse. The way he talks leaves something to be desired but... he would be a welcome addition to our tribe," said Moki. He watched Flynn's head whip around, his eyes shoot daggers at him. "But he did not give any indication that he wished to join us. He seems content to be with you."

Flynn's shoulders relaxed and he smiled a little. "Well, it was nice to meet you, I guess. Even if it was just for a little bit. Good luck out there."

"Before I go, I have a question for you," said Moki.

"Um, sure. Go ahead."

"I must say... you are a master field commander. The tactics you used during that last battle were magnificent!"

Flynn smiled, his cheeks turning a slight reddish color. Flynn picked up a few of the World War II books he had lying on top of his bed covers. "They weren't really my ideas."

"Perhaps not, but you knew enough to read about the success of others and pass along those tactics," said Moki.

Flynn opened up one of the books, flipped it open to a page showing maps of the German occupations of Europe during the war. Moki peered over Flynn's arm to see images of soldiers with guns, tanks, and planes.

"I see. What was the tactic called where you had Viho's tribe attacking us so fast, in waves?"

"Ahh, hang on a sec," said Flynn. He flipped through several pages of the book to show Moki. "See, the Nazis fought differently in World War Two than the first world war. Instead of moving slowly and setting up camps and digging trenches and stuff, they just rushed in and fought hard. It was called the Blitzkrieg."

"Blitzkrieg? Strange term."

"Well, it's German, so…"

"What does it mean?"

"It means, well, kinda what they… well, we did to you guys… a quick, fierce and intimidating surprise attack. Most armies tend to fight each other slowly. Like your two tribes just firing arrows back and forth. Then, after a while, you get bored with that and you all sort of rush in. With a blitzkrieg, you focus on just one point of attack and you're supposed to be quick and maneuverable and brutal. It can be kinda scary when someone comes at you like that. When it frightens the enemy, they tend to run."

"That was your goal with us? To get us to run?"

"Yeah, my hope was to scare you guys off once and for all," said Flynn. "But that was before I knew you were fighting for your kid. I can't imagine I would ever give up trying to get my son back."

"Indeed," concluded Moki. "I must ask, if Viho decides to attack again, how would we counter this strategy? This *Blitzkrieg*?"

"Hmm. That's a good question. The first thing is that you now know about their tactic, so they've lost the element of surprise. The second thing that will help is that they need sort of a wide-open area to do this in. If you can put up impediments to slow them down, that takes away the speed advantage. Air superiority helps a lot, too. Having more planes than them, or at least better pilots, affects them a lot. Finally, you got to cut off their supply lines."

"That all makes for a good strategy, Flynn. I thank you again," said Moki.

"There's another thing that works. When the Nazis invaded Russia, at the battle of Stalingrad, they met a fierce resistance from the people in the city. The Russians were determined to win, or die trying, so they countered the Blitzkrieg with something the Germans called *Rattenkrieg*."

"Rattenkrieg? As in… rats?"

"Yep. It means Rat War."

"What an unfortunate name," mused Moki.

"Anyway, while the Nazis thought they could fight quickly but also slightly farther away, the Russians decided to get up *real* close to them. Since the

Nazis had air superiority, they first bombed the heck outta Stalingrad and figured the people would leave. But they didn't. So, the Germans had to go in and fight, like, from house-to-house," said Flynn.

"And that… slowed down these Germans," added Moki.

"Yes! This gave time for more Russians to show up and to attack the German flanks, coming around from both sides of the city. They cut them off from their supply lines, so they eventually had to surrender."

"Interesting," said Moki.

"What was supposed to take a few weeks took five months," said Flynn. "And it cost over two million lives. It was not pretty."

"War is never pretty, Flynn," stated Moki.

"Yeah. So, well… I'd avoid the *Rattenkrieg* option if you can," said Flynn.

"Wise words from a wise young man. I thank you for your help," said Moki. "I will let you rest now."

Flynn watched the powerful warrior mouse leap off the bed, land on all four paws, sprint across the floor, and disappear behind the dresser.

On Monday, Mark tried to reach Amy Regula through her office phone. When she didn't answer, the call was transferred to her colleagues in the office of the Franklin County Child Services.

Mark was hesitant to leave a detailed message with anyone else in Amy's office for fear of getting her in trouble. She had been rather kind to him, and since he had no idea how one of her charges ended up on his front porch on a cold winter evening, he simply asked that Amy return his call. He was reasonably sure Flynn had driven himself from his previous foster home. Through the frigid temperatures and heavy snow. Whatever had happened with the previous foster family it was severe enough – either due to the actions of the boy or the parents – that he needed to get away quickly. Mark refused to jump to any conclusions because he really liked Flynn. He seemed like a great kid. Laura liked him and she was an excellent judge of character.

After he hung up, Mark watched Flynn as he showed the young girl how to put together one of his model planes at the dining room table. Laura liked to take things apart, but she seemed content to watch the boy in the wheelchair assemble the plastic model using his pen-shaped hobby knife and tube of modeling glue.

If Mark were honest with himself, he really did not want to report Flynn's presence to Child Services. He was convinced they would load the kid up and haul him back to the foster facility or, even worse, to the previous home. But he knew Flynn was most likely considered missing and they were looking for him. It probably explained why Miss Regula was out of the office most of Monday.

He tried calling her again the next day. When she did not pick up her direct line at the office, he decided to talk to someone.

In the Franklin County Child Services office, dozens of people chatted away on phone calls and hustled about the room. Paul Julian heard the phone stop ringing at Amy Regula's desk. He continued typing away on his whirring Smith Corona electric typewriter until his phone rang. He let the phone ring a few times and then, with a sigh, picked up.

"Child Services. Paul Julian," he announced as he checked the piece of paper rolled up in the typewriter for errors.

Mark cleared his throat, unsure how to start the conversation. "Um, hello. Can I speak with Amy Regula?" Mark stared hard at the business card in his hand to make sure he pronounced her name correctly.

"Amy is out of the office this morning. How can I help you?" asked Paul, still checking the form in his typewriter.

"Uh, do you know when she'll be back?" said Mark.

"She's got a full case load as far as I know. Probably this afternoon. Maybe this evening," said Paul. "Can I get your name and number? Have her call you?"

"Could you let her know Mark Dobson called? She's got the number. I'll try again this afternoon."

"Okey-doke," said Paul to the phone receiver as he hung up the phone and grabbed his trusty bottle of correction fluid to fix one of the errors on the form. His phone rang again as soon as he dabbed the fluid on the paper, causing him to mess up the entire sheet. He torn it from the typewriter, started over with a fresh form.

Mark rolled his eyes and dropped the handset onto the phone base. He doubted the man at Child Services even wrote down his name. He pulled on a pair of gloves and headed out of the house to bring in more firewood.

He managed another call that afternoon, in between his chores and a quick sandwich for lunch. Amy Regula was again out, and he left his name and number with a woman. From what Mark could determine, it sounded like she was at least writing down his contact information.

On Tuesday morning, Mark was caught up in the weather report on his transistor radio as the sun was coming up. The radio weatherman warned of a winter storm front coming up toward the North from Texas as another front was moving down to Ohio from the Northern Plains states of Montana and Wyoming.

"We've had an entire winter in the month of January," Mark announced to himself, shaking his head. He knew he had an exceptionally long day ahead to prepare the farm for yet another storm.

Before he headed out the back door, Mark remembered he needed to call again. He dialed the number on Amy's business card and left another message with the guy he had talked to the first time he had called. Paul was his name. To make sure the guy took down his information, Mark made Paul read his phone number back to him.

That afternoon, Amy finally made it back to the Child Services office. She was weighed down by her purse and a stack of manila folders. She plopped everything on her desk and fell into her chair. She glanced at the new stack of folders that had filled her inbox shelf while she had been out trying to track down Flynn Myers.

Paul strolled over to her desk and dropped a handful of phone messages on her desk and if looks could kill then Amy's glare would have dropped him right there on the office floor. He smiled, sat on the corner of her desk. She sifted through the messages.

"Seems like you have an admirer," stated Paul, sipping coffee from a small Styrofoam cup.

"I don't have time for a mystery, Paul. Spit it out," sighed Amy.

He glanced down at her messages, selected one and held it up to her. "This fella has been quite persistent. I think he's called five times, in the past two days, looking for you," said Paul.

She took the small piece of paper out of Paul's hand. "Mark Dobson? Dobson…" repeated Amy, leaning back in her squeaky wood chair.

"Dobson. Dobson," she placed the piece of paper on her forehead to try to kickstart a memory. "Oh, yeah, I know this guy."

"If a guy could sound good-looking then… he sounded good-looking," said Paul. She gave him another glare. "What?"

"Don't start the match-making again, Paul. I'm warning you," said Amy, through gritted teeth.

"Hey, I'm all about the women's lib, Amy. But going out on a date, for the first time in what must be years, would not be a terrible thing for you," said Paul, holding his hands up in surrender. "You're still young. Ish."

She wadded up a piece of paper, threw it at Paul's face.

"Did he say what he wanted?" She examined the phone message.

"He just said to give him a call and gave his number," said Paul. "So, is he good-looking?"

"Well… yeah, I guess."

"Ding-ding! We have a winner! Call him!" shouted Paul.

"But he's a bit of a rube. A farm boy. Not really my type," sighed Amy. "He probably just wants a date. He'll say he wants to meet me for coffee or something."

She slid the phone message down under the bottom of the pile.

Paul gave her a sad, pouty face. "Too bad. So sad."

She shrugged and rolled her eyes as Paul shuffled off to the paperwork waiting on his desk.

While Laura was taking one of her forced afternoon naps – and they were always forced because naps are for little kids, she would inevitably argue – Flynn read a favorite World War II book with Gray. Flynn had parked his wheelchair in the living room so he could look out onto the porch and driveway. Gray would look up at the road that passed in front of the house, as vehicles passed back and forth, and then go back to staring at pictures in the boy's book. They were both expecting the worst – a car driving up that would take them away.

"The German Panther and Tiger tanks were nearly unstoppable during the war. They had better armor and more firepower than the Sherman tanks the Allies fought with," said Flynn, pointing to tank pictures in the book.

"Then how come the Germans didn't win?" asked Gray.

"Well, we got really good at making a *lot* of tanks and we kinda overwhelmed them with quantity over quality. Both sides kept trying to come up with better and better versions, but the Germans eventually ran outta time," said Flynn. He flipped to a page showing large, heavy tank. "But they also made a lot of bad decisions. They came up with one – the Panzer Maus – that was one of the heaviest tanks ever built."

"Wait. They called the biggest tank ever... the Mouse?"

"Yep, it was four times heavier than the biggest ones the Allies were developing," said Flynn.

"Ha! That's rich!" snorted Gray.

"That's sarcasm. I think," said Flynn.

"Kid, it's amazing to me how much time and effort the animals on this planet put into finding ways to kill each other," stated Gray.

"Yeah, but you have to protect yourself, too."

"I know, I know. You either gotta beat the other guy to get the food or... you become the food," Gray mused.

The mouse looked carefully over the photos in the book as Flynn looked down at his friend.

"Hey, kid. Did I ever tell you the one about the German soldier in the wheelchair? He was blown up by an Allied bomber because they thought he was a small tank! I bet he did *Nazi* that comin'!"

Flynn laughed out loud.

"Get it?! Not-see? Nazi?!" shouted Gray, laughing to himself.

"Yeah, yeah. I get it..." said Flynn. "Gray, I gotta ask... Are you going to leave?"

Gray closed his eyes. "I'm not goin' anywhere, kid. Unless you want me to go. You got a real good thing here, it seems. If you want me gone, I'll skedaddle."

"No!" Flynn bellowed out. He immediately realized his response was too loud, too quick. "I mean, you can hang out. If you want. For, you know, as long as you want."

Gray grinned, patted Flynn. "Thanks, kid. But, if you ever get tired of me or don't want me around, I'll be all right."

"That would never happen, Gray. Never."

"That's good to know. Let's just get Moki's tribe on their way and see if a little peace and quiet don't do us some good… for a change."

33

The Calm Before

Dark clouds rolled in on Wednesday morning and the temperatures curiously crawled higher and higher. Amy had spent part of her day at the police station, tracking down leads on Flynn's disappearance, and the other part placing a girl in a new foster home. As the afternoon turned to evening, she headed to her office for the first time.

The sun was long gone and, to add to the misery, rain began to fall. The bright white snow turned to murky gray slush under the wheels of her rusty green GTO. Her back tires didn't slip on icy roads at every turn like they had the day before.

She ran into the drab, gray building with file folders over her head to protect her hair from the rain. The day had been long enough without wrapping it up looking like a drowned rat.

Paul stood waiting at her desk, holding up her phone handset with his hand covering the mouthpiece. He held it out towards her as he mouthed out "It's him!" with a big smile on his face.

Amy stopped in her tracks, too tired to even roll her eyes, then marched forward and threw all her paperwork on her desk. She pulled the handset out of Paul's hand and took a deep breath.

"This is Amy Regula," she said, her fingers rubbing at her temples.

"Um, hi. This is Mark Dobson," she heard the man's voice on the phone say.

"Yes, what can I do for you, Mister Dobson?" she asked. Paul was doing a happy dance right behind her. She used her free hand to shoo him away.

"Well, I was wondering if… we could meet?" said Mark.

"Meet, Mister Dobson?" She wanted to ask why but knew that would not be the most professional way to handle the situation.

"I, um, have some questions for you," said Mark.

"Questions?" asked Amy.

"Yes, I can't talk about it now but was hoping, maybe, we could, uh, meet for coffee this evening?" said Mark.

Finally, she had the strength to roll her eyes. She pretended to sip coffee with her free hand – I told you so! – to Paul and he immediately threw his arms up like a cheerleader, doing rah-rahs, and spinning his hands with imaginary pom-poms to root her on and make her break out in a smile.

"Mister Dobson, I don't think that's a good idea—" started Amy.

Mark cut her off. "It's very important."

Back in his kitchen, Mark looked over his shoulder. Flynn had been watching *Sesame Street* with Laura over on the couch but was now staring directly at him. The boy knew something was amiss, but Mark could not bring himself to say his name during the phone call.

"Very important," Mark added.

"Is this… is this about Flynn Myers?"

"Yes," confirmed Mark.

"And he's there now?" asked Amy.

"Yes," Mark said. He looked over to Flynn, who was pretending to watch the TV show again.

"I'll be there in twenty minutes!" screamed Amy.

"No, but—"

Amy slammed the received down on the base. She scrambled to dig out Flynn's case file and find Mark Dobson's home address.

Mark looked at the phone, over to Flynn, then held the handset back up to his ear. "Okay, that'll be fine. Coffee tomorrow morning," he said to the dial tone buzzing in his ear.

Flynn snuck another peek at Mark, who had hung up the phone and tiptoed out of the kitchen and disappeared out the back door.

Amy's tired old windshield wipers struggled to keep the falling rain clear as she raced through the streets of Columbus. She kept checking the scribbled directions and address she had written down weeks ago on a folded sheet of legal paper.

With rush hour traffic and all the rain added to the wintry mix, it had taken Amy over an hour to get to Mark's house on the outskirts of town. When she finally pulled onto the long driveway and drove up between the house and barn, she spotted Mark deftly slinking out the front door.

Inside, the kids sat at the dining table, eating their macaroni and cheese. Flynn watched Mark slip out of the house.

The warm weather and cold snow on the ground created a thick fog which made it hard to see more than ten feet in front her. Amy was in such a frantic hurry that she left the headlights on and car door open and ran up onto his front porch.

"Where's Flynn?! Is he okay?! Show me where—"

Mark held up his hands, stood between Amy and the front door. "He's fine. Everything's okay."

"But—"

"Miss Regula? Can I talk to you for a second?" He was very calming, talking slowly and smiling.

"Yes, I'm sorry. It's just that he's been missing, and I've been so worried," she said, placing her hands on her hips and taking in deep breaths.

Flynn stared at the closed front door. He could sense that Mark was nervous, trying to hide something. With a quick whisper to Laura, who was concentrating on her macaroni, he wheeled his chair away from the table.

"Flynn is fine. He came here on his own on Friday and—"

"Friday?! It's Wednesday! Why didn't you call me? Call the police?" asked Amy.

"I've been trying to reach you. Like I said, he's fine. But I don't know anything about his situation. I don't know what happened to him or how he got here. And I couldn't just hand him over to the police. That might be way too traumatic. I knew I had to talk with you since you were his… case worker, or whatever you call it," soothed Mark.

"Okay. Okay, I get that. Sorry, I've just been freaking out over this. Not knowing where he is or if he's safe," said Amy.

"That makes total sense. He's a very smart, young man," said Mark.

Flynn wheeled up close to the front door, put his ear near the frosted glass of the sidelight next to the door.

"How did he know to come here?" asked Amy.

"He must've seen a list of potential foster parents. He literally attached a makeshift motor to his wheelchair and drove here through the snow and freezing weather," said Mark. "But I've got a favor to ask."

"What?" said Amy.

"I know you need to take him back to Child Services. I understand that. You need to sort through what happened. But if you could consider us, as a foster home, we'd love to have him. My daughter, Laura, just loves him to pieces. They get a long great and… I think he's a great kid. I'd love a shot."

"I'll see what I can do," she said, looking through the window to try to get a look at the boy in his wheelchair.

"I know you will. But I think it might be best, for him, if you could leave him here tonight? Let me break it to him that he has to go back? Give him a chance to mentally prepare?"

Amy looked up at Mark. She could see it in his face, his expression, that he really did want the best for Flynn. She exhaled hard, then gave him her best fake smile.

"Yes, that's no problem. Like I said, I'm just glad he's safe. Yes. Tomorrow morning is fine with me," said Amy.

"Listen, I'm an early riser. Farm boy, ya know?" said Mark. He smiled and it made her laugh a little. "Why don't I meet you somewhere close, for coffee?"

She smiled at him again, suddenly aware of that dimple in his chin and his cute, blond buzzcut hair. "Coffee would be great. Seven o'clock tomorrow morning? Where?"

"There's a little diner down the road called Stan's. I'll meet you there."

Flynn pushed his wheelchair quietly away from the front door.

"It's a date," said Amy. She heard herself say it. She couldn't believe she said it, but she did. She was aghast. "I mean, I'm... What I meant to... oh my God."

He grinned down at her. "I know what you meant. It's okay. I'll see you tomorrow morning."

He politely shook her hand while she stood there, mortified. After he went back inside the house, she balled up her fist and pounded the side of her own head.

"Stupid, stupid!"

Amy staggered back to her car. She noticed that her trunk lid was open. She didn't remember opening her trunk. Without thinking about it, she slammed the lid down and climbed into her car.

Viho and his tribe of mice waited behind a snow pile, in the rain, as they watched her back out of Mark's driveway and disappear into the foggy night.

He turned to his troops. "My warriors! The Matwau are here! The cowards are hiding in the barn. Set up camp under the porch! We attack at first light!"

The tribe shouted and raised paws in the air. They gathered their weapons and supplies and began to carry their radio-controlled planes and war supplies toward the house.

34

The Blizzard

The Blizzard

The oddly warm temperatures, rain, and fog from the day before had faded away during the night. They were replaced by a frigid cold and a fierce wind. Ice formed quickly on the roads but were covered by a heavy, blowing snow that began to fall before the sun came up.

Moki stood at the barn window over the tool bench, the cracked lens from the broken glasses held up to his eye, trying to get a better view of the house. It was still dark outside, and the wind was creating dozens of moving shadows.

Tala slid up onto the windowsill next to him. "Any sign of them?"

"Other than their stench? No... Not yet," said Moki. He wiped at the ice crystals that quickly formed on the window glass. "But they will attack soon. It is a certainty."

Tala looked around at all the barriers they had erected throughout the barn as well as the many traps. The tribe was scattered about, resting or sharpening spears or eating food, waiting for the battle to begin.

Under the front porch of the house, Maska lumbered up to Viho and Zaltana as she slid arrows down into the chief's quiver.

"We are ready for the assault on the barn," Maska said. "The airplanes have been fueled and primed. That wind may cause problems but we'll—"

Zaltana slammed the last of the arrows into the pack, moved precariously close to Maska. "That will not be a concern. We are not attacking the barn. We march on the house!"

"The house? You mean we are going to strike at the humans?!"

"And that traitorous mouse who helped the Matwau!" stammered Zaltana.

Viho slithered up next to his mate. "They are expecting us to engage them in the barn. They have had time to prepare. We will not fall into their trap."

"But… you think it wise to attack humans?"

"We will hurt them – or worse – if we can," snarled Zaltana.

"And we will draw the Matwau out of the barn. We shall end this once and for all," announced Viho. "Let the others know."

Maska stared at the chief and his mate. She put her paws against her sides, cocked her head to the side, and bared her teeth. Maska nodded, backed away toward the rest of the troops as they prepared for battle.

In the kitchen, Mark listened to the transistor radio as he buttoned up his flannel shirt and pulled on his heavy winter coat.

The weatherman sounded worried. "Folks, this is as bad as it gets. We've had two major storm systems converge over Ohio. We're experiencing a record-low pressure system; so low that some stations don't *show* a reading. This usually only happens during a hurricane! Snow is starting to come down heavy – we may see four to twelve inches fall today. And that wind is no joke, with forty to sixty mile-an-hour gusts possible. Be careful out there today. Don't leave the house if you don't have to. It's going to be one nasty blizzard!"

Mark threw on his baseball cap and grabbed his gloves and keys off the counter. The sun was just coming up, but he knew he had to leave early for the diner. Even with a four-wheel drive truck, the weather was not going to make for an easy trip.

He marched out of the house, across the porch, and into the harsh wind and blowing snow, to climb into his pickup truck.

Viho and Zaltana watched the big truck start up. The sturdy man climbed back out to scrape all the ice off the truck glass.

"It appears we have one less human to worry about," said Zaltana.

"Apollo smiles upon us, my beloved," said Viho. "We will have our revenge."

Smiles spread wide under their whiskers as they watched as the pickup carefully crawl along the snow-covered driveway to the main road.

Amy really hated the snow this morning. Like really, really hated it this time. The winter storm was causing absolute chaos on the streets. Those who were out in this blizzard were sliding off the roads or rear-ending other cars stopped at traffic lights.

Visibility was limited to no more than a dozen feet ahead of her car hood. She turned up her wipers, desperately trying to brush away all the new snow that was blowing hard onto her windshield.

She crawled through the city avenues and out toward the country roads to make her meeting with Mark on time.

Gray slept on a pillow next to Flynn's head when a host of familiar scents wafted past his nose. His eyes were wide-open as soon as he recognized the smell of mice. He hopped onto all fours and began tugging on Flynn's hair.

"Hey, kid! Holy smokes! Wake up!" Gray screamed.

"What? What is it?" mumbled Flynn, still lost in a sleepy daze. "Five more minutes..."

"No! You gotta get up! Now!" added Gray. He leaned in close to whisper in the boy's ear. "The Halona are here."

Flynn immediately opened his eyes. He sat up fast. Gray, who was still holding Flynn's hair, was flung down to the foot of the bed.

"The Halona? Wait... the bad guys we thought were good guys or the good guys we thought were the bad guys?!"

Gray rolled himself back over and sat up. "The former. I think. Whatever! The bad guys are here!"

Flynn pulled his wheelchair close and leapt over to the seat. He placed his cast on the leg rest and waited for Gray to jump over before backing up. They wheeled to the door and cracked it enough to see down the hallway. It was quiet, except for Laura who snored away, on her princess bed, in her bedroom.

"I don't see anything."

"They're here," said Gray. His whiskers ruffled as he sniffed the air. "I can tell."

"I believe you. What should we do?"

Gray realized Viho's tribe was between the bedrooms and Moki's field mice out in the barn. His mind began racing. They could lock themselves in Laura's bedroom, but Gray immediately conjured Bodaway and his flaming arrows catching the door on fire to smoke them out.

Gray took a deep breath. "Okay, kid. Here's the plan. We let the girl sleep, draw them away from her side of the house, and hope she doesn't wake up, ya know?"

"Couldn't I just run over all of them with my wheelchair?"

"You might get a few but they're no fools. A well-placed arrow or spear in your eye or one of their homemade bombs and you could be in a world of hurt, kid. Let's keep Laura safe for now and see how it plays out..."

Flynn's head nodded fast. Gray could tell the boy was frightened.

"Let's make a break for the back door. It leads to the barn, right? We'll warn Moki's people. Get 'em to scare these fools away. Everything's gonna be okay, kid."

Flynn quietly pulled his door open and rolled his wheelchair, by hand, across the hall to avoid the noise of the motor. It was nearly impossible to push across the wood floor with the heavy motor and battery attached.

He closed Laura's bedroom door as Gray stood watch, searching for movement from the living room.

The boy aimed his wheelchair down the length of the hallway, placed his fingers on the joystick controller, and turned to Gray. The mouse gave a quick nod – let's do this!

Flynn jammed the controller forward. The wheelchair rubber wheels bit into the wood floor and launched them down the hall.

Viho heard the whine of the motor. "Here they come! Attack!"

A group of archers lined up in the living room. Others held their spears at the ready.

The wheelchair raced out of the hallway and onto the foyer carpet. The thick shag slowed his electric wheelchair down, as they passed the front door and headed around the couch. Flynn and Gray kept their heads low. The metal chair zipped past the fireplace, toward the back door.

A volley of arrows whizzed through the air. Grunts came from the mice as they hurled their spears.

Flynn steered his wheelchair around the rack of fireplace tools, over a few of Laura's toys lying on the carpet, and into an ottoman near a chair in the living room. The wheelchair bounced off the ottoman, which went spinning off toward the couch.

A few arrows from the mice hit the wheelchair, glanced off. Many arrows hit Flynn's pajama shirt, falling harmlessly to the carpet. A few hit Flynn's neck, his arm, and some landed in his hair. They stung but were ineffective. One spear struck the boy's forearm and stuck, drawing blood.

"Ow!" screamed Flynn. He grabbed at the spear hanging from his arm, plucked it out, but Flynn accidently rammed the wheelchair into the recliner chair.

More arrows followed.

Gray ducked as they rained down from above. "Go, kid! Go!"

"I'm trying!" yelled Flynn. He pulled back on the joystick and the wheelchair zoomed backwards on the carpet. Several mice jumped out of the way of his rolling wheels.

Dozens more arrows fell on them as they raced on. Flynn slid his wheelchair to a halt next to the back door.

Spears and several arrows sunk deep into the wood as the boy threw open the door to the backyard and barn.

Flynn and Gray stared straight up at the opening – their mouths fell open.

The entire doorway was filled with snow, from top to bottom. They looked at each other in stunned silence.

The blizzard outside had blown snow up against the house, covering the entire back porch.

Flynn and Gray turned and looked behind them.

Viho's troops were marching toward them, bows and spears drawn.

When Amy's car slid up into the parking lot of the diner, she only saw one other car and Mark's white and copper truck. Since everything was covered by blowing snow, she created her own parking spot next his pickup.

She adjusted her rear-view mirror for one last check of her hair and makeup, but as soon as she opened the car door her hair was quickly rearranged by the severe wind. By the time she walked into the diner, the windshield of her car was already covered by snow.

Mark was alone, at a booth, with his breakfast plate and cup of coffee. Betty, the sad and weary waitress, looked up from the horoscope section of the newspaper and sighed. She plastered on her finest fake smile, grabbed the coffee pot, and shambled out from behind the counter.

"Um, I'm with him," Amy stated. She pointed at Mark. He stood up and waited for her to sit at his booth. She smiled to herself that he had stood for her arrival.

Betty shrugged as she flipped over and filled a coffee cup. "What can I get ya?"

"Coffee is fine. Thanks," said Amy.

Amy self-consciously made attempts to fix her wind-blown hair but then noticed the bacon on his plate.

"Are you going to eat that?" she asked, as she picked up a bacon strip and bit into it.

He grinned. "I guess not."

"Okay, look. We've got to move fast. This weather is getting worse by the minute. You told Flynn I was coming?"

Mark squirmed a bit in his seat, avoiding eye contact. "Well, yes. No. I mean I didn't think it was the right time—"

"You didn't tell him?! That was the whole point of giving you until this morning! Geez. I thought he needed time to process this?"

"It's just that he's a great kid. And I—"

"And you were hoping that I would just let him stay because you're such a terrific guy, right? He is a 'missing persons' case with the cops right now! We've been looking for him for days! I need to produce a body," Amy stated. Then she winced when she realized how that sounded. "Well, so to speak."

"I know. I know," said Mark. "I'm worried that he'll get tossed around again and end up in a bunch of different homes. He's really happy with me and Laura. Just ask him."

"I have a job to do, Mister Dobson. My hands are tied. I need to take him back to Child Services. It was your job to soften that blow."

Amy grabbed his fork and took a quick bite of his scrambled eggs. Mark could only stare at the snow pelting the window of the diner.

"Why this kid? What's so special about him?" asked Amy.

"I've been in his position. I kinda know what he's going through," said Mark.

"You were in the system?"

"No, not really. My dad died when I was six months old. But my mom? Oh, she was a piece of work. She hit the bottle hard, probably after my dad passed. She'd go on these benders for days. She couldn't hold onto a job. We eventually lost the house…. when I was about Flynn's age. For a while, we were living out of the car. Anyway, long story short, I joined the Air Force before I could get drafted into the Army, I guess, and—"

"So, you were in Vietnam?" She grabbed a slice of his wheat toast off the plate and took a bite.

"No, I was actually stationed in Guam and eventually Hawaii. I worked in logistics mostly."

"Logistics? That would bore me to death." Amy grabbed his fork and stabbed several bites of scrambled eggs.

"Actually, it saved my life. I was responsible to distributing food. I learned a ton about it – how to grow it, transport it, and the quantities needed," said Mark.

"Speaking of food…" said Amy. She pulled his entire breakfast plate over and began eagerly eating the rest of it. "Go on," she said, between bites.

"When I was done, I came back to Ohio and bought my farm. It gave me a sense of purpose. Who knows what would have happened to me if I hadn't learned what I did?" said Mark.

"Cool story but how does it apply to Flynn?" asked Amy. She waved her empty coffee cup at Betty the reluctant waitress.

"Right now, he's got no purpose. He's alone. He's scared. And growing up in the foster care system probably won't help matters."

"Thanks," she said, dripping with sarcasm.

"You know what I mean. Besides, my wife always wanted to have two kids. And, well, since that's not going to happen, I thought I'd restore the balance," said Mark.

"Restore the balance? Whoa. That's some Grade-A, kung-fu, Confucius stuff right there," whispered Amy.

Mark laughed. "Well, I think the term you're looking for is Buddhist. While all the other airmen went off to the chapel on Sunday mornings, I visited the local temple."

"You keep getting more and more mysterious and intriguing, Mister Dobson. Carry on, soldier."

"Airman," he corrected.

She pointed his fork at him and winked.

"Well, since I'm not getting married again, I figured why not try being a foster parent. And when you told me about Flynn's case, I—"

"Wait, wait, wait… you're not getting married again?" asked Amy. "Like *ever*?"

"No, ma'am. Candace was the one. She was my soulmate," stated Mark.

"So, there are five billion people on this planet. More than half of them are women. And you only get *one* soulmate? That doesn't sound fair," said Amy, finishing off his toast.

"Like I said, Flynn's a good kid. And we want to help. Laura really likes him and she's the very definition of the word *picky*," admitted Mark. "Anything you could do to—"

"Relax, Mark. We're going to make it happen. I'll recommend you as his next foster parent. But I still need to go through the motions and take him back to group home until we sort it all out. Okay?"

"Okay," he said. "Thank you."

"So, back to this whole 'never getting married' thing…"

35

The Final Battle Begins

Flynn sat in his wheelchair guarding Gray, who was hunched down in his lap, with his arm around the mouse. A half dozen spears and arrows were stuck in his forearm and the back of his hand. Another half dozen had struck the palm of Flynn's hand as he held it up to protect his own face.

Maska notched another arrow to fire it from his large bow but paused, turned to look back at his chief. "Viho, this does not seem fair!"

Viho rushed to push his nose and whiskers in close to Maska's face. "Losing my child was not fair! This is war, Maska!"

Reluctantly, and not with all his strength, he drew his bow string back and fired at the child cowering in the wheelchair.

Gray popped up from behind Flynn's arm, cupped his paws over his mouth. "We gotta get outta here, kid!"

"We can't leave here! They'd find Laura and attack her, too!"

"We have to do something!" shouted Gray, ducking back behind Flynn's arm as another arrow flew by his head.

The wall of snow in the doorway behind them began to crumble. A huge chunk fell, with most of it falling down Flynn's back and into his pajama shirt.

The boy sat forward, eyes and mouth wide open. "Oh! That's cold!"

Through the new opening in the door, a flood of field mice poured into the room. Moki's tribe rushed over the snowbank, firing arrows as they jumped to the carpet.

"Attack!" Moki shouted, rushing forward with a spear in his paw.

The tribe took up a defensive position around the wheelchair, firing their arrows and launching spears at Viho's warriors.

"Fall back!" shouted Viho.

His mate, Zaltana, rushed to his side. "We must not give up our position! We have them cornered!"

"I was expecting Moki's arrival, my dear," Viho said as his paw patted her arm. "Launch the toys!"

Maska raised his massive arm to signal little Wamblee, by the open front door. Wamblee spun around to throw his arms into the air.

Snow had already covered the path, cleared by the mice, on the porch. But they threw the propellers down, starting the primed engines, and backed up as the planes rushed forward.

The Fokker Dr.1 triplane was the first to take off because it needed less runway space.

The Mustang P-51 fighter was right behind. Wind buffeted the wings but the engine revved higher, pushing it through the doorway. Once in the house, the Mustang lifted off and veered off to the living room.

Flynn and Gray immediately recognized the buzzing sound of those remote-control planes. They saw the two planes flying right at them. Flynn could see mice in the cockpits, but a quick search revealed no one on the floor holding the remote transmitters.

"They put the controls inside the planes!" shouted Flynn.

"What?!"

"Look! The mice are flying the planes! They're able to go around walls with no transmitter interference. And I don't see anyone operating them on the ground," said Flynn.

The Fokker triplane and the Mustang monoplane zoomed straight at the mice trapped by the back doorway.

The Mustang had two Roman candles taped under the wings. Inside the cockpit, Fala flipped a homemade switch next to her seat. A wire led out of the cockpit, under the right wing, to the multi-colored cardboard fireworks tube. It emitted a spark, lighting the wick of the candle.

"That's not good," said Gray, moving back behind Flynn's forearm.

"Oh, crap… Get down!" Flynn shouted.

Moki and his mice dropped to the carpet, paws over their heads.

Roman candles are made up of a long cardboard tube that is filled with colorful pyrotechnics. The balls of fire shoot out at intervals as the wick burns through the tube. The first ball fired from the wing of the Mustang was red. A loud whistle echoed out as the flaming ball shot directly at Flynn. He tucked his head down as the ball whooshed into the bank of snow behind him, sizzling and melting the snow. When it exploded, snow and ice chunks sprayed over everyone in the living room.

The second ball was blue. It fired from the plane and exploded on the carpet next to Flynn's wheelchair. Chuchip was closest to the blast – he was lifted off the floor and flipped through the air, landing several feet away. He staggered to his hind legs, dazed from the blast. Flynn used his good leg to stamp out the blue-burning flame on the carpet.

Fala pulled her controller to the left, sending the Mustang off deeper into the living room to avoid hitting the wall.

Sitting in the Fokker triplane, made famous by the Red Baron, was the warrior Tarsha. She steered the slower plane directly at the mice near the doorway. The strong blizzard winds rushing in buffeted the airplane, but her paws held strong on the joystick helping to maintain control.

Tarsha gave a quick look behind her. In the rear cockpit, Taima was fast asleep.

"Taima! Wake up! Now is not the time!" bellowed Tarsha.

Taima stirred in her seat, grabbed a small bag, filled tight with gunpowder, and touched the bomb's wick to a live electrical wire positioned next to her seat. The wick lit and she peered over the edge of the cockpit.

Tarsha banked her triplane as they flew over Flynn and the mice. Taima dropped her first bomb and picked up another lying at her feet. She lit the next one and dropped it over the other side of the cockpit.

Both bombs exploded in front of the wheelchair. One sent chunks of carpet flying everywhere. The other went off next to the ottoman, shattering the wood leg. The ottoman lurched to the side, causing the mice that were perched on top to topple to the floor.

As Fala steered her Mustang back toward the front door, in order to make another bombing run, a yellow firework shot out of the Roman candle under her wing.

Viho and his troops ducked down to avoid the blast. "Fala, be careful!" Viho screamed.

Fala shrugged in the cockpit. "It is beyond my control once it has been lit!" she bellowed back down.

The next blue flaming ball shot out and bounced off the front window of the house and back down to the floor, rolling along and whistling until it exploded on the far side of Flynn. He held his hands up to shield himself from the blast.

"Fire!" commanded Viho to his warriors.

His archers took up their positions and pulled back their bows. They sent a volley of dozens of arrows down on their enemy.

Gray popped up from behind his arm. He noticed that Enola, the albino mouse, had been struck in the back by an arrow. He watched her limp to the back of their defensive line to allow Hinto to remove the arrow and patch up her bloody wound.

"This is crazy! We've got to do something!" Flynn shrieked.

"Right on, kid! Grab everybody and let's book!"

"No, I mean we gotta get our planes! We need to fight back," said Flynn.

"Fighting is not the answer, Flynn!" shouted Gray.

Flynn ignore his friend and scooped up Moki in his hand. "I'm going to go grab our planes. Can you cover us?"

"I would understand if you did not return, Flynn. This is not your fight," said Moki.

"I'll be back! I promise!" said Flynn. "We just can't let them have air superiority."

"We have your back, my brother! But I fear it may be time for... Rattenkrieg," stated Moki.

That word sunk deep into Flynn's mind. His shoulders sagged; his head dropped down. He knew what that meant.

"Can't you jerks just high-tail it outta here?!" pleaded Gray.

Moki ducked as an arrow whizzed past his ear. "No, brother. They would hunt us down from behind and we would be doomed. If we are to die today, we will be facing our enemy."

Hapless, Gray threw up his paws and turned away.

More arrows fell on them, dragging Flynn back into the moment.

A flash of anger crossed his face and he pointed to Moki. "Take cover in the living room! Move behind the couches. No Rattenkrieg until I get back!"

Flynn set Moki down behind the broken ottoman. Moki waved to his troops and they followed him deeper into the living room, with its couch and chairs and tables providing cover from falling arrows and bomb-dropping planes.

Betty poured out coffee refills for Amy and Mark and gave a long look out the window.

"Now, this is just me talking... but if I had somewhere to be... I'd be trying to get there, quick like," said Betty.

When they looked up at her, they quickly followed her gaze out at the massive amount of snow continuing to pile up against their vehicles.

Mark and Amy gave each other a quick look.

"Check, please," said Mark.

"Smart man, there," said Betty. She winked at Amy and schlepped her coffee pot back behind the counter.

They quickly stood, wrapping themselves up for the severe weather outside. Mark looked around the empty diner and pulled out a ten-dollar bill and set it on the table. Amy took notice that he was going to over-tip to make up for Betty's lack of customers. She let another smile slip out as she wrapped a scarf around her neck.

Mark waited for her at the door, pulling on his gloves. "I should probably drive you. It's going to be rough out there."

"I'll be fine. You take care of yourself, soldier."

"Airman," corrected Mark. He smiled back when she grinned at him. "Follow me. Visibility is bad out there, so keep your headlights on so I can see you. Okay?"

She nodded. He shoved the door open but met serious resistance from the strong wind.

They pulled their hats down and rushed out into the blizzard.

36

The Mouse Trap

Flynn blasted through the huge bank of snow that had filled the back doorway. He kept the joystick controlling his wheelchair jammed forward and they raced across the small porch.

Snow had built up against the steps, creating the perfect ramp. They launched off the porch and landed in the snow. The thin wheelchair wheels dug deep, gripping the gravel on the drive. Big chunks of snow blasted Flynn and Gray as they plowed along. Biting cold wind blew through the fur on the mouse and boy's thin pajamas.

They bounced and fishtailed their way straight to the barn. Flynn struggled to pull open the door but managed a big enough gap to fit his chair through the opening.

Gray put his paws on Flynn's hand, before the boy could drive them into the barn.

"What are you doing?! We've got to hurry!" shouted Flynn over the wind.

"Moki may have booby-trapped the joint!" replied Gray. The mouse slowly pushed the wheelchair controller forward and they inched across the threshold.

The small front wheels ran over fishing line that had been stretched across the doorway. This triggered a big concrete block, attached to a beam above, to drop. The concrete block pivoted and swung down toward Flynn's wheelchair.

"Look out!" shouted Gray. He pulled the joystick back. The chair wheels spun on the gravel, grabbed hold, and pulled them out of the way. The concrete block swept in front of them, just missing Flynn's cast.

"Whew! That was close." said Flynn.

"Too close. They were expecting Viho's tribe to come marching through the front door. We gotta be careful in here, kid. There may be more."

The mouse pushed the joystick ahead with both paws. They both looked high and low as they slowly moved into the barn.

"See anything?" asked Flynn.

"No, nothing."

The wheels drove over something buried under the gravel on the barn floor. They both looked at each other. Gray shoved the joystick hard, to the right, toward the tool bench up against the wall.

A wooden beam, attached to ropes, dropped from a hiding spot behind a beam supporting the hay loft. It plunged down and swept across the barn floor, designed to clean away a tribe of mice walking in.

The wheelchair raced to the side as the beam moved down and then along the gravel floor. The end of the wooden shaft caught the big wheel on the wheelchair as it passed by. Flynn's chair spun around in a complete circle. Gray held onto the arm as Flynn put his arms in front of his eyes, screams streaming from both.

They came to rest right in front of the tool bench. Gray immediately hopped from the arm of the chair to the surface of the table. He pushed the Sopwith Camel remote-control biplane toward the edge of the tool bench. Flynn grabbed it off the table. His fingers were able to touch the transmitters and he pulled them to his lap.

Gray returned for the P-47 Thunderbird model. He rolled it along the table until Flynn could pick it up. He quickly jumped onto Flynn's lap. He climbed to the arm to control the joystick, pulling hard to take them in reverse.

"What about the booby traps?!" shouted Flynn.

The wheels spun on the gravel and bit hard. They launched backwards.

"There's no time for the booby traps, kid!"

The wheelchair backed to a stop just past the open barn door – triggering another trap. A large hole had been dug to the side of the door and covered with a thin tarp and small sticks. Flynn's left side wheel broke through one of the flat sticks. The tarp fell in and they nearly toppled down into the hole. Both looked down in terror to see sharp wood spikes, sticking up in the air, waiting for them to fall in.

"Lean right! Lean right!" shrieked Gray.

Both the boy and the mouse shoved all their weight to the right side of the wheelchair. But they stayed there, suspended over the terrifying hole. Teetering. On the edge.

Flynn extended his arms, holding out both remote-control planes.

They slowly rocked back over, and the right wheel touched back down on the barn floor.

Gray shoved the joystick forward. The left wheel spun in midair, but the right rubber wheel dug into the dirt floor and yanked them away from the deep hole.

He pushed the controller to the right, they zoomed out of the barn and back into the deep snow and hard-driving wind.

Amy wiped at her fogged windshield as her wipers rattled back and forth, trying to keep up with the blizzard. The strong wind pummeled her car as she drove slowly behind Mark. Visibility was terrible – she couldn't see anything ahead.

They inched along through the dense slush as wind and falling snow blasted across the two-lane road. No other traffic was out on the streets this terrible morning. The Department of Transportation plows were busy working the main thoroughfares in the city, dropping salt and pushing snow. They would not get around to these country roads until much later, if ever.

Amy grew impatient. He was driving too slowly. Fears of getting snowed-in or trapped somewhere flooded over her. She pulled her Pontiac out to see if anyone was ahead of him that was slowing him down. No one was in front of his truck.

She returned to her lane but her right front tire lost traction.

253

"Oh, no! No, no, no!"

Amy turned the wheel to the left, but the car kept sliding. She gently applied the brakes. The wheels grabbed the road for a second. Then she hit another patch of ice. She continued sliding. She turned the wheel farther to the left, hitting the brakes again.

The Pontiac skidded off the road, down into a rain ditch that ran along the side of the road. So much snow had fallen and been blown over into the channel that the side the car was completely buried. Her left wheel was suspended in the air, spinning uselessly. The weight of the car shifted, pulling it farther down into the embankment.

"Tell me you saw that, Mark!" she screamed at the white truck slowly driving away from her, down the snowy road. "Mark!"

She honked her horn, but the sound was muffled by snow that buried the front end of her car.

37

The Cornered

Flynn and Gray burst through the snowbank on the porch and into the farmhouse. Flynn ducked down to avoid spears and arrows, gripping both planes in each hand, as Gray steered the wheelchair around the ottoman and to the back of the living room.

Moki and his tribe were surrounded. They took advantage of cover provided to them, hiding under the couch, coffee table, an armchair, and an end table. They would randomly rise up or peek around the corner to fire weapons only to hide when the enemy would rain arrows down on their position. And they were closing in.

Gray halted the wheelchair behind the worn couch. Flynn bent as far forward as he could to avoid getting shot in the eye.

Moki rushed to greet them. He had an arrow that had pierced his skin, just under the fur. Like someone swatting away an annoying fly, he yanked the arrow from his shoulder.

"We are out of time, brother," snarled Moki. "They are using the Blitzkrieg tactic again, moving towards us quickly in waves."

"I know. I've got the planes now," said Flynn, holding up the remote-control biplanes. "We need to push them back with bombs of our own and cut off their supply lines."

"Supply lines?"

"They had several days to prepare for this battle. They have a huge supply of arrows, spears, and fireworks. They probably stored it under the front porch," said Flynn. "Which means they're bringing it all in through the front door. If we can take that out—"

They both ducked as the Fokker triplane flew overhead and Taima dropped several small bombs on them. One detonated on the top of the couch, sending foam pieces flying into the air.

"That will not be enough, brother! We are nearly surrounded, and they are upon us!" shouted Moki, his tiny ears ringing from the small but devastating explosions.

"Kid, we got no runway! How are we gonna launch these suckers?" asked Gray.

Flynn took a quick look around the room. "I've got an idea. Prep the planes, Gray. Moki, did you guys bring those bombs you made?"

Moki turned to Dyani and Hakan who were standing behind the couch. He nodded to his mate. Dyani and Hakan pulled off the packs on their backs, opened the flaps, and revealed homemade bombs made from the fertilizer they had found in the barn. Hakan had a huge grin plastered on his little mouse face.

"Good! Get 'em loaded in the planes! And we're going to need pilots! Go! Go!" yelled Flynn.

Flynn returned his attention to Moki, leaning down farther as more arrows fell on their position. "I need you to flank them. Send a team along the back of this couch and hit them from the side. That gives them two fronts to fight on instead of advancing on just one! Got me?!"

Moki bowed. He called Chuchip to his side. The young warrior ran to his chief, nodded, and ran off.

"I trust you, brother," said Moki. Flynn blushed but doubts crept in – he hoped he was doing the right thing.

Mark could only see a few feet in front of his truck. Snow was falling and blowing so hard that everything ahead of him was pure white. He strained to make out the road ahead to avoid driving off an edge.

For a brief second, he checked his rear-view mirror. The headlights from

Amy's car were gone. He slowed down but did not want to come to a complete stop, or she might ram him from behind. When she did not catch up, he realized something was wrong.

"Whoa. That's not good," whispered Mark. "Not good at all."

Mark looked for a driveway to turn around in but found nothing. He made an instant decision to risk turning around in the middle of the road. He made a wide, quickly shifted into reverse when his truck was at the edge, backed up, and dropped it into drive. He was finally able to breathe again once he was headed back toward town.

He found her car quickly. She had slid into a ditch on the side of the road and even his four-wheel drive would not be able to pull her out. It was going to take a tow truck and there was zero chance of that happening during the blizzard.

Mark pulled into a driveway close to where she had crashed. The wind tried to pull the handle out of his hand when he opened the truck door. He managed to push it closed and moved as quickly as he could through snow that had drifted above his knees.

"Amy! Can you hear me?" screamed Mark, over the heavy wind. "Amy?!"

His gloved hand knocked against the window. He yanked off the glove, hit his knuckles hard against the glass. There was no response.

Mark realized that her car was still running. Amy had probably left it on to supply heat.

Ice had formed on the glass and it was steamed-up from the inside so he could see nothing. He yanked on the door handle, but the door was either locked or stuck.

He pounded on the window again but got no reaction from her. "Amy! Open the door, Amy!"

The glass was too thick to shatter with his bare hand. He rushed back to his truck to find a tool, any tool, to break her out.

Inside the car, Amy was laying back in her seat with her eyes closed. Exhaust fumes floated in through the rust holes in the trunk. She thought she had heard some thumping or pounding sounds, from somewhere off in the distance, but she was so tired. Sleepy. Just wanted to keep her eyes closed and sleep. Forever.

Chuchip and a dozen warriors emerged from the far side of the living room couch with their arrows notched. The Blitzkrieg maneuver kept the focus on Viho's troops on the front lines, heading directly toward the coffee table. They were not expecting an attack from the side. Chuchip ordered his troops to fire arrows.

Tate noticed movement to their flank. "Everyone, down!"

The tribe around Tate stopped marching forward and hunkered down, their shields held over their heads. Arrows fell on them, striking and sticking into their homemade shields.

Flynn waited until the crude bombs had been loaded into the cockpits of the planes. He watched Sakari climb into the P-47 Thunderbird "Razorback" monoplane and wave that she was ready.

Tala hopped on the wing and into the cockpit of the Sopwith Camel biplane. She nodded to Flynn and gave a wink to Gray. Hinto scrambled to the propeller of the Thunderbird, primed it a few times, and gave it another hard pull. It cranked right up. Hinto moved over to the Sopwith to repeat the procedure.

"Gray! Drive the wheelchair from behind here and then down along the couch as fast as we can go!" Flynn shouted over the buzzing from the propellers.

Gray quickly realized the kid's plan, nodded, and hopped up to the arm of the wheelchair to grab the joystick. Flynn set the transmitters on each side of his legs, then scooped up the planes and gave a wink to Gray, which made the mouse roll his eyes. Flynn smiled.

His tiny paws pulled the joystick to the right, rotating the wheelchair, and then shoved it all the way forward. The rubber wheels hooked hard into the thick shag carpet, driving them along the couch with the small front wheels up in the air.

"We're doin' a wheelie!" screamed a gleeful Gray.

Flynn held up both planes. "Faster!"

"The pedal's to the metal, kid!"

Tate and the front-line troops had to jump out of the way to avoid being run over by the rolling chair wheels. Chuchip and his team cheered as Flynn raced by. When they got close to the fireplace, Gray veered them to the right with the wheelchair accelerating along the way.

Flynn threw both planes high into the air. Both Sakari and Tala gripped their paws to the sides of the cockpit, their eyes wide, as they started to drop down. Flynn handed Gray a controller. They both hit the accelerators and lowered the flaps, causing both planes to fly faster and rise toward the ceiling.

Arrows and spears from Tate's warriors fell upon them once again. Maska's second wave, behind Tate, released their volley.

Flynn used his thumb to operate the transmitter with his left hand while the fingers on his right hand gripped the wheelchair joystick. He managed to back them out of the line of fire while keeping the Thunderbird in sight. Flynn backed them behind one of the chairs in the living room as Chuchip's band surrounded them, providing cover.

"Aim Tala toward the front door!" shouted Flynn.

Gray steered his controls to adjust the course of the Sopwith Camel. In the biplane, Tala grabbed a match from a small stack by her side. She struck the match against the rough wall of the cockpit, lighting the flame. With her other paw, she grabbed one of Hakan's homemade bombs.

Standing on the kitchen counter, overlooking the living room, Viho studied the trajectory of the enemy planes. He looked back at his tribe's stash of stolen fireworks as well as their huge stack of arrows and spears that they had made while waiting in the trunk of the vehicle.

Viho pointed toward the Sopwith and the Thunderbird. "Stop those planes! Stop them!"

As Tarsha made a pass by the kitchen to turn around, she noticed Viho shouting and waving his arms. She followed his claw, which was pointed at the enemy planes headed toward them. She steered her Fokker triplane up and out of the kitchen.

Sakari had her small bomb ready to go but froze when she saw the triplane flying directly toward her.

"I did not sign up for this!" Sakari screamed.

Flynn noticed the triplane. "Look out for the Fokker!"

Gray saw the enemy plane on a collision course.

"Watch your language, kid." He chuckled to himself.

The Sopwith Camel veered to the left and the Thunderbird to the right as Tarsha's triplane flew between them.

"Do not mess with me!" screamed Tarsha.

Taima, trying to nap in the back cockpit, shifted around to get more comfortable. "Calm down, Tarsha."

Flynn had no choice but to fly Sakari, in her Thunderbird, out the front door. The small plane was instantly struck by the strong wind outside, throwing her into a deadly spin.

Gray forced the biplane into a spin, sending Tala against the cockpit as she struggled to keep her match flame away from the balsa wood. He cut back on the throttle, pulling the Sopwith Camel around again. Tala sat up, lit the fuse on her small bomb.

Flynn tried to locate the Thunderbird out the front window. Without seeing her and knowing of the fierce winds outside, he flew the plane to the left and gave it more throttle. He finally saw a wing dip down from the sky. He pushed up the flaps and ailerons, shifting her farther to the left. Sakari's P-47 Thunderbird sailed back into view. The tiny plane was buffeted by the wind from the storm, pushing her back toward the house. Flynn bit his lower lip, trying to line her up with the front door.

Tala was about to drop her bomb when the P-51 Mustang, with Fala in the cockpit, swooped in next to her. Fala rammed her wing against the biplane's lower wing, veering it wildly off course. Tala inadvertently dropped her homemade bomb - which tumbled to the floor below, detonating on the seat of a reading chair next to the front window. Tala rolled her eyes and gave the wind-up motion to Gray, back in the living room, demanding that he make another run.

Mark fought his way through the deep powder that had accumulated on the side of the road. The wind had driven snow across Amy's car to the point that it was part of the landscape.

He smashed through the driver side window, with a hammer from his toolbox that he kept behind his truck seat. Shards of glass showered the unconscious Amy, who was slumped over and held in place by the lap seatbelt at her waist.

"Amy? Can you hear me? Amy!" said Mark.

He unlocked her car door and struggled to pull the damaged door free from the car.

"Wake up, Amy. Stay with me," he said. He felt for a pulse on her neck, then pushed up her eye lids to see if there was a pupil response.

Wincing, Mark slapped her cheeks as light as he could. She moaned, murmured, tried to push his hand away.

"There you are," said Mark. "Let's get you out of here."

Mark unclipped the seatbelt and put both strong arms underneath her. He managed to pull her up out of the car without slipping down the side of the ditch. After laying her in the thick snow, Mark adjusted her position and then hoisted her over his shoulder. Slowly and carefully, he began the long slog back to his truck.

"Whoa, this is not easy," said Mark to himself.

"Did you… just… call me… fat?" slurred Amy.

He smirked as he fought against the wind, carrying her on to the pickup.

38

The Rat War

Moki took advantage of the confusion in the skies above. He summoned his tribe close with a high-pitched scream and a wave of his paw.

"My warriors! If we are to survive, it is time to follow the strategy from brother Flynn! We will take away the advantage of their deadly arrows and fight them up close. It is time for the Rat War!"

Though many were injured, every mouse lifted his or her paws in the air and feverishly screamed.

"Attack!" screamed Moki.

He ran past his troops with his sword held high, and they spun around to follow him into battle. Their loud screams echoed through the house.

Tate and his first wave of mice were unprepared for the assault. Moki's troops were on them in an instant, while the first wave still held their bows. Several managed to fire arrows at the onrushing mice but most of the shots bounced off shields or missed entirely.

Maska, in the second wave, held up his paw as his troops aimed their bows at the attackers. There was no way to avoid hitting the first wave. He grimaced, pulled out his sword.

The third wave of Viho's tribe lowered their bows as well, unsure of what to do next. Viho was pre-occupied with the planes battling overhead.

Sakari's claws dug deep into the sides of the cockpit as her plane fell through the front door, carried along by the strong winds outside. Flynn's fingers furiously worked the plane's transmitter but could not regain control.

The Thunderbird tumbled toward the wall.

Tarsha steered her triplane directly toward the Sakari's uncontrolled remote plane.

Frustrated, Flynn looked up from the transmitter. "Jump! Sakari, jump now!"

Overcome with fear, the small mouse looked back toward Flynn and then way down to the floor below. The wall was getting close, closer.

Sakari stood in her cockpit, pulling out the small cloth napkin attached to her shoulders by four long strings. She closed her eyes, said a quick prayer to Apollo, and lunged off the seat.

The P-47 Thunderbird crashed hard into the wall. The wings snapped and struck the wall. The small plane bounced back away from the hole it had created in the plaster and spun down to the carpet below.

Sakari's napkin unfurled as she fell. The strings went taut. She let out a screech. The momentum of the plane carried her so close to the wall. Sakari watched in fright as the plane dropped out of the air from above. She squeezed her eyes shut, but the broken plane fell past her. Air filled her homemade parachute. She drifted down and down, rocking back and forth.

Tarsha flew the Fokker triplane past Sakari, balled her paw into a fist and shook it at her defeated enemy, shouting out in victory. She veered the makeshift yoke over, banking the plane to the right and back toward the fight.

Flynn gripped the arms of his wheelchair as he watched her slowly land near the wall, behind a potted fern. Relief washed over him when he saw Sakari scurry around the corner and away into the living room.

In anger, he threw the useless transmitter at the triplane as she flew into range. Tarsha rolled the plane, tipping up her wing to the side, to avoid the flying plastic box. It harmlessly bounced off the far wall, next to the front window.

Flynn could see Gray, teetering on the edge of the armrest, still steering

Tala's Sopwith Camel biplane.

"I'm out, Gray. You got this?" stated Flynn.

"Yeah, yeah, kid... I got this," whispered Gray. All of his focus was on that biplane.

He steered the Sopwith back around toward their target – the supply of arrows and the stash of unused fireworks. He brought her in low to avoid the enemy planes.

From the corner of his eye, Gray spotted the P-51 Mustang on an intercept course with Tala's plane.

"Oh, crap!" muttered Gray.

Flynn noticed the Mustang closing in. He leaned down to whisper. "Go faster, Gray."

Gray gave the boy a quick glance, pushed the right-side control on the transmitter forward.

Tala's biplane buzzed even louder, with the throttle almost all the way open, and she accelerated rapidly behind enemy lines.

The Mustang was caught by surprise at the new speed of the Sopwith. Fala slammed her throttle hard but it was too late. She fell in behind the biplane, playing catch-up.

From her vantage point, Tarsha could see the biplane soaring low and fast at their supply lines. She had circled into the kitchen and decided to meet the Sopwith Camel head-on. She shoved her throttle as far as it would go.

Tala looked over the edge of the cockpit and saw she was moving close to the supplies of the house mice. She lit the fuse on a small ammonium nitrate bomb and waited as Gray flew her in lower and faster.

Flynn tapped on finger on Gray's little shoulder and pointed at the Fokker and Mustang closing in from both directions. "You got trouble..."

Gray took his small eyes off Tala's Sopwith for a fraction of a second, shrugging the boy off.

"I got this." But he was not sure that he did have it. Both enemy planes were going to beat him to the target.

Tala held the small bomb above her head, waiting for the right moment.

The Fokker triplane was headed for a direct collision with the Sopwith.

Fala kept the Mustang on the tail of the biplane, hoping to catch up and nudge Tala off course again.

At the last second, Gray pitched up the plane's nose and applied the ailerons. Then he adjusted the rudder. The biplane began to roll. He kept the Sopwith on the same course but let the fuselage spin over until the biplane was upside down.

"Drop the bomb," whispered Gray.

Tala was not expecting the roll. She nearly fell out of the plane. The wick was burning dangerously low, but she had to grasp a paw on the inside of the cockpit.

The roll helped the Sopwith avoid the oncoming triplane. Tala sailed right over top of Tarsha and Taima, who exchanged glances as they flew by.

The Mustang was too close to avoid collision. Tarsha steered her slow triplane away but it was too late. Fala screamed, jammed her joystick to the right but the Mustang wing took off a large section of the lower two wings on the triplane. Fala's plane lost a large section of her left wing.

As Tala pulled the bomb back in, she lost her grip. The strong wind flowing past the cockpit caused the bomb to roll back into the balsa wood fuselage.

"Oh, that is not good," said Tala, her eyes wide and her mouth hanging open. "No!"

Tarsha had little control left to keep her airborne, but she was flying at full throttle. She struggled hard with her joystick but guided the Fokker down. The wings and fuselage bounced off the seat cushion on the chair near the front window. The triplane dropped to the carpet, slid along, and struck the wall, spinning it around several times.

Tala tried to reach the lit bomb at the back of the fuselage – it was too far away. She gave up. One paw grabbed the cloth napkin, the other gripped the fuselage. Tala threw herself from the plane. The wick burned down to the bomb.

Fala gripped her joystick hard as it rattled back and forth in her paws. The Mustang spun wildly in circles. She stood up in her cockpit and unfurled a silk handkerchief that she had turned into her homemade parachute. As the spinning plane nearly overwhelmed her equilibrium, she half-fell over the side. She caught just enough air and tumbled off the wing. The Mustang crashed hard into the wall, breaking into numerous chunks of wood and metal. Fala's parachute expanded and she spun slowly to the floor.

Tala's Sopwith Camel exploded in midair. A bright fireball lit up the foyer. Flynn and Gray closed their eyes – they lost their last chance to drop a bomb on the enemy supply lines.

Gray hunched down on all fours, letting the remote-control transmitter drop off the wheelchair armrest.

"Wait! Look!" shouted Flynn.

Gray watched the fiery wreckage of the Sopwith biplane fall down onto the supply area used by the Halona. Flames spread out, torching their huge stack of arrows and spears. The mice around the stash scrambled away from the fire.

"Yes!" Gray screamed, pumping his fist high into the air. "Can you dig it?!"

"All right!" agreed Flynn.

"Slip me some skin!" said Gray. He held out his paw and Flynn slid a finger across the pad.

Gray's grin faded in an instant. His attention turned to Tala. She was floating down near the front door.

"Tala…" murmured Gray.

Wind was blowing strong through the open front door; the blizzard was raging away, bringing the outside in. Tala's parachute was pushed past the foyer and into the front of the living room.

She sailed over the wreckage of the Fokker triplane. Tarsha stood in the cockpit, trying to wake Taima, and glared at the enemy mouse as she floated past.

Without saying a word, Gray vaulted off the wheelchair and raced across the carpet toward the front of the living room.

Flynn placed his hand on the controller for his electric wheelchair – he wanted to help Gray rescue Tala. But he knew Gray was on a mission. Flynn returned his focus to the battle before him.

The explosion caused all the warriors on the carpeted battleground to pause, but only for a brief moment. After the fiery plane crashed down, they were back to the grind.

Enola turned to the three archers before her. The blazing fires growing throughout the room flashed in her pink eyes. Her bloodied fur stood up, making her look even larger. She bared her teeth, let out a vicious scream, and sprinted directly at the house mice holding their bows at their sides. All three turned and ran in fear.

Chuchip leapt into a crowd of house mice, his sword held high, screaming at the top of his lungs. Two warriors swung swords down on him as he rolled and popped back up. He parried their swings, sending sparks flying. Another soldier jabbed at Chuchip with a spear, but he deftly sidestepped it and hacked off the tip with his blade. As he parried a sword strike by one of the mice, Chuchip was struck in the back of the head by a shield. The mouse fell to all fours, dazed from the blunt trauma to his skull. Several house mice pounced, slashing downward with their swords. Dyani hurdled over two mice, jutting her sword over Chuchip and deflecting their blades. With a warrior's shriek, she fought them off with the fury of ten field mice. Without looking, she reached her paw back and pulled Chuchip off the floor. He shook his head to clear the cobwebs. Dyani took a brief moment to nudge him, flash him a grin, and then went back to battling the house mice.

Moki parried away the attacks of the mice surrounding him when his sword broke at the hilt. He grunted and threw the handle at one of the mice, then threw his shield at another, knocking the mouse out cold. Moki seized two mice by the heads and slammed them together, leaving them groggy and staggering away. His tail wrapped around another warrior and threw him away. He roared at the remaining house mice and chased them across the living room floor.

Ahiga and Chayton stood, back to back, facing their enemy. Ahiga parried a sword swing. Chayton threw back his war hammer with his one good shoulder – striking Ahiga on the top of the head. Chayton heard Ahiga grunt in pain and spun around to check on his friend. When he spun, his hammer struck Ahiga on the side of the head which sent the mouse to the floor.

"I am sorry, Ahiga!" screamed Chayton, holding out his paw. "Let me help you up!"

"No! No! I will just lay here. Just pretend that *they* are *me!*"

Chayton laughed. As he stood upright, his hammer knocked out an approaching house mouse from behind.

Ahiga could only shake his head and roll his eyes.

Flynn smiled, leaning forward and holding out his hands, as he saw Gray and Tala run up to him. He scooped them up and set them on his leg cast.

"Things are going well!" said Flynn.

"Are they?" questioned Gray.

Flynn followed Gray's gaze as the mouse looked out on the ravages of the battle throughout the house. Beyond the small fires and thick black smoke, the boy could see the carnage. He heard the clanking of tiny swords, shields clashing, arrows whooshing through the air, the harsh cries of pain. What stood out to Flynn were the splotches of red on *everything* – blood stains on their battle jackets and matted fur, on their sword tips and tin shields, across the carpet, and up against the furniture. Injured mice were being dragged away by comrades, screaming out in high-pitched agony. A mother wept over her daughter, who was being triaged for a serious spear wound. He saw one mouse limping away, holding the stump on his shoulder where his left arm had been.

"This is a *real* battle, kid. This is life and death. It's not all the cool tanks and planes. It's pain and misery," stated Gray.

The boy looked away, closed his eyes.

Away from Flynn's scrutiny, behind one of the living room ferns, Nodin cautiously rounded the ceramic pot with his spear in both paws. Moki's shaman was over three years old but still had a little fight left in him.

Nodin came face-to-face with Sani, the Halona tribe elder, who held up his short sword with a shaky arm.

When the two old mice squinted hard enough to recognize one another, they both let out long raspy sighs.

"Oh, you…" said Sani.

"Thank, Apollo! I do not have another fight in me," groaned Nodin.

Sani took a seat on the drainage saucer for the fern pot, rubbing his aching back.

"How is your back, old one?" queried Nodin.

"Old one? Me? You are several seasons well-past me, *ancient* one," grinned Sani. "My back will be the death of me. How are your knees?"

Nodin slowly lowered himself to the carpet, rubbing the knees on his hind legs. "As bad as ever."

"This fighting must stop. With the worst winter in a hundred generations, we should be focused on survival," said Sani.

"I do not even remember why they are fighting," admitted Nodin, as he stretched out his sore legs.

"Pride, jealousy, revenge," said Sani. "Everything we were guilty of when we were young and strong. And stupid."

"How can we end this?"

"I have no control. They hear me, out of respect, but they no longer listen," said Sani.

"It is the same for me," acknowledged Nodin.

"Then… all is lost," exhaled Sani, shaking his head. "All is lost."

Mark managed to kick open the passenger door to his pickup without dropping his precious cargo. Amy stirred as he set her down in the seat. The wind whipped hard around him and snow blew into the cab as he strapped a seatbelt around her.

"Amy? You with me? I'm taking you to the hospital," announced Mark.

She shifted in her seat, opened her eyes. "No, not the hospital. I'm fine. I'm fat, apparently, but… I'm fine…"

"You're not fine. Or… fat. You have, however, inhaled a lot of carbon monoxide from the exhaust," said Mark.

Amy grabbed the sides of her head. "That's explains this massive headache. But I'm gonna be okay. You've got to get back to the kids. This storm is getting out of hand."

"Are you sure?" asked Mark.

She nodded her head while rubbing her temples. "The kids. They're home. Alone."

He closed her door and rushed around the truck to climb into the cab. He backed the truck onto the street, all four wheels struggling to bite into the deep snow. Ice-encrusted trees bent over the road from the heavy wind gusts. Power and phone lines swayed back and forth. Huge drifts had piled up against nearby houses as high as his pickup. The white-out conditions made it hard for Mark to see more than a short distance ahead.

"These winds are so bad, the power is probably out at home," said Mark. He cranked the defroster on high to clear the ice that had formed on the windshield.

"And no power means no heat, right?" asked Amy.

Mark nodded. She noticed how tightly his jaw was clenched. His hands gripped the steering wheel so hard that his knuckles were white. His worry had shifted from her to the children.

39

The Hostage

Laura snuggled down under her covers, leaving only her forehead and a few locks of curly red hair sticking out. But she was still freezing cold. She could not stop her teeth from chattering, no matter how hard she tried.

And the noise. So much noise coming from outside her closed bedroom door. Banging, clattering, high-pitched squeaks… as if her dad was building something *inside* the house.

She could smell smoke, as well. Like someone had burned a whole lot of toast.

Laura examined her alarm clock on the nightstand. She smiled. Daddy had let her sleep in so it must be another snow day! She loved snow days. That meant no school. No teachers talk, talk, talking, on and on, for hours and hours. No annoying Bobby Marsh making fun of her red hair or throwing snowballs at her during recess.

She threw the blankets back and hopped out of bed. The floor was too cold, so she jumped into her fuzzy bunny slippers.

After a big yawn, she felt her tummy grumbling. It was cereal time.

The six-year-old padded down the hallway.

When her balled-up little fists had finished rubbing sleep from her eyes, she could see everything taking place in the foyer and living room.

She blinked several times.

Laura saw dozens of mice, wearing uniforms, fighting all around the carpet and on the furniture. Broken toy planes were scattered around, one was on fire. Snow was blowing into the house from the open front door. Small fires smoldered and a few blazed up high. Tiny sticks and arrows were stuck in the furniture. Pictures had fallen and she saw big burn holes in the walls. A mix of ash, smoke, and snow flurries swirled about both rooms.

Laura blinked hard one final time – unsure of what she was seeing – and vigorously shook her head.

Carefully watching the child, Zaltana climbed onto the kitchen counter that overlooked the dining room and placed her sword in her teeth.

Still reeling from all she was seeing, Laura spotted Flynn by the fireplace. He was staring at her with his mouth wide open. She saw two mice, standing on his cast, observing her.

Everything rushed scattershot through her mind all at once. There was a little voice in her head that was telling her to just go straight back to bed – this was all a bad dream. But her body told her to take a step forward, go to Flynn.

Before Laura could take that step, Zaltana leapt from the counter and landed on Laura's shoulder. The little girl screamed, spun around to try to see what was touching her.

Flynn shoved his wheelchair remote-control joystick forward. Gray and Tala both stuck claws into Flynn's leg cast to keep from falling off.

"Laura!" shouted Flynn.

The wheelchair bowled straight through the middle of the battlefield. Mice from both tribes threw themselves out of the way to avoid the rolling rubber wheels.

Ahiga ferociously dueled with a house mouse when Chayton pushed him out of the way of the wheels. Chayton jumped to safety. But Ahiga was not so lucky.

A loose bolt on the wheelchair wheel caught the back of Ahiga's battle vest and swept him up in the air. He went around in a complete circle. When he reached the floor, Ahiga was pounded hard on the floor.

"Oh, come on!" screamed Ahiga. He was lifted up again and swung around on the rolling wheelchair wheel. He crashed down once again, knocking the wind out of him.

Ahiga managed to unhook his vest but was immediately thrown backward as the wheel revolved up once again. He sailed away and landed flat on his back, groaning in pain, with just a small squeak the only sound he could emit.

Zaltana bounded along Laura's shoulder and up close to her face, holding a sharp sword against the girl's skin.

"Do not move, little one, or you will die where you stand," whispered Zaltana.

Laura could immediately feel the blade as the mouse pushed hard enough to draw blood. Tears welled up as she tried, in vain, to get a look at the mouse. The freezing house and the adrenaline pumping through her veins made her shake uncontrollably.

Flynn shut off the power to his wheelchair when he saw Zaltana on the girl's shoulder with the sword dangerously close to the vein in her neck. The chair rolled to a stop several feet from Laura.

"No, Zaltana!" Flynn pleaded. "She has nothing to do with this!"

"Neither did you, human!" seethed Zaltana. "But you could not resist interfering and now... you must pay!"

Flynn and his chair were parked in the foyer, causing the wind blowing into the door to swirl in a new pattern.

"Please! I'll give you anything you want! Just please, please let her go!"

The wind fanned the flames of the burning wreckage of Tala's biplane and the engulfed pile of arrows and spears.

"Tell Moki to surrender! Have them drop their weapons immediately!" demanded Zaltana.

The red-hot flames scorched the carpet until it caught fire.

Flynn looked around the room for Moki, spotted him fighting off three of Viho's warriors. "Moki! She's got Laura!"

Moki shoved a mouse away, hit another in the head with the handle of his sword, and swung his heavy paw into the nose of the last warrior.

"What?!"

"Look!" Flynn shouted. He pointed at Laura, standing frozen in fear by the kitchen.

Moki instantly spotted Zaltana holding a sword to the child's throat. "By Apollo…"

The old warrior dropped his sword immediately.

Behind the front door, the flames spread out away from the burning Sopwith Camel and across the carpet.

"Tell your tribe to surrender! Please!" implored Flynn. Tears were streaming down his face.

Gray held onto Tala's paw as they both looked on in horror.

Moki leaned back and bellowed. "My warriors! Drop your weapons!"

His booming voice brought the many skirmishes across the house to a standstill. Moki's troops, one by one, let their bows and swords and spears fall to the floor.

The massive warrior Maska turned away from his opponent, who had stopped fighting. His eyes quickly locked on Zaltana, standing on the shoulder of the human with her sword held tight to the girl's neck.

"No…" sighed Maska. He threw his sword away in disgust.

His eyes scanned the living room, looking for signs of Viho, and spotted him trying to fight, at the back of the battle, with a warrior who had already dropped his weapon. Maska ran toward Viho as fast as his strong legs could carry him.

The fire moved close to the huge stash of fireworks that Viho's troops had brought along from the Ciminello house.

Laura reached her arms out. "Help me, Flynn!"

"You're gonna be okay. I promise. Just don't move," soothed Flynn.

Gray walked slowly to the end of Flynn's cast, standing on the boy's toes to get as close as he could to Zaltana.

"Look, lady. I get it. You hate me. What do ya say I switch places with the girl? Take me hostage and let her go?"

Zaltana threw her head back, laughed. "That is a very generous offer! This adorable little human for a worthless city mouse no one cares about!

274

Thank you, but... no."

Tala rushed up next to Gray's side. "I care about him!"

"Ah, young love! How sweet," mocked Zaltana.

Maska pushed the poor field mouse away who was fending off blows from Viho. The big mouse loomed over the chief.

"End this! Now!" snarled Maska, pointing up at Laura.

"You will not talk to your leader that way," scoffed Viho. Still spoiling for a fight, he aimed his sword at Maska.

Maska's paw immediately went to the ball bearing gun strapped to his back.

Zaltana shouted out to her tribe. "Take their weapons away, my warriors! The battle is won!"

Reluctantly, Moki nodded to the field mice as the house mice scooped up the swords and bows from the floor and used the weapons to prod their enemy closer to Zaltana.

The flame on the burning carpet reached the first few wicks on several Roman candles.

A huge red ball of fire shot across the foyer and into the dining room.

Then, a blue flaming ball launched into the living room. Explosions rocked the house.

Next came the brick of firecrackers. Loud pops echoed through the rooms. Fire flashes and sparks lit up the foyer. More roman candle fireballs were unleashed. Smoke was everywhere.

In a panic, all the mice scattered in every direction to avoid the sure death. The entire stash of fireworks was engulfed in flame. Bombs exploded.

When Zaltana crouched down and covered her ears with her paws, Laura reacted – she flicked the mouse off her shoulder, ran toward Flynn.

Laura jumped onto his lap, knocking Tala and Gray off the cast and to the floor. Her momentum nearly rocked the wheelchair over. The front wheels lifted up off the carpet. Flynn leaned forward to keep them upright.

High-pitched screams from the mice mixed with the loud cracks, bangs, and whooshing Roman candle fireballs. Black smoke filled the room. Sulphur burned their eyes.

Flynn pulled the joystick back and the wheelchair zoomed away from the foyer. He yanked it hard to the left to turn the chair around, toward the back door.

Gray grasped Tala's paw and they scrambled for the back door, running underneath Flynn's wheelchair to avoid all the other mice racing around them.

Jamming the joystick ahead, Flynn directed the wheelchair forward. Then it lurched. Shuddered. The engine whined as the battery ran out of juice. The chair rolled forward on the carpet and then stopped moving entirely.

The battery was dead.

Flynn looked back as a Roman candle ball shot past, close to his ear.

The front window curtains were on fire. Flames raged across the front door and foyer carpet. More smoke filled the room, making it hard to see and breathe.

Laura coughed hard. Flynn's eyes watered as he looked around for a way out of this situation. He put both hands on the rubber wheels and tried valiantly to roll across the carpet.

But the carpet was too thick, wet, too full of debris. The battery and engine underneath his seat weighed too much.

He grabbed Laura's shoulders. "Laura! Listen to me! You've got to get outta here! Run to the barn!"

"No! I'm not leaving you here! You'll die!" screamed Laura, tears running down her cheeks.

"You have to. The wheelchair is broke and it's too heavy to roll out of here!" Flynn argued.

The flames quickly raced across the walls of the house, lighting the old wallpaper on fire.

"Nope! Not gonna. You can't make me! But... I can help! I'm a good helper," stated Laura.

Laura slid off Flynn's lap and onto the floor. She peeked under the wheelchair to look at everything strapped in down there. She rubbed her eyes as the smoked continued to burn them. As quick as she could, she scanned the floor until she found what she needed.

Flynn coughed, watched the flames crawl across the ceiling. A sitting chair caught fire next to him. He pulled up his pajama shirt to cover his mouth.

Using a small sword dropped by a mouse, Laura went to work. She used it as a screwdriver, turning the small metals screws that held the makeshift frame that Adriel had built for the battery. She turned and turned until several screws dropped to the carpet. She pulled hard on the battery and it plonked to the floor. Then, she went to work on the engine. When the sword did not fit the bolts holding up the engine, she discovered a spear with a triangular tip, buried in a table leg, and used that as a tool.

Flynn kept trying to roll the wheelchair but all he did was rock back and forth. Flames raced through the living room and the couch caught fire.

Most of the mice had scurried from of the house. Moki stood in the doorway, pushing mice out the door and into the snow. Gray and Tala scampered up to the back door when Gray turned back to see Flynn stuck in the middle of the room.

"We're the last ones!" said Tala.

"Out, you two! Head to the barn!" bellowed Moki.

Tala coughed. "Come on, Gray! We must flee!"

"Naw… No can do, beautiful," Gray whispered. "I can't leave the kids."

Tala sighed, knowing they would most likely not make it out of the quickly burning house. "I understand. It is not our way either."

Moki looked up at the burning structure of the house. "Tala… you must hurry!"

"Get to the barn! Take care of the others! Please?!"

Moki grimaced. "That is not how it works, my dear."

He jumped down from the snow drift and ran with Gray and Tala back toward Flynn and Laura.

Pieces from the burning ceiling dropped on Flynn's lap. He pushed the embers off his lap and shoulder and hair. He turned back to Laura, who was busy working away, with elbows and shoulders casting about under his seat.

"There! All done!" said Laura. The heavy engine thudded hard onto the carpet. As smoke seized her little lungs, she coughed hard to clear them.

Laura got behind Flynn's wheelchair, her small hands holding the handles. "Ready?"

Flynn nodded and she pushed with all her might. Flynn thrust the rubber wheels forward as hard as he could, and they finally rolled over the debris and across the thick carpet.

Tala, Moki and Gray arrived, grasping the bar that connects the big rear wheel to the smaller front wheels, and helped push the boy toward the back door.

A huge, burning chunk of the plaster ceiling dropped onto the carpet where Flynn had been parked. The old carpeting easily burst into flames.

They built up enough momentum to carry the wheelchair over the threshold of the door. They rolled onto the porch. Flynn could barely see the ruts in the snow from his previous journey to the barn because snow was blowing so hard. Luckily, the retreating mice had followed the same path.

"Head to the barn!" Flynn shouted over the howling winds driving across the porch. Cold, wet snow pelted their faces as they pushed onto the driveway.

40

The Accident

The heavy wheelchair and rubber wheels had packed down enough snow to make hardened grooves. Flynn and Laura sailed down the porch and over the snow-buried steps and onto the gravel drive. Laura kept pushing, with her head down and fuzzy slippers driving into the thick snow. Flynn's arms pumped forward, over and over, causing his shoulders to burn with pain. Moki, Tala and Gray held onto the bar below and used their hind legs to drive them forward.

The fire spread throughout the main floor of the house. Thick flames shattered the glass in the windows as they belched out in search of fresh air, hungry for more fuel.

Winded, muscles screaming, coughing hard to get out the smoke remnants, they made it to the barn door. Laura rushed around the wheelchair to push open the door all the way.

"Be careful!" yelled Flynn, holding his hands out at her as a warning.

Laura looked at him quizzically after she had opened the door wide enough. "Why?"

"There are booby traps in there!" said Flynn.

She tilted her head to the side, rolled her eyes, and then moved back behind the chair to push him all the way inside.

Flynn pushed ahead just enough to get the entire chair inside and then locked the chair brake. Laura gave up trying to move him any farther and returned to the door to shut out the blowing snow and freezing cold wind.

He carefully inspected their surroundings as Tala and Gray climbed back on Flynn's cast. Both tribes had hauled their wounded through the snow and had created temporary encampments only a few feet from each other. Exhausted from the battle and the race through the blizzard, the weary warriors sat doubled over or leaned up against anything sturdy. Others hovered around the seriously wounded, desperately trying to save lives.

As was her way, Taima laid down against a hay bale to take one of her many naps.

Moki lowered his aching body down to inspect Chuchip's wound. Dyani wrapped a bandage around a deep bloody cut on his shoulder. When Moki finally looked up, his eyes locked on Viho across the barn.

Viho snarled and leapt to his hind legs, sword in hand. Moki drew his bloodied sword and marched across the wooden barn floor.

Before the two could commence their attack, Flynn rolled his wheelchair forward as fast as he could.

"Stop!"

Both Moki and Viho froze. The tribes, who had already stood up on exhausted and sore hind legs and had drawn weapons to begin the battle again, looked to Flynn.

"This... this whole thing is over!" shouted Flynn. "The war stops now!"

"None of this concerns you, human!" screamed Viho, waving his sword at the boy.

"Oh, I think it does! You just burned her whole house down!" said Flynn, pointing back at Laura. "You nearly killed both of us!"

"Stay out of it, boy!" cried Zaltana, drawing her own sword.

"No, I will not. Look at what you've done to your tribe. Look!" said Flynn. He pointed to both sides.

Moki turned back to looked at his mice. Nearly every single one had blood matted on their fur. Many held on to injured shoulders, cut sides, damaged legs, and slashed faces.

Viho examined his own troops – they were as weary, wet, bloodied, and hurt as Moki's warriors. They had no fight left in them.

"And what for? What have you accomplished?" pleaded Flynn. "The fighting ends today."

"Yeah, you guys should just kiss and make up!" chimed in Laura.

Coming from her, that almost made Flynn smile.

Her announcement did make Gray grin. "You tell 'em, kid!"

"This is over when I say it is over!" screamed Viho. He screamed and held his sword up high.

Viho started to sprint toward Moki but was lifted up in the air.

The giant Maska stood behind his chief, his paws gripping onto Viho's fur, and hoisted him up higher.

"What are you doing?!" said Viho. "Put me down!"

"We are done. Like the boy said... this is over," proclaimed Maska.

Zaltana slid up beside Maska, pointing her sword at his head. "You traitor!"

"It is you two who are the traitors," said Maska.

She gasped.

Viho grunted, tried to look over his shoulder to determine if his big warrior was serious. "How dare you!"

Maska dropped Viho to the barn floor. The chief whirled him around until they were face to face. Maska pulled out the homemade ball bearing gun he had strapped to his back.

"I know you are hurt and have suffered great loss. But you will not destroy this tribe to get your vengeance!" snarled Maska.

"*You* speak for the tribe now?" asked Zaltana, her sword edging closer to the giant warrior.

His grip tightened on the trigger to his ball bearing gun.

Maska turned on Zaltana. "I speak for the good of us all! If I am wrong, then you can kill me or banish me. But this is what I feel is right, in my heart."

He pounded his chest and bent down so that his eyes were lined up with hers. His glare pierced right through her until she looked away.

Viho rushed at Moki, pointing at his nemesis, and shouted to Flynn. "What of his crimes?!"

"You kidnapped his son!" said Flynn.

"Because this demon killed *my* son!"

"What?!" screamed Moki.

"You did! You killed my only son! I know it!"

"What is he talking about?" asked Flynn.

Moki sighed. He collected himself, strode across the wood floor toward the wheelchair.

"Before all this started," said Moki, gesturing to the weary tribes on both sides. "Our tribes have helped each other for generations. They have provided with food from inside houses and we have given them shelter, food from our stores, and protection outdoors."

"Tell him what you did to my son!" demanded Viho.

"I am getting to that, Viho," said Moki, holding up his paw to calm the chief. "Last summer, we were all in the fields. I was gathering apples. I have a taste for the fruit. His son, Wakiza, was curious and followed me up a tree. I did not know he was there. I had climbed very high to retrieve a particularly ripe apple…"

"And when you saw him, you pushed him out of the tree!" shouted Viho, as he paced back and forth.

Both tribes gathered around their leaders to listen closely.

"I did nothing of the sort. Once I had the apple, I turned and Wakiza was right behind me. I did not smell or hear the boy. When I saw him, I dropped the apple I carried in my mouth. Wakiza tried to catch it and he fell out of the tree," said Moki. He looked off into the distance of that memory.

"So, it was an accident?" asked Flynn.

"Lies!" screamed Viho.

Gray followed Tala as she moved into the circle of tribes around the two leaders.

"When Viho arrived at the apple tree, he saw his boy lying dead at the base. He acknowledged my presence up in the tree but did not talk to me. I never had the chance to explain what had transpired. The next day, the house mice left our camp. And they stole *my* son, Yuma. I had no idea why, but we had been chasing them all Fall and into the Winter to get him back.

And that is when you became involved."

"Do you even hear the utter nonsense pouring from your tiny lips, Moki?! Do you?" seethed Viho.

"Why would I lie about the death of your son?" asked Moki.

"You were jealous!" stammered Viho.

"Jealous?"

"Yes! My son was confident, proud, and strong. He was going to be a great warrior. Your son is nervous and weak, overly attached to his mother. And, as she has given you nothing but a few litters of females, you knew your days of fathering a great warrior were nearly over! You had no one to take your place as leader!"

Moki eyed Tala, who had moved in next to him.

"Do you hear your own bile, sad little cretin? You took Yuma away before he had a chance to open his eyes! We have no idea what kind of mouse he will turn out to be," said Moki.

Moki pointed a single claw at Viho's face. "All I know is that you are responsible for the death of my beloved son!"

The two leaders began circling one another.

"His death was a calamity. Of disastrous proportions. And I am sorry for your loss. But I am not responsible," declared Moki.

As they shuffled around the barn floor, Moki stepped over the sleeping Taima without taking his eyes from Viho. They circled around until Viho was forced to step over her. Both of them gripped their swords tighter and tighter. They moved closer and closer; their eyes locked.

Maska tightened his own grip on the ball bearing gun. He could not let this go on – he was prepared to eliminate Viho.

"He would still be alive if not for you. Your time is at an end," raged Viho, exposing his teeth.

Tala noticed Viho's sword begin to strike. "Father, watch out!"

Viho thrust his sword directly at Moki's gut but Tala's blade parried the blade away, spinning Viho to face her. She was ready to take him on, but Moki held his arm in front of her. He would not let Tala fight his battle.

"Father?" muttered Gray.

At that moment, Taima awoke from a scary dream and sat straight up, eyes wide.

Reacting instinctively to her movement – Maska pulled the trigger on his ball bearing gun.

Gray heard the trigger click. His eyes followed along the path of the barrel of the gun.

The spring released – the ball bearing launched.

Gray threw himself in front of Tala. The gun had been pointed directly at her even as Maska had been watching the two chiefs circle each other.

The ball bearing struck Gray in the belly, sending him flying backward into Tala. They rolled backwards into the hay bale.

"No!" screamed Flynn, as he watched from above.

All the mice gasped or screamed out in horror. Maska dropped his gun as if it were on fire.

Taima scurried off in fear.

Moki bounded in to help Tala off the barn floor. She immediately turned her attention Gray, rushing to his side.

Flynn felt desperate to help as tears poured from his eyes. Without thinking, he rolled off his wheelchair and landed with a thump on the hard deck, sending up a plume of sawdust. Dragging his heavy leg cast behind, he crawled across the wood floor to be close to the lifeless mouse.

"Gray! Gray! Wake up!" cried Flynn.

Tala gripped Gray's fur in her claws. "Gray! Can you hear me?!"

Flynn scanned the floor. Between his fingers, he picked up the small ball bearing that struck his friend.

"Wait! This hit his front, right?" asked Flynn. He held up the bearing to Tala.

She nodded. Tears had formed in her eyes as well. Gray's eyes were closed, his mouth hanging slightly open.

"This probably hit his chest! And maybe stopped his heart," said Flynn. "We had to... to do this thing in health class where we breathe into the mouth for them... to give them air. And push on the chest t-to start their heart!"

"Well, then… do that!" screamed Tala.

"I can't! I'd overfill his lungs and break them or something. And I'd crush him," admitted Flynn. "You have to do it!"

"Tell me what to do!" begged Tala.

Flynn walked her through the steps of the cardiopulmonary resuscitation technique he had learned in school. Tala placed her paws on Gray's fur and, after a deep sigh, began compressions on his chest. She put her weight into it and pushed down over and over.

"How much longer?" breathed Tala.

"I don't know. We've got to try to restart his heart," said Flynn. "Check to see if he's breathing?"

Tala placed her ear to Gray's mouth but heard no sounds, felt no air. She shook her head.

"Okay, give him a breath with your mouth on his."

Tala blew air into his mouth but much of escaped through his nose.

"Oh! Sorry! Cover his nose!"

She breathed deeply into his mouth a few times, then went back to chest compressions.

Moki and both tribes squeezed in closer, watching intently for signs of life from Gray.

After dozens of compressions, Tala began to wear down.

"Here. Let me help," said Moki. He placed his paw on her shoulder. Reluctantly, she conceded and let him take over.

Moki pushed down repeatedly on Gray's chest. He would stop to let Tala breathe air into Gray's lungs.

"Come on, Gray! Don't leave me," pleaded Flynn.

But the hope that had initially filled his heart quickly drained away.

"Flynn, I do not… think… this… will work," wheezed Moki.

"Keep trying! Please," said Tala.

"We can't give up," whispered Flynn. "Not yet."

Moki renewed the vigorous chest compressions. Tala continued trying to exhale life back into Gray.

Flynn closed his eyes, knowing his friend was gone. Laura laid down on the floor, next to Flynn and patted his shoulder.

Tala blew her breath into Gray one last time, placed her forehead against his whiskers.

Gray opened his eyes.

He sucked in air in a massive gasp, then coughed. But the coughing caused him serious pain from the ball-bearing damage and the compressions. His paws gripped his broken ribs.

"Gray!" shouted Flynn.

"Yay!" screamed Laura.

Gray rolled to his side, trying desperately to breathe in more air, but it hurt with every inhale.

"You live?!" exclaimed Tala.

"Yeah, still kickin'. Must've been your kiss that brought me back to life," muttered Gray.

Tala playfully smacked him, and a wide grin slid across her face.

"Yes! You live to fight another day!" bellowed Moki. Without thinking, the big warrior plucked Gray up and squeezed him hard.

Everyone, at once, held up their hands and paws – "No!"

"Put him down! He's injured!" screamed Flynn.

"Oh," said Moki. He dropped Gray back to the wood floor in a heap. "Sorry."

"Ow…" cried Gray, writhing in even more pain. "Ya really know how to kick a guy when he's down."

Flynn smiled, which quickly turned into infectious laughter.

Tala beamed as she hugged Gray's head, careful to avoid his injuries.

Laura clapped, excited that the mouse would live after all.

Viho pushed his way into the circle, shoving away members of both tribes.

"Come fight me like a real mouse and not hide behind your daughter like a rat!" yelled Viho.

Moki bared his teeth, tightly gripped his sword.

As he laid down on the floor, Flynn was now very close to Moki. He leaned in and whispered to the chief.

Moki stood up straight, sheathed his sword, and gave a look to Flynn.

"Enough is enough," whispered Moki.

Viho was flabbergasted that Moki had put away his sword. When he relaxed in that moment, Moki punched Viho square in the nose. He gave a look back at Flynn and shrugged as if that was the best he could do. The boy gave him a stern look.

Viho staggered away, falling on his back, blood spurting from his nose. Zaltana rushed help Viho to a seated position.

"That is the last of the violence today, Viho." Moki pointed a claw at Viho's head.

Viho held a paw to his nose to stem the blood flow. "I will be the one who decides—"

"You will be... banished," stated Moki.

Several of the mice in the crowd gasped.

"You-you cannot banish me from my own tribe!" said Viho.

Moki turned to face all the mice that were assembled around him. "Listen to me, warriors! This... mouse has led you astray. He has involved you in his vendetta against me without caring about the well-being of his tribe. On this most terrible winter day, I invite you to join our tribe. All are welcome... with the exception of Viho and his mate Zaltana!"

Viho was speechless. Zaltana gulped, clutching her paw to her chest.

"Who do you think you are?!" screamed Viho, spit flying from his mouth as he bared his teeth.

Moki ignored the two on the floor. "These two... are not worthy to lead you. Our tribe will take you in, provide for you, and only take actions that ensure your safety. I believe that most of you will take me up on this offer because you are tired of fighting and wish to live in peace. For those who do not, you are free to leave with Viho and Zaltana. But know that if you come back – for either goodwill or ill – we shall consider you the enemy and will act accordingly!"

"Stop!" screamed Viho. He tried to stand on his hind legs but slipped in his own blood and collapsed on the barn floor.

"From this time forward, I propose that Viho and Zaltana be banished!" proclaimed Moki. "We must be a majority! Does anyone protest this proclamation?!"

No one, from either tribe, said a word or protested in any way.

Viho scanned the crowd gathered around. His eyes landed on Koko. "You? You as well?"

Koko bowed her head, closed her eyes, and said nothing. She quietly slipped away from the crowd. She had loved Viho as a father but knew that Moki was right…. this had to end.

"We are unanimous! They are banished and shall be sent forth from this barn today and never will return to the tribe, no matter where we roam or eventually settle…"

"I will not go without a fight!" seethed Viho. He searched the floor to find his sword. When he spotted his blade, he reached down for it but Moki stood on Viho's arm. He leaned down close to the disgraced leader.

"I will not fight you. Because I will kill you. And this would force me to banish your mate to the cold alone. So… leave with some dignity intact. Go quietly before I lose my temper. Again…"

Standing in the back of the crowd, the wizened Sani leaned over to whisper in the old shaman Nodin's ear. He nudged him with his elbow and pointed at Moki with his cane. "We are going to be fine. He is a smart leader."

"I know," said Nodin.

Tate stepped up to Dyani, causing her to recoil slightly and grab the handle of her sword.

"Hey, do you guys have anything to eat? I am starving," asked Tate.

Dyani grinned at him, pointed to their food stash under the tool bench.

41

The Exile

The big tires on the Chevy truck plowed slowly over the snow that had blown across the road on the way to the Dobson home.

Through the barren ice-covered trees that lined the road, Amy spotted the problem first. "Is that smoke?"

"What?! Where?" asked Mark.

He saw the black smoke billowing up as soon as she pointed down the street.

"Oh, no…" The color drained instantly from Mark's face. His foot jammed hard on the accelerator and the truck slipped and slid as the tires sought traction.

Amy held on tight as the trucked bounced along the road.

The truck fishtailed onto the driveway. Mark over-corrected the steering and they went into a spin. The back of a truck hit a giant snow drift that had built up against several trees.

He threw open his truck door, sprinted to the house through snow up to his knees. Amy raced along behind him, trying not to fall.

"No, please! No!" screamed Mark.

The entire house was engulfed in fire. Flames flicked out of every window. Smoke billowed up and was swiftly scattered by the strong blizzard winds.

"Laura!" he bellowed. "Flynn?!"

Amy caught up, holding onto his shoulder for support while her hand intertwined with his.

Mark started to run toward the house.

"No! You can't go in there!" yelled Amy. She held on tight to his hand, pulling him back from the leaping onto the porch.

"Laura!"

Amy looked all around the house, the fields, and then noticed the barn.

"What about the barn?!" said Amy.

"Come on!" yelled Mark. Still holding her hand, they ran through the heavy snow as fast as they could.

The united tribe of mice stood at the back door of the barn. They watched in silence as Viho, Zaltana and two other mice marched slowly across the field toward the ice-covered trees. They had small sacks with food slung over their backs. They leaned hard into the heavy wind as they walked atop of several feet of snow.

Moki slowly slid the barn door closed. Dyani held the long staff up to her mate – it was the staff that the leader of the tribe always carried. He looked down on it and sighed.

"Perhaps, someday... I will be able to pass this on to my son," said Moki.

"Or... your daughter," grinned Dyani.

She turned and pointed to Tala, across the barn floor, who was leading the injured Gray toward the boy in the wheelchair.

"Possibly," pondered Moki. "Possibly."

Dyani put her arm around her mate and leaned her face against his shoulder. They watched as the mice scattered to dark corners of the barn to deal with their wounds and to rest.

Laura helped Flynn roll onto his back and then tugged on his arms to help him sit upright. She looked at him, then his wheelchair. She had no idea how she would get him back into it.

Tala supported Gray with her arm around his back. She helped him shuffle up to Flynn.

"Hey, there you are. How are you feeling?" asked Flynn.

"Anybody get the license plate off the truck that ran me over?" mused

Gray.

"The license numbers are actually stamped on your forehead, Gray," said Flynn, with a grin.

Gray laughed out loud but doubled over in pain, holding his sides and coughing. "Oh, man. It's okay. It only hurts when I laugh, kid. Or breathe."

"The house is probably toast, isn't it?" pondered Flynn.

"Yep. I bet you lost your suitcase… the last of all your stuff," said Gray. "Sorry about that."

Flynn thought about it for a second. "Eh, I lost my Bicentennial shirt. It was my favorite. But I mostly just lost the books on war… and I think I'm done with war."

Tala shifted the weight of Gray leaning against her arm, to better support him. She could only stare him, amazed he was still alive.

Flynn's smile faded. "You're staying with them, aren't you?"

Gray sighed, unable to look at the boy in the eyes. "Yeah, kid. I am. I think I finally found my people. My family."

Sadness swept over him. His emotional roller coaster had finally entered the station. He looked around the room, at Laura, and then out through the barn door and pictured the burning house outside.

"I think I found my family, too. But then… I lost them," said Flynn. "I burned their house down, dude."

Laura stared at Flynn and then looked back toward the barn doors, realizing her burning home was just beyond. She held her finger up to her mouth. "Shhh!"

"What?" said Flynn.

"You remember our game of *Life*? Don't worry. I'm not gonna send you to the Poor Farm. I promise. Just stick with me. Okay?" said Laura.

Flynn gave a sympathetic smile to the young girl. He knew she had no concept of how much trouble he was in. "Okay."

Tala gave Laura a look, causing the young girl to tilt her head to the side. "Hi, Laura. Can you help me find some bandages for Gray? I need to support his ribs."

Laura was excited to help. She held out her hand so that Tala could climb on. Tala gave Gray a look as they left the boy and the mouse alone together.

"So, I gotta ask… what did you tell Moki that made him put away his sword… after Viho called him a rat?" asked Gray.

"I told him that a wise military strategist once said that the art of war is to beat your enemy… without fighting."

"Sun Tzu! Nice!" exclaimed Gray. "Nice."

An awkward silence fell on them. They both had so much to say but had idea where to start.

"Hey, kid. Did I ever tell you about the guy in the wheelchair who broke up with his girlfriend? No? He broke up with the dame because all she ever did was push him around and talk behind his back."

Gray laughed but Flynn's smile quickly faded. Tears welled up in his eyes. Gray was going to add something flippant but knew that was not the time. Everything caught up with the boy all at once.

Sitting on the floor, Flynn sobbed. He covered his eyes, but the tears fell between his fingers. He wept for the first time for his mother and father. For his loneliness. For the fear of what was to come. It all came pouring out, all at once.

Gray hoped that the kid had maybe… just maybe… let go of some of that anger. And the sadness of it all had finally caught up with him. He knew Flynn could finally grieve.

He hugged Flynn's knee and just held on, letting the boy know he was there for him. For now.

"Hey, kid. You're gonna be just fine. I know it," said Gray.

"Hey, Gray. I-I… Take care of yourself," said Flynn.

"I love you, too, kid." Gray grinned at him.

Laura returned and set Tala on the barn floor. She held out a handful of rags that she had found to tie around Gray's injured ribs. Tala helped him slowly walk off to join the rest of the mice.

"Thank you for being there for me," whispered Flynn.

Gray gave one last look over his shoulder, winked at the boy and gave a short nod. You too, kid. You too.

From outside, over the harsh wind whistling through the barn, they could hear people shouting out their names. He wiped at the tears that had streaked his face.

"Flynn?!"

"Laura!"

The barn door slid open and swirling cold wind and snow blew hard across the floor. Amy rushed in first, with Mark right behind.

"Thank God you're okay!" shouted Amy.

Mark sprinted across the barn, scooped up Laura, and swung her around in circles.

Amy dropped to her knees, hugged Flynn as tight as she could, then put both hands on his face and inspected him for burns. She wiped away soot and tears on his cheeks and then hugged him again.

"Did you get burned? Are you kids okay? What about smoke – did you inhale too much smoke?" asked Mark. He quickly completed his inspection of Laura.

He set Laura down to move on to the boy sitting on the barn floor. Mark and Amy picked him up and set him back in his wheelchair. Mark adjusted the Flynn's cast back onto the wheelchair leg support.

Amy looked into Flynn's eyes, her hands holding up his face. "Flynn, I have to ask. Did you set that fire?"

Flynn froze. His eyes were wide, fearful. He wanted nothing more than to run away as fast as he could. He opened his mouth but had no clue about what to say next. Then he sighed, relaxed, ready to accept blame and punishment for what the mice had done.

"It was all my fault—"

Laura stood next to Flynn's chair, putting both hands on his arm. "No. I won't let you, Flynn."

Flynn was confused. "Huh?"

Laura turned around to look her at dad, but she could not make eye contact.

"I was playing with fireworks, daddy," said Laura so quietly.

"What? Fireworks?" said Mark. "What are you talking about, honey?"

He dropped to both knees to address her on her level. Laura gave a look to Flynn and then focused on her father, putting her hands on her hips.

"Where did you get fireworks from?" asked Amy. She had asked the little girl but watched Flynn's reaction. She knew fireworks had been involved at the Ciminello house before the boy had fled. And she remembered the smell of sulfur that had lingered in the air.

"Bobby Marsh," stated Laura. She hated Bobby Marsh.

"Bobby? What are you talking about, baby girl?" asked Mark. He could not focus on her words but was simply amazed she was alive, unharmed.

"Bobby brought fireworks to school, to show off. But he's an idiot. I thought he was gonna blow us up, so I took them from him," announced Laura. She turned to Amy. "He's a bully. He pulls on my hair and punches my arms at recess."

"I see," said Amy.

"I figured we had a snow day today so I... I wanted to know what the fireworks looked like. What kind of colors they had? You know? I was only gonna light one but then they all blew up. All at the same time!" said Laura. "I'm so sorry, daddy!"

Flynn noticed that Amy was no longer focused on him. She was watching the little girl's masterful performance. She was either going to be some kind of great lawyer, like he had seen on TV, or a really good actress.

"Oh, honey, I don't care! As long as you're okay!" said Mark. He hugged her hard, squeezing the air from her.

"Okay. As long as you're in a good mood I also ate all the peanut butter last night," said Laura.

This made the others laugh out loud as the adrenaline had finally worn off.

"What's so funny?" asked Laura. This got her even more hugs from dad. Amy even shuffled over on her knees to get in her own bear hug.

"Come on now," said Mark. "Let's get Flynn back to Child Services before this storm shuts us in for a month."

"But can't Flynn stay with us? I want him to stay with us, daddy! You promised!" said Laura.

Amy grabbed Laura's hand as the two adults stood up. "Laura, I promise you… I'm going to do everything I can to get Flynn placed with your family."

"You promise?" she asked.

"Yes," said Amy. She looked Flynn up and down. She still had her suspicions, but she trusted the boy. There's was just something about him. He was a good person in a terrible situation. "I promise you, Laura. We're going to make this happen."

They worked their way to the barn door. Amy pulled it open far enough to fit the wheelchair through the opening. The four of them stared at the burning house, which was merely an engulfed wooden frame at that point.

"But first… you're going to need a place to live," said Amy.

"Oh, I don't know… it's not too bad," said Mark. "A few nails, some drywall, a little duct tape… it'll be good as new."

They watched the house burn for a few seconds.

"Shoot," said Mark.

"What?" asked Amy.

"That would've been perfect timing if the house completely collapsed as soon as I said that…"

"You mean like it always does in the movies?" said Amy.

"Yeah," said Mark.

"That never happens," she sighed.

The burning frame of the house completely collapsed, leaving only the fireplace standing in the flames.

"Oh! You were so close! Your timing is a bit off," said a smiling Amy.

"Story of my life," said Mark.

Flynn rolled his eyes at how sappy both the grownups were being and made the puking motion to Laura. She chuckled to herself and squeezed his hand.

"Ugh. I really don't want to go back out in this blizzard," said Amy. The wind whipped her face with snow blowing in and landing on her eyelashes.

"Yeah. I'm over this winter," said Mark.

"Me, too," said Amy. "But I don't care anymore. I'm headed to California."

"California, huh?" said Mark. "That sounds nice…"

42

The Bet

"And the rest, as they say, is history," said Flynn.

He dug his hand in the dirt where a house had once stood. He was sweating but the temperature was only in the mid-eighties. He was used to the hot summer sun in California but had forgotten about the Ohio humidity, where you would still be hot standing in the shade.

Mia stood on the stone hearth of the fireplace, the only remnant of the house, staring at the *Lava Run* game on her smartphone.

"Did you hear anything I said?" asked Flynn.

She flashed a stern, penetrating glare from those hazel eyes she had gotten from her mother. Despite her mere fourteen years on the planet, she had the ability to make him feel like that student who had forgotten to do his homework. And Flynn had been out of school for thirty years.

Mia rolled her eyes as she tied up her long, straight strawberry blond hair with a hair tie and then fanned herself to cool off.

"Can we go now?" asked Mia.

She went right back to the game on her phone. Flynn was convinced that phone was permanently attached to her hand. He could never figure out how her battery lasted twice as long as his, when he rarely used his phone.

"And, yes, I heard you," added Mia.

Flynn stood up and rubbed the ache in his left leg. He wasn't sure if it was because a summer thunderstorm was on the horizon or all the memories flooding his brain had suddenly blessed him with some sort of phantom pain.

"We can go soon. I just needed to check out the condition of the property. When Grandpa Mark passed away last month, this farm was one of things he left to me," said Flynn.

Mia looked around her. The fields were full of corn. There was a gravel driveway and a big white barn that had seen better days. The only signs a house had ever been there were some iron pipes sticking up through the weeds and the blackened brick fireplace and chimney.

"Doesn't look like he did you any favors," said Mia.

"Well, we can keep making a little money leasing the land out to local farmers. But I might want to hang on to the property. Just so no one knocks down the old barn," said Flynn.

"What do you care about some stupid old barn?" said Mia.

"Because of the mice, of course."

"The mice?"

"Yeah. When Grandpa Mark, Aunt Laura, and I moved out to Sausalito to be with your grandma Amy, the mice had set up a permanent camp in the barn. I doubt the tribe ever left," said Mark. "There's plenty of food around here and no people to bother them."

Mia stared at her father for a long time. Suddenly, she was worried about him. Had the death of his adoptive father knocked a screw or two loose? Had he fallen recently? Was dementia setting in? He was pretty old now, but he was not *that* old.

"Please tell me you don't actually believe in talking mice," said Mia.

Flynn laughed. "Oh. You thought I was just making that whole story up?"

"Well…. yeah! Mice don't talk, dad."

"That's what many people think," mused Flynn.

She watched him stroll off toward the barn. He had a slight limp, as he favored his left leg a little. Mia opened up her phone again. She began texting mom that she was concerned that dad may be going insane.

She heard him unlock the padlock and slide the old barn door open as she typed away on her phone.

"Psst!"

Mia jumped up off the hearth, worried a snake was about to strike. She didn't even know if Ohio had poisonous snakes, but she wasn't taking any chances.

"Psst!"

She heard the hissing sound again.

Close to the crumbling chimney, she spotted a small gray mouse. He held his paws together and stood on his hind legs.

"I was wondering if you could help me settle a bet?" asked the young mouse.

Mia gasped, took a step back, and dropped her phone.

"Is that man really... The Flynn?" said the mouse. "My sister says it cannot be him. We have a sunflower seed bet."

"Y-you... you c-can talk?!" stammered Mia.

"Of course. Did you not hear him tell the story? It has been a legend in our culture, passed down for many generations," said the young gray mouse.

"Oh, God... *I'm* the one who's crazy!" said Mia. She looked all around, unsure if she was really standing there in the middle of a rundown farm.

"I enjoyed his version of the story. I learned a great deal that I had never heard before," he said.

"This is insane," said Mia.

"Is he The Flynn?" asked the mouse.

"*The* Flynn? Well, his name is Flynn but..." Mia paused. She closed her eyes, took a deep breath. "Ohmygod... I am *talking* to a mouse."

A large tan-colored female mouse rushed up to the younger male. She covered his mouth, stared up a Mia for several seconds, then pushed him along until they disappeared into tall weeds surrounding the fireplace.

Mia stood staring at the empty fireplace. Her legs went weak; she swayed back and forth. Despite the heat, a chill ran up her back and the hair on her arms rose up.

"Dad?" she whispered.

She looked all around her feet, at the fireplace, the surrounding weeds, and then her eyes landed on the old, weathered white barn across the gravel driveway.

"Daddy!" screamed Mia.

As fast as her shaky legs would carry her, Mia ran toward the open barn door.

The End

The Great Blizzard of '78

Starting on January 25th, 1978, a most deadly and severe blizzard hit Ohio, Illinois, Indiana, and Wisconsin. Between one and three feet of snow fell in a very short period, on top of the twenty-four inches of snow that had already fallen. Winds averaged between fifty and seventy miles per hour, which created snowdrifts as high as twenty-five feet. With temperatures hovering around zero, the deadly wind chill reached sixty degrees below zero. The storm system produced some of the lowest barometric pressure readings ever recorded in the United States, not associated with hurricanes, with pressures falling below the chart scale in some cases.

When the storm moved eastward, it brought warmer temperatures that converted snow to ice and paralyzed most of the area for weeks. Over one hundred and seventy thousand homes were without power and many people were stranded in their cars and houses for several days. For the first time in its history, the Ohio Turnpike was closed. Thirty-one thousand miles of roads needed to be cleared. One truck driver was buried inside his semi and he was not found until after a week. Five thousand national guardsmen were called in by the governor to help rescue people trapped in their homes and cars.

Seventy people were killed by this storm, with over fifty of victims in Ohio. Nearly half of the victims were killed trying to leave stranded cars. Schools and businesses were closed for several weeks. Nearly two thousand homes were destroyed and the worst storm in Ohio's history caused more than one billion dollars in damage to the country.

CPSIA information can be obtained
at www.ICGtesting.com
Printed in the USA
BVHW040029131220
595587BV00022B/1717